D0850114

The Heart of a Hero

"Susan May Warren whips up a maelstrom of action that slams Jake and Aria together and keeps the pages turning. Twists, turns, and constant danger keep you wondering whether this superb cast of characters can ride out the storm."

James R. Hannibal, multi–award winning author
of *Chasing the White Lion*

Praise for *The Way of the Brave*

"*The Way of the Brave* grabbed me at the first chapter and never let go. Susan May Warren is a master storyteller, creating strong, confident, and compassionate characters. This book is no different. The healing of Jenny and Orion as they brave the elements of Denali is a perfect mirror of our journey in Christ. Daily we must go 'the way of the brave.'"

Rachel Hauck, *New York Times* bestselling author
of *The Wedding Dress* and *The Memory House*

"Warren lays the foundation of a promising faith-influenced series with this exciting outing."

Publishers Weekly

"The first in Warren's Global Search and Rescue series combines high-adrenaline thrills and a sweet romance. Perfect for fans of Dee Henderson and Irene Hannon."

Booklist

Praise for the Montana Rescue Series

"Pitting characters against nature—and themselves—in a rugged mountain setting, Susan May Warren pulls readers in on page one and never lets go."

Irene Hannon, bestselling author
and three-time RITA Award winner

"Warren's stalwart characters and engaging story lines make her Montana Rescue series a must-read."

Booklist

"*Troubled Waters* is a story that will not be easy to forget and one that you will read again."

Fresh Fiction

"Everything about this story sparkles: snappy dialogue, high-flying action, and mountain scenery that beckons the reader to take up snowboarding."

Publishers Weekly

Books by Susan May Warren

MONTANA RESCUE

Wild Montana Skies

Rescue Me

A Matter of Trust

Troubled Waters

Storm Front

Wait for Me

GLOBAL SEARCH AND RESCUE

The Way of the Brave

The Heart of a Hero

THE HEART OF A HERO

SUSAN MAY WARREN

a division of Baker Publishing Group
Grand Rapids, Michigan

Published by Revell
a division of Baker Publishing Group
PO Box 6287, Grand Rapids, MI 49516-6287
www.revellbooks.com

Printed in the United States of America

Library of Congress Cataloging-in-Publication Data
Names: Warren, Susan May, 1966– author.
Title: The heart of a hero / Susan May Warren.
Description: Grand Rapids, Michigan : Revell, a division of Baker Publishing Group, [2020]
Identifiers: LCCN 2019036301 | ISBN 9780800735852 (paperback)
Subjects: GSAFD: Romantic suspense fiction.
Classification: LCC PS3623.A865 H43 2020 | DDC 813/.6—dc23
LC record available at https://lccn.loc.gov/2019036301

ISBN: 978-0-8007-3870-9 (casebound)

20 21 22 23 24 25 26 7 6 5 4 3 2 1

CHAPTER 1

IN THE DAYLIGHT, Jake Silver wasn't the devil.

He didn't hear the screams.

Didn't smell the pungent residue of gun smoke tinging the air.

Didn't destroy lives.

In the daylight, he was just Uncle Jake, the guy who knew how to fly.

Jake tucked his feet into the toe straps in the trampoline of his Hobie 16 catamaran and glanced at the sky.

A perfect day. Blue skies overhead, a high in the low eighties, a scattering of cirrus that lent just enough shadow to escape the July heat.

This morning, when Jake rose, gulping back a familiar scream, his body sheened with sweat, the sunrise had cast a glaze over the platinum water that lapped the fifty feet of shoreline of his parents' lakeside home, leaving a beckoning trail of brilliant orange-and-golden sun. He'd had no choice but to surrender to the lure and drag out his cat, hopefully before the crazies hit the lake with their high-powered ski boats that dragged wakeboarders through the chop of Lake Minnetonka.

Deceiving, maybe, but the cool blue suggested a quietness that might calm the buzz that hummed right under his skin. Always, but especially since he'd come down from Denali a week ago.

No. Since he'd taken down a terrorist in the lobby of the Summit Hotel in Anchorage, Alaska.

A clean shot. A good kill.

But it awakened the demons.

Jake's plan was easy—keep outrunning them. And for the last hour he'd heard nothing but the wind, felt the sun kiss his face, casting deep into his soul. The fragrance of the lake—brine and seaweed, the fishy scent of bass and sunnies that lived in the shallows—seasoned the air.

Yes, Jake could die happily out here, in the water, away from everything that landlocked him.

He guessed the wind at about 10 knots, enough for a sweet joyride from one side of the lake to the other, past the massive million-dollar homes that edged the shoreline.

He glanced over at the little girl sitting beside him. "How ya doin', kid?"

Ten-year-old Aggie Jones wore her dark blonde hair in two tight braids down her back under a Twins ball cap his mother had found for her, along with a swimsuit and life jacket. He'd clipped her to the trapeze so she wouldn't fly off should they catch a gust, but she sat on the lip of the trampoline, her feet tucked into the toe straps, gripping the edge.

Like she'd been sailing her entire life.

Now she looked at him and nodded. No grin, but he didn't expect one. She might not even understand him. Aggie Jones hadn't spoken a word since her father found her in Italy a week ago.

Of course, Hamilton hadn't even known his daughter existed until he received a call from the air force base in Sigonella. The only survivor of a yachting accident, Agatha Jones was found by the Italian coast guard amidst the debris on shore. Although she identified herself to the American doctor serving at the clinic, she clammed up the minute Ham showed up.

Hadn't said a word since. Just clutched her only possession, a grimy unicorn that had weathered the crash.

Ham was getting desperate. But the kid just needed time. After all, she'd just lost her mother. Jake knew what it felt like to have your entire world ripped out from under you. Hence his suggestion that Ham and Aggie join Jake and the Silver clan for today's Fourth of July picnic.

When Jake had spotted Aggie up early, sitting in the sunroom, he'd invited her on his morning cruise. Asked permission from Ham, who'd spent way too long mulling over the answer.

Ham was out of his element for the first time in his life. Poor guy—the man could plan an op against a Taliban stronghold, execute and extract key prisoners, and escape through the mountains. But he didn't know how to talk to a ten-year-old.

Worse, he was shaken by the fact that the woman he'd married had escaped the bombing that he thought had taken her life.

That she'd borne him a child.

That she'd spent the last decade in hiding.

And that he'd been too late, again, to save her life.

Yeah, Ham had his own regrets to run from. A snarl of unspoken confusion. And not that Jake knew much about kids, but being the favorite uncle of his sister's rascals, he knew that sometimes you just had to stop trying so hard.

Probably advice he needed to give to himself. Let it go, let it go, according to his twin nieces, Lola and Darcy.

Someday, maybe.

"Hang on, sweetheart," Jake said now. "We're going to fly the hull!"

The cool spray of the water glistened on his surf shirt as he let out a little on the jib sheet. The catamaran rode up, skimming across the waves on the opposite hull. He held the tiller and the mainsheet in his left hand, controlled the jib sheet with his right, the sails on a broad reach.

"Woohoo!" He glanced again at Aggie. No smile as she hung on, her braids flying.

Tough crowd.

The cat rose to a forty-five-degree angle, nearly past the point of no return as they sliced through the waves. A few ski boats bobbed in the distance in Smith's Bay, one of the favorite wakeboarding spots. He'd probably be buzzing his two nephews through it later today, or maybe farther, under the bridge and into Crystal Bay.

Now, he kept heading west, toward Big Island, along the shoreline of St. Louis Bay. The wind burned his ears, and he pulled in the jib as the cat picked up even more speed.

Yeah, this day had all the makings of a restart. Erase the crazy two weeks he'd spent nearly dying on Denali. And maybe too, stop obsessing over the fact that every time he found something good, he managed to screw it up with his stupid, impulsive behavior.

Like the fact that he'd finally met a woman—*the* woman—and . . . well, he wasn't sure what happened, but the fact that the last time he'd seen her she was practically *running* from him should tell him that hadn't quite worked out.

Let it go, let it go . . .

Today was the day of freedom. New starts. Taming the wind and moving on.

The jib caught a gust and the cat jerked.

He needed more control. Or maybe it was simply the call of the wind, but he shouted at Aggie, "Stay put!" Then, Jake scooted out and braced his feet on the edge, letting the trapeze hold him as he leaned out over the water. Pulling in the jib, he slowed them just enough for him to set his feet, then let the sail out again.

The wind grabbed him, shot the hull up.

He was flying, water spraying up, his body hanging over the water.

Hooyah.

Better than sky jumping, better than diving, hanging ten on his cat made him feel like Aquaman, master of the waves.

A noise breached the wind and he looked down to see Aggie looking up at him.

Was that a smile? It turned her entire countenance to sunshine and light, her blue eyes luminous. Wow. Jake thought she looked like Ham when she was serious, all intensity and focus, but when she smiled, Jake saw the man who'd led and inspired SEAL Team Three for the better part of a decade. A person of strength and hope.

The kid just might be okay, if they all played this right.

Jake grinned back at her. "Fun, right?"

She nodded.

Well, well.

He angled them around a fishing boat and into the wide-open chop of Lower Lake South.

Jet skiers chased him down the shore, lifting their hands. Early wakeboarders had arrived, surfing behind double-engine boats churning up wake.

A chilly breeze made him glance behind him. A brouhaha of black clouds gathered at the far eastern end of the lake, rolling like fists over the horizon, tumbling his direction. And judging by the sheet of dark blue, rain.

They still had time, but the way the wind bit the bare skin of his legs with icy teeth, probably he should steer them home.

Besides, if he knew his mother, she'd be waiting with a pile of French toast.

A scream jerked his attention down. Aggie was pointing—

A tuber had cut in front of his cat.

Jake pulled in his line and cut hard with his rudder, just missing them.

They lifted their hand, as if to apologize, but he was busy righting himself, the cat slowing fast.

He danced back to the center, drawing in the main and the jib sheet, and gathered himself, tasting his thundering heartbeat.

Maybe taking Aggie out for a run wasn't the safest idea. But she was looking up at him, still grinning.

Having fun.

And he wanted more of that smile. So he let out the main, coming back around.

Jake moved back, adding more weight and leverage to his hold on the main and jib sheets. There was more chop in the open water, and he had to keep the jib in tight. He wrapped the line around his gloved hand, moving the rudder slightly to head toward St. Albin's Bay, and home.

Their white legacy-farmhouse-turned-stately-home sprawled along the shoreline with a massive lawn that made for excellent youth group parties as a kid. His pastor father had lucked out with his lineage—the only child of a doctor, he'd inherited the family wealth.

They were skimming across the waves again, Jake standing on the flying hull, when he spotted Ham standing on the dock, still too far away to attempt shouting. His short dark blond hair blew in the wind and he wore cargo shorts and a T-shirt, trying to be casual. Jake hoped Aggie kept her smile for him when they docked.

Motorboats cut in front of him, jet skiers jumping their wakes. This time a water-skier raced him across the water.

The lake was turning into a traffic jam.

He had lowered the hull down to skim the waves, pulling in the main when a cruiser—something built for a day on the lake—sped by, churning up a frothy wake.

And right then, the storm gust caught him.

Maybe it was his balance—off from the sudden gust—or even the tumult of waves from the ski boat, but the cat's opposite hull rode up the wave, dipping his side downward—

The water snagged him. Bracing, fast, quick, it sucked him under, stole his breath, stung his bones with the chill.

Not a problem—he was wearing a vest—but attached to the trapeze line, his weight dragged the mast with him. The momentum of their ride catapulted the cat forward.

The mast speared the water and just like that—

They capsized.

End over end, the mast pointed downward, turtling in the water.

The jib wrapped around him, the mast hit his head, and in a second, he was cocooned under the clutter of the lines, the sail, the gear.

Water filled his eyes.

His breath burned in his chest as he unclipped his vest. But the nylon of the sail tangled into his legs and he fought to free himself of the mess.

His lungs burned. *Aggie!*

He finally skimmed his hands down his legs, dove down, and kicked free.

Swimming hard, he surfaced. Breaths razored into his lungs. "Aggie!"

Water chopped over him, and he spat it out, blinking to clear his vision.

No little girl bobbing in the waves. "Aggie!"

She'd been attached to the cat. Which meant when it turned over, she would be caught underneath.

He dove down, under the mess, pushed past the soggy mast, and followed the lines to the trampoline.

She must have fought the trapeze line snagged onto the mast because she was tangled in the lines. Her hands pushed on the mesh of the trampoline, her mouth against the tiniest sip of air between waves.

She looked at him with an expression that could tear out his soul.

"Hang on!" He grabbed her vest and unhooked the trapeze line. Then took a breath and fought with the lines around her legs.

Where was his scuba knife when he needed it?

The cat sank deeper into the water, forcing her under.

She was going to drown.

Not on his watch.

He wrestled with the ropes, his lungs burning.

In BUD/S, the boot camp for SEALs, he'd learned to live without breathing, half-drowning most of the time.

Frankly, it felt like he lived that way his entire life.

But now he was seeing spots, fighting not to let his body take a natural breath.

No—he wasn't leaving.

Her legs came free and he kicked hard, dragging her out by her vest, forcing his jaw shut as he propelled them under the hull.

He shot to the surface. His body gulped air, his lungs searing.

She wasn't breathing, her body limp in the water.

"No! C'mon!"

Please, God!

Then, suddenly, she coughed.

A motorboat sped up and he heard a splash.

Aggie started to cry. Such a blessed, wonderful sound Jake wanted to cry too. She covered her face with her hands, still coughing, crying.

"Give her to me!" Ham was in the water. He grabbed his daughter, such a wrecked expression on his face that Jake felt ill.

The boat came closer and Jake looked up to see his buddy North leaning over the side. "I got her, Ham."

Ham didn't seem to want to give her up—Jake could hardly blame him—but Ham lifted her to North, who grabbed her arms and pulled her into the boat.

Ham swam around to the back and hoisted himself up on the deck without a ladder.

Jake treaded water, watching as Ham scooped his daughter into his embrace.

Her arms went around his neck.

Then, Jake watched the bravest man he knew sink down into a seat, trembling.

"You okay, bro?" North said. "Need some help with that?" He wore a blue GoSports T-shirt, his dark brown hair slicked back, a pair of Oakleys on a lanyard on his head. He nodded toward the capsized catamaran. It lay spent, the mast spired down into the depths.

Oh, this would be fun. "No. Take Aggie in. She probably needs to go to the ER and get checked out. See if she has water in her lungs. Don't worry about me. This is my mess. I'll clean it up."

North considered him a moment. "I'll be back." He sped off.

And as if on cue, the skies opened up and started to weep. Rain spat upon the water, and thunder rolled in the distance.

Jake grabbed the hull of his sunken ship, not sure how to rescue it from the depths.

■ ■ ■

Inside, Dr. Aria Sinclair was running.

"Dr. Sinclair, are you okay?"

No. Aria stood under the shower in the locker room of Methodist Hospital, her hands braced against the tile, her head down as the water sluiced over her plastic cap. "I'm okay, Devon. You don't have to follow me into the bathroom."

Nothing she said to her resident was going to change the fact that little Leo Richter had died.

Her patient. Her procedure. Her fault.

"It's a unisex locker room and I'm not following you. I mean, not completely . . ." Devon's voice slipped through the steam as heat rose, soaking into her bones.

No matter how long she stood here, she couldn't wash away the haunting wails of Lenae Richter.

Maybe Aria shouldn't have returned to work so quickly.

Maybe not at all.

"You did everything you could."

She could imagine him standing in the main locker room area, shouting, dressed in his scrubs, distress on his handsome face.

He'd stood beside her as they tried to console the Richters. But that was over—what else did he want from her?

"You're a resident, Devon. You're going to have to get used to this kind of thing."

She didn't mean to be harsh, but frankly, that's what it took to be in this specialty. Pediatric cardiothoracic surgery meant taking chances, sometimes losing lives. Knowing when to move on.

"I know, Dr. Sinclair. I was just . . . wondering how you are."

"I'm fine." These things happened.

Except, well, it *wasn't* supposed to happen.

She hadn't exactly made promises, but this had felt like a win. She might have even . . . relaxed.

Let the victory into her bones.

After all, she had practically pioneered this procedure. A balloon atrial septoplasty, *in utero*. Groundbreaking. Lifesaving. A procedure she'd refined and published in the *International Journal for Pediatric and Congenital Heart Surgery*. She'd received teaching offers in Sydney, British Columbia, and even Johannesburg. The one from Texas Children's was still sitting on her desk, her acceptance letter in her outbasket.

Number one children's hospital in the world. The next step on her quest to be at the top of her field.

But really, she knew better than to offer hope. Especially since she'd never seen a case so dire in a preterm baby—both interior walls of the heart sealed shut, the main arteries reversed.

If little baby Leo Richter had been born naturally, he wouldn't have lived long enough to make it to the surgical theater to make the repairs.

But he had.

Because she'd convinced Lenae and Jeremy that she could insert a needle through Lenae's womb, right into their baby boy—Leo—and place a balloon in his tiny heart, making a hole that would open the heart's interior wall so oxygenated blood could pass through. He would live long enough for her to give him open-heart surgery to correct his misaligned arteries.

And it worked.

Even the surgery to correct the congenital defect, four days after his birth, worked.

Until it didn't.

"He threw a clot. Pulmonary embolism. We couldn't have stopped it," she said now, for Devon.

"I know." Devon's voice sounded closer. "I just . . . I wanted to make sure *you* knew."

And with his words, Aria just wanted to sink down, into the corner, and weep. "I know, Devon. I know. Go home."

It wasn't her first loss. Not by far. The deaths were brutal but sometimes expected in her specialty.

But on top of everything else—

"Aria, come out and talk to me."

Not Devon's voice this time. This male voice belonged to Dr. Lucas Maguire, chief of surgery.

"Lucas? What are you doing here?"

"Come out and I'll tell you."

So, Lucas was worried too.

Worried, because he was her boss.

Worried, because he was the husband of her best friend.

Worried, probably because only a week ago, she'd nearly lost her life on a mountain.

Maybe she had no business operating on baby Leo. Not with her ankle still rocking a splint and her body still exhausted from her twenty days above fourteen thousand feet.

But no one else knew the procedure.

Oh, her arrogance.

He probably should suspend her. She turned off the shower and grabbed her towel. "I'm . . . I'll be out in a minute."

She shivered as she pulled on her robe and stepped out into the private dressing cubicle. Her sundress hung from a hook and she pulled it on, grabbed her cardigan, and exited into the mirrored area.

Stripped of makeup, she looked about eighty-two. Fatigue lines etched around her eyes, and as she pulled off the plastic cap, she could definitely see white streaks in her dark hair.

She pulled it back into a messy bun, then threw the towel into the bin and hung her robe in the locker beside her toiletries. Grabbed her satchel.

She needed her bed. A pillow over her head.

The dreamless sleep of the dead.

And maybe when she awoke, she'd find a new day, a fresh start, without drama, disaster, and grief.

Without regret. No, without fears that she would do it—life, medicine, relationships—wrong.

Lucas was waiting in the staff lounge, his back to her. He ripped open a stevia packet and added it to some sludge-slash-coffee. Outside, the night had given way to morning, but rain spat on the windows, a dour, gray greeting.

That felt about right.

Devon sat at a round table, drinking a Diet Coke from the machine. He wore the fatigue lines of the trauma in his face. A handsome man, brown hair, dark skin, beautiful pale green eyes, he'd started his medical career late, after being an army medic for the first five years out of high school. Now, he sat at the table, his scrub hat in his hand, and watched her, his gaze a little too probing.

"What is this, the Spanish Inquisition?"

Lucas didn't smile. "Mmmhmm," he said instead. Over six feet, still built like the former navy doctor he'd been, Lucas wore a beard, his light brown hair cut short, his hazel-brown eyes containing a texture of worry. He was in his street clothes, no scrubs, and it occurred to her that he was supposed to have the day off.

She looked at Devon, then Lucas. "Am I in trouble?"

Lucas frowned.

"The baby threw a clot. It wasn't the procedure—"

"Listen," Lucas said, "Devon filled me in. You spent the night by his bedside and worked on him for over an hour. In front of his parents. I got worried." Lucas walked over and pulled out a formed plastic chair. "Sit."

"I'm buzzing." She walked over to the coffeepot and poured out the last of the dregs.

"That'll help."

"Coffee is my favorite food group."

"It's your only food group." Lucas was still pointing at the chair. He raised an eyebrow.

Fine. She slid onto the chair, dropping her satchel beside her. Glanced at Devon. "You're as tired as I am. Go home." She looked away from him, to Lucas. "And I thought you had the day off. Independence Day—you should be celebrating with Sasha."

"I am. I will. And—that's why I'm here."

She took a drink, made a face. "Did one of the new interns make this?"

Lucas tried his coffee. But he'd doctored his with creamer and sweetener, so—

"Oh yeah, that'll peel hair off." He set down the coffee. "Listen, I need a favor."

She scrubbed her hands down her face. Perfect. Dr. Maguire probably needed her to take on his patients while he and Sasha jetted off to another vacation—

Oh, that wasn't fair. Sasha had nearly died a week ago. Yes, probably they needed a break. Warm shores.

Cancun. Aria let herself laugh, at least on the inside—the joke she shared with Jenny Calhoun and Sasha as they heated snow for water and tried to survive in their flimsy tent as a blizzard socked them in. Next girls' trip—Mexico.

Outside, the rain was letting up, but an errant wind rattled the window.

Aria shivered, a by-product of spending twenty-one days in subzero temperatures.

"How's your ankle?" Lucas pulled out another chair for her to prop her foot up.

Tender. Swollen from standing on it for hours.

"It's fine."

"It's not. She took off her brace and limped all the way down here," Devon said.

She shot him a look. "Go."

"Stay," Lucas said.

"What's the favor?" She didn't mean to bark at him, but . . .

Okay, she didn't like herself much lately, to be honest. Didn't like the fact that she'd nearly done something colossally stupid in Alaska, with a charming guy who probably hadn't thought about her since she'd practically fled from him. Didn't like the fact that her sleepless nights had more to do with the memory of Jake Silver's stupid smile, his charisma, and the way he'd made her feel—

Well, not like the uptight cardiothoracic pediatric surgeon she'd left back in Minneapolis.

She'd lost her mind, just a little, in Alaska—especially around Jake. Embarrassed herself, badly.

Escaped home, trying to find herself again.

Not quite. And baby Leo might have paid the price.

She could be ill, right here, and pressed her hand to her stomach. "Sorry. I'm just tired."

Lucas was watching her. "You probably have a little PTSD after what happened on the mountain."

"What happened on the mountain?" Devon said.

"She blew off the top of Denali, is what. She and her team survived a fall down a glacier. Spent three nights on the back side of the mountain and would have died up there if—"

"Hit the showers, Devon." She looked at Lucas. "Don't you dare mention his name."

He startled and she wanted to wince. She'd never win at poker.

"Who? Hamilton Jones?"

Right. Jake's boss, the SAR guy who had led the team who'd found and saved them. She swallowed. Nodded.

"Oh wait . . . you mean Jake Silver."

"Thanks for that."

Lucas grinned and wore a not-so-subtle twinkle in his eye. "Yeah, I saw you two together. Did something . . . happen there, Doc?"

Almost. And shoot, if God had mercy her face wouldn't heat, wouldn't—

"Wow," Lucas said. "So, that's a yes."

Again, no poker for her.

"We . . . he . . . so, no. Nothing important happened."

Because Jenny, her roommate, had walked in. Right before she'd nearly . . .

And now *she* should probably flee the room.

She sipped her coffee, letting her silence do the work of making Devon leave. He headed for the locker room.

Lucas's tone changed. Softened. "Aria, are you . . . okay?"

She drew in a breath. Her hand went to her neck, to the bare skin there. Made a fist where the missing necklace should be. Right. She didn't have her half of her heart anymore, either.

Thanks for that, Jake.

Probably she should stop blaming the guy for her own bad behavior.

But if she never saw him again, it would be too soon.

"I heard you were offered a job at the Texas Children's Hospital."

She stilled. "You heard about that?"

"It's my job to know. Besides, they called me before they extended the offer." He gave her a wry smile. "Head of pediatrics. Teaching, your own grant funds for research. And you haven't said yes yet?"

She drew in a breath. "I am. I will. I—"

"Is that what you really want?"

His question brought her up. "Yeah. Of course. It's the next step, right?"

"To where?"

"To . . . well . . . just the next step."

He nodded and took a sip of coffee.

"I mean, that's the goal, right? To be the best?"

He set down his cup. "You tell me."

She frowned. Shook her head. "Well, yes, I'm going to take the job. I just . . . I just need to get my feet under me is all. I'm just feeling—"

"Like you lost your mojo."

She stared at him. "No. I . . . I'm fine—"

"I know. That's why you're going to the beach," Lucas said quietly.

Oh. She raised an eyebrow. "I, no . . . *what*?"

"Key West. I signed you up to speak at a Cardiology and Pulmonology for Primary Care conference."

"I'm not prepared—"

"Of course you are. You eat and breathe the balloon atrial septoplasty. Just show up and talk."

"My patient *died*, Lucas. I don't want to talk about it."

He made a grim line with his mouth. "I know. But it was still another landmark surgery . . ."

And now her eyes filled. She was just tired. So . . . tired. "He should have lived."

Lucas didn't move.

"Maybe I wasn't ready to come back."

"You're one of the best, Aria. Talented. But you need a break."

"I can't go to Key West."

"Yes, you can," Lucas said. "I'll take your patients. Devon can fill me in. You still have vacation time, and frankly, as your boss, I'm telling you that you're going."

She got up, picked up her coffee, and limped over to the trash can. Oops, she probably shouldn't have sat down. Now her ankle burned, and the idea of taking a week off— "How long is the conference?"

"Just two days, but my travel agent booked the resort for a week."

No. *Really.* No.

"You could sleep the entire week."

She glanced at Lucas. "I don't—"

"Sleep? I know, Aria. You're the hardest-working—"

"Need a vacation."

"You've needed a vacation since I met you. You take vacations that you need vacations from, for crying out loud. And your last vacation"—he finger-quoted the words—"tried to kill you. Listen, I'll help you cheat. You have to work before you get to play. That should satisfy the perfectionist workaholic in you."

He probably didn't mean for his words to sting but . . . okay, maybe.

But people given second chances had a responsibility to *do* something with their lives.

Devon emerged from the locker room wearing a pair of jeans and a black T-shirt, smelling good.

Lucas got up. "Your plane ticket is already purchased. Flight leaves on Friday—"

"Next week?"

"In two days."

"Lucas!"

"No one is going to die without you."

She knew he didn't mean for it to sting. But, *ouch*.

Devon came back to the table. "I'll fill Dr. Maguire in on your patients, and you can call me anytime to check on things. You already have my number."

Outside, the rain had stopped, sunshine streaking through the gray clouds, burning away the gloom.

Maybe she did need sunshine. Beach.

And about two thousand miles between her and her regrets.

Namely a six-two, blond former SEAL who lived somewhere in Minneapolis. A city big enough for her to avoid him. Forever.

Please, God.

And maybe a break would help her shake free of her recent string of disasters.

Find her mojo again, as Lucas said.

Help her say yes to Texas.

"Now, here comes the bad news," Lucas said.

"What? Tickets to Disneyland? Or better, you're buying me a house."

"Funny. Sasha sent me to pick you up. We're going to a party."

"No, I—"

"Jenny's back from Alaska with Orion. She texted Sasha and invited us to a Fourth of July party. On the lake." Lucas came over to her and eased her satchel off her shoulder. "With cake."

"I don't like cake."

"Everybody likes cake."

She sighed.

"I can't go home empty-handed. Help a guy out here."

She winced, pressing her thumb and forefinger into her eyes.

"Devon, come with us. You need a break too."

What—no! But she looked up just as Devon nodded.

"Great. Let's go." Lucas stood up. "I promise, you're going to have a great time, whether you like it or not."

She'd bet on not.

CHAPTER 2

THE MAST STILL LOOKS INTACT."

Orion Starr stood on the shore, his knee in a brace, watching as Jake towed the Hobie cat onto the sandy shoreline next to his family's dock. Orion leaned on a pair of crutches, his face still sunburned in a reverse raccoon look, the white around his eyes evidence of the summer sun on top of Denali. He'd gotten a haircut, leaving his brown hair shorter on the sides and longer on top. Jake had a swift memory of the way Orion had lain shattered at the bottom of a crevasse, his knee at a brutal angle. To see him up and walking . . . maybe Jake had done something good when he'd helped rescue him.

Even if he'd like to forget the rest.

"The Hobie is pretty tough. It's taken more than one cartwheel across the lake." Jake climbed aboard the cat to take down the sails. "I've had it since I was a kid. When did you get to Minneapolis?"

After their adventure in Alaska, Orion had stayed behind to pack his gear for his big move to Minnesota to join Hamilton Jones's private global search and rescue team.

It didn't hurt that his girlfriend, Jenny Calhoun, lived nearby. And according to Ham, she was going to join the team as their team profiler and climbing pro. Which meant Jake would get a constant reminder of the Girl Who Got Away.

Aka Aria Sinclair, Jenny's roommate.

He clamped his mouth shut, refusing to ask about the pediatric surgeon who lived just across town.

Aria hadn't so much as texted him.

Then again, the running away from him should have been a dead giveaway that they were o-*ver*. Before they'd even begun.

Probably for the best. She didn't need a guy with his demons.

The foamy residue of the storm lapped around his ankles as he unhooked the lines and tied up the jib sail. If he took the kids out on the lake today, he'd take the ski boat.

"We got in last night," Orion said. "Ham texted this morning and invited us to your shindig."

Of course he did. Although Ham could have held the party at his place, just down the shoreline, his lawn twice the size of the Silver family home. Jake had a feeling Ham's presence at the Silvers' party had more to do with Aggie and his panic over his sudden fatherhood.

Not that Ham panicked easily, or even betrayed his emotions at all. But Jake knew the story behind Signe, Aggie's mom, and the fact that after all this time Ham found himself with a daughter had hit even Jake in the chest like a fist. No wonder Ham was reeling.

"How's Aggie?" Jake unhooked the mainsail, drawing it down.

"Rattled, but she'll be okay. Ham took her into urgent care. She was checked out and released. I think they gave her antibiotics in case she ingested water. She's inside watching television, eating your mom's chocolate chip cookies."

"The sure cure for trauma."

"Ham grabbed a few for himself too. He's up at the grill talking with your dad. And North is making moves on one of your sisters, I think. Blonde, pretty—"

"Take your pick, buddy. That's pretty much all of them."

"That's rough. Being the big brother of all that beauty."

Jake tucked away the mainsail into its cover. "I got into more than my share of fights trying to keep the hungry away."

He didn't look at Orion, but he knew this game—keeping the conversation easy, away from the fact that he'd nearly *killed* Ham's kid. Jake's stomach was still woozy and aching from where he'd lost it in the lake.

Jake could have probably used North's help when his former swim buddy and fellow GoSports employee returned in the family ski boat to help him, but he wanted to reckon with the disaster alone.

His mess. His problem.

It took him the better part of two hours to right the cat, get the lines reattached, and sail her back in.

At least it had stopped raining.

The sun had even emerged, drying the grass. Smoke stirred from the grill on the stone patio, up near the house, and the shouts of his nephews playing catch with a pigskin drifted down to the beach.

And oh, he couldn't stop himself— "So," he said, still keeping it casual, "did you see . . . uh . . ."

"Aria?"

For a second, just her name uttered from Orion's lips swept back the memories Jake had been trying—clearly not hard enough—to burn from his mind.

Aria's dark, wet hair playing through his fingers as she stepped up to him, those beautiful doe-brown eyes in his, her hands on his shirt, the smell of a shower fresh on her skin. *"Mornin', Hawkeye."*

Of course, those words were spoken more in his fantasy than

memory, but she could have said them, given the fact that they'd spent the night camped out on her hotel room floor.

Innocent. At least in action.

Not hardly in his head.

"Uncle Jake! Look out!"

The shouts from his twelve-year-old nephew, Scout, jerked him out of the rest of the memory just in time to throw up his hands to deflect the football arrowing for his head.

In fact, with more instinct than effort, he made a spectacular catch, nabbing the ball and falling back into the water with a splash.

"Cool!" Scout ran down onto the beach, wearing only a pair of swim trunks, barefoot and tan, his blond hair long around his ears. "Great catch!"

Jake pushed himself to his feet and shook the water out of his eyes. "Yeah, well, I wasn't all-state for nothin', kid." He tossed Scout the ball and saw Orion smirk. "What?"

Orion nodded at Scout, who ran back up the lawn toward his brother, Bear. "I see a little hero worship there."

Jake was winding up rope and glanced at the two boys. "Their dad, Mark, works a lot—he's a computer geek. Great guy, but not super athletic."

"And their uncle is a SEAL."

"Was. Now I teach swimming lessons to kids." He tied down the last of the lines. "And occasionally nearly drown them."

"That wasn't your fault."

Jake lifted a shoulder. "Doesn't matter. I was responsible for her. My watch, my mistake."

Orion said nothing.

Jake joined him on the beach, grabbing a towel to scrub his face. He then pulled off his surf shirt, wringing it out.

"I didn't see Aria," Orion said finally. "But I didn't go by Jenny's apartment—she dropped me off at the hotel last night. But . . ." Orion made a face.

"What did Jenny say?"

"Enough. I know what happened in Alaska. That's tough."

"Seriously." He hung the towel around his shoulders.

"Dude, I get it. Aria is a grown woman, but apparently Jenny thinks you took advantage of her. She was on pain meds, and still suffering from altitude sickness, and—"

"I did not. She—" And what could he say? That she made him lose his mind with her soft suggestion that he stick around and take a shower in her hotel room and . . .

Okay, so maybe that suggestion didn't quite fit her persona as a bigwig baby doc, but maybe they'd both been suffering from the aftereffects of nearly dying on a mountain.

Or maybe he'd simply read way, way too much into that suggestion and embarrassed both of them.

"She—what?" Orion asked, frowning.

Jake shook his head. "Nothing. Just . . . I handled it badly. But I . . ." He'd thought they could have something more than just right then. More than a fling that could stay in Alaska.

He'd even started hoping for it, sometime during the days he'd been trapped with her in a tent.

So, yeah, when he kissed her, when he'd reached for the belt securing her bathrobe, he'd been thinking about something more than just a tawdry one-night-stand. Jenny's sudden appearance in the hotel room had snapped him back to reality. To the fact that he was about to take them both someplace they might—probably, yes—regret.

But that was his MO. Dive in and think about the consequences later.

"Nothing happened. But Jenny is probably right. Aria might

not have been in the best place emotionally. She freaked out, and then Jenny practically threw me out of the hotel, and . . . aw, shoot. I just wish I could hit reset. Start over. Show her I'm not that guy."

Orion raised an eyebrow.

"Not with her. She's . . ."

"Way out of your league?"

Jake grinned, nodded. "That, yeah. You're probably right. I should let it go. She isn't exactly trying to track me down."

Orion gave him a strange look.

"What?"

"Nothing. I just . . . nothing."

Jake frowned but climbed up to the dock and onto the freshly mowed grass. He headed up to the house, Orion behind him.

The farmhouse had been overhauled, the exterior updated with new paint, fresh windows, and an expansive stone patio complete with fire pit, built-in grill, portico, and a bright-red picnic table.

His father, Chuck, stood at the grill, the tangy smell of his sweet rib recipe stirring the air and Jake's appetite. His father always reminded him of an older Jeff Bridges. He wore his hair scandalously long for a preacher, but then again, he'd grown up in the hippie era. Wealthy doctor's kid turned druggie, saved at a Billy Graham crusade, ministering to the lost in downtown Minneapolis.

He was Jake's hero.

Jake never deserved the forgiveness his father offered him, and he knew it.

His father wore a pair of jeans, a T-shirt, and a mitt over his hand, which gripped a barbecue fork. "Ribs will be ready in an hour," he said to Jake as he approached.

"Hey, Jake." This from his sister Dinah, who sat in a nearby Adirondack chair paging through a magazine. She wore her long blonde hair back in a sleek ponytail and was dressed in lightweight linen pants, a teal tank top, and fingernail polish matching her toes. "The boys are hoping you'll take them out on the cat today."

"We'll see," Jake said. "When is Mark getting here?"

"I don't know. He's having some internet security breach at the office." She looked up. "By the way, I'm having the twins' birthday bash at the Mall of America—next Saturday. Don't forget."

Right. Mandatory Silver Family Event. "I'll be there."

"Good. And I have a few more listings for you to look at when you're ready."

Listings. For the condo she wanted him to buy.

Probably his sister was right. He still occupied the bedroom in his parents' house six months after returning to Minneapolis. He just . . . well, he wasn't sure he was down for that kind of long-term commitment. "Yeah, sure. Whenever."

The picnic table held a bowl of potato salad covered in plastic and a plastic container of pickles. Jake stole one while Orion fished a dripping can of Coke from the nearby cooler.

Jake crunched on the pickle as he watched North help his sister Selah set up the volleyball net. He debated warning off the guy—Selah had given her heart and future to Jesus and had spent the past four years teaching English in foreign lands.

Or maybe he should simply stop trying to babysit everyone.

Ham stood beside his father at the grill. He'd changed out of his wet clothes—had probably stopped by his house after the urgent-care trip—into a pair of jeans and another T-shirt with the red GoSports logo on his chest.

"Hey, Jake," Ham said. "Can I get a sec?"

Jake nodded, finishing off the pickle. "Let me change and I'll be down."

He went into the house, through the back porch, and up the stairs from the basement and found his mother in the recently remodeled kitchen on the main floor. It opened to an expansive view of Lake Minnetonka, with wide windows that captured the blues of the lake and sky, the towering elms that shaded the yard, the green grass that had beckoned him home after the chaos of war.

The kitchen merged into a sunroom—wicker chairs, blue pillows, and, with the exception of his father's old recliner, a nautical feel to a room that had once been the home of a farmer. The smell of chocolate chip cookies caused Jake to swing by the island and snag one off the white quartz countertop.

Vegetables before dessert.

"You okay?" His mother, her white-blonde hair cut short, wearing a jean shirt over her tank top and leggings, slid a couple warm cookies off the hot sheet. "I heard about the accident." She met his gaze.

Out of everyone, his mother had the ability to pull him to the ground, root him there, and find the truth.

Now he nodded. Swallowed.

"She's okay. She's watching some Barbie horse patrol with the twins in the den. But Jake, accidents happen. This wasn't on you."

He gave her a thin-lipped nod, his jaw tightening. Took another cookie.

He passed the den and saw the girls cuddled up on the sofa, Aggie sitting between Dinah's six-year-old twin girls.

He was heading upstairs at the front of the house when his sister Phoebe came into the house holding a paper bag on her hip. Her button shirt was open over her baby bump. She wore her blonde hair long and sported a pair of short shorts, her legs long and tanned. She was probably still modeling, even six months pregnant.

"Hey, let me help you." He grabbed for the bag as she came in. "Where's Stephan?"

"He's got a meeting this morning—he'll be over later. Partner stuff." She handed him the bag. "Were you out training for your next Ironman?"

"Funny. No. Sailing."

"You mean flying." She winked at him. "Glad you're back. Dad said you were mountain climbing? In Alaska?"

"Something like that." He put the bag in the kitchen, then headed up the stairs to his room overlooking the garage, his window the exact height for surreptitious escapes in his high school years. After grabbing dry clothes, he jumped into the shower and was out and dressed by the time his other sister, Chloe, had arrived.

She sat on one of the stools in the kitchen, her hair shorn short, wearing what looked like an African scarf on her head. Tanned, she wore no makeup and peeled an orange onto the counter. Her satchel sat on a nearby sofa.

"When did you get back?" she asked as Jake came through the room, his feet bare on the wooden floor.

"A week ago. You?"

"Same."

"Where did the paper send you this time? Or don't I want to know? You're looking pretty tan—I'm guessing it was to a continent south of the equator?"

"Sudan."

"See, no, don't tell me those things." He leaned in and kissed her cheek. "Please don't make me have to come after you someday."

She patted his chest. "Calm down, big brother. You take your job too seriously."

She left her hand there, maybe because she knew her words stung, even inadvertently. He patted it but didn't say anything.

Because, even after twenty years, the wounds could still be as raw as the day Hannah had gone missing.

Ham came into the house. "Ready?"

Jake nodded and gestured into the living room, off the kitchen.

"Hey, Ham," Chloe said, and Jake noticed her gaze follow the tall SEAL as he walked through the kitchen.

"Chloe," he said, clearly oblivious. Or maybe just preoccupied.

Jake followed him into the room, shutting the swinging door behind him. "Ham—"

"She's fine." He turned to Jake, plowing a hand through his hair. "Because of you, she's fine."

Oh. He hadn't expected that. "I'm so sorry—"

"I saw the entire thing—it wasn't your fault."

"I strapped her into the trapeze line."

"And if you hadn't, she might have been thrown off earlier or . . . anyway . . ." Ham took a breath. "Thanks."

Oh. Jake's chest eased.

"But, are you okay?"

The question clipped him, drew him up, and he stared at Ham. Swallowed.

"You know I'm not talking about today."

Jake nodded.

"It's just . . . if you need to talk to someone—"

"I'm sick of talking, Ham. I just . . . I just need to keep moving."

Ham leaned against the fireplace mantel, folded his arms.

And why not, really, voice the question churning in his chest, the one that lingered in the light of day. "I'm thinking about re-activating."

Ham's brow creased.

"I don't know what I'm doing here, Ham. Sleeping in my old bedroom, teaching kids how to swim—I need to be out there, doing something." He walked to the window, shook his head. "I don't know who I am anymore."

"You're the same guy who separated from the navy six months ago—"

"I hope not," Jake said, turning. "Because that guy was a mess, and we both know it."

Ham nodded. "Okay, agreed. But you've done the hard work. And you've found your way back. North was right about you—you're a good man, with integrity."

"He's supposed to say that—he was my swim buddy."

"But I worked with you too, before I took over my own platoon. You were young, but eager and dedicated, and, truth is, I wouldn't have invited you to join Jones, Inc., if I didn't think you were right for this team."

Jake steeled himself. Swallowed.

"Oh," Ham said. "This is about the shooting in Alaska."

"If the press finds out it's me—"

"They can't connect you. They won't. It was classified."

"They found out anyway. And called me the devil." He looked away. "Maybe I am."

"Jake—stop." Ham walked over. "You were doing your job. End of story."

Jake nodded. "I know. And I miss it—being a part of something bigger than myself. I had a mission. A purpose. I felt like . . ."

"A hero?"

Jake lifted a shoulder. "A SEAL."

"Jake. You don't have to wear your dog tags to be a SEAL. That's in here." He put a fist to his chest.

Jake sighed.

"Listen, I need you, Jake. More than you realize. I need to go out of town."

"Now?" Jake said, sitting on the arm of the sofa. "What about Aggie?"

"I won't be gone long—just a few days, maybe a week."

Jake frowned. "Does this have something to do with Signe and her death?"

Ham shook his head, emotion flickering across his face. "No. It's something else."

"Really?"

"Yeah."

"So, you're not going to even look into—"

"What am I going to do? The Italian officials said the yacht she was on blew up. Aggie is lucky to be alive." Ham looked out the window, shaking his head. "I still can't believe that Signe didn't tell me."

"Ham. You didn't even know she was alive. Maybe Signe *couldn't* tell you."

And that was clearly not the right thing to say because Ham's mouth tightened around the edges. Yeah, Jake was imagining some dire scenarios too.

"I should have kept looking," Ham said quietly. "I shouldn't have let myself believe—"

"You can't hang on forever," Jake said softly. Something the family counselor had said, so long ago. He still wasn't sure she was right, but it sounded good, so, "You had to move on."

A muscle twitched in Ham's jaw. "I need a favor."

Jake raised an eyebrow. "What do you want me to do?"

Ham ran a thumb under his eye. "Watch Aggie for me."

"What—me?"

"Yeah. I already cleared it with your mom for her to stay here. But Aggie . . . she trusts you. And I need her to feel safe right now. She does, with you. With your family. I . . . I need you, Jake."

Wow, and that felt like a lot for Ham to admit.

"I . . ."

Ham just looked at him, those dark blue eyes pinning him down. He knew that look.

"Listen. Ham. I'm not . . . I don't . . ." His gaze went to the pictures on the wall. The ones that hadn't moved for twenty years. Family pictures when their family was still intact. Of course, Ellie wasn't in them.

But Hannah was. Forever young, missing her two front teeth, grinning in the center of the family picture, taken at the beach the summer she went missing.

He was in the picture too, buck teeth, gangly in his thirteen-year-old awkwardness, looking too smug for his own good, a football under his arm.

What an idiot.

Ham followed his gaze and went quiet.

Jake ran a hand behind his neck.

"I trust you, Jake. With my life. With her life."

Jake couldn't look at him. "I don't know anything about taking care of a ten-year-old girl."

"Neither do I! But you have all these sisters—"

"They're my *sisters*. My job was to annoy them and protect them."

"So . . . protect my daughter. Ellie will be here, right? Maybe she can . . . I don't know, make cookies with her."

"Ellie barely lifts her head away from her cell phone," Jake said, but he sighed, nodding. "But I'll figure it out."

"Would it help if I told you I was following up on a lead about Royal Benjamin?"

Royal Benjamin, a former SEAL teammate under Ham's command who'd gone missing after an op-gone-south in Afghanistan three years ago.

"My friend Senator Isaac White has a contact in Europe who

he thinks might be him. Says he's working for the CIA. I made a promise to Orion that we'd try and find him, bring him home."

Orion, who'd tried to rescue Royal during that same op, and failed. The Taliban had captured Royal and another SEAL, Logan Thorne, and although they'd eventually been rescued, Royal had vanished.

Orion was still plagued by the nightmares of leaving a man behind.

"I don't get a chance at redemption often, Jake. I gotta do this."

Jake glanced out the window to where movement caught his attention. A car had pulled up. He watched as Dr. Lucas Maguire stepped out of the driver's seat. From the other side, Sasha emerged, and—

His breath stopped.

Aria Sinclair.

She looked good too. Brown hair down, wearing a sundress and flip-flops, her ankle in a walking brace. She flipped her hair back, and for a second, he could nearly feel it, silky between his fingers.

Redemption. Walking down his front walk.

Except, beside her emerged someone else. Another man, dark hair, his gaze on Aria.

Oh goody, she'd brought a date.

This day was just getting better and better.

He turned back to Ham. "You can count on me, bro. I won't let anything happen to Aggie."

■ ■ ■

If Aria just made it through the next four hours, she'd never have to see the man again.

But Jake Silver was hard, oh-so-very-hard to ignore.

Especially with his *Top Gun* beach volleyball impression.

First, his parents had a rockin' backyard facing the lake, although if she'd known Lucas was dragging her to Jake's house—

Except, Jenny was there, and Sasha, and a slew of Jake's sisters, and family, as well as a few other guys from GoSports, Ham and North, and maybe . . . okay, maybe Aria was having a good time.

Especially watching Jake and Devon wage some kind of testosterone war with their two-on-two volleyball game.

Two, as in North and Devon against Ham and Jake. They'd set up a volleyball net in the yard, and the rest of the family had pulled up chairs around the perimeter, acting as line judges to the contest.

She wasn't exactly sure how she'd gone from wanting to flee the moment Jake opened his front door to diving into the trash talking and fun.

Maybe it was because when Jake's blue-eyed gaze slid over her, the man acted as if . . . well, as if he barely knew her.

And frankly, she didn't know whether she might be hurt, or just ticked that he'd so easily written off their near tryst. She shouldn't have let herself get so twisted up about this guy. Charming Jake Silver.

See, she knew, just *knew* she was one of his many flings.

What happened in Alaska really did stay in Alaska.

As if to prove it, Jake had given her another cursory glance, then one at Devon, then flashed them both a smile, completely, infuriatingly unaffected by her appearance.

Whereas she just stood there like an idiot, staring at him, no, completely bowled over by the change in him.

First, he smelled good—freshly showered, his Alaskan beard shaved, his blond hair cut. As if the moment he left Alaska he'd shed the persona of mountain man for this preppy boy from the suburbs. He stood barefoot, his legs tanned, wearing a T-shirt and a pair of cargo shorts.

Well, it wasn't like she looked the same, either. Last time he saw her she'd been wearing a bathrobe.

Now, she was Dr. Aria Sinclair, and two could play at this game of charades, thank you.

"I'm Jake," he said, extending his hand to Devon, who took it.

And she didn't know why, but she put her hand on Devon's arm. "He's my resident."

Devon glanced at her, frowned, then, "Dr. Devon McMillan. I work with Dr. Sinclair."

A spark had lit in Jake's eyes then, one she probably should have predicted, but, well, someone—hello, Lucas—should have told her that they were going to Jake's house.

Jake's jaw had tightened at Devon's introduction. Or maybe she simply imagined—hoped—it, but he just nodded. "Super. Welcome to our little Fourth of July party."

She might have given Devon too much encouragement because he touched her back as they entered Jake's lair.

And what a lair. The house wasn't exactly sprawling, but compared to the tiny bungalow where she was raised in Iowa, the place felt massive. A grand kitchen with wooden flooring, a vaulted ceiling, and a towering white fireplace filled the great room, and a sunroom led out to a deck with a stone patio underneath.

Jake had led the others down the stairs to the patio below.

She'd stood on the deck for a long moment, breathing in the scent of the lake, the oak trees, the English roses climbing up the lattice along the wall of the house.

"Hi." His mother had followed her out onto the deck. "I'm Georgia Silver. And you must be Aria?" Slim and pretty, Georgia wore her blonde hair short, a jean shirt open over a tank top, a pair of leggings. "Ham said you were in Alaska, with Jake."

"No. I was on the team of women Jake and Ham rescued." She

might as well get it out into the open, admit the bald truth. "We were blown off the mountain and Jake saved my life."

His mother just stared at her. "Oh. I didn't . . . I didn't know that." She found a smile, however, quickly, and glanced at her ankle splint. "Are you okay?"

She looked down at the gathering on the patio. Jenny stood with Orion, who leaned on his crutches. Sasha was laughing, her arms around Lucas's waist.

They'd survived. She should be celebrating.

Hard to do when a woman was making funeral arrangements for her four-day-old child.

"Yeah," Aria said. "Just a rough night at work."

Georgia nodded. "I understand rough nights. But God's mercies are new every morning." She patted Aria on the arm. "I think the ribs are about ready. Or, you could just stay up here and enjoy the view."

Probably she meant the view of the lake, with the jet skiers and the speedboats, but of course Aria's gaze went to . . . well, Jake.

He'd gone over to Devon and was talking to the resident, and just the comparison of the two . . . well, it really wasn't fair to compare Devon with a former navy SEAL.

Devon wasn't exactly a slouch. He probably worked out, lean and trim in his jeans and his black T-shirt. Handsome, really, and about her age.

Frankly, she'd heard the hospital rumors that Devon liked her.

Jake had picked up a volleyball and was twirling it in his hands. He stood, legs apart, confident as he bumped the ball with his fist, caught it. Laughed at something Devon said.

He had such a nice laugh—

Shoot. Wake *up*! Dr. Aria Sinclair had no room for a guy like

Jake in her life. Jake was charming and fun, the kind of guy meant for a vacation fling.

Not for real life.

Her sister Kia would have been a perfect match for Jake. But Kia wasn't here, and even if Aria did have Kia's heart beating in her chest, it didn't mean she had to follow it into the arms of trouble.

Even if trouble did know how to kiss. And turn her into a warm puddle with one glance of his blue eyes . . .

Stop. Because Jake was also impulsive and dangerous. Aria had no room for either in her world.

She should be focusing on a guy like Devon. Steady. Tucked in.

Except, an hour later, she wasn't sure who was the steady, tucked-in one. Devon had stripped off his shirt, revealing exactly the toned physique she'd guessed. And then there was Jake, also stripped down to just his shorts, his shoulders thick with muscle as he dove to bump the ball up to Ham.

Who jumped and spiked it onto the grass on Devon's side of the court.

"In!" shouted one of Jake's sisters—Dinah, she thought, the oldest one, a real estate agent who reminded her a little of Gwyneth Paltrow. Pretty, smart, long blonde hair.

"No way, that was out." This from Ellie, the youngest, who'd come home halfway through lunch. Also blonde, she held one of her nieces on her lap, bouncing the six-year-old.

Ham's daughter sat on the picnic table behind them, watching.

Aria's heart went out to her. She knew too well what it felt like to sit on the sidelines.

Aria sat next to Selah, who wore her blonde hair in a long, singular braid. Chloe, her twin, had excused herself to take a phone call.

"Out," said Chuck, Jake's dad. "Next point wins."

"Bring it, Yankee," Ham said, taunting North as he sent the

ball over the net. Ham bumped it up, and Jake sent it over. Devon dove, scooped it up, and set it for North, who tipped it over.

Jake slapped it back.

North blocked it and Ham dove for it, scooping it up. Jake sent it over with a backward bump. It flew high over the net.

Devon let it go, and it hit the grass behind him.

"What was that?" North said.

"Out!" Devon said. "It was out."

"It was in," Jake said. "Ask Aria. She's sitting right there."

Oh, uh.

She looked at Devon, then Jake. "I didn't see it."

Jake ran his arm across his forehead, breathing hard. Looked over at her. "C'mon, Aria. Is the game over, or not?"

She didn't know why, but his words tunneled inside, stirred her.

And she didn't know why, but suddenly, "Not."

He smiled at her then, and she hated how the clouds parted.

She should *not* like this man.

Ham got the serve.

He aced it, the ball landing in a wide spot between North and Devon.

"And that's the game!" Jake slapped Ham's hand, and then flexed, wearing a stupid grin that she knew she shouldn't like so much.

What was her problem that around Jake she lost her brains?

She got up and headed toward the picnic table, scooping up a handful of potato chips and grabbing a rib. She sat down on the bench, her back to the table.

Jake came over and sat beside her. He was still breathing hard, and now smelled a little ripe. But even in his sweaty persona, his eyes shone. "Thanks for the second chance."

"It was probably out."

One side of his mouth slid up. "Really?"

She lifted a shoulder. "You were trying so hard."

"I wasn't trying. I'm just that awesome."

She laughed, shaking her head. "Okay, Captain Awesome."

He stole a potato chip off her plate. "So, you okay?"

Crazily, her eyes started to fill.

"Oh no. What did I do now?"

She looked away. "Nothing. Just . . . I'm tired. I had a long night with a patient. Lucas wants to send me to the Keys for a conference. Says I'm still wiped from Alaska."

Jake nodded. "You should go diving while you're down there. There's a great state park in Key Largo with a reef."

"I don't scuba dive. It freaks me out."

"It's amazing, I promise."

"Said the navy SEAL."

"I started diving before I was a SEAL," he said. "But if you don't do that, at least go snorkeling. You'll love it. It's like flying, only on water."

She looked at him, touched by his attempts at friendship. "Jake, I, uh . . . you know, about what happened . . ." Oh, shoot, what was she doing?

His mouth tightened, his voice dropping. "I'm sorry, Aria, for . . . well, I'm just sorry. It was a mistake."

Oh. Yes. Right.

A mistake.

Dr. Aria Sinclair knew that.

Really.

Except, sitting here, so close to him, she didn't feel like Dr. Aria Sinclair. For a moment, she was the girl he'd held in his arms as he'd helped her escape a mountaintop.

And Jake was the hero who'd stayed with her when she'd been terrified her best friend would die.

No, it hadn't been a mistake. Not then.

Now, however . . .

"You're right. No big deal, just a mistake."

Jake drew in a breath. "Friends?"

She found her voice. "Yeah. Sure."

"Hey, listen. Text me when you get to Florida. I'll tell you where to go."

"I don't have your number."

"Give me your phone."

She handed it over and watched him put in his digits.

He handed it back, winked at her. "It'll be dark soon. I hope you're sticking around for the fireworks. We have a perfect view from here."

He stood up and ran back to the volleyball court, where his nephews were starting a game, his skin tanned under the setting sun.

Yes, really this was the perfect view.

Oh brother.

Because clearly Jake was over her and whatever had happened between them in Alaska.

Friends?

Yeah, perfect. Swell.

But she was an idiot because she wasn't in the least over Jake Silver. Or his stupid, intoxicating charm.

But clearly, she didn't need to run. Because there was nothing to run from.

Just like she thought, she meant nothing to Jake Silver.

▪ ▪ ▪

He wouldn't win any awards for father of the year.

Ham sat on a blanket, leaning back on his hands, staring at the sky as fireworks exploded over Excelsior Beach. The spray of red and white dripped down the velvet sky into the dark waters below, lighting them on fire.

What had started dire had turned into a glorious day. The temperature had fallen to the high seventies, the sun turned the lake to a rich blue, and everyone managed to get a tan. Jenny and Orion were back—and by the looks of them snuggled together on a stadium blanket, his instinct to hire Orion as his medic for Jones, Inc., was right on. And he'd hired psychologist Jenny Calhoun as his team profiler and climbing pro. He'd talked to North—apparently Jenny had broken some GoSports speed ice-climbing record a few months ago.

Aria was sitting with Lucas and Sasha, next to Devon somebody. Jake's occasional glances their direction weren't lost on Ham. Poor guy. Something had gone down between those two on the mountain, and Ham still hadn't figured it out.

Jake's nieces and nephews lay on the grass, and Dinah's husband, Mark, had finally showed up, still dressed for the office in his khaki pants. Apparently internet security analysts didn't get days off.

Phoebe's husband hadn't arrived, but no one said anything. She sat with Chloe, her hand on her swollen belly.

Yeah, a perfect day. Except for the fact that Aggie still hadn't spoken. To him. To anyone. And honestly, he wasn't really watching the sky. Ham's gaze was on his daughter.

His amazing, beautiful, broken daughter who seemed afraid of him, more comfortable in Jake's lap than with her own father.

Because Unca Jake had saved her life.

Or maybe because Jake was fun. Jake made her laugh. Jake gave her ice cream.

Never mind that Ham had flown halfway across the world at the suggestion that he was her father.

He would be less than honest if he didn't wonder whether she was really his.

Signe hadn't told him she was pregnant.

Frankly, the odds were slim. Except for . . .

Well, there was at least one possibility.

He'd spent ten years trying to forget the way Signe felt in his arms. His wife, the one he should have never let go.

The woman he'd failed.

Looking at Aggie, who clutched her soiled stuffed unicorn to herself, her blonde braids fraying out of their bonds as she sat tucked into the center of Jake's folded legs, leaning against him as she watched the sky, Ham couldn't help but see Signe in her profile.

Yes, definitely Signe's daughter, at least. And that was enough. The nearness of Signe's presence, even in death, pressed into his chest. *I'll take care of her, I promise.*

North sat down beside him. His name wasn't actually North—deep in Ham's memory was lodged his real name—Neil Gunderson. But the guy hailed from some small town in North Dakota, and the location had stuck around as a moniker. When North joined the team as their point man and navigator, something about him worked as their due North.

His faith, maybe.

North had spent the day hanging around Selah Silver, listening to her talk about her adventures in Africa working in a refugee camp. Frankly, she reminded Ham way too much of Signe. Idealistic, the kind of enthusiasm that could only get her in way over her head.

Trap her in a country that would turn on her.

"How you doing, boss?" North was solid, the kind of guy who listened first, spoke later. Ham knew his question was more than casual.

So, "I keep running it through my head. How did I miss the fact she was pregnant?"

North was reading his mind, as usual. "You couldn't know she was still alive, boss. That was a direct hit on the Chechen base."

Ham's jaw tightened. "If I had known she was in that bunker—"

"Stop. You didn't know. And clearly, she wasn't there, was she?"

"She didn't tell me she was pregnant," he said quietly. "I should have made her leave."

North let out a laugh, more of a grunt than humor. "Right. Even I know Signe better than that. There's not a hope you could have made her leave."

"Maybe. But I was her husband—I should have kept her safe. Made sure the baby was safe."

North looked at Aggie, her head drooping back into Jake's arms. "Looks like she is."

Ham's throat filled. "And I intend to keep her that way." He glanced at North. "I have to go out of town. I got a call from Senator White. He has a friend who got into a pickle in Russia, and I need to do a quick in-and-out."

"In Russia?"

"Apparently she needs an escort out of the country. It's an easy op, but here's the kicker—the senator has a lead on Royal. Says he's the one who contacted him about his friend in trouble."

"Royal Benjamin? I know he vanished after you liberated him from the Taliban. Along with Logan Thorne."

"Yeah. Except Thorne showed up in Alaska last summer, hiding out. Told Orion a story about him being set up by the CIA to do wet work. I think Royal got pulled in too, somehow. Orion has always blamed himself for the events that caused Royal's capture. I made him a promise we'd find Royal and bring him home."

"Then let Orion go," North said.

"He's still healing from his knee injury. Besides . . ."

"This isn't just about Royal, is it? You want to look into Signe's accident, in Italy."

"I don't know. Maybe. Ten years ago I think I've accidentally killed her in an air attack in Chechnya, and suddenly I get a call that she was in a boating accident in the Mediterranean? Except, they can't find her body, and the only witness is a ten-year-old girl who claims I'm her father, but won't talk to me when I show up in Italy to get her."

"Claims?"

Ham lifted a shoulder. "I don't know what to believe."

"She looks like you, Ham. She has your blue eyes."

Ham glanced at him, frowning.

"You're not the only one trying to figure it out. But I see her in you, dude. And, um . . . well, it's possible isn't it? I mean, I remember you two—"

"Yeah, I know." He didn't want to remember that weekend.

He could hardly believe he'd found her again, only to lose her three weeks later.

"It's possible she didn't even know she was pregnant when Tsarnaev and his rebels overran the hospital," North said.

"I need to find out whose yacht she was on, and how she got there. What happened in Chechnya, and . . ."

"You think she's still alive."

Ham stared overhead as the finale approached, the explosions of a number of popcorn blasts that reminded him too much of gunfire in the thick of the night. He didn't much like fireworks, really. He didn't want to nod.

But, yeah.

"I just need some answers. And some closure."

Silence.

"Aggie still isn't talking?"

Ham shook his head.

"And you tried speaking Russian?"

He nodded. Silence, then, "I don't know what I'm doing here. I'm not a dad. I never . . . thought about being a dad, I guess."

"Not even when you married Signe?"

"We got married on a crazy weekend of shore leave, in Vegas. I had no thoughts other than being her husband, if you know what I mean."

"Right."

"It was impulsive. And stupid. And I didn't think about what was best for Signe—"

"She was your high school sweetheart, right?"

More than that. "I've known her since first grade. She was there when . . . well, my mom died when I was nine. Cancer. She was my best friend. When I had no one else, I had Signe."

And wow, that sounded sappy. "We used to slap around the puck on the pond behind my house, build tree forts, even compete in track. She was tough, and I liked that about her."

"Looks like her daughter inherited her toughness. She was a fighter today."

Today. He'd nearly lost it when he'd seen the cat cartwheel. And when he realized she was trapped under it—

Okay, that still sent a shudder through him.

But she'd lived. Because she was tough. Like her mother . . .

"Signe grew up with her grandparents—her mother was sort of in and out of the picture. A little wacky." See? He had memories he could talk about without curling into the fetal position.

"She went to Berkeley, wanted to be a lawyer and fight for human rights or something. I lost touch with her after my first deployment."

"But you were married."

Ham took a breath. "Yeah. Well, there's a story behind that, but the important part is, I didn't see her again until we ran into each other at the hospital in Chechnya five years later. But she was always feisty, always the defender of the weak. And smart. Valedictorian of our class. She could do anything she put her mind to, so I wasn't surprised to see her working as a translator. I was worried about her—it was a hotbed for insurgents fighting Russia, but she wouldn't listen to me. She could be emotional and bullheaded." He cast another glance at Aggie. "Not unlike her daughter. I wish she'd talk to me."

"She seems to like Jake," North said.

"Everybody likes Jake." Ham glanced at North. "I asked him to watch her while I'm gone. But . . ."

"I've got his six."

"Thanks, Yankee."

Ham lay back, one arm curled under his head. And for a second, Signe was there, lying in his arms, her head on his bicep. *"Hey sailor, miss me?"*

He stared at the sky, seeing the stars. *Yes. More than you know.*

She rolled over, and he could nearly feel her lips on his neck. *"Ever think about the what-ifs?"*

Constantly.

He shook her image away before it sank in, grew talons. *If you're alive, Sig, I will find you. And I'll bring you home.*

CHAPTER 3

"YOU'RE SUCH A JERK!"

The voice of his sister shooting up from outside and through the open bedroom window woke Jake from where he'd dozed off, on Dinah's bed, in the room down the hall from his. Aggie was curled on the bed, asleep, her stuffed unicorn clutched under her arm, the book he'd been reading to her fallen on the floor in their slumber.

A Wrinkle in Time. His mother's suggestion—a story about a little girl who goes in search of her father. It sounded like something appropriate for Aggie, although Jake hadn't a clue how much she understood.

Three days since Ham's departure and she still hadn't said a word. Jake had spent the weekend playing checkers with her, taking her out in the speedboat, teaching her how to play croquet—he was a regular super uncle.

Still, even Jake was starting to worry. "What happened to you, little one?"

But maybe he had other problems, like what had caused his sister Ellie to slam the car door outside, shoot off the words to her boyfriend, then bang her way into the house.

He looked at the clock. After 10:00 p.m., which meant his folks were probably asleep. His mother had started going to bed at 9:00 p.m., which had him a little worried. Her last cancer scans had declared her still in remission, but he feared that someday she'd gather the family around the table with the news that the breast cancer had returned, in force.

He saw the worry in his father's eyes too, sometimes.

In truth, he worried about all of them. Dinah's marriage felt a little off, what with Mark showing up so late to the party a few days ago, not to mention Stephan not showing up at all for Phoebe. But he'd just made partner in his law firm, so he got a pass.

Chloe seemed off—quiet. Jake wanted to ask her about her last assignment. After all, he still had his SEAL security clearance. But Chloe always played things close to the chest, so who knew what she might be brooding over. She saw a lot of dark things in her job as a war correspondent. He had long lived in fear that he'd show up in a country on an assignment to rescue hostages, and one of them would be his too-tough-for-her-own-good kid sister.

And then there was Selah. She and North had taken a walk down to the beach after the fireworks, and maybe that should have given him pause, but frankly, North was a good guy. A man of faith, and Selah could do worse. Maybe there was room for a man in that heart dedicated to Jesus. She'd inherited the family do-gooder gene, so North better buckle up. Being with Selah meant joining her on her quest to save the world, or at least the downtrodden and hurting.

But Ellie—she was an enigma to Jake. Mostly because he'd missed the majority of her childhood. When he'd left home, she'd been all of four years old. Now, at seventeen he recognized a smidgen of himself in her, and frankly, that scared him.

He got up and shut the door, moving down the hall to find her.

She was standing in the kitchen, the glow of the fridge light bathing her as she pondered her food choices.

"Ice cream is in the freezer."

She pulled out the milk and set it on the counter. "Not every girl needs ice cream when she breaks up with a guy." She gave him a look.

"You two broke up?"

She went to the pantry and took out a box of Lucky Charms. "Yeah, we broke up."

"Why?"

She poured out the cereal. "Just because." But she didn't look at him, and her voice wavered. And he'd been through enough breakups with Dinah and Phoebe to know the look of a stiff upper lip.

"You need to talk about it?"

"With you?" She looked up. "No."

He frowned. "Yeah, with me. I'm your big brother."

"Listen, Jake. I know you're my big brother, but frankly, we barely know each other. You moved back six months ago and were gone for the last month, so really . . ." She lifted a shoulder.

"It doesn't mean I don't care. I'm still your big brother."

"Fine." She set the box on the counter. "I'll tell you why I broke up if you tell me why you separated from the navy. Mom says we're supposed to give you time to get your feet under you, but frankly, I'm trying to figure out what took you out in the first place."

"What's your deal? Did I wrong you somehow?"

She looked at him, her eyes glistening. Then looked away. "No. I'm sorry. I'm just . . . mad."

Yeah. He got mad.

He spent most of his life, lately, mad. "Do I need to go have a talk with this guy?"

She gave him an eye roll.

"I'm serious."

"Like I'm going to send my big brother around to shake some sense into him?" She poured in the milk. "No thanks, Jake. You don't need to save everyone."

"I'm not trying to—"

She picked up the bowl, but it slid out of her hands and dropped onto the counter, sloshing milk everywhere. She let out a word.

"Hey—*hey*." Jake came around and picked up a towel. "Listen. I'll get you more cereal. Go sit down."

She turned away from the counter, covered her face with her hands, her shoulders trembling. "He's just such a *jerk*!"

Oh. He said nothing, cleaning up the milk, pouring the cereal down into the sink. Then he got a new bowl and set it on the counter.

And because she was still standing there, crying, he reached over and pulled her to himself. She sort of leaned in, pressed her forehead to his chest.

"I'm happy to shake some sense into him."

She sniffed, and her body trembled. "Can you make it hurt?"

"Probably."

"Without marks?"

He held her away, raised an eyebrow. "What happened, El?"

"He . . ." She winced, and looked away.

"Okay, now I'm serious. What did he do?"

"Nothing. I mean—nothing. I don't know. I guess I just let him in too far . . ."

He froze, although his heart gave a hard thump, betraying him. "Too far."

She pushed out of his arms. "Calm down, big brother. I don't mean *too far*. I mean . . . you know. I let him into my life. I . . . let him know me." She cocked her head. "And not in the biblical sense, so you can put away your Ka-Bar."

He held up his hands. "I'm unarmed."

"Hardly."

His voice softened. "What happened?"

"Nothing. I don't know." She turned her back to him. "I . . . I told him about Hannah and he didn't say *anything*—"

"You told him about Hannah? Why?"

She rounded on him. "Because, I don't know, it *matters*?"

"Fine."

"And now you're acting weird. What's the big deal?"

He poured her cereal, added milk.

"Jake?"

"Nothing. Here are your Lucky Charms."

She put a hand on his arm. "Really? Just like that you go from being all great to being a jerk."

He glanced at her, his mouth tight. "I just don't think . . . well, that's family business. Besides, you weren't even around."

She drew in her breath. "Thanks." She grabbed her cereal. "Thanks for that."

"El—"

"Listen, truth is, I wouldn't be around if she was still here, so there's that, Jake." Her eyes were hard in his. "Try being me. The replacement for the sister you never knew. The sister everyone lost."

She pressed past him.

Not everyone. Him.

The sister *he* lost.

"Ellie—" He followed her into the den. She sat down on the brown corduroy sofa. "Listen. We don't know what would have happened—"

"Six years says they were done having kids. Then, three years after Hannah goes missing, I'm born. Seriously, Jake. Don't think I don't live with that fun fact every day. I'm a replacement child."

"You're not, Ellie. You're your own person." He sat on the end of the sofa. She drew up her feet, but he picked them up and put them on his lap. "Listen. It was really hard after—well, after. No one talked about it, but Mom . . . she spent days locked in her room. So maybe they thought having another kid would help. But then you were born and you are *nothing* like Hannah. She was quiet and—"

"Sweet and obedient and never threw a temper tantrum—yeah, I know it all—"

"You're amazing and beautiful and feisty and exactly who you're supposed to be." His throat tightened at the way her eyes glistened. "I miss Hannah. But I would miss you too, Ellie, if you weren't here."

She stared down at her cereal. "You're such a sap, Jake."

"All this estrogen in the house. It's hard to escape."

She looked up at him. "You know, you don't have to always fix everything."

He reached over and stole a marshmallow. "It's the curse of the oldest child."

The television had flickered on, turned to the Weather Channel.

"Oh, for Pete's sake. Dad's been watching *Storm Chasers* again." She went to pick up the remote, but he put his hand over hers.

"I want to hear this."

The weather map showed a swirl of storm moving in from the south of the Atlantic, toward Florida. He pumped up the volume and listened to the female redhead on the screen give a rundown. "It looks like the storm is building—it might go up the coast and miss Florida completely, but until then, we're keeping an eye on it." The screen flipped to a local report and he turned the volume back down.

"Were you going to do some diving or something?"

"No. Just someone I know is down there right now, and . . . I'm sure she'll be fine."

"You're such a worrywart." She threw a pillow at him.

Yeah, well, he had good reasons. For a second, his gaze landed on the wall of family pictures, some before Ellie, some after. He hadn't really noticed the change in his mother until he saw them lined up. She'd lost hair and weight after Hannah went missing. Never really regained it. The rest of them, too, looked wrung out.

And then there was Ellie, a beaming cherub in the midst of them. Maybe she had been a replacement.

Maybe she'd saved them all.

"Who is it?"

He looked at her. "Who is—?"

"The friend." She pointed her empty spoon at him. "The *girl* you're worried about."

"I'm not . . ."

She took another bite of cereal and raised an eyebrow.

"Okay, fine. Just a woman I met in Alaska."

"One of the women you *rescued*?" She wagged her eyebrows now.

"Fine. Yes. I rescued her. But she's a doctor and pretty capable. She was just hurt, so—"

"Okay, whatever, Superman. Stop being modest. You like this girl."

He lifted a shoulder.

"Wait." She set her spoon down. "Was she at the party? The dark-haired one in the yellow sundress? What was her name—Aria? I saw you talking to her."

He looked at the television. They were showing the storm front again, a circle of wrath moving up the shoreline.

"Yeah, I remember her. She let you win the volleyball game."

"She didn't let me win—"

"And she was with that handsome doctor—what was his name?"

"Devon." Aw shoot, his tone gave him away. "She wasn't with him, I don't think . . ." Except, what if she was? It didn't matter. "We're just friends. It's nothing."

"Mmmhmm."

He looked at her. "Really. It's nothing."

"Right. That's what all that flexing was about."

"I was not flexing."

"It was blinding."

He shook his head.

"You do like her."

"We . . . I thought . . . we . . . we got along, okay?"

"Oh. You . . . *told* her things, didn't you?"

His mouth closed into a tight line.

"You let her in too far!"

"I—" But, okay, maybe he did. He glanced at her. "People do stupid things when they're under trauma. We were stuck in a tent together for two days, trying to keep her friend alive during a blizzard. We shared stories."

And yeah, there'd been more, but maybe his sister didn't need to know that.

Problem was, he hadn't exactly stopped thinking of the *more* for the past three days. Aria had just looked so . . . so put together at the party. Pretty in that sundress, her smile exactly why he was, yes, flexing.

Clearly, he still liked her. But she had a different life here in Minneapolis, one that included buttoned-up doctors like Devon McMillan.

Jake might be the least buttoned-up person he knew.

Dr. Aria Sinclair was a world-renowned surgeon.

He was a has-been SEAL who taught ten-year-olds how to swim.

Oh boy, he needed someone to grab his feet and pull him down to reality. "Sometimes that's all there is . . ."

"Nope." Ellie shook her head, disentangled herself, and got up.

"Where are you going?"

"Stay here." Ellie left the room and he sat there, watching as the storm swirled at the bottom of the screen. Maybe he should just text Aria, make sure she was safe.

Because they were friends. And that's what friends did.

Yeah, right.

He wanted to be her friend like he wanted to let a truck drive over him.

Ellie returned holding the box of Lucky Charms. She handed it to Jake.

"What's this for?"

"The girl you like, the one you spilled your heart to? Yeah, she showed up at our Fourth of July bash with a date. You need these Lucky Charms, bro, because like it or not, the great and awesome Jake Silver has been dumped. Feel free to cry, tough guy."

He looked at her.

Took the box.

"The green ones are especially tasty," she said.

■ ■ ■

Aria was probably going to die. And it was all Jake's fault.

Okay, that might not be entirely fair, but his description of snorkeling as "flying" had her intrigued and made Aria sign up for the snorkeling tour out of Key Largo on her first day off.

Two days of teaching in paradise and she felt like she'd found her way back to herself, just a little. Distance from the loss of Leo had helped, and the fact that her peers packed her class on the advanced techniques of in-utero septoplasty had made her wake up to the idea that really, she did know what she was doing.

Hello, mojo.

The fiasco with Jake hadn't completely knocked her off her game.

And paradise might be exactly the place to forget him, move on. Delegate him to the *just friends* section of her heart.

"Jenny, you're right," she'd said into her friend's voice mail after the first night on the island. "No more slogging through ice and snow. Our next great adventure will have to be in Cancun."

Or Key West.

She might be in love with the tiny island on the southern tip of the United States. After flying into Miami, she'd driven down Highway 1, past the swamplands that boasted mangrove and alligators, then farther south into the sandy strips of beach that bisected the Atlantic from the Gulf of Mexico. Boats and resorts whitewashed with a summer glare, stores that boasted surfing and snorkeling attire, and beach restaurants heralding the catch of the day evidenced that she'd left the great white north behind.

The wind smelled of the sea and salt, a sweet heat in the air that came from lazy afternoons with toes tucked into the sand.

When she reached the final key—after driving through Key Largo and a dozen other keys—she'd felt her body begin to relax, her muscles shake out, the coiled stress of the past month loosen.

Lucas's travel agent had booked her a deluxe room at the Bahama Mama resort, a sprawling two-story tiki hut complete with grass roof. She just wanted to take a dive off her veranda, which overlooked both the sparkling aqua pool and the endless blue ocean. The pillow on her bed read "Relax" on the printed burlap, and by the time she changed into a sundress and flip-flops and headed down to the beach, she decided to agree.

She'd spent the first two days tucked into an air-conditioned room at the resort, overlooking the blue, listening to speakers, serving on panels, and delivering her talk.

In the evenings, she'd commandeer a lounger and face it west to catch the final wink of the sunset. She was healing, her body uncoiling. Even her ankle felt stronger—she had taken off her brace and was walking with the barest of limps.

Yesterday, she'd taken a walk into the borough and found Ernest Hemingway's house. Drank a fruity drink on the shoreline and chatted with a pregnant woman working on a watercolor on the beach. The woman wore her hair in blonde dreadlocks and had a cool name—Evangeline, or something like that. She possessed a smile that made Aria sit down next to her and watch the sunset as she painted. Aria purchased a postcard from her basket of offerings, addressed it, and slipped it into the mail for Jenny.

She'd made a few friends at the conference too. A redheaded doctor from Cincinnati named Drey had invited her to dinner the first night with his friends. It only brought her thoughts back to the Fourth of July volleyball game.

To Jake, and his quiet "You okay?"

She might be, after a few more days in paradise. The concern in his blue eyes had found her bones.

Yeah, she might be able to be his friend. Someday. Once her heart figured out how to let him go.

His suggestion to go snorkeling sat inside her, nudging her.

She made the mistake of mentioning the excursion to Drey after a dinner of crab cakes and fresh squid, raw oysters, and buttery lobster.

Drey caught up the idea like he'd thought of it and suddenly she found herself in a bus headed up to Key Largo at 8:00 a.m. on her first day off.

She purchased a laminated fish-finder guide and boarded a scuba boat around 11:00 a.m. with the sun high, the waves choppy but endlessly blue.

"Ever been snorkeling before?" asked a guy named Joe, lean and tanned, wearing a swimsuit and a rash guard surfing shirt. He wore a mask backward on his head and was issuing her gear—a snorkel, a mask, an optional life preserver. She took it, not sure how she felt about the swells of the ocean as their boat split the waves, motoring out to the reef offshore.

Drey sat across from her. "You're looking a little green, Aria."

He was a handsome man. Less than six feet tall, but lean with short hair and magnetic blue eyes. He'd headed up a discussion on the technical aspects of segmentectomy and lobectomy, including some new methods for vessel transection.

She'd read about most of them in the *Journal for Thoracic and Cardiovascular Surgery*.

Aria gripped the railing of the boat. Not a big vessel, maybe forty-five feet, it held oxygen tanks in slots on either side of the boat behind benches where clients hung on, their faces turned to or away from the spray. A few people had climbed to the front of the boat, sitting on the hull.

"You could go up top," Drey said, pointing to the captain's roost.

"No, I'm okay." Aria put her hand to her stomach, wishing she'd eaten more than a hard-boiled egg for breakfast.

"What are you reading?"

"It's a guide about the fish on the reef."

Drey shook his head. "Wow. I'll bet you were the top of your class. You could just enjoy the view, you know. There won't be a test."

"Or, I could actually know what I'm looking at."

Drey lifted a shoulder. "Sometimes the fun is in the discovery. Be impulsive. Let go."

They hit a swell and the boat rammed hard into the wave, the water splashing the deck.

Her hand tightened on the railing.

The last time she'd let go, she found herself in the arms of a guy she was trying hard—and failing—to forget.

Thanks, but she was done with impulsive. Life was better preplanned. At least that way she knew what disasters to expect.

They arrived at the site. A few other boats bobbed in the water, snorkelers and divers already fighting the waves. Joe helped her gear up. He semi-inflated her life vest and helped her slip on her fins. "Listen, I'll be nearby, but just stay in the area and make sure you listen for the boat's horn. And if you see any sharks, don't panic. They're harmless."

Sharks?

Drey was grinning at her with a gleam in his eye. Sort of reminded her of Jake.

Except, she wasn't supposed to be thinking about Jake.

The icy chill sent a shock through her, but she warmed up fast and set her face in the water.

"Just breathe normally," said Joe, who was treading nearby.

Normally.

Hard to breathe *normally* when a whole new world transformed before your eyes. She'd never considered, really, what might live in the ocean depths, except, of course, for the aquariums and Animal Planet specials. But to see it up close—the vivid colors of the reef, the fish swimming just out of reach—

She gasped, got a mouthful of water, came up sputtering.

Joe lifted his head and spat out his snorkel. "Listen, if you have water in your snorkel, just blow out hard. The key is to just float on top of the water and let your body relax. You can do this."

"It's amazing, I promise."

She didn't know why Jake's voice slid into her thoughts, but she put her face back down and forced herself to float.

The world turned magical. Below her, maybe twenty feet down, a pink-and-blue coral reef teemed with life. White coral spires and dark green or brilliant red ferns shifted in the current, and around them, fish searched for food. Blue-and-green triggerfish, red-striped hawkfish, saddleback butterflyfish with the black markings on their tails. Angelfish and tangs flitted around a large rock, and a lobster peeked out with its spindly antennae and beady eyes.

The waves undulated around her, moving her in the water, and her stomach tried to rebel. But she ignored it and focused on a sudden scattering of sand in the distance. Joe pointed and she nearly stopped breathing when a stingray emerged from the dust and, like an eagle, glided away, the water rippling its gray skin in a gentle caress.

Oh, Jake, you were right. She did feel like she might be flying, high above, weightless over the earth. So maybe letting go had its merits.

A hand closed around her wrist and she looked over to see Drey pointing to his right.

Deep in an underground grotto, a statue of what looked like Jesus, his hands raised to the heavens, was covered in barnacles and algae.

And swimming around it, as if stalking its prey, was a snub-nosed shark.

Drey's hand tightened as if he realized she might bolt. But a small crowd had gathered, watching the sleek creature as it skidded along the blue-sandy bottom and under an overhanging reef.

After it vanished, she surfaced and spat out her snorkel. Drey, Joe, and a few others came up also.

"That's a nurse shark," said Joe, treading water. "They populate the area. Sometimes we might even see a loggerhead turtle."

The waves had picked up, turned choppy. A blast from the boat sounded across the water.

"Time to head back," Joe said. He ducked into the water again.

She kicked hard to follow him, aware now of the pull of the waves, tossing her off course. The wind, too, had picked up, and by the time she reached the boat, it was bobbing hard in the water.

She got knocked in the face with the ladder when she missed her grip. Joe came up beside her and helped her tug off her fins. He lifted them up to the divemaster on board, and she hoisted herself onto the ladder and out of the water.

"If you're going to hurl, do it over the side," Joe said as he climbed up behind her.

"I'm not going to—oh . . . shoot . . ." She grabbed the railing and found herself on her knees, starboard side, emptying her meager breakfast into the ocean.

Nice.

She staggered back to the bench and sat back, letting the sun warm her bones.

"You going to live, Aria?" Drey said as he sat down opposite her.

"Mmmhmm."

Except, by the time they returned to port, she just wanted to die a quick death.

"Maybe it's something you ate," Drey suggested as they walked to the bus.

She never wanted to eat again.

Someone in the group passed her a couple Dramamine, and in desperation she downed them with a sip of water.

Then she curled up in the back of the bus and rued her life.

So much for impulsiveness.

Night had pitched the resort into darkness, cloud cover blanketing the sky by the time they returned. She staggered to her room while Drey and the others headed to the tiki bar by the pool to finish off their adventure. The wind stirred the night, whispering through the palm trees, crashing the ocean onto shore. She fell onto her bed in the fetal position.

The room swam.

Maybe she did have a touch of food poisoning, because her stomach still convulsed, every pore in her body repulsed by the thought of food, movement, even life.

A rush of nausea made her fall to her knees, and she crawled to the bathroom and lay with her face on the cool tile floor.

Oh, this was gross.

Suddenly all she could think about was the way she'd felt on the mountain, when altitude sickness had swept in and her entire body had wanted to curl into her sleeping bag and never move again.

Except for Jake, she might have perished on the mountain, frozen to death. He'd made her laugh and kept her hydrated, and when she shivered nearly out of her skin, he'd kept her warm.

A gentleman, really.

Then, to save her life, he'd picked her up in his arms and helped lift her into a chopper, then stayed behind to find her friend Jenny.

The guy was a hero and shoot, she might *never* get him out of her head. Not if, when she was drunk on Dramamine and woozy with illness, she still wished he were here to hold her hair back as she—

Oh. Yeah, she could call it quits on her tropical vacation any time.

She heard her phone buzzing somewhere in the room, and after she rinsed her mouth, she crawled back out and found it on her bedside stand, where she'd left it.

Calls. From Devon. And Jenny.

She thumbed open a voice mail from Devon. "Just checking in. Hope you're having a great time. Nothing to worry about here. I was just . . . well, checking in."

Huh. She wasn't unaware of the way he'd sat next to her, purposely, at the picnic.

Jenny's voice mail was more to the point. "Listen, you'd better be out having a good time and not in your room reading some medical report on aortic valve repair or something. Call me."

Rolling onto the bed, she opened her contacts. Hit J and scrolled down to Jenny's name. JC, for Jenny Calhoun.

She opened the texting app and used her voice-to-text. "Hey, J. I wish you were here. Went snorkeling today. I spent the day throwing up and now I feel like I have the flu. I could use some TLC, LOL. This is worse than Denali. Why do I always get myself in over my head? Anyway, try and stay out of trouble until I get back. See you in a few days."

She pushed send, then turned off her phone. Dropped it on the bed.

Rolled over.

And told herself that next time she came to paradise, she'd stay away from the fish.

CHAPTER 4

"DON'T LET GO, ARIA! Don't let go!"

Jake's own voice thundered through him as he lay on the snow, peering over the edge of the crevasse.

Aria hung from her belay line, her feet fixed into the snow, horizontal to the sky.

Below her, the crevasse fell thousands of feet into blackness.

His head swam as he reached out for her. "Grab my hand!"

She dove for him and missed. Again. "I can't!"

"You can, just reach for me!"

Her dark brown eyes fixed on his. "You reach for me!"

He dug his ice axe into the snow and leaned down, straining.

At his waist, snow began to fall. He started to slide.

Aria's eyes widened. "No, Jake, go back, *go back*!"

Around him the icy ridge cracked, broke free.

Suddenly, he was falling, past Aria, his screams lifting—

"Jake!"

His door banged open, and in a second, Jake sat up, blinking into the darkness.

His sister Ellie stood outlined in the frame of the door. "Are you okay?"

So no, he wasn't falling into a crevasse on the back side of Denali to freeze to death. He was in his bedroom, the rain pinging against the window, wind blowing, a chill invading the dark room.

Still, sweat drenched his body, and his covers fell to his waist. He was trembling, the dream felt so—well, even his bones were frozen.

At least, however, this nightmare wasn't a memory.

In this nightmare, no one died.

He ran his hand through his hair, blowing out a breath.

"You were shouting," she said, pulling her sweater around her. She wore a pair of flannel Minnesota Vikings pajama pants and a T-shirt. "I was afraid I'd find you on the floor or something, hunkered down with your M16."

"I don't have an M16. It was just a dream."

She raised an eyebrow and tucked her hair back behind her ear. "Right. Well, I'm going to make myself some hot cocoa, so . . ."

He swung his legs off the bed, his feet finding the cold of the wooden floor as she closed the door behind her.

His body still shook, Aria's screams in his ears.

He hadn't fallen into a crevasse, although when he and his team had found Aria and her friends on the mountain, she had been dangling above a jagged slash in the ice that was three thousand feet deep.

Seeing her like that had scared the skin off him. He had fixed himself into the snow, dug in with his crampons, attached the ascender to the line, and hauled Aria up to safety.

And right into his life.

He could still see her, sitting down beside him, looking over at him, her dark hair frozen as it fell from her cap, those brown eyes wide, trying to hide her fear. "Thanks."

That was all she said until later, when he'd seen her grimacing, hiding bruised ribs and a horribly sprained ankle.

"First, you drag me up a mountain to rescue you, and now you're coming up with reasons not to dance with me."

He wasn't sure why he'd said that, but somehow, he knew she had just enough competitive spirit in her that he wasn't taking a look at that ankle without a dare.

So he referenced how they'd met—him asking her to dance during a country music jam back in the little Alaskan town of Copper Mountain.

"I'm fine. And I don't want to dance with you again."

"Sure you do. You've been thinking about me since you left the dance floor. Now stop your crybabying and lean back and let me look at your ankle."

She'd fought him. Accused him of wanting to look up her shirt.

He wasn't exactly sure she was kidding.

It ignited feelings inside him he hadn't known how to manage. Then, she'd started calling him Hawkeye, from the TV show *M*A*S*H*.

It only made sense that he followed up with Houlihan. And later . . . Hot Lips.

Yeah, they'd been playing some crazy game up there on the mountain. But Ellie's words spoken last night pinged back to him . . . *"Like it or not, the great and awesome Jake Silver has been dumped. Feel free to cry, tough guy."*

Her words had dug into his chest and irked him.

Aria hadn't even given them a chance, in real life. And sure, they had that hiccup in the hotel room, a misstep that could have taken out any chance at something longlasting, but the fact was, they *hadn't* danced outside the lines.

He deserved a chance to try again.

He got up and reached for his jeans and a T-shirt and found himself nearly tripping over his backpack. Although he'd unpacked his dirty clothes, he still hadn't emptied out his pockets, and now as the pack fell on the floor, he heard a jangle.

His shoe polish tin. Where he kept his military identification tags. "*You don't have to wear your dog tags to be a SEAL. That's in here . . .*"

Whatever. He was still giving serious thought to reactivating. It had only been six months—he could pass the psych evaluation now, he was sure of it. Besides, he'd never been broken. Just angry.

Just the devil—if he were to believe the press.

Okay, sometimes he did.

He unzipped the pack and pulled the tin out.

Opened it.

Inside lay his tags. And a necklace. A half heart.

Aria's.

The memory whooshed in, brusque, jolting.

"*My necklace. It's gone.*" Her panic had grabbed hold and taken him under. He'd searched the tent with her, and finally found the gold chain in her sleeping bag, broken. She'd taken it from his hand, held it to herself. Tried to pass it off as nothing until he pried it out of her.

She broke his heart with her explanation. "It's just a trinket my sister gave me when we were kids."

Her sister. Her *dead* sister. Her *twin* dead sister who'd given Aria her heart. Literally.

He'd put the necklace into his pack for safekeeping. Then promptly taken it home and forgotten it.

He needed to give it back.

He put it back into the tin and set it on his nightstand. Got up, went to the bathroom, and scrubbed his face. Outside, rain lashed his window. Hot cocoa sounded good.

In the kitchen, the microwave was humming. Ellie stood in front of it, in the glow, watching her cup circle inside.

"Hey, Jake," said his mother, who sat at the counter.

"It's a party," he said. "Did I wake you?"

"My kids can't get up in the night without a mother knowing." She pushed a plate of oatmeal cookies his direction.

He sat on the stool next to her. "You okay?"

He braced himself for something negative, but she just nodded, blew on her cocoa. "Aggie seems to be doing okay. When is Ham getting back?"

"I don't know."

"I still can't believe he has a daughter he didn't know about. How does that happen?"

The microwave dinged and Ellie retrieved the mug, then set it in front of him along with a container of whipped cream.

"See, we have a vibe going, you and me," Jake said, and picked up the can, swirling the foam into his cup.

She laughed, then filled another mug and added a packet of cocoa before putting it in the microwave. "So, what's the yelling about?"

He shook his head. "Just . . ."

"The war?"

He looked at his mother before he answered Ellie. "No, actually. I was on Denali, falling into a crevasse, if you must know."

She held up her hands. "Sorry."

"Not everyone who comes back from war has PTSD, El."

"Fine."

He didn't look at his mother.

She gave him the grace of not looking at him, either.

"By the way, you left your phone down here. It buzzed a while ago," his mother said quietly.

He walked over and retrieved it from the counter.

A text had come in. He read it, frowning at the unknown number.

Hey J. I wish you were here. Went snorkeling today. I spent the day throwing up and now I feel like I have the flu. I could use some TLC, LOL. This is worse than Denali. Why do I always get myself in over my head? Anyway, try and stay out of trouble until I get back. See you in a few days.

He read it again, trying to make sense of it, wondering if it might have come from Ham.

But, snorkeling.

Aria?

"Who's texting you at this hour?" his mother asked.

He looked up at her. "Uh . . ."

"Is it that girl?" Ellie said, bringing her cocoa over to the counter.

"What girl?"

"He got dumped by that brunette at our party."

"I wasn't dumped. We weren't even dating." He texted her back.

Aria? Is this you? Are you okay?

He waited for the sent notification to change to delivered, but it didn't go through.

"That doctor?"

He set the phone on the island. "Yeah. She was one of the women in the party in Denali. She went down to the Keys this weekend to, I don't know, unwind, I guess."

"I might need a trip to Florida if I got trapped on a mountain-top," Ellie said.

"The Keys?" His mother put her mug down. "Your father has been following the storm coming in. Lucy, I think they're calling it. They upgraded it to a Cat 4 hurricane right before we turned it off."

"There's a Cat 4 headed to Key West?" Ellie said. "And your not-a-girlfriend is there?" She reached out for his phone. "What did she say?"

"Hey!" He made a swipe for it but she pulled away.

"Wait. She said she wishes you were there?" She looked up at him. "She's sick and needs some TLC!"

"It's weird, isn't it?"

"What happened on that mountain, Jake?" His mother raised an eyebrow.

"Nothing. I mean—" He shook his head. "Nothing. We're just friends."

"She doesn't sound like just a friend," Ellie said. "'Try and stay out of trouble'? Sounds like she doesn't want you rescuing any other women." She finger-quoted "rescuing" and winked.

"Give me my phone."

"Are you sure she's okay? Is she by herself? It sounds like she's pretty sick."

"I texted her back. There's not really much else I can do at the moment."

His mother picked up the remote and aimed it at the kitchen television. The Weather Channel, of course, popped up, with an update on Hurricane Lucy.

"It looks like it's still headed north, away from the Keys, so she'll probably be okay."

But the swirl on the screen had his gut in a roil.

It was a weird text. Aria didn't do helpless or needy. At least not with him.

And she was by herself.

He texted her again.

Aria, this is Jake. Just text me back that you're okay.

They sat in silence, him holding his phone as they watched the predictions roll in.

"They say that the biggest killer with hurricanes is the fact that no one leaves," his mother said. "It's all blue skies and sunny, and no one believes that a storm is heading their way until it's too late."

"Thanks for that, Mom." Jake got up and pressed dial. The call went right to voice mail.

So, her phone was off. That at least gave him answers.

But what if she was *really* sick?

Like, the kind of sick that was more than seasickness, or food poisoning, or even the flu.

Her heart had taken quite a beating up there on Denali.

Her transplanted heart . . .

Jake got up, dialed his phone, and walked out into the sunroom, staring out the window into the darkness. Wind lashed the trees, the rain sending the lake to the shore in frothy, dark waves.

Not a twenty-foot swell of death and debris to swamp an island. Trap people. Drown them under collapsing houses and uprooted trees.

"What?" Orion's voice came on the line.

"Where is Aria staying?"

A pause. "Jake?"

"Yeah. I got a weird text from her, and I'm worried."

"It's after midnight."

"I know, but . . . listen, let me talk to Jenny."

Another pause, and he imagined Orion sitting up. "Dude, what are you thinking? Jenny isn't *here*. I'm not staying at her place. I got a hotel room. You want to talk to Jenny, you have to call her. But what's going on?"

Jake sank onto the arm of his father's recliner, aware that his mother had turned up the volume on the Weather Channel. *Thanks, Mom.* He ran a hand through his hair. "I don't know. I'm just . . . I'm worried, okay? Aria seemed pretty rattled when she was here for the Fourth of July party. She said she was okay, but—"

"Aw, Jenny found out that Aria had lost a patient. A baby she'd operated on."

Oh, Aria.

"Lucas sent her down to the Keys for some medical conference, but mostly to get away."

He wanted to ask, but probably shouldn't and then couldn't help it—"Did she go with that Devon guy?"

Silence. "Who?"

"That guy—the resident—who came with her to the party."

"I don't know, dude. I'm not in charge of her social life."

"Well, ask Jenny!"

"She's not here. Sheesh, bro, breathe. I'm sure Aria is fine. Relaxing—"

"There's a Cat 4 hurricane heading her direction." He was on his feet now. "Okay, just . . . listen, calm down—"

"I'm calm. You're the one yelling."

"I'm not yelling—"

"You're yelling," said Ellie from across the room.

He shot her a glare but cut his voice down and turned away, toward the window. In the reflection he saw a guy who might need to yes, calm down. Unshaven, his blond hair in rats, his eyes a little wired. He pressed his hand to the cool glass. "Listen. I just . . . she's not picking up and I thought I'd call the resort and see if I could find her."

"Why?"

"Because she texted me and said she was sick, okay?"

He heard rustling. "Sick?"

"Yeah. And the symptoms of heart-transplant rejection are flu-like symptoms and nausea . . ."

"What?"

"Aria is a heart-transplant recipient. And females have a higher chance of rejecting hearts. And after Denali, it's possible that maybe her heart was damaged, and I'm just worried—"

"The only one with a damaged heart is you, buddy. Listen, it didn't work out between you. You need to just deal with that."

"It's not—I'm not—I'm *worried* about her!" Oh joy, the shouting was back. "I just need to know where she is, okay? Just talk to her, and then . . ."

"You'll be a normal human being? Right. Okay, hang up, Jake, and let me call Jenny. She'll know what to do."

"Fine." He hung up. Tapped the phone on his leg.

"Okay, you're all set."

He turned around.

His sister was leaning over his mother's shoulder and now glanced back at him. "We got you booked on a 5:00 a.m. flight to Miami. Go pack."

He stared at her, and his mother turned and met his eyes.

Oh.

"We'll watch Aggie," she said softly. "You go."

His throat thickened. "This is stupid, isn't it?"

His sister picked up the container of whipped cream. Opened

her mouth. Shot a wad in and closed it. Grinned as she swallowed it down. "Sometimes you just gotta follow your heart, bro."

■ ■ ■

She'd turned the bedsheets into a soggy mess.

But at least she wasn't dead.

Aria rolled over onto her side, thankful that her stomach didn't protest and decide to send her scrambling again to the bathroom.

The room didn't swim.

She smelled rank, felt like the living dead, and given the shadows banking through her window she'd slept well into the day.

Maybe longer. She didn't want to guess.

Sitting up, Aria pressed her hands to her face. So, she might live. But not if she didn't eat something.

Crackers, maybe. Some soda.

She shuffled to the bathroom and brushed her teeth, stared at her reflection in the mirror. She hadn't so much as tanned her nose during her day at sea. In fact, she'd gotten a better tan in Alaska, albeit raccoon eyes.

A quick shower, a change of clothing, and she decided she was alive enough to trudge down to the restaurant and order a coffee.

She walked outside. Overhead, the sky had clouded over, and a fierce wind had tumbled a few deck chairs poolside. Palm fronds floated in the water. She must have slept through a storm.

Oddly, no one walked the beach.

She headed along the upper deck, took the stairs down to the cobblestones, and wandered around the resort, toward the cabana cafe. Closed. She peered inside, but no one manned the hostess stand, no patrons ate lunch.

Overhead, gulls cried, and the ocean sounded angry as she tucked her head down and scurried across the walkway to the main resort headquarters.

Inside, the gift shop was dark. She walked down to the main desk, but it was empty.

She half expected Jack Nicholson to jump out and say, *"Here's Johnny!"*

"Hello?"

Through a door behind the desk, barely ajar, voices lifted.

Phew.

"I don't care what everyone else is doing, girl. I'm not leaving. This is my home—"

"Mimi, don't be stupid. You remember what happened to those folks in New Orleans—"

"This isn't New Orleans—and we've weathered tougher storms than that. When Irma hit, I was sitting right here, listening to her wail."

"Oh, for the love of—"

"Hello?" Aria leaned over the desk. "Hello, front desk?"

The door opened and a woman emerged. Maybe early twenties, dressed in a teal collared shirt with the Bahama Mama logo on the breast pocket and a pair of faded jeans. She might have the most beautiful skin color Aria had ever seen—a light brown, almost golden. She looked at Aria with deep, dark brown eyes that betrayed a hint of panic. "What are you doing here?"

For a second, Aria had nothing. Then, "I'm . . . in room 217."

The woman approached the desk and typed into the computer. "You're with the medical conference group?"

Aria nodded.

"I'm sorry—they all checked out this morning. We have your room as vacated. I didn't realize . . ."

"Yola! Who is that?"

Yola turned. "Room 217, Mimi. She didn't evacuate yet."

"Evacuate?" Aria noticed rain starting to pelt the windows. "Is there a storm coming?"

Yola turned back to her. "Yes—"

"It's nothin' to worry about!" said Mimi, the voice from the back room.

Yola rolled her eyes. "She's lived on the island for nearly fifty years and thinks she knows best."

"There isn't anything we can't handle. We just have to hunker down." Mimi appeared in the doorway. Thin, her skin tanned to leather, her long white hair flowing down the back of a tie-dye maxi dress. She hung on to the frame. "A hurricane is nothing to be afraid of."

"Did you say *hurricane*?" Aria said. Outside, the sky appeared eerily green, the rain sheeting down in gusts. The palm trees at the front of the property had started to blow.

"Oh, don't you worry. Those are just the outer rain bands. They'll pass soon enough."

Water ran down the street, emptying into rain gutters. The parking lot was empty, save for her rental Honda and the resort van.

"Mimi, sit down."

"I'm fine. We're all going to be just fine." She approached the desk. "But it might be a good idea to raid the cabana for fresh water bottles and some of that shrimp gumbo Sonny makes. I'm sure he's got leftovers in the freezer." She ended her speech with a cough, her breath rattling in her chest.

Yola eased her down into a high-top chair. "My grandmama has COPD." She looked at Mimi. "Because she *smoked* for twenty years."

"And not just cigarettes," Mimi said, looking up and winking.

Oh. Uh.

Yola rolled her eyes. "Mimi is a child of the sixties."

"Oh, calm down. That was then. Now, I believe that nothing soothes the soul like prayer and a daily dose of sass."

Yola grinned, shaking her head. "See what I'm dealing with here?"

"I'm a little worried about your grandmother's cough. Mimi, how's your chest? Is it tight?"

"Oh, honey, I've had it called a number of things, but tight isn't one of them." She laughed. Coughed.

"Mimi! She's trying to help."

"Can I come around?" Aria asked and when Yola nodded, she came around the desk and turned Mimi to face her. "Can I take your pulse?"

"My heart is beating just fine."

Aria took her wrist, felt the rhythm there. Fast, maybe too fast, but given the storm building outside, maybe Mimi wasn't as calm as she'd like to convey. Aria turned her hand over. Her fingernails were gray with a tinge of blue.

The woman probably needed oxygen.

"What stage is her COPD?"

"I don't know—"

"The 'I don't worry about it' stage," Mimi said but ended in more coughing that had her reaching for a tissue on the desk and putting it to her mouth.

Aria noticed the mucus she spat out.

Mimi wadded the tissue and threw it into the trash.

"Ma'am—"

"You can call me Mimi. Everyone does."

"Do you have a nebulizer here?"

"Doc said I should get one, but I have the beach. That's fresh air enough."

Aria looked at Yola, who just shrugged. "It's like trying to tame a cat."

"Okay, Mimi, I think it would be good for you to go to the ER. Get some oxygen. Maybe a bronchodilator, just to help you breathe easier." Mimi's breaths were raspy as they filtered out, long, almost painful. Aria would guess her at a stage three, if not four.

"I'd like you to take a spirometry test. Just to see how far your COPD has progressed. Do you have a primary care doctor?"

"Good old Doc WebMD," Mimi said.

"All right, that's it. You're going to the ER," Yola said.

"I'll go with you," Aria said. "And then I probably need to leave for Miami."

"Oh, honey, it's too late for that. If the storm is headed our way, you don't want to get caught on the overseas highway during a hurricane. What we need to do is finish boarding up these front windows."

Aria stared at her. "I . . . I need to go home . . ."

Mimi lifted a shoulder. "Sorry."

"I'm going to get my stuff. I'll meet you here in ten minutes."

She stood inside the door, waiting for a break in the storm. The rain was sheeting down now, blowing the palm trees, their fronds twisting in the gusts. The sky had turned an eerie green, the ocean frothing onto the shore.

The wind had piled more chairs into themselves around the pool, and broken glass from a poolside light littered the cement.

Rain blew by in gusts.

There was no escaping it. She ducked her head and ran out into the deluge, across the cobblestones, and finally under the balconies. Her clothing was plastered to her body by the time she scooted up her stairs.

She tried her room key.

The door didn't open.

She tried again.

Nothing.

They must have checked her out, zeroed out her key.

Perfect.

She raced down the stairs and back out into the pelting rain, shivering violently by the time she slammed the lodge door behind her. "I'm locked out!"

Her voice carried across the lobby even as she followed it to the front desk. "I'm locked out of my—"

Mimi lay with her head on the desk. Yola stood over her with the phone pressed to her ear. Drool ran from Mimi's mouth.

"What happened?" Aria ran around the edge of the desk, pressed her fingers to Mimi's jugular. A rhythm, fast and thready.

"She just collapsed. What's wrong with her?"

"Mimi?" Aria kneeled before her. "Mimi, can you hear me?"

Her eyes opened, and she took a breath. "Oh, my . . . um . . ." She lifted her head, clearly disoriented.

"Maybe she just passed out from lack of oxygen," said Aria. She helped Mimi sit up. Her skin was crepe-paper thin, despite the leathery look. "Mimi, can you smile for me? Show me teeth?"

Mimi frowned at her.

"Mimi, please."

She made an exaggerated smile. No facial weakness.

"How about lift your arms for me?"

"I'm fine!" She went to stand up but fell back into her chair.

"You're not fine."

"I'm just a little dizzy. I haven't eaten lunch, with all the excitement around here."

No slurring of speech. And aside from the balance . . . maybe she wasn't having a stroke. Still— "Do you have keys to the van?"

Yola opened a drawer and pulled out the keys. "I don't have a license."

"I do, let's go." Aria hoisted Mimi up and pulled her arm around her shoulder. "Get her other side."

Yola ducked under her grandmother and helped her up.

"This is ridiculous," Mimi said, but when she stumbled, her grip tightened around Aria. She said nothing as they approached the door.

The van sat on the far side of the parking lot, lashed by rain. Across the street, water had pooled in the sports shop parking lot, and a fleet of kayaks floated free.

"Wait here," Aria said and lowered Mimi down onto a nearby bench. Then, ducking her head, she ran for the van.

She unlocked it on the way, dove into the driver's seat, and fought to get the key in the ignition with her trembling hands. Rain bulleted the front windshield.

The engine turned over and she pulled out, then alongside the resort entrance. Yola had Mimi up and headed to the van by the time she came around. They loaded Mimi onto the bench seat and Yola climbed in beside her.

"The Key West hospital is up the road a couple miles, on Stock Island, just off Highway 1," Yola said.

"We had a tour a couple days ago," Aria said and put the van into drive.

The wind howled, shivering road signs, tearing palm branches from trees, sheeting water down the road. It had risen to maybe six inches—not so deep she couldn't drive through it—but she eased out onto the road slowly. A kayak had dislodged from the pack in the lot across the street and edged out into the road. Farther down, the traffic light blinked red, and a tree limb partially blocked the road.

"There's no signal," Yola said, pocketing her cell phone. "Maybe the lines are down."

"She'll be okay. We'll get her to the hospital, get her on oxygen, give her a treatment, and . . ." Aria didn't want to suggest anything else, like monitor her for a stroke, but COPD patients had a myriad of potential problems, from stroke, to lung cancer, to heart disease. "I'm sure she'll be fine, but we can't be too safe."

"Yeah," Yola said as she hung between the seats. "That's why I came down here this summer. I go to college in Queens, but I thought I'd spend the summer here, you know. I lost my mom to cancer a few years ago, and Mimi is all I have left. She tries to run the place by herself—"

"I'm just fine!"

Yola cut her voice down. "Frankly, I'd like her to sell the place, but she's had it for over forty years, so there's no budging her. She and my grandpop bought it, fixed it up after a hurricane came through in the early seventies."

"Tropical Storms Dorothy and Felice. Only two weeks apart. Tore the Mama to shreds. Rollo and I took it on from the owner and worked for free for years to pay him back, but we built something. We believed in something—" Mimi doubled over, coughing.

Aria glanced in the rearview mirror. Yola was rubbing Mimi's back.

"Mimi and Pops rebuilt the place. Pops said it could be a little piece of paradise. He died about twenty years ago, but Mimi refused to move. This place has always been home, at least in the summer."

Mimi sat up. "I'm not selling, Yola."

Aria crawled through the entertainment district—past the closed tiki bars, the pubs, the museums, the seafood restaurants—and toward the business district on Caroline Street. As they passed the beach she noted the sky had turned darker, the waves now crashing against the cement barriers, spraying fury into the sky and over onto the boardwalk. A tree branch skittered across the road in front of her.

She cut right, down to Eaton, and followed that to Palm Avenue Causeway.

Waves crashed over the two-lane road, the Garrison Bight harbor furious as it drenched the road.

"Go back," Yola said, and Aria was already backing up.

They doubled back on Eisenhower and took Truman east. They passed the empty parking lot of the Parrot resort, the car rental place, Home Depot—advertising an empty display of plywood and hurricane protection—the Pizza Hut, and another empty hotel lot.

The road narrowed near the ballfields, the ocean to the left crashing over the breakwater and onto the highway. Boats moored in the causeway slammed into the barriers that tethered them. The palm tree fronds blew horizontal.

"This is just the outer bands. Good thing the eyewall isn't going to hit us," Mimi said.

Aria kept her eyes on the road, the windshield wipers on full as she motored down Roosevelt and the long stretch of unprotected highway. She hazarded a look once and the foamy torrent of the sea put a hand in her gut.

She might prefer a blizzard to this chaos.

A gust nearly knocked them into the ditch, but she gripped the wheel, righted the van. Stepped down a little on the gas.

They passed a medical building and a set of three-story apartments facing the Salt Pond Keys, then finally made the turn south to Highway 1.

The bridge stretched over the water, between Key West and Stock Island.

"There's the hospital." Yola pointed to a three-story building on the north of Stock Island.

Two miles away.

Waves splashed against the bridge, spittle flying into the air, crashing down onto the pavement in a tumult of power that could wash their van right over the edge.

"Maybe we should go back," Mimi said.

Aria glanced at Mimi. Her lips appeared blue. She turned back, watching the surge, timing it. "Hang on. But you might not want to buckle in case we go over."

"What?" Yola shrieked.

Aria gunned it. The waves had receded, and she slammed the gas into the floor, praying the van had the get-up-and-go she needed.

The water was rushing back, the rain blinding on the windshield. She leaned forward, willing the van past the surge.

The wave crashed down just as they reached the other side, a frothy explosion of fury that could have certainly washed them out to sea. She eased off the gas, afraid to tap her brakes and hydroplane. But they slowed enough for her to turn left onto College Road.

They passed the Monroe County Sheriff's department and detention center, and she noticed lights on in the building.

"Those poor inmates," Mimi said. "They must be terrified, stuck in their cells."

Huh. Aria hadn't thought about the fact that the prison might not evacuate.

The vegetation here was nearly washed away, the road littered with shrubbery and debris. She eased around the litter, kept her foot on the gas, the gusts hitting the van hard, fresh off the ocean some twenty feet away.

An electrical pole sparked right in front of them, and she swerved, nearly plowed into the sand and mud on the side of the road.

"You have some kind of spunk, girl," Mimi said, her voice weak.

Yeah, well, she was channeling her inner Kia, the sister who had possessed enough spunk for both of them. She, on the other hand, was the brainy one. The one who got straight As and landed at the top of her class.

The one who didn't get in over her head. Usually.

They passed the teal-and-gray buildings of the elementary school, a fine arts center, then finally—

"There it is!" Yola said.

Aria pulled in on the right, across the parking lot and right under the overhang entrance of the three-story orange-and-white building.

The hospital was evacuating.

A massive coast guard chopper sat in the lot, under bright lights washed by the raging winds and rain. A handful of people—staff, maybe, dressed in scrubs and street clothes—waited under the shelter of the awning. A few more held umbrellas, moving a handful of patients in wheelchairs out to the chopper.

The few onlookers parted as she braked and got out.

Yola had already opened the door.

"Aria, what are you still doing here?" She looked over to see Drey, dressed in a pair of khakis and a collared shirt, moving around the front of the van. "I thought you'd left with the others."

"I was sick, but I'm fine now. I need help." She reached in and helped Mimi out of the van, Yola on the other side. "What are you doing here?"

"I stayed to help. The others left for Miami. But now everyone is leaving. The hospital has been evacuated. You can't stay here." He said this as they moved Mimi toward the doors. They opened, and she stepped into the cool air-conditioning and relative quiet of the lobby.

"Where's the ER? She needs oxygen."

He gave her a look, then pointed down the hallway.

She set Mimi down into a nearby wheelchair. It was wet. Aria turned to Yola. "Take her to the ER. Get her on a bed. I'll be right there."

Yola hustled her away and Aria turned to Drey. "I agree. But I need to stabilize her first."

"The chopper is leaving now." Drey glanced toward the door. "The highway is closed—you can't get out by car. You need to go now."

"What about Mimi?"

He looked back at her. "I'll see if there's room, but they've already agreed to take the staff on this flight. We stayed because they promised they wouldn't leave us behind. I think the chopper is full."

"She's in danger of having a stroke, Drey. I can't leave her here."

He held up his hands. "I don't know what to tell you. I can ask if they'll come back—"

"Yeah, do that." She shook her head. "I'm not leaving her behind."

"If she didn't already evacuate, then she doesn't want to leave—"

"It doesn't matter. She needs help, and I'm not going to abandon her."

"Fine. I'll ask if they can come back for you. But are you prepared to stay here if they can't?"

Yola had emerged out into the hallway, soaked to the bone, her shirt plastered to her body, her hands wrapped around her waist. Clearly she'd gotten Mimi settled.

Or maybe not, because she was trembling, worry in her eyes.

"Yeah. I'm not going to trade my life for someone else's, thanks. You go. We'll be fine."

His mouth tightened in a grim line. "I don't like this—"

"You could stay."

He drew in a breath.

"Doctor?" A nurse had stepped inside the building. "They're leaving."

He cocked his head. "I'm sorry, Aria."

"It's fine. It's not my first storm. We'll be fine."

"I'll ask them to come back—"

"Just go."

She headed down the hallway to Yola.

"She's over here," Yola said and directed her to an ER bay where Mimi lay on a gurney. Her eyes were closed.

First things first. She opened the drawers, searching for an oxygen mask, found one in a package, and ripped it open. Then, she turned on the pulse-ox monitor and attached the clip to Mimi's finger.

The reading was 62mm, dangerously close to hypoxia. She turned on the oxygen and heard it hiss as she affixed the mask to the hose, then tucked it over Mimi's mouth and nose.

"You're going to feel better in a bit," she said. She'd like to get a FEV/sec test, along with a spirometry test, but for now, she just wanted Mimi to breathe.

Outside, she heard the roar of the chopper as it lifted away, disappeared.

A hand reached out, gripped her arm. She looked at Mimi.

"Don't you worry about a thing," Mimi said, drawing away the mask. "God always shows up in a storm."

Huh. She didn't know why, but the words settled inside her, found her bones.

She covered Mimi's hand with hers.

"Uh-oh," Yola said quietly.

Aria looked at her.

Yola was standing in the hallway, looking at her feet.

Her white tennis shoes were covered with an inch of water, dribbling down the hallway.

■ ■ ■

The smells of fried chebureki turned in Ham's gut as he walked down Victory Avenue on his way to Pushkin Park.

Ukraine, the city of Kiev, the place of his last, worst mistake.

Okay, he'd made more since then, but none of them of the epic nature of losing, for the final time, the woman he loved, right here in this city.

Well, the end had started here.

The grand finale happened in the mountains of Chechnya.

He stuck his hands into his jacket pockets, head down, trying not to draw attention. Not that the local militia had any reason to look for him, but attracting attention wouldn't do anything to fix his current op-gone-south.

He was supposed to be on a train to Moscow to rescue a woman who'd been accused of an international crime. And everything would have gone off as planned if her brother, a navy SEAL named Ford Marshall, and his girlfriend, Scarlett Hathaway, hadn't turned Ham's well-oiled plan into a tangled mess, causing him to have to stay behind and sort out their exfil details.

It did, however, give him time to track down Royal Benjamin.

How Senator White had gotten a bead on Royal, he didn't know, but apparently Royal was masking his identity with the code name Prince.

Which felt a little on the nose, but the guy hadn't been known for his creativity, just his ability to get the job done.

Ham had a dark feeling that he knew exactly what Royal's current job was.

Unfortunately, he'd missed their planned meeting in Prague, where Royal told Ford how to find his sister.

Ham wasn't going to miss this one. Not with Royal, but a contact Ham had made through his SEAL connections, namely former teammate Luke Dekker, now a private security contractor with Stryker International. Luke had set Ham up with his boss, Chet Stryker.

Right here in Kiev.

Ham walked past a hospital, a music academy, and then into the park with its paved paths, tall oak and linden trees, and the smell of wild raspberries thick on the vines. Mothers walked their children in prams, a cool breeze rustled the foliage and carried in it the sound of an accordion and the smells of more fried street food.

"I miss hamburgers." Signe, tugging on his hand, her green eyes finding his. "And french fries. What do you miss?"

"Besides pizza?" No, besides her smile—healing, moment by moment, the terrible gash inside him that he'd lived with for the past five years, since he came home from his deployment to find her gone. Vamoosed. Without a trace or a forwarding address. She'd warned him—he just hadn't believed her.

Never stopped looking for her.

"And country music. I can't believe you got me hooked on that."

He wanted to pull her into a two-step right there on the sidewalk.

Ham put a hand to his chest at the memory, took a breath. It didn't do him any good to rehash it. It still ended up the same way, every single time, no matter how much he reworked it.

They simply didn't see the world the same way.

Didn't see their relationship—their *marriage*—the same way.

The music he heard was coming from a street performer, a man in a ragged pair of pants and a grimy jacket. Ham dropped a couple hryvnia into his upturned hat and kept going, toward the benches near a playground where he planned to meet Chet. The brightly colored equipment had seen better days, the paint peeling, the wooden teeter-totter worn, the wood rotting.

"Let me down, Ham!" Signe, trapped at the top, banging the board, him at the bottom, grinning up at her. He wanted to leave her there, trap her so she couldn't leave him again. Couldn't scare him.

"Not until you agree to go home." Stupid words, he couldn't believe he let them emerge.

A darkness crossed her face, her smile vanishing. "That's like me asking you to quit the teams. I have a job to do." She lifted her leg over, hopped off, and stalked away.

Brilliant, Ham.

Now a dog barked in the park and he watched a little girl, maybe age ten, her hair in pigtails, wearing a school uniform, chase after it.

Reminded him of Aggie, her laughter with Jake at the party.

His little girl had been like a board when he hugged her goodbye later that night. He'd bubbled an "I'll be back," and even to his ears it felt cold, a little like Arnold Schwarzenegger in *The Terminator*.

"Vera! Come back!" The voice of her mother called the little girl back. In Ukrainian, of course, but Ham's rusty Ukrainian was coming back to him. He glanced over, spotted the woman—midthirties, wearing a short skirt and heels, holding a jacket, her hair short behind her ears.

Signe would have been in her midthirties by now. He held her in immortality in his head for some reason, young, her blonde hair long and twining between his fingers, her laugh a balm for his soul.

What were you doing in Italy, Sig?

But right now wasn't the time because he spotted Chet sitting on a bench across the play area. A former Green Beret turned private security operator, Chet Stryker had worked in the eastern European theater, namely Georgia, just south of Chechnya. So he knew Russian, not to mention the right people to help get Ford and his friends out of Russia via Kazakhstan should they need to travel south.

But more, Chet had connections—the kind who could track down an under-the-radar wet-work operator.

Chet wore a black dress shirt, a suit coat, and a pair of jeans and met Ham's approach with a nod.

Ham sat down beside him and extended a hand.

"Never thought I'd see you again in this part of the world," Chet said. "I heard you were in Afghanistan."

"I'm retired. Live in the States." *With my daughter.* Naw, that felt too fresh to say. "I run a private global SAR team now."

"Interesting. Finding tourists who wander off?"

"Something like that. How've you been?"

"Good. I just got done consulting on a job and Dekker shot me a text, said you wanted to meet up. I'm on a train out tonight, back to Prague."

"You're HQed there?"

"Yeah. My wife and I just had our second kid." He pulled up his cell phone and opened it to a couple redheaded rug rats, the oldest no more than two. "Finally got Mae to agree to sit out a few missions, although she's aching to get back into the cockpit."

"I get it. Signe never was one for sitting still, either." And wow, he didn't know why he'd said that, like he was a married man, with a wife who wouldn't quit.

Except, that was sort of the truth. Or would have been if everything had gone according to plan.

But nothing, it seemed, went according to his plans.

"So, what brings you to Ukraine?" Chet asked.

"Right now, I'm working on extracting three people from Russia, possibly across the southern border into Kazakhstan."

"I have a few contacts, people in immigration, some friends inside their security forces. I'll have my guy Artyom send you a number."

"Great. Can I ask another favor?"

"Give it a try."

"I'm trying to track down a buddy of mine—Royal Benjamin. He was mixed up in something in Afghanistan and sort of disappeared. We think he's working in Europe, going by the name Prince."

Chet gave a half-grin. "That's a terrible code name."

"Agreed. But he might be in trouble, and I just want to check on him."

Chet folded his arms, his gaze on a couple kids kicking a soccer ball down the pavement. "Did you hear about the assassination attempt in Russia?"

"Some general—"

"Boris Stanislov. One of the troika. The leadership. I have a contact in Russia who thinks the Bratva, the Russian mob, is behind it."

No wonder Ford needed to find his sister, get her out, if the Bratva were after her—or framing her—for the attack. But he didn't add that to Chet's words.

"There is some conversation on the dark web suggesting the Bratva was behind the recent assassination attempt on Senator White."

"The one in Alaska?" Ham didn't mention that he'd been there, that he and Jake had been the ones to take down the terrorist. "I thought he was acting alone."

"Maybe. But there was another in San Diego, at the national convention."

Ham had heard about that—a thwarted bombing. "You think Russia is behind this?"

"I think Russia has always been interested in our politics. It's the game we play—we spy on them, they spy on us, but now . . . well, it's getting personal."

"Yes, if they want to try and assassinate our presidential candidates."

"Didn't we just try to assassinate their general?" Chet said.

"I don't know." Ford seemed to think his sister was innocent, that she'd been set up.

"Have you ever heard of the NOC list?" Chet asked.

"Of course," Ham said. "The list of agents working non-official cover for the CIA."

"No immunity, no protection if they're caught, but patriots, in the employ of the US government, defending our country. Acting as diplomats and humanitarian aid workers and journalists and photographers and international employees and even occasionally simply going dark, becoming ghosts."

"In other words, spies."

Chet nodded. "And according to the dark web, the NOC list is out, and up for sale."

"How did it get out?"

"We're not sure. But imagine if Russia got their hands on it."

"Where is it now?"

"The offer went out about a month ago, but there's been no movement on it, and the sale is still open, so we're not sure what's going on. Artyom has been monitoring the sale."

"You think my friend Royal might be on that list?"

"If he is, he's in trouble, along with everyone else on that list—a list Russia or the Bratva would very much like to have. And a list that might include who made the attempt on General Stanislov. The

Russians—or the Bratva—getting their hands on that list would ensure that they could take out anyone who might get in their way."

"Including Royal. Can you figure out a way to reach out to him?"

Chet considered him. "I'll try. No promises, but Artyom can tap a few private message boards. Prince, you said?"

Ham nodded.

The boys kicked the soccer ball into the yard. Chet got up and stopped it with his foot, kicked it back. Stood in the shadows of the playground, his hands in his pockets. "Tell me again why you're here, Ham?"

Ham stood up. "Just helping out a friend."

"Okay. I'll get you in touch with my contact in Kazakhstan. But listen . . . if your *friend* is in trouble with the Bratva, they're not slowed down by any borders. You find her, and you tell her to hide."

"I will." He shook Chet's hand.

"And you tell that pretty wife of yours hello. I met her in Italy a few years ago, when Luke spotted her. She had your daughter with her, if I remember correctly."

Ham stared at him. For a moment the words didn't fully engage and he nearly let them slide off him.

And then, "What?"

"Your wife. I saw her in Italy."

"When?"

"I don't know. It was before Mae and I were married, so . . . maybe eight years ago? We were working a kidnapping in Italy at the time. Luke was sort of freaking out when he saw her, I'm not sure why."

Because he'd been with Ham in Chechnya when Ham thought he'd *killed* her?

A hand pressed Ham's chest, took out his breath.

"She said you'd been spun up but were working out of Sigonella and she'd come to see you."

The lie felt so believable, he almost nodded.

What if she'd been in Italy all this time?

All this time, with his child, and never said a word. Never contacted him.

Never cared.

"I'll tell her," Ham said, the Terminator voice back again.

"Your daughter's, what—"

"Ten. Her name is Aggie."

"Cutie pie, if I remember right. We're lucky men, Ham." He checked his watch. "I'll let you know if I find out anything about Royal too."

Ham nodded and watched him leave, unable to move.

He sat back on the bench. The sun was cresting down, casting goldenrod fingers through the trees. *"I love you, Ham. I always have. But we . . . this can't be any more than right now."* Signe, in silhouette against the hotel window, her back to St. Michael's Golden-Domed Monastery, the setting sun glinting off it, blinding him. Watering his eyes. He'd arranged this getaway to help them find their footing again. For him to remind her that once upon a time, they loved each other.

"But we're married, Sig—"

"Only because you didn't annul the marriage. That's why we got married in Vegas, for Pete's sake—so it would be easier to annul."

"I married you because I loved you."

"You married me because you said we couldn't be together unless we were married. Because of your black-and-white sense of morality." She turned away from him. "I can't be married to a navy SEAL."

"What? Why?"

She sighed. "You know why. I can't watch you die. I can't . . . I can't do that, Ham."

Was she kidding? "What about you? You're working as an aid worker in a refugee camp in the middle of a country in a civil war!"

She folded her arms.

"C'mon. Why are you even here?" His own voice, reverberating through the tiny room.

"You don't understand . . . " She'd started, then stopped herself, her voice cresting low. "I have to be here."

He'd forgotten about that conversation. Had swept it away into his subconscious, had told himself it was one of her justice-for-humanity causes that made her say it.

As in, she was compelled to be there.

But what if . . . what if it was her job?

"Have you ever heard of the NOC list?"

"No immunity, no protection if they're caught, but patriots, in the employ of the US government, defending our country. Acting as diplomats and humanitarian aid workers . . ."

No. Except, after their hurry-up wedding in Vegas, he'd been deployed, and she'd suddenly stopped writing. Then she'd graduated and vanished.

It had taken him five years to find her. In the back hills of Chechnya, of all places. Somehow, he'd convinced her to sneak away to Ukraine to sort it all out.

His phone vibrated and he tapped it.

A text from Ellie, Jake's sister. He opened it. A picture of Aggie filled the screen, sitting on the sofa, cuddling with Arthur, the Silver family's goldendoodle. Smiling, of course.

The night was descending. Ham got up and headed back to the hotel.

But he couldn't help but see Signe again, in his mind as he walked. Her arms folded, her mouth tight, her eyes bright, as if she too might be holding back tears as they fought during their getaway to Kiev. All he wanted to do was cross the hotel room and take her into his arms. Again.

Keep them both safe, forever.

"You don't have to be here. This is a dangerous place, with dangerous people. I know you're tough, and brave, but . . . I can't lose you, Sig." He couldn't stop himself from advancing on her, taking her by the arms. Meeting her beautiful eyes. "Please, please go home."

She put her hands on his chest, warming his beating heart, and in a gesture that he thought might be a yes, lifted her face to kiss him. "I'll be safe, I promise."

And his foolish heart believed her.

CHAPTER 5

JAKE WAS SOME KIND OF IMPULSIVE IDIOT to truly believe that hopping on an early morning flight to Miami to save a woman who not only probably didn't need to be rescued but also was trying to forget him was a good idea.

Okay, so maybe she wasn't trying to *forget* him. After all, "I wish you were here" and "I need some TLC" didn't exactly sound like "*I'm over you.*"

But she probably didn't need *rescuing*. Aria, if anything, was a capable woman who saved little lives with groundbreaking, courageous procedures.

She'd just needed help that one time climbing off a killer mountain.

In fact, she was probably caught in the throng of traffic he'd met while driving US 1 from Miami to the Keys.

Blue skies overhead, but all of southern Florida seemed to be makin' for them thar hills—aka, the mainland. He'd rented the last vehicle in the lot—a jeep—and after sitting in morning traffic in Miami, found himself rehearsing exactly what he might say to her when he showed up.

Hi, Aria. Um, so, need help with your bags?

Hi, Aria, I was in town.

Hi, Aria, about the TLC you needed—

No, *no*. This was a very bad idea. Only the law of diminishing returns kept him from turning his car around when he reached Key Largo and saw the swarm of traffic inching their way north. He'd come this far, and frankly, well . . .

Even if she didn't need to be rescued, maybe they could *talk*. Even start over. He could woo her with a beachy sunset. Maybe get his hands on a catamaran and take her out sailing.

Aw, Ellie was right. He just had to fix everything.

Jake pulled in for gas at a station in the median of the two-lane highway. A man in a caravan with Alabama plates was pumping across from him. He sported a baseball cap and a killer sunburn on the back of his neck.

"Where's the fire?" Jake said, and the guy looked over at him. Frowned. So, clearly no sense of humor. A few clouds bumped together, and a slight wind bullied the heat, but, "It doesn't look like the hurricane is anywhere near here."

"That's the thing with hurricanes," the man said. "It'll be gorgeous until it isn't. And then suddenly, you're in the thick of it. You don't want to be caught on the bridge when the storm hits."

He finished pumping and climbed into his car, a few kids peering at Jake through the window.

"If you're going south, I'd put your foot down. They might close the highway if this thing heads inland, and then they'll turn you around."

Jake didn't stop for gas after that. He noticed a few state patrol vehicles on the road, probably watching the bumper-to-bumper lineup north. He kept it at the speed limit, mostly, watched the sky, and by the time he hit the bridge over the Sugarloaf Channel, the waves had turned nasty and dark.

The local Key West police were set up on the southern side of the channel. Jake slowed and rolled down his window. A man in a rain slicker approached his car. He was clean-shaven and bore the build of a linebacker. The wind plastered his slicker to his body.

"Sorry, sir, we're going to have to turn you around. Looks like the storm might be heading this way. We don't want to take the chance you're stuck on the island."

He pointed to a turnaround spot just down the road, past a coffee shop.

"Listen. I have a medical emergency. My . . . friend is sick. And she's stuck in Key West and I need to get down there."

The cop was shaking his head.

"It's five miles away. C'mon, dude—"

"Sorry—"

Jake glanced at the line of cars inching along in the opposite lane. "Listen, here's the deal, traffic is completely backed up. I turn around now, I won't be north for hours, and I might get trapped on the bridge when this storm hits. There's a woman five miles down the road who called and told me she needed me. Now, she's pretty, man. Really pretty, and I think I have a shot with her. But if I don't show up, it's over. Done. Are you going to tell me you're willing to kill what could be true love to make me sit in this line of traffic for hours?"

The cop pursed his lips but seemed to be listening.

"Do me a solid, bro. Let me go down there. We'll hunker down someplace safe. Or, if you want, I'll find her and we'll drive back out, pronto."

He considered Jake. "Fine. We haven't closed the road yet. Go now." He stepped back and Jake didn't wait.

He drove past the naval air station; the runways and chopper pads looked empty. Overhead, the sky had turned an eerie green. It started to rain, something of a patter, and he flipped on the wipers.

He crossed Stock Island and pulled into the empty parking lot of a Hilton, thumbing up his voice mail app.

Jenny had left him a message, which he'd downloaded earlier. He listened to it now.

"Jake. What are you doing? Are you sure Aria texted you? Because . . . well, I know what happened between you two but she's pretty embarrassed. She said that you guys agreed to be just friends at the party, so . . . okay, fine. I can't get ahold of her either. She sent me a card, though, and it said she was staying on the beach. I called Lucas at work and he said his travel agent booked it for him. He can't remember the name but says it was something like Piña Colada Resort, or maybe Rum Runner—a fruity drink name. Anyway, just remember, the Aria you met in Alaska might not be the Aria in real life. Stay safe." She hung up.

He frowned, not sure what to think of Jenny's words. But with the wind picking up and the palm fronds starting to waggle in the breeze, he guessed that the outer fringes of the storm had hit. Maybe they'd just scoot by the island, leave behind sunny skies.

Until then, the clouds had cut off cell reception and his GPS wouldn't pull up a map. He got out and headed into the Hilton to ask, but the lobby was empty. He did grab a map of the area, however, a cute watercolor tourist brochure with destinations, eateries, and a few resorts marked.

Coconut Colada Beach homes sounded like a possibility. And Tequila Shores Resort. Clearly not all the hotels and resorts on the island were marked—probably only those that paid for the advertising. But it was a start. Both resorts were located on the southern side of the island, near the airport.

He headed back out and got on the road circling the island. Maybe he'd just stop in at all of them.

Or maybe this was a wild-goose chase and he should turn the jeep around.

He stopped by Tequila Shores Resort, a massive complex of condos, beach homes, and boat slips. A few cars remained in the lot and he parked and got out, running against the wind to the front office.

It was dark, but he spotted a light in the back and when he rang, a man emerged wearing a rain slicker. "What are you doing here? We're not taking guests."

"I'm looking for someone. Aria Sinclair. She was with a medical convention."

"Sorry." The man pushed past him. "No convention here. And we're closed. If she was here, she isn't now." He stepped outside, and Jake followed. He headed down to the docks, maybe to tie off the boats. Jake stood, looking out to sea. A dark swath of clouds boiled up in the distance, a line of gray signaling a wall of rain heading this direction.

He stopped at two more resorts—the Best Western, the Sheraton. No medical conventions. *C'mon, Aria, where are you?*

Coconut Colada was a lineup of townhomes that looked like long-term rentals. Most of the homes had metal hurricane windows and a few owners were outside, hanging plywood. He drove up to a man wearing seersucker shorts and a wifebeater. "Hey! I'm looking for some sort of medical convention. You heard of anything around here?"

"This is a fifty-five-and-older community." He wandered to the car. "But you could try Margaritaville. They have a big conference room. It's at the western end of the island."

Margaritaville. "You're brilliant, man."

"You'd better find a place to lay low. It's going to get wet." He headed back toward his house.

Jake drove out of the lot and around the southern side of the island. The ocean was kicking up against the breakwater, splashing against a long pier that jutted out into the sea. A couple onlookers sat on the beach, their hair blowing back.

He followed the road around the southern end of the island and found himself lost inside a neighborhood. Military houses, utilitarian with picnic tables between them, a few cars in the mostly empty lot. Farther in rose two-story beach homes, with verandas and balconies that extended around the square homes. Many had plywood or hurricane coverings over the windows, their furniture tied up or covered. Grills strapped down. The neighborhoods were tight, houses closed, and it gave the island a hunkered-down feel, as if the inhabitants might be used to surviving together.

Amidst those were smaller, one-story homes with towering oak and palm trees, a few boats covered up, parked in the yards.

He had to get out of this tangle and back to the shoreline. Spotting a church, he headed toward the spire and emerged from the clutter of streets at a marine sanctuary, the ocean on the other side, angry and churning.

But he found a road and followed it northwest.

The road led him along the harbor, where sailboats and fishing boats were moored, tied down, covered. A couple float planes also tied tight thrashed in the waves.

Oh, those wouldn't last long if things got nasty.

He was just passing the harbor when he spotted the sign for Margaritaville. He pulled into the massive lot and parked. A few cars remained in the lot and he ran in, through the thickening rain, to the lobby.

The Margaritaville resort lodge was a grand two-story plantation house, with cobblestone walkways and blue awnings. He ducked under one and found the door. Tried it. It was boarded up and locked.

"C'mon!" He stood there a moment, not sure what to do.

Not that he expected it, but he could use a little help.

"What's going on?"

The voice turned him and he spied a man walking toward him. A big man, dark hair, with a scrape of vacation whiskers, he wore a rain slicker over a gray shirt and carried a newspaper over his head to ward off the rain.

"I'm looking for a friend of mine."

"No one here, man. Unless they're local. All the tourists up and ran north."

"My friend was here for a medical convention. She was staying at a place named after a drink." He gestured to the sign.

"Did you try the Bahama Mama? Mimi never shuts down—been through dozens of hurricanes. If anyone is still operating, it's her. But you better get under cover soon. We're hours from the eye, but the outer bands are starting to hit."

"Where's the Bahama Mama?" He had to shout as the rain thickened.

The man pointed down the shore, past the aquarium. "The giant tiki hut."

"Thanks!" Jake ran out into the parking lot, got into the jeep. The rain thundered down onto the pavement now, turning almost horizontal in the wind.

He pulled out, driving past an aquarium, then a paved square that looked out over the ocean. Giant waves slammed against the embankment, splashing down onto the square. Palm fronds littered the lot of the Bahama Mama, one lonely car parked under a palm tree. He got out and found the door unlocked, the building relatively unprotected from the storm. Inside, the place was empty, quiet. "Hello? Aria?"

Silly. He could barely hear himself above the thunder of the rain.

He stared out at the beach through the glass doors at the other end of the lobby. The sky had turned dark, the water a cauldron of froth and chaos.

And—wait. Sitting on a chair, under the alcove, staring out at the water, a person.

Just sitting there, under the gale, unmoving.

Aria?

He quick walked, then jogged down the corridor and opened the door. "Aria?"

The woman turned. Blonde, her hair in dreadlocks and enormously pregnant, she looked at him with a sort of confusion. "Baker?"

"Ma'am. What are you doing here?"

She said nothing at first, frowning. Then she turned back to the ocean. "I . . . I don't know. I didn't know where else to go."

His gaze fell on a bag at her feet, bulging with what looked like art supplies. A backpack sat next to it. "We got in a terrible fight. I never thought . . ." She looked back at him, her eyes big. "He left me. I came back to the hostel and he was gone."

Jake crouched next to her. "Who was gone?"

She swallowed, and her gaze tracked over to him. "Baker. My . . ." Her mouth tightened and she looked down at her belly. "I guess I thought he was my boyfriend."

Aw.

Only then did he see that she was barefoot. Blood dripped off her foot onto the cement, only to ripple away in the wash of water. Around them, the wind began to howl.

"What happened to your foot?"

She looked down, as if seeing it for the first time. "I cut it."

"Can I see it?"

She nodded and he moved to take a closer look. Maybe from broken glass, the wound cut through the heel of her foot, a deep slice that could probably use a couple stitches.

"I think we need to go to the hospital."

"I don't have any money."

"Don't worry about that. C'mon." He held out his hand. "What's your name?"

A trash barrel rolled by on the wharf.

"Evangeline, but people call me Angel." She took his hand, but when she put weight on the foot, she cried out, shrinking back.

He caught her and in a second, swooped her up into his arms. "Sorry. We need to get out of here. Hope it's okay if I carry you."

She looped her arms around his neck. He'd put her in her early twenties, maybe younger. He didn't want to imagine how much younger. He bent low enough that she could pick up her bags, cradling them against herself as he walked her back through the building.

The sky had turned nearly black by the time he secured her in the jeep.

"Do you know where the hospital is?" he asked.

"It's at the far end of the island."

On the way out of town. Where he should be heading. He eased out of the lot and onto the flooding streets, winding through the neighborhoods to stay away from the surging water. When they reached the outskirts of town, he debated the run back over the bridge to Stock Island, but he belted her in and put the gas to the floor, plowing through the foot-high water and clearing the surge before it crashed into the bridge.

She was looking at him, something of horror on her face.

Yeah, well, that was him—act first, think later. And fix it when he could.

"Turn here," she said.

He drove down College Road, noticing the lights off at the county detention center—hopefully they'd evacuated any prisoners. Already the yard was starting to flood with the surge.

A foot of water covered the hospital's parking lot, but the drive-through area was clogged with cars so he drove into the lot, parked, went around, and pulled Angel back into his arms.

Seawater rose past his ankles as he waded into the dark lobby. "Hello?"

His voice echoed down the hallways of the vacant hospital.

"They must have evacuated," Angel said, still holding on to him.

"Yeah. Probably. Let's see if I can find something to close that wound."

He headed toward the ER bay, wishing he had his Maglite. Finding a gurney, he was setting her on it when a boom shook the building. Angel's arms tightened around his neck.

It was followed by a bright and resounding crash, a shattering of glass.

"What was that?" Angel put a vise hold around his neck.

"Probably a window breaking—"

But on its tail, a scream lifted, something primal and terrified and . . . oh no.

He *knew* that scream.

It came straight out of his nightmares.

Aria!

■ ■ ■

Aria just couldn't break free of her bad decisions. She had stood too long at the window, her hands folded over her waist, watching the torrent. Watching for the chopper Drey had promised.

No, not promised.

"You should have left with the other doctors," Yola said. She sat next to Mimi's bed, holding the nebulizer mask to her face.

Aria shook her head, refusing to agree, at least outwardly.

How she always got in over her head, she had no idea, but here she was again, trapped by a storm.

At least she wasn't freezing to death on a mountain.

And like Mimi said, she'd lived through storms before. Still, "I've never seen horizontal rain before," Aria said.

"Me either," Yola said. "It's creepy."

The entire sky was creepy. The horizon had darkened to an evil gray and water flooded the parking lot, cars starting to move like toy boats.

She guessed that the surge from the oncoming storm had filled the storm gutters of the low-lying key, which was how the first floor of the hospital flooded so quickly. Now, the wind came in terrible gusts, ripping down palm fronds, and in the distance, a power line sparked, fireflies against the darkness.

Mimi lay on the bed, her breathing better now. Her pulse ox was up to 68mm.

The moment Yola had noticed the water rising, they'd packed Mimi up and headed upstairs to the second floor—a med-surg floor with a nurses' station in the center. The patient rooms were separated into two wings with rooms on each side of the station. A supply room and a nurses' lounge were located at the end of the hall. A tiny waiting room flanked the other end, with a couple of purple sofas and a teal-and-purple rug with seashells stamped into the design.

Aria had settled Mimi into a vacant and clean room opposite the nursing center. That the hospital had vacated quickly was evident in the disarray of a number of rooms—bedsheets and pads in a mess, empty packets of sterile wipes, their contents in wads on the metal bedside tables, IV bags left behind.

She'd found a pharmacy on the first floor and discovered the door left unlocked—clearly an oversight, but she propped it open, just in case. Water was already up to her ankles by the time she found a box of albuterol and a nebulizer kit and brought it upstairs.

Assembling the kit, she plugged the hose into the oxygen line. The familiar hiss and steam from the mask seemed to settle over them like a blanket, a comforting reminder that as the world fell apart around them, right now, Mimi could breathe, and they were warm and drying.

Aria then left them to find scrubs in the supply room and returned wearing dry clothing, with scrubs for Mimi and Yola. Yola had pulled up a chair to Mimi's bed and was holding the mask over her face. Mimi had her eyes closed.

"My mother was diagnosed with melanoma two months before she died. It was all over her body. I was sixteen, and the day she died, I remember standing by her bed thinking . . . what now?" Yola's hand whisked Mimi's hair back from her forehead. "Mimi just somehow appeared, right in the middle of all that. Told me that I might not be able to see the future, but right now, we were safe, together. And we'd just take one moment at a time." She reached out and took Aria's hand. "Thanks for bringing us here. And for staying."

Oh.

Yola squeezed her hand, then let her go, and that's when Aria walked to the window.

She thought she'd seen lights flash in the lot, but maybe that had been lightning. Although she hadn't heard any thunder. Just the roar of the wind, gusting against the hospital. She picked up a nearby television remote and tried to turn on the flat screen. It flickered on, but just static filled the screen. Perfect.

"I'm going to find some food. With any luck, they'll have Cheetos in the vending machine," Aria said. "You let me know if she has any trouble breathing, chest tightness, or even a pounding heartbeat, okay?"

"Thanks, Doc," Yola said.

Aria headed toward the staff room. The tiny room at the end of the hall contained a couple round tables, a fridge, a microwave, and a small sink. A window overlooked the side parking lot, illuminated by the tall streetlights. And yes, the obligatory staff vending machine with Cheetos bags stacked in the coils.

Of course, she hadn't brought any money.

She opened the fridge and found a few containers of lunches, all of unknown date and origin. She decided on the frost-bitten box of macaroni and cheese.

The microwave was still working. Her stomach roared to life as the machine hummed, the plastic turning on the glass table.

God shows up in the storms. Maybe. She certainly hadn't expected Jake's face to appear at the top of the mountain, hadn't expected him to be pulling her up from the depths of a crevasse.

Maybe God had sent him, Ham, and Orion to save them.

But God couldn't just keep rescuing people, showing up over and over. At some point, people simply got in over their heads.

And needed to figure their own way out.

Better to not get in trouble in the first place. Plan ahead for the storms.

Besides, Jake wasn't going to show up here, now. She was on her own.

The microwave beeped and she opened it, pulling the container out onto the counter, then peeling back the rest of the plastic to vent it.

Yay for comfort food. She just might live. And if Mimi was

right, and this storm was just the outer bands of the hurricane, the rain would pass and maybe the chopper would be back for them in the morning.

She found a plastic fork and brought the meal to the round wooden table, slid onto the vinyl chair, and was about to dig in—

A crash trembled the entire building. Shattering glass, then a roar as wind whooshed into the hallway outside the break room.

She ran to the doorway.

One of the streetlights had crashed through the second-story window of the patient room across the hall, its massive broken light spraying fireworks into the room. Horizontal rain chased it inside, past the jagged teeth of the broken glass of a massive two-paned picture window. Wind tore at the blinds, banging them against the wall.

Sparks spat from the broken lamp, onto the bedclothes, the floor, the debris left on the table.

The bedside table ignited.

"Oh!"

And then, just like that, the room flamed. Fire dripped onto the bedsheets, the pads.

The mattress flashed over.

Aria screamed.

She didn't know why—it just bubbled out of her, maybe its own combustion from the stress of the past day, but she let out a shrill that shook through her.

Found her bones.

Galvanized her.

"What?" Yola appeared in the hallway.

"Go back to the room. Shut the door!" Aria raced down the hall for the fire extinguisher. She found it inside a cabinet halfway down the hall.

It wasn't locked. Grabbing the red canister, she raced back to the room, pulling out the pin as she went.

The bed was nearly an inferno, the heat kicking her back. She turned her face away and held up the hose, shooting blindly into the room. The fog swelled, the fire battling against it.

She squinted her eyes, but they watered against the cloud.

"You gotta sweep it," said a voice over her shoulder. A man. He stepped up next to her and took the hose, directing it into the room.

Somehow, she handed over the canister too and then stood back as the man disappeared into the fog, battling the fire.

Then, to her horror, the door closed behind him.

"Hey!" She pressed on it, but it didn't move, as if he might be standing against it. "Hey! Don't get trapped!"

Smoke had filled the corridor, and she bent over, coughing. Only then did she see a woman standing in the hallway, next to the nurses' station. Rain soaked and wide-eyed, she held her pregnant belly.

She looked vaguely familiar too.

Aria slapped on the door. "Let me in! Hey! Are you okay?"

The door jerked open and a man stood there, breathing hard. Soggy and blackened from head to toe. Her gaze slid past him to the room.

The fire was out, the bed steaming, charred, the plastic blinds twisted, the light fixture dead. The rain had lessened, the gale wind dying just a little. As if somehow the fury had surrendered.

She could see why. Because the man just stood there like some kind of mythical hero, a knight fighting fire-breathing dragons and the hounds of the underworld. His chest rose and fell, his blue eyes fierce in hers, pinning her to the spot.

Recognition jolted her like a slap. He was tall, over six feet, with sculpted shoulders, and wearing a soggy T-shirt that outlined every muscle in his lean torso. He wore cargo shorts and a hat backwards on his head, a spray of dirty whiskers, and the look of so much concern it simply took out her voice.

Just like he had when he'd pulled her out of death's mouth on Denali.

"Jake?"

"Aria."

He stepped forward and closed the door behind him, then dropped the fire extinguisher to grip her upper arms. "Are you okay?"

She just stared at him, wanting very much to reach out—okay, she gave in to that urge—and put her hand on his chest. His soggy, firm chest, with the heart banging against his ribs. "What are you . . . what are you *doing* here?"

He blinked at her. "What am I doing here? I was worried about you. You said you were sick and—" He looked her over. "You said you felt like you were going to die."

What?

"Wait—first, that was hyperbole! I was seasick, for Pete's sake. But—how did you . . . wait . . ." She pushed away from him. "Did you call Jenny to check up on me?"

"What? No! You texted me. Said you missed me. That you wanted TLC. That . . ."

Oh my . . . "Jake, I . . . no, I didn't text you. I . . ." She pressed her hand to her head. "I texted Jenny."

His mouth turned into a grim line. "No, you didn't. You texted me. Said you wished I were here—"

What in the world? Jake was a gung-ho, passionate man, but . . . really? "So you jumped on a plane and came down here?"

Oh joy, they had an audience. Down at the end of the hall both Yola and the pregnant girl—wait . . . She did know her . . .

What was Jake doing with the painter from the beach?

But clearly, that wasn't top in his mind. "I didn't just . . . okay, yes, I might have done that, but like I said, I was worried about you." He blew out a breath. "I kept thinking about your heart, and then, how being at altitude probably hadn't been good for it, and then I started worrying that maybe you were going into rejection and—"

"You thought my body was *rejecting* Kia's heart?" She knew her voice sounded a little crazy, but— "Jake. Seriously. What is going on?"

"Nothing. Just . . ." He held up his hands, as if to stop their argument. "Listen. We need to get out of here. The storm is going to get worse, and we don't want to get trapped down here."

"Are you kidding me? The only way out is the highway. We'd be stuck on the bridge for hours."

"We can't stay here."

"Why not?"

"Because you're sick."

She recoiled. "Do I look sick to you, Hawkeye?" She stood back, held open her arms. "Soggy maybe, but trust me, I'm just fine."

What? No, she did *not* say that! But his stupid nickname just bubbled out, and now it only served to ignite something inside her she didn't want to acknowledge.

Jake was back. Right here, showing up in the storm.

Like some sort of ethereal, almost creepy ESP conjuring.

Oh boy . . .

He grinned then, something that tweaked his blue eyes and sent a spark to them. "Whatever you say, Houlihan."

No. Oh, she should have guessed that was coming. Heaven help her, she'd have to keep her wits about her if she didn't want to end up exactly as Jake had suggested.

With her heart in dangerous, dangerous trouble.

CHAPTER 6

ARIA JUST WALKED AWAY.

Again.

Jake stood there for a moment, watching as Aria stalked down the hall, practically in a run.

What—?

Okay, so he could admit to his impulsiveness, but . . . hello, she'd sent him that text . . .

Or . . . *"I texted Jenny."*

Shoot, he'd done that before—sent the wrong person a text. And that person hadn't jumped on a plane . . .

Clearly she wasn't sick, or incapable, and he'd simply followed his impulses, again. Or rather, his desires.

He'd wanted to see her. And had talked himself way too easily into the idea that she was desperate to see him too.

Apparently, she *meant* just friends.

Nice, Jake.

Still. It wasn't like he hadn't just found her trying to extinguish a *fire*, for Pete's sake. Badly, he might add.

So, "Aria, what's the matter?"

He bit back a cough, despite his efforts to hold his breath, keep from inhaling smoke.

She'd met Angel and now had her arm around her, leading her into a nearby room. He sprinted down the hallway, came alongside them. Held open the door, then picked up Angel and placed her on the bed.

Aria just looked at him, then left the room. He might even call it sprinting.

Angel stared at him. "Was that who you were looking for?"

"Yeah," he said and made a face.

She raised an eyebrow. "Sorta sounds like she wasn't expecting you."

"I'm getting that vibe."

Outside the rain was dying, the howl of the wind haunting as it moaned through the darkness.

Aria came back in, pushing a supply cart. "I can't find a suture kit. Can you go down to the ER and see what you can scrape up?"

Oh, was she talking to him?

Apparently, because she looked over at him.

"Sure, Doc," he said.

"Thanks." She turned her back to him.

Oh, this was fun.

She might be a tad overly angry here. Jenny's words swept back to him as he headed toward the stairwell. *"Just remember, the Aria you met in Alaska might not be the Aria in real life."*

You think?

The water was up to the second step from the bottom and he stepped down into the chill. It bit at his bones as he pulled out his phone and flicked on the light.

He wrestled open the door, and water poured in and filled the stairwell nearly to his knees. The lower floor was silent, the water gleaming as his light licked over the reception desk, the reception area, the double doors of the ER bay. He waded through the expanse to the ER doors and pushed them open.

His phone light illuminated the empty bays, the gurneys, the movable cabinets filled with supplies. Sloshing over to the nearest one, he opened it, fishing through the supplies.

"What are you doing here?"

And now he couldn't dislodge her tone of voice, the incredulous way Aria had looked at him.

What *was* he doing here?

Yep, he was an idiot. Because she hadn't meant to text him, which meant . . .

She was over him.

Dumped, just like Ellie said, and here he was, stuck in a hurricane, cold, hungry, wet, and trying to find—what did she want again? A suture kit?

He knew what a suture kit looked like. Alcohol wipes, tweezers, forceps, needle and thread. He found a plastic pack in one of the drawers. She'd probably need some lidocaine too. That, he'd probably find in the pharmacy.

He waded down the hall.

Probably she was right—they wouldn't be able to get out onto the bridge. And if Hurricane Lucy really was headed their way, being inside a building like the hospital, with its cement outer walls, seemed like the best option.

The pharmacy door was wedged open with a chair, and he climbed over it and searched the shelves, three huge metal racks filled with all manner of meds and supplies.

Flashing his light over a locked cabinet, he found a shelf of pain meds—Oxycontin and other drugs that could too easily get lost on the street. He finally located a box of lidocaine on another shelf and grabbed a couple along with a bag of needles in plastic.

Holding up the supplies, he climbed back over the chair and out into the mess of water. It probably wouldn't be long until the electricity went out, depending on where the breakers were, but hopefully the engineers put generators on the roof.

He climbed back up the stairs and came out by the scorched room. Down the hall, he found Aria holding a gauze pad to Angel's foot.

"I found some supplies." He dumped the stash onto the other bed.

She wore purple gloves, had tied her hair back, and looked so in her element, he just stared at her for a moment. "Thanks, Jake." She removed the gauze, examining the wound.

What was he thinking, really? The Aria he'd met had been on vacation.

This was the real Aria.

A woman like Dr. Aria Sinclair wasn't exactly going to get serious with a guy like Jake. She should be with a lawyer. Or a CPA. Or . . .

Aw, he should have expected this.

He would just hunker down with her until the storm passed, make sure she got home safely, and walk away.

"How did this happen?" Aria said to Angel.

The woman leaned back against a pillow, her hand over her belly. "I . . . I was walking on the boardwalk and I stepped on some glass."

Aria opened the suture kit and began to lay out the items on a tray. She smiled at Angel, her voice calm, as if they might be ordering lunch. "In the middle of the storm? Why didn't you take cover?"

"I . . ." She glanced at Jake, then away. "I had nowhere to go."

Aria was cleaning the area with benzine, the dark liquid making Angel wince.

"Where are you from? Do you live in Key West?" Jake said, stepping up to her, wanting to take her mind off the procedure. He'd lacerated his foot once. Not a picnic.

"No. I'm from Wisconsin, actually. I met Baker during spring break a year ago and we . . . I thought we fell in love. We've been staying at the Seashell Youth Hostel for the past six months." She ran her hand over her belly.

Jake said nothing but looked over at Aria. She had filled the needle with lidocaine.

"I'm just going to numb this area. Little prick . . ."

Jake offered his hand and Angel took it, squeezed. One eye closed as Aria administered the shot.

"Okay, you did great. We'll wait a moment here, and then get you sutured up." She looked at Jake and gestured with her head toward the hall. Then, she pulled off her gloves, tossed them in a garbage can nearby, and left the room.

He followed her out. She shut the door. Turned to him. "How in trouble are we?"

For a moment, he had nothing, caught in those brown eyes, the way she looked at him as if she actually needed him.

As if they might be in this together, just like before.

"I don't know," he said. "Last I heard, the storm was heading north, up the coast. This could just be the edges of it. It might pass right by us."

She nodded. "Okay." Then, she blew out a breath.

"Aria—?"

"I'm not an obstetrician, but her blood pressure is pretty low, and her lips are blue. I'm worried the baby isn't getting enough oxygen. I'd like to find a fetal monitor, if we could. But really, I'd like to know how long we might be here."

He glanced down the hall, toward the giant picture window near the other area. "The rain seems to be diminishing—"

"According to Mimi, hurricanes come in rain bands."

He raised an eyebrow.

"There's an older woman in the next room. She has COPD. That's why I'm here. She needed medical help."

"And that's why you didn't evacuate."

She lifted a shoulder. "I couldn't leave her here. Even if she insisted on staying."

"I've met those types. The stubborn ones."

"Really, Jake? Should we not talk about the ones who jump to conclusions? What should we call this . . ." She gestured to him—as in, his presence. "Panic?"

"Friendship," he said.

She cocked her head at him. Blew out a breath. "Right. Okay."

"Aria."

She looked over at him. For the first time he noticed the wells under her eyes. And he couldn't stop himself. "I'm . . . I don't know why I'm here. I guess I thought you needed me. Call it a reflex, I don't know. But that's what friends do. Maybe it's just my history on the teams, but when a teammate needs help, we show up. So, I'm here, and I'll help you. We'll get through this storm, and everything is going to be fine, okay?"

She stared at him, and he had nothing when her eyes filled.

What?

She blinked hard, forced a smile. "Yeah. Sorry, Jake. I am glad you're here."

He wanted to give her something sarcastic like, *Don't leap into my arms or anything*, but actually, she looked like she needed a hug, so instead, "That's what I do."

She gave a tiny laugh then, and somehow, just like that, it was all better. Her eyes cleared, and she nodded. "I know. You can't help but be a hero."

And there she was. The woman he'd left in Alaska. Sweet, brave, funny.

Wow, he'd missed her.

She turned toward the room, her hand on the door. "As long as you're predicting the weather, do you think you can predict us some food? I'm starved, and my guess is that Angel hasn't eaten much. There's a vending machine in the staff lounge."

"As you wish."

She rolled her eyes, but he got the slightest grin and disappeared into the room.

Food. He headed down the hall and found the vending machine in the employee lounge.

No money. And the machine didn't accept credit cards. But it hosted a few candy bars, bags of Doritos, Cheetos, unpopped popcorn, juice boxes, and protein bars.

Maybe he could shake some of the items loose. He unplugged the machine, then braced his arms on either side and threw his weight into the box.

He barely budged it.

Where was his demo guy when he needed him?

"My money is on the machine."

He turned. A young woman stood at the door. Golden brown skin, brown eyes, her hair in a turban. She wore a pair of green scrubs.

"Do you work here?"

She laughed and came into the room. "No. I'm Mimi's granddaughter. I came in with Aria. Who are you?"

"I'm Jake." He held out his hand and shook hers.

"What are you doing here?"

He turned back to the machine, surveying it. "Good question. I'm not really sure. I thought . . . well, it's a long story . . . Aria sent me this text, only it wasn't for me, apparently, so . . ."

"So you weren't with the medical conference?"

He shook his head. "I'm just a friend from Minnesota."

"You came from Minnesota down to a hurricane? C'mon. She's not just a friend. You got a thing for Miss Aria." She folded her arms and leaned against the door frame.

Oh. So clearly there was nothing getting past her. "What's your name?"

"Yolanda."

"Well, Yolanda, it's complicated. We . . . I . . ."

"Yeah, it sounds complicated. I'll simplify it for you." She leaned up. "When a man loves a woman . . ."

"It's not like that."

"Huh. So that's why you're busting up property, because she wants some Cheetos." She walked over to the machine. "It's got a lock on it. You could probably just pick the lock and open it."

Pick the lock.

He pushed past her, toward the door.

"Where'ya going?"

"Outside."

She followed him into the hallway. "There's a storm outside."

"So I'll get a little wet." He disappeared down the hallway, back down the stairwell.

Because if Aria wanted Cheetos, she was getting Cheetos.

■ ■ ■

"He was searching the entire island for you."

Aria looked up from her work, the intricate sutures on Angel's heel.

"What?"

"Jake. He was searching the entire island for you. He would have kept searching if he hadn't seen me. He was really worried."

Aria looked back down at her work. A deep laceration, nearly to the bone of her heel. Angel would need antibiotics, which meant another trip downstairs. "He's prone to that. He works for a search and rescue team, so, it's in his bones."

"If any guy came looking for me, I think I'd be glad to see him."

Aria frowned, looked up.

Angel was looking at her. Her blonde hair hung in wet, thick dreads, her hazel-green eyes meeting Aria's. "He's really cute too."

Aria let out a breath, a sort of laugh. "Yeah, he is. And he knows it. Listen, Angel, Jake is a great guy, but he's . . . well, he's not the settling-down type. Not the I-want-a-family, get-married, buy-a-home, get-a-dog, and volunteer-to-be-a-baseball-coach type. He's the guy who shows up to save the day . . . and then walks away to the next damsel in distress."

She looked back at her work. "I just happened to have been the most recent damsel."

"Really? He rescued you?"

She finished off her stitch. Reached for the scissors. "I was stuck on a mountain with a couple of friends, and he and a couple of *his* friends showed up to help us. So, yes." She snipped off the thread. "But that's all we were—friends."

"Mmmhmm. Then why did you text him?"

She looked up again. "I didn't text him."

"Didn't you?"

"No, I . . ." She got up and reached for the supply cart. "No. I thought I was texting my friend Jenny."

"Or, you subconsciously wanted him to find you so you texted him . . ."

"I didn't text him."

Angel raised an eyebrow.

"I didn't. I don't want him here."

"Not at all?"

She sighed. "I guess . . . I mean . . ."

Angel grinned. "I thought so. Because you know, you're awfully angry at him for no reason."

"I'm not mad at him, I'm just . . . well . . . he totally overreacted and—"

"It was sweet, wasn't it? Him coming down here?"

She unwrapped a bandage and pressed it over her wound. Stood up. "It was sweet." She snapped off her gloves. "But I don't have room for sweet and charming and . . . well, anything but *just friends* in my life." She tossed the gloves into a nearby garbage can. Looked at Angel. "You don't know it, but your life is about to get very busy. And sometimes, when you have something super important to you, other things just . . . well, they have to be sacrificed."

"Like love?" Angel's hands curled over her stomach.

"Well, maybe some kinds of love. I love my job. My patients, my life. I just don't . . . I . . . Jake is a great guy. But he is very different from me. The real me, not the me he met on the mountain. He is funny and charming and everybody loves him. But he's also impulsive. And frankly a little frightening sometimes."

Angel's eyes had widened.

Aria held up her hand. "No, I don't mean scary, as in he would hurt someone, although he was a navy SEAL, so maybe he would, but I never felt anything but safe with him."

"He was a navy SEAL?"

"Yeah. So, he's got a bigger protection gene than the average man."

"And that's why you're mad at him?"

Aria took some gauze and began to wrap it around Angel's heel, the question sinking inside.

"No. That's not why I'm mad at him." She looked at the window, seeing herself dimly lit in the reflection. It looked tired and bedraggled, and she felt it. She wasn't up to fighting the feelings Jake stirred in her.

Wasn't up to fighting the longing to give in to his charm.

"He broke a deal we made."

"What deal?"

And she didn't know why she was trying to justify herself to this girl. Or maybe, it was just to herself.

"The unspoken deal we made in Alaska that what happens in Alaska stays in Alaska. That I could be one person there, the person that could laugh at his jokes, and dance with him, and kiss him—"

"You kissed him?"

Aria smiled, glanced up at Angel. "Yeah."

"Oh." Angel grinned. "I'll bet he's a good kisser."

Aria looked away, warmth spreading through her. "Good enough. But see, that's the thing. I don't go around kissing guys. In fact, I can count the number of times I've been kissed on one hand, and I let myself sort of . . . I don't know. Kiss Jake and tell myself that it didn't matter. That it was all in fun."

"But it wasn't in fun. You like him."

Aria reached for the tape to secure the wrapping. "No. I mean, yes. One part of me liked him, but the other part . . . no, I can't like Jake. And *he* was supposed to forget about me. He wasn't supposed to care. And he certainly wasn't supposed to follow me to Key West. He broke our deal."

"Does he know that?"

The voice came from behind them, and she turned to see Yola entering the room. "So that's what that was about."

"What was about?"

"Complicated." Yola walked into the room. "Jake said things between you two are complicated. But they don't sound complicated. Jake likes you, you like him—"

"I don't—"

Yola gave her a look.

"Fine. But like I was telling Angel, it won't work between us."

"You'd better tell him that, because he's breaking the law for you down the hall."

"Huh?"

"He was wrestling the vending machine. I told him that maybe he just needed to pick the lock instead of beating it up, and he took off like a man on a mission."

"Where did he go?"

"He said he was going to get wet." Yola walked over to the window. "Yep, he's down in the lot. The light's on in a car."

Aria walked to the window. The parking lights illuminated the lot, rippling with running water, in some places past the windows of the parked cars. No, there was no getting off this island—by car, at least.

She spied Jake in the back seat of an SUV. He climbed out and shut the door.

But instead of heading toward the hospital, he stopped, slung his backpack over his shoulder, and headed out into the lot.

He stopped by a car and leaned over, looking in. Then he reached into the door through an open window and unlocked it.

"What's he doing?" Yola said.

He opened the door. Pulled out something and tucked it into his jacket.

"Maybe he found some food or something," Aria said and turned away as Jake ran for the building.

She walked over to Angel. "I'm going to try and find an ultrasound machine, but until then, let me get your blood pressure again." She pulled the cuff from the wall and wrapped it around her arm.

"I think you should give him another chance." Angel pressed her hand onto her abdomen. As if warmed by the heat, her stomach moved, the body inside pressing back.

Aria watched, a warmth coursing through her. Life. Hope.

"Some things are worth the risk," Angel said. "Right? Even if he's not the settle-down-and-have-a-family, get-a-dog type. He still showed up for you."

Yes, he had.

And if she were honest— "I just don't want him getting hurt because of me."

Angel frowned but didn't answer because of the footsteps squeaking down the hallway. They passed the room without entering.

Aria couldn't help the slightest twinge of disappointment.

"He looks pretty sturdy," Yola said, walking to the door. "Not the type to get easily hurt."

"Yeah, well, you don't know Jake like I do."

Yola turned. "I think that's the point. If Jake is the guy you say he is, maybe that's exactly why he isn't letting you go. Why he chased you to Florida."

"I don't think—"

Yola stepped back as the door opened.

Jake stood in the frame. Soaking wet. Grinning. Wearing his backpack and holding up a bag of Cheetos as if he'd brought home dinner from the wilds.

Yola folded her arms and looked at Aria, a told-you-so in her expression.

"Here you go, Doc," he said and tossed her the bag.

She caught it. "I suppose you want a tip."

"Nope."

"How'd you get into the vending machine?" Yola asked.

"I picked the lock." He turned to Angel. "And I got something for you too." He walked over, and from his coat drew out a—

"Oh my, it's a puppy!" Angel said.

Soaking wet and shivering, the little black dog appeared to be a poodle, with curly hair but droopy ears and big brown eyes. He looked about three months old, about the size of a football.

"Where did you find him?"

Jake set his pack down, leaned it against the wall. "He was in this car. I don't know if he climbed in, or maybe the owner left him there, but he was barking, scared to death."

"He's trembling," Angel whispered and pulled him to herself.

"I thought you might like some practice before the little one shows up," Jake said.

"He's so sweet," Angel said.

Aria stared at Jake. Water dripped down his face, into his beard, his baseball hat saturated, his clothes equally wet. He shivered a little, but he was watching Angel, grinning.

Yes, he was.

Oh, boy. "I'm going to find you a blanket," she said and pushed past the infuriating man and out into the hallway.

He turned and followed her down the hallway, of course. "Aria, what's the matter?"

She didn't look back.

"Hot Lips. Turn around and talk to me."

Oh, for— "Don't call me that." But she turned, her hands on her hips.

He skidded to a halt. "Then tell me what I did."

"What you did? What you . . ." She shook her head. "Stop being so . . . charming. You sweep in here like you're Superman, carrying a pregnant woman. Then you put out a fire, find a puppy—for crying out loud, and bring me Cheetos. I mean, what's next, donating a kidney?"

He just stared at her.

"You can't do this, Jake. You can't follow me around the world and make me . . . just, you can't."

"Make you what?" His voice had dropped, his blue eyes holding hers.

Her mind went blank. Shoot, those eyes had magical powers. "Don't."

"What?"

"Look at me!"

He moved his eyes off her, up, over, down, over—

"Stop." But she bit back a smile. "You're like a two-year-old."

He grinned. "A very tall two-year-old."

She sighed. "Jake, don't you get it? What we had in Alaska was . . . it was a time-out from life. It was . . . fun. And yeah, I . . . I liked you."

His smile fell. "I liked you too." He made to reach out for her then, but she stepped back.

"But that's the point. That wasn't . . . me. The real me doesn't, well, she doesn't do impulsive, or unexpected, or even really—"

"Have fun?"

She lifted a shoulder. "I tried to have fun and ended up stuck in a tropical storm. And, before that, on a mountain."

"That was a little fun."

"And see, that's why we don't belong together. Because no, it wasn't fun. I mean . . . yes. I liked talking to you—"

"That's not all we did—"

"Don't. I mean, I *know*." And now she couldn't look at him, her face heating. "But see, again. To you, that was all fun. To me . . . I . . . I don't behave that way. I don't just kiss people and walk away."

"Except that's exactly what you did." He drew in a breath. "Was it because . . . well, because of what happened, or didn't happen, in the hotel room? Because I made you feel, I don't know . . . unsafe? Because if that's what it was, then I'm not only sorry, but yeah, I'll walk away from you, Aria. I never want you to feel unsafe with me."

"No, Jake. No." She put her hand on his arm then. Squeezed. "I felt safe. Too safe, probably. And that's why I suggested . . . well, again, I wasn't myself. I don't know what I was thinking, but I do know that I'm back in my real world now, and in this world, I work 24/7. I barely have a social life, my patients are my world, and I like it that way. I know I'm not being fair to you, but . . . but you don't really want a woman like me anyway."

He frowned at her.

"No, Jake, really. I'm all preplanning, schedules, to-do lists, and by the book. You're . . . well, you're the guy who climbs mountains for fun, jumps from a plane on a whim, and breaks into cars to rescue puppies."

"You would have broken into a car to save a puppy," he said.

She shook her head.

"What if I'm good for you?"

She looked up at him, softened her voice. "No, Jake. You're not good for me. You get me in over my head."

He drew in a breath, and his jaw tightened. But he nodded, something hooded coming over his face. "Yeah. Okay. I'm sorry. I'm really, really sorry, Aria. For everything. For Alaska. And for following you down to Florida."

She didn't know why, but her chest tightened and her throat burned.

"We'll get through this storm, and back home, and I promise, you'll never see me again."

Then he turned and walked down the hall.

CHAPTER 7

THE SOONER JAKE GOT OUT OF HERE, the better. Because watching Aria stare at the dregs of her Cheetos, avoiding his gaze, only burned a hole through him.

"No, Jake. You're not good for me. You get me in over my head."

His sternum might have actual bruising from the way her words hit him.

He got her in over her head. He could attach a slew of other words to that. He scared her. He was dangerous. He was, um, bad for her.

In fact, boil it down and Jake was nothing but trouble.

Nice.

Yes, this little excursion was quickly turning into a trip through H-E-double-hockey-sticks. Despite his attempts to lighten the mood.

"So, what did the football coach say to the vending machine?" Jake sat on the windowsill, rooting around in his Doritos bag, looking for the last full chip.

He looked up to the silence in the room. Mimi lay on the bed, breathing oxygen through a mask, hooked up to a ventilator. But she'd demanded that "whatever party y'all are having, you'd better have in my room," so he'd wheeled Angel's bed in next to the older woman's.

He liked Mimi. She reminded him of his grandmother—feisty, to-the-point, determined. Probably an older version of Aria, at least on the inside. On the outside, Aria was probably going to die in a pair of scrub pants.

"I want my quarter back," he said to his waiting audience.

"I like it!" Angel was sitting up, petting the puppy—whom she'd named Toby. The little guy had finally stopped shivering, warmed in the nest of blankets Aria had found.

Angel had dried off too, although her dreads were still soggy. She looked desperately young. He'd like to get his hands on Baker, the guy who'd knocked her up and abandoned her.

"You should do stand-up," Yola said. She sat on a chair next to Mimi's bed. "There's this great comedy club in my neighborhood in Queens. They have open mic every Wednesday."

"You know, I know a lot of jokes about unemployed people but none of them work." Jake found a chip, crunched it, waiting.

A pause, then Mimi started to laugh.

Jake winked. "You know why the shrimp wouldn't share his treasure, right?" He lifted a shoulder. "Because he was a little shellfish."

Mimi bent over, her hand to her stomach, laughing. It turned into a cough.

"Okay, that's enough, Jake." Aria got up from where she was sitting on the floor. She washed the Cheetos grime off her hands in the sink and went over to Mimi. "We don't want to have to give her another nebulizer treatment."

"Sorry," Jake said, but the rest of the women were grinning at him. And as long as he kept everyone smiling, everyone laughing, he didn't have to think about—*no, it wasn't fun.*

Wow, he'd judged that wrong.

Because he remembered being trapped with Aria as being very, very fun. At least when he didn't think about the parts where someone could have died.

"Where did you learn all those jokes?" Yola asked.

"BUD/S. We had a guy—we called him Seinfeld. He was hilarious and we'd be dying, just trying to breathe and he'd come up with a one-liner that would take us out. He tapped out during hell week, but his jokes stayed."

"How long were you a SEAL?" Yola asked.

"Twelve years. I got out about a year ago."

He didn't look at Aria. Because during one of the not-fun parts of their two days trapped together, he'd told her exactly why. One of a handful of people who knew the facts, even if he hadn't told her *everything*.

But talk about letting someone in too far . . .

"Thank you for your service," said Mimi.

He looked over at her, smiled. "Thanks, ma'am."

"My Rollo wanted to go in, but I was too afraid he'd be shipped over to 'Nam, and we already had Yolanda's mama, so he agreed to stay out. And they hadn't started the draft yet, when he came of age, so . . . but he always felt like he shoulda served."

"It's not for everyone," he said. "But it was a life I . . . well, it fit me. I liked being on the teams." He got up then and went over to the remote near the bed. "Let's see if we can get some reception, Mimi. Get us some Weather Channel."

He turned it on but found static.

"We already tried that," Aria said. "Probably the cable station is down."

"Hopefully we're past the worst of it," Mimi said. "The storm sounds like it's dying."

The rain had gusted in bursts of fury over the past hour. Outside, one of the lights had gone out, broken. Jake reached for his cell phone, checking again for reception. Nothing.

He walked toward the window—one bar appeared, and with it, a message. He opened it before the reception died.

Jake. Hope you found your girl and are out of danger. Cat 5 hurricane headed for the Keys. Call us when you get to Miami. Dad

He stilled, then closed his phone and slipped it into his back pocket.

"You know," he said, taking a breath, "I was thinking that if the storm gets worse, we probably don't want to be near these windows." He turned, a smile on his face. "I'm going to try and find a better room for us."

He petted Toby on the way out of the room.

Aria followed him. "Jake?"

He looked over his shoulder. "'Sup?"

"What was in the text?"

He opened an inner door—supply room. Not big enough to accommodate all of them. "Nothing. My dad, checking in."

She'd caught up to him. "You're acting weird."

He opened another door, a tiny bathroom. It could work, maybe. "Did you see any other rooms here that don't have any windows?"

"There's a chapel on the other side, sort of by the nurses' station."

He turned to her. Debated. But she'd said she liked to plan, didn't want anything unexpected, so, "Lucy has been upgraded to a Cat 5, and with the intermittent rain bands, my guess is that it's going to hit soon. Which means there will be a storm surge and pretty violent winds. We need to stay high and get someplace without glass."

She was just staring at him. "A . . . Cat 5. No. That isn't . . . that can't . . ." She reached out and braced her hand on the wall. "No, this can't be—"

"Aria?"

"This isn't happening, this . . ." She pressed her hand to her head, turned, and wandered down the hall.

He caught up to her, grabbed her shoulders. "You okay?"

Her expression looked a little wild, her eyes big. "I'm supposed to be on vacation! Drinking margaritas and sunbathing, and . . . eating raw oysters."

"Raw oysters. Now I know how you got sick."

"Jake!" She focused on him now. "How does this happen to me? I go on vacation and suddenly . . . I'm in trouble? It's like—"

"Maybe you like it. Trouble."

She narrowed her eyes. "Really? You think I *like* this?"

"I'm just saying—you did choose to stay here. Mimi told me that you could have flown out on the last chopper."

"Yeah, you're right. I *love* trouble. It's my favorite thing. In fact, after I get everyone buttoned up, maybe I'll go out and do a little surfing in the thirty-foot storm surge. Or maybe I'll swim with sharks—by the way, I did see one on my oh-so-fun snorkeling adventure."

"You going to blame me for that too?"

She frowned. "What—?"

"Nothing. Just, I'm not responsible for all the trouble you get in."

She blinked at him. "No, no, you're not."

He stood there, and there was clearly something wrong with him, because he still wanted to kiss her, the way she stared up at him, a little spark in her eyes. She'd impressed him on the mountain with her courage. Now, he didn't know why he liked her . . .

Except, he just couldn't take his eyes off that little pulse in her neck. And the way she looked so small and delicious in her scrubs and—

He wouldn't even call them friends anymore after what she said to him. But he couldn't get his heart to stop wishing she'd stop glaring at him and let him kiss her.

She drew in a breath and stepped back from him. "I guess I owe you an apology. It didn't even occur to me that maybe I led you on in Alaska."

He frowned. Oh, wait— "Aria, that's not what I was—"

"No, no, you're right. I was . . . well, I was just like every other woman you met—"

"What? No, are you kidding me? You're nothing like the women I—" And oh, that's not what he wanted to say at all. "Listen, Aria, I just meant that you didn't know you were going to fall off a mountain. Or get caught in a hurricane. Those things happen—they're nobody's fault."

"Yeah, well, I'm tired of them happening to me. And people I love getting hurt because they want to, I don't know, save me."

And click, suddenly her anger made sense. She thought he was going to get hurt. Because her sister had died, and because of it, Aria had lived. At her core, that had to ache. He lowered his voice. "Aria, I'm not going to get hurt because I came down to Florida after you."

"Really? Because you're stuck here, in a Cat 5 hurricane. Because of me."

"I came down here because I wanted to—"

"It's a Cat 5?" Yola stood in the hallway. "Oh, I knew it. I just knew it—"

Aria turned. "It's okay, Yola, we got this. We'll put everyone in the chapel. Right? Okay?" She turned back to Jake. "We need to get these people to safety." She took a breath. Smiled. And suddenly, all the panic had flushed from her expression. "Can you help me?"

Jake just stared at her. Aria had morphed right in front of his eyes, turned into a surgeon, the boss.

Huh. *"That wasn't . . . me. The real me doesn't, well, she doesn't do impulsive, or unexpected . . ."*

Then who had he met on the mountain? The girl who laughed with him and called him Hawkeye?

The woman who had kissed him as if she'd been starving.

That woman laughed and teased and . . . *lived*.

"Yes. Of course," Jake said, morphing into the operator he'd been. Because two could play at this game.

"Good. Angel's blood pressure is back to normal, and I got a heartbeat from the baby, so she just needs to be comfortable. Mimi, however, needs her ventilator—"

"I'm on it, Doc."

She nodded and headed down the hall.

He followed her into the patient room.

She was already piling supplies—the nebulizer, some pharmaceuticals, the leftover foodstuffs—onto Mimi's bed. Yola was maneuvering Angel's bed out of the room, but Angel had hopped off.

"I can walk." She started to limp but made a sound so Jake picked her up.

"You're such a hero, Jake," Angel said, the puppy in her arms.

He didn't feel like a hero. So far, he'd become a stalker, a womanizer, a troublemaker, and maybe even a jerk.

What a fun trip.

And now, he'd somehow made Aria feel like all of it was her fault.

He carried Angel down to the chapel, a tiny room with six chairs, a small altar at the front, and a cross hanging at the end of the room. He set her down on a chair. When he scooted out, Yola followed him. "What can I do?"

"Let's get some mattresses and build us a bunker."

They pulled off mattresses from nearby beds, dragging them into the room. Yola made a bed for Angel, one for her grandmother.

Jake retrieved his backpack from the staff room, then helped Mimi, who insisted on walking, into the room. Aria wheeled the ventilator behind her.

Outside, the wind had picked up, a terrible moan filling the corridors.

"We should get some juice." He deposited his pack, then returned to the staff room and emptied the vending machine of the juice boxes, piling them into his shirt.

A crash sounded at the end of the hallway. He ran out and found Aria sprinting toward him, her eyes wide, wind blowing in behind her through a broken window at the end of the hall. Rain bulleted in with a howl.

Aria's hair had turned wild around her face. "It's here!"

And just like that, she transformed back into the woman he'd pulled from the crevasse. Unguarded, her eyes full of emotion and definitely not afraid of him as she reached out and grabbed his hand.

The wind tore through the building, shaking it, ripping papers and supplies from the nursing station.

He clutched the juice boxes in his shirt as they raced to the chapel. Then he let them fall, shut the door, and braced a mattress against it.

Aria grabbed the back of his shirt and pulled him down, his back to the wall.

Hunkered down next to him.

And then, confusing him completely, she reached out and grabbed his hand, threading her fingers through his.

Ho-*kay*.

He tightened his hand around hers. Maybe it didn't matter who she was in Alaska, or even in Minnesota.

She could be whomever she wanted to be, really. As long as she was alive.

And, frankly, with him.

The lights flickered off as the wind around them raised its voice and roared.

■ ■ ■

Aria leaned her head against the wall of the chapel. The A/C had cut off with the electricity, although generators were keeping the ventilators still running. Outside their tiny spiritual enclave Lucy tore at the building. It shuddered, and with it, the wind moaned, haunting the hallways with shrieks and wails.

She wanted to press her hands over her ears.

Glass shattered all over the building, tearing at the metal frames. Rain pounded the building, the storm surge outside rising and falling with what sounded like great gulps of destruction.

She drew her knees to herself. She'd take a blizzard any day.

And, please, with Jake. Because he sat with her. She'd let go of his hand, but he was close enough for her to touch, if she needed.

Oh, she needed.

She was painfully, keenly aware of the way she'd practically launched herself at Jake, holding on to him like he might be dragging her out of a crevasse.

Again.

After she'd taken his hand and escaped to the chapel, after Jake had secured the door, and after she caught her breath, she'd tucked Mimi and Yola in, making sure they had blankets, checked on Mimi's pulse and blood pressure. She'd done the same for Angel, then crawled back over to Jake, who'd held his cell phone flashlight on her activities.

She sat on the mattress next to him, his scent radiating off him—part seawater, part male exertion, part just Jake, a sort of force of power and safety that she could recognize anywhere.

Memories of Alaska kept sweeping into her brain, especially the way he'd held her, kept her warm inside the sleeping bag as the blizzard tried to bury them.

Yeah, any sort of misbehavior, any *over-her-head* with them had been all her doing, because even now, the man just sat there, his hands to himself.

Oh, she wanted to weave her hand back through his. Or better, lean her head against his shoulder.

And this was why she needed to stay away from Jake. And vacations. Because somehow they always combined to find her behaving exactly opposite of herself, as if she flipped a switch and became someone else.

Became . . . well, actually, her sister, Kia.

So, "I'm ready. Tell me one of your corny jokes."

"What?"

"A silly joke. I need one." She was whispering, just in case the rest of the women were sleeping.

"Okay. How do hurricanes see?"

"Tell me."

"With one eye."

She laughed. "Okay, that was clever."

"What did one raindrop say to the other?"

"I have no idea."

"Two's company. Three's a cloud."

She could almost see him in the darkness, leaning against the wall, his hands folded on his lap. How many times had she woken up in Alaska to see him watching her? Funny that when skies were clear, he was the storm. But in the middle of the storm . . .

He was the calm.

"Okay, here's a riddle. What goes up when the rain comes down?"

"I . . . I don't know."

"An umbrella."

She wished they had lights—she would have liked to see his smile. But frankly, darkness gave her a measure of safety. Allowed her to loosen the hold she had on herself.

To relax and lean a little in his direction. And maybe . . .

"Okay, Jake, this is the last time I'm going to talk about it, but . . . what happened in Alaska wasn't your fault. I know Jenny blames you, but the fact is, sometimes . . . well, sometimes I don't know who I am. I want to be Kia, who flings caution to the wind and embraces life in the moment. But the prudent side of me says think it through. And right there, any spontaneity dies."

"And in Alaska, you were Kia?"

"Yeah."

"So, Kia is your heart, and Aria is your head."

She'd never heard it put that way, but . . . "I guess so. Because literally, you know—"

"Your heart is Kia's. I know." His voice was closer now, as if he'd turned to her. "But it's not, you know. It's yours. She gave it to you. Your heart belongs to you."

She frowned, not sure what to say.

"I have something for you," he said and moved away from the wall. She heard a rustling, a zip, as if he were digging into his backpack. Outside the room, the wind howled, rattling the door.

Come back, Jake.

He finally resettled next to her. His shoulder touched hers and she felt his hand trace down her arm to find her hand.

"Here," he said and opened her hand, dropping something cool into it. "I should have given this back in Alaska, but . . . it sort of got missed."

She ran her thumb over the coil of what felt like metal, and a flat object— "My necklace."

"Yeah. Sorry. I put it in my shoe polish canister and forgot about it. I got you a new chain. It's just a cheap gold one I found in the Miami airport, so if you want a better one, I'll upgrade it."

She fumbled with the latch—

"Here." He found her hand again and reached for the necklace. "I'll put it on you."

She let him have it and turned her back to him, lifting her hair.

He maneuvered his hands over her head, his body close to hers, then latched it around her neck. The half-heart charm fell against her neck, cool and familiar.

"Now you have your heart back," he said.

She wasn't sure, suddenly, why his words hit her. Why, suddenly, she wasn't sure she wanted it back. Her hand went to the charm, tracing the jagged edge with her thumb, an old habit. "My sister gave this to me on our thirteenth birthday. I have the other half at home—I could never bring myself to wear it."

She'd turned around again but somehow ended up leaning against him.

He didn't move away.

"You mentioned a motorcycle accident. Kia sounds like she was pretty adventurous."

"Yeah. Completely opposite of me. We could have been fraternal twins for the differences, but I blame my faulty heart. She was born first, and she did everything first. Walked, talked, danced. Well, I never really danced—"

"You danced with me, in Alaska."

"If I remember correctly, I stepped on your toes."

He made a low humming noise. "I liked it."

Oh, Jake. Stop, please. Because a rush of warmth spread through her.

She'd liked it too.

"Kia was on danceline, knew all the guys, knew how to flirt—she did all the fun things—"

"Everything you couldn't do because of your heart."

"I don't know. She was brave and beautiful and adventurous. I like to read about adventures, not go on them . . ."

"I beg to differ. This from the woman who climbed Denali."

"Yeah, see, that was for Kia. Because she would have wanted to."

"Mmmhmm."

"What?"

"It just seems like a lot of commitment to adventure for someone who just wants to stay home."

She had nothing. Her hand went to her charm, ran it up the chain.

"I was really jealous of Kia." She didn't know where that came from, and pitched her voice low when she said it, but there it was, the truth.

And it occurred to her that Jake had this knack of pulling the truth out of her, whether she wanted him to or not.

"She used to come home after dance practice, or a date, or even some crazy thing she did and come into my room, and she'd tell me every detail. Even the kissing."

"Yeah, that sounds like sisters," Jake said, and she heard a smile in his voice. Then, it turned soft. "But my guess is that maybe it was hard for Kia to watch you suffer. Maybe she did all those things because she wanted you to live them too."

She hadn't really thought of that.

"In fact, if I understand sisters at all—and I have five of them, remember—they would do just about anything for each other. I'll bet Kia is in heaven right now smiling down on the fact that you've started to live the adventures you only got to dream about."

"With her heart beating inside me."

"With *your* heart beating inside you. The one she gave you."

She dropped the charm, his words settling inside her.

"You don't want to hear that, do you?"

"I don't want to think about the fact my sister had to die for me to live. And I can't help but feel I'm a poor substitute for her."

He said nothing then but slid his hand down to hers, took it, and wove his fingers through hers.

Squeezed.

Something a friend would do, maybe, but it ignited a fire through her, right down to her veins, the feel of his warm skin, the slight hairs of his arm brushing hers, tickling.

And right then, the awareness of him—solid, sturdy, bold, safe, sitting right next to her in this terrifying storm—swept over her.

Jake. Was here. In the storm.

Again.

Like God had decided to providentially send him.

"Jake?"

"Mmm?"

"Why did you . . . why did you come to Florida? Really."

Silence, and in it, thunder cracked, the rain pounding, wind whistling, high and sharp.

"I just . . . didn't want your last memory of me to be the one where I made you run away."

Huh? But yes, maybe she had run from him. From the overwhelming sense that with this man, she was someone different.

Someone she didn't quite recognize.

She slid her other hand over his. Then she leaned her head against his shoulder. Solid, a little sweaty, but in a second, he unlatched his hand from hers and curled it around her shoulders, pulling her against him.

"I'm not going to let anything happen to you, Aria," he said softly. "We're going to get through this."

Yeah. He'd said that before. Only earlier, he'd added, *"And I promise, you never have to see me again."* She held her breath, waiting.

He didn't add the words, and she didn't remind him.

"Thank you, Jake," she said quietly.

"For?"

"Everything. Alaska, but . . . I'm glad you're here."

He gave a little chuckle. "I'm glad I'm here too, Houlihan."

■ ■ ■

Ham couldn't decide between the stuffed elephant or Gaius the Roman Turtle.

He stood across the street from the Baroque cathedral in Piazza del Duomo in the Mediterranean port city of Catania, the heat of the day pouring down his back, listening to the chatter of tourists as they strolled the square.

Not the tourist attraction of Rome or Florence, Catania sat in the shadow of Mount Etna, the live volcano to the north, and was built on lava flows. Still, the city bore the marks of the modern age, with trolleys and rail trains bisecting the city, bicyclists mingling with scooters to whip in and out of traffic. The smells of the sea rose from the nearby port, but he wasn't here to see the beach.

He stepped inside the cool shadow of a kiosk that sold plush toys of gladiators, key rings of swords, picture books that detailed the epic history of Rome, and most importantly, burner cell phones.

He pointed to a phone, then to the turtle. *"Per favore."*

The dark-haired teenager handed him the items and Ham handed over the euros.

Just in case he needed a secure way to call the Prince, whose number he got from Chet's text.

The Prince, who may or may not be the man named Royal, who'd helped get Ford and his sister, along with Scarlett, out of Russia.

So much for needing Ham's help, although he had secured them passage on a boat in the Caspian Sea. But admittedly, he'd dropped the mission ball, so to speak—focusing too hard on his quest to unearth information about Signe.

A quest that had sent him down to Sigonella to meet with the doctor on base who'd called him about Agatha. When he'd picked up his daughter, he'd been too stunned to dig deeper into his wife's death. Now, he had a list of questions. However, Lt. Marilyn Hollybrook had nothing more to tell him.

The trim officer, who appeared to be in her midforties, folded her arms over her uniform and leaned back in her desk chair.

"We got a call from the Italian coast guard, who said they found her on a beach, wearing a life jacket, a little shell-shocked. She said the yacht she was on blew up, and that her mother was dead. Identified you as her father."

"Did the coast guard find any wreckage, any bodies?"

She nodded. "Two men washed up a couple days later, and they found the wreckage of a yacht farther down the coast."

"No body of a woman, midthirties?"

"You'll have to call the local authorities." She wrote down a number. "Salvatore D'amico. He's the coroner in Catania, and a friend. Tell him I sent you."

He'd given Salvatore a call, and thankfully he'd spoken enough English for Ham to explain his situation. No female bodies, but he took Ham's number.

And that's when a text from his old SEAL buddy Luke Dekker had come in.

Ham took the bag with the turtle in it, pocketed the cell phone, and headed down the piazza to the Caffe Opera, a small outdoor espresso bar that served fresh croissants, coffee, and gelato.

He took a seat on a wicker chair under an umbrella and watched the square. Pigeons waddled over the cobblestones, the fragrance of the potted peonies and ferns mixing with the aroma of fresh-baked bread. A server came out, and he ordered a cappuccino.

While he waited, he sent Jake another text. The man hadn't texted him back in three days, although Ellie had kept Ham stocked in pictures of Aggie. And while he wasn't exactly panicked—clearly she was having a great time—it did irk him that Jake wasn't answering, especially since Ham had left the man to care for his daughter.

His daughter. He still didn't know how to wrap his head around that word. Or the idea that Signe hadn't mentioned a word.

Maybe Aggie wasn't his. Maybe that's why she hadn't said anything. It wasn't unheard of for children to claim soldiers as their fathers to escape a foreign country.

And it wasn't an idea unique to Signe. Her own father had been a soldier stationed at Fort Benning, a man she'd never met.

Which made it even more strange that she'd keep his daughter from him, knowing her wounds.

Jake. How are things going with Aggie?
Check in.

Ham closed the phone just as he spotted Luke crossing the square.

Dekker still walked like a spec ops soldier, confidence in his gait. He wore sunglasses, a T-shirt under an unbuttoned collared shirt, cargo shorts, and a pair of flip-flops—his baseball hat on backward with blond hair curling out the back.

Ham grimaced. The man had American written all over him. Then again, they were less than thirty miles from the naval base, so maybe Catania was used to seeing Americans.

Maybe this was the best kind of cover for a private security operator.

Luke came up, grinning. "Hamilton." He held out his hand.

Ham took it, then pulled him close, slapping his back.

"You look good," Luke said. "A little thick around the waist, but—"

"At least I'm not impersonating a beach bum."

"I live on the Mediterranean Sea. Of course I'm a beach bum."

Ham noticed the ring. "You're married?"

"Yeah. I met her on assignment a few years ago." He pulled out a chair. "So, what are you doing on my side of the ocean?"

"I had a gig."

"You're working private security too?"

"No, I started a global SAR company. Occasionally we do extractions from undisclosed countries."

The waiter came out and Luke ordered in Italian.

"You're living here now?" Ham said.

"No. I live in a small town north of here called Santa Margherita. It's private and I don't bring my work home. It's safer that way." He nodded to the waiter who brought him his coffee, a frothy drink with a design on the top. "I make enemies in my job."

He added a sugar cube, then pushed it through the froth with a spoon. "When you texted me, I was just coming off a job in Greece, so . . ." He lifted a shoulder. "What are you doing in Sicily?" He crossed one leg over the other, leaned back.

Ham had known Luke back when they both served on Team Three. "Do you remember Signe?"

Luke gave a small laugh. "Do I remember the woman who nearly cost us our lives? Uh, yes."

Right. Because he'd dragged along Luke and Jake and North for an unsanctioned op to rescue his wife.

"I thought she was in that village."

"Me too. I don't know how she survived that bunker buster, but I couldn't believe it when I saw her—here, actually—a few years later. I mean—when HQ issued that air strike, I was pretty sure it was all over."

Ham drew in a breath. "Yeah. Me too."

Ham could still taste the acid that had stripped his throat as he watched the air strike, as the bunker burned, his screams to abort still echoing into the radio.

He didn't remember too much after that, how Luke and the others had gotten him back to their exfil, onto the plane.

Didn't remember the trip home.

Only remembered waking, for six months afterward, every night, screaming.

"I should have realized that you were crazy about her when we showed up at that refugee camp," Luke said now. "I'll never forget the look on your face when she drove up that day in that old truck, like you'd seen a ghost."

"She was surrounded by three men toting Kalashnikovs. Of course I was freaked out."

"Ham, what are you doing here?" She'd said the same thing

climbing out of the truck as she'd said to him six years earlier at Berkeley. Except, instead of holding her book bag, she was helping carry a wounded child to the hospital her NGO had set up on the border of Ingushetia and the Republic of Georgia.

He didn't want to tell her that he'd arrived to help train the very people who were climbing out of the truck with her.

"I'm with NATO," he said, and that was accurate enough.

She had changed. Lost weight and wore no makeup, her green eyes weary, her long blonde hair in a grimy braid. She wore fatigues and a loose hijab, a thousand miles from the hippie he'd known.

But still his Signe.

He'd followed her into the Quonset hut, a makeshift medical unit with twenty or so beds, a small surgical area in the back. She was speaking Russian as she made room for the boy—maybe ten years old and crying.

"They say they're done fighting, but you know the Russians," she said, glancing at Ham. "They don't give up when they think something belongs to them."

And he just . . . he couldn't breathe. He'd found her.

Then she put her hands around her waist and dismantled him. *"I knew you'd find me. But what took you so long?"*

"I felt like I had seen a ghost," he said now to Luke. "I'd spent about five years looking for her, and then, there she was. I mean, I'd heard she was in the region, but . . ." In fact, he might have arranged for his team to be assigned to this particular op, hoping . . .

But he could have never imagined what he found.

Luke ran his thumb down the handle of his cup. "She is something. Pretty, for sure. And brave. How many languages does she speak?"

"Three, fluently, besides English. French, Italian, and Russian."

"And a local dialect. I also remember her walking away with our money after playing darts."

"I taught her that. We had a dartboard in the barn growing up. She has an amazing eye."

"I do remember you two sneaking off for a number of personal debriefings." Luke winked.

Ham looked away, heat filling his chest. Yes, their Kiev trip. When Aggie was conceived.

"So, how is she?" Luke asked. "She was pretty cryptic when I last saw her. Said you were stationed at Sig, but I knew that wasn't true. A good lie, though, for anyone who hasn't been on the teams."

Ham sighed. "Listen, here's the truth. I thought she died. Until two weeks ago when she showed up here, with a kid—"

"Wait—you didn't know she was alive?"

Silence.

"Wow." Luke leaned back. Shook his head. "That's brutal. And the little girl? She had blonde hair, blue eyes."

"Her name is Aggie. She survived a yacht crash, and when they found her, she named me as her father."

Luke had leaned forward. "And Signe?"

Ham shook his head.

"Aw, that's rough, man. You lost her all over again?"

When Luke said it like that, it was a spear, right in the middle of Ham's chest. He nodded.

"Are you sure she's dead? Because she did survive last time."

Ham looked at him. "And how did she do that? When we showed up in that village, Zara told us Tsarnaev had taken her to his bunker."

Of course, by then it had been too late to call off the air strike.

The one his commander ordered after his team found a cache of Russian munitions, enough to start another invasion.

It hadn't been Ham's order, but it felt like it.

"Apparently, he didn't," Luke said. "So, was she with Tsarnaev all these years?"

That thought sent a shudder through Ham. But Chet's words swept back to him. *Acting as diplomats and humanitarian aid workers . . . and even occasionally simply going dark, becoming ghosts.*

He didn't want the word to linger, but frankly it had been lodged there for days.

Spies.

"What do you know about Pavel Tsarnaev?"

"Just rumors. Wealthy. He's half Russian, half Chechen, and heavily involved in the Russian mafia."

"The Bratva."

Luke nodded.

"Why would Tsarnaev hold her hostage for ten years?"

Luke looked at his cup. "I hate to ask this, but is the kid even yours?"

The question came in like a blow.

"When you saw her, how did Signe seem?"

"Fine. Maybe a little surprised to see me. I asked how you were, and she said fine—like you two were together. While I knew she was lying about your whereabouts, I thought you were at least together. Since I was off the teams by then, I didn't know."

"Healthy. Not hurt."

"And she didn't seem like she might be a prisoner, held against her will."

Ham looked away.

"Sorry."

"That's okay. I'm just . . ." He lifted a shoulder.

"If the woman I loved came back from the dead with my kid, I'd want to find her too." Luke finished his cup of coffee. "If you need help, let me know. Don't be a stranger."

He got up and Ham did too.

But as he walked away, he turned. "Ham, buddy. That little girl—she *did* look like you. Why don't you get a DNA test? Then you'll know for sure."

Ham forced a smile and waved at Luke, his last conversation with Signe playing in his mind.

"Signe, why here, in Chechnya?"

She was sitting on a bluff overlooking the valley where the camp, with its five thousand inhabitants, was located.

"I came as a translator with a group of Doctors Without Borders about six months ago, and then . . . I don't know, I just stayed. Because . . . well, they needed me."

"It's Caesar all over again."

She grinned at him. "Stupid dog."

"Lucky dog. He picked the right girl to follow home from school." He wanted to reach out, tuck the errant strand of her hair behind her ear. "He wasn't the only stray you took in."

She seemed to consider him. The sun had long ago kissed her face, dappled it with freckles, deepened her tan. If anything, she'd grown even more beautiful since her college years, from spunk to substance. "Yeah, but he wasn't easy. He used to try and bite me if I reached out to him."

"He was just afraid of getting hurt."

"He should have trusted that I knew what I was doing."

He drew in a breath. "I thought I lost you."

She leaned close. "You'll never lose me, Hamburglar. No matter where I am."

He kissed her then, because he'd been a little lost without her, because he still ached for her.

Because he didn't care if he got hurt.

She kissed him back, sweetly, as if she expected it. As if she'd seen him yesterday.

But he couldn't escape the memory of her words, now turning him cold. *"He should have trusted that I knew what I was doing."*

What, Signe, were you doing?

CHAPTER 8

SOMEHOW, JAKE HAD GOTTEN Aria into his arms. Nearly. Not that it had been his goal, but . . .

Jake tried to still his heartbeat to get a fix on the weather—anything, really, to not focus on the feel of Aria's body edged up next to his. Warm. Soft. And it stirred up way too many memories of their days in the tent, especially that last night when the blizzard roared. To keep her warm, he'd pulled her into his sleeping bag, fully clothed, and tucked her against him, trying to quell her shivering.

He'd been so worried that she might be going into shock, or worse, starting to suffer from altitude sickness. At least here in Florida he just had to worry about the weather.

The wind had stopped wailing, the thunder of the rain dying. The storm surge still raged, sounding eerily like an engine revving, in cycles. But maybe . . .

"Why did you say that I ran away from you?" Aria asked.

She'd been quiet a long time after he'd called her Houlihan, and he'd listened to his pulse, condemning him for going there, again. The nickname just emerged, something sweet, and well, he thought of her like that. Determined, smart, unafraid, just like Hot Lips Houlihan on *M*A*S*H*.

Aria didn't move away, however, and he began to hope that maybe she'd stopped being angry with him. So, quietly, "Well, what I remember is that I was kissing you, and then Jenny walked in, and then you looked at me with an expression I'll never forget and took off for the bathroom. So, I guess to me, that was running away."

She made a little noise. "I was just . . . I was embarrassed."

He tightened his arm around her, not really meaning to, but not knowing what else to say. "Sorry."

"No, again, that wasn't your fault. But, Jake . . . why did it matter? Although, I remember Jenny practically ordering you from the room and I felt terrible, so . . ."

"I guess it just reminded me of, well . . . something that happened when I was a kid."

He wasn't sure why that slipped out. Maybe the darkness. Or maybe just Aria. Because being around her just seemed to unlatch something inside him.

Still, he winced, painfully aware of Ellie's words. *I let him in too far.*

Then Aria put her hand on his arm, the warmth of it sinking into him, and another piece of himself broke free.

"My kid sister ran away from me when she was six years old."

He hadn't said those words aloud . . . well, probably ever. But with the telling, it felt as if a hand had unloosed around his lungs. He swallowed, and, "We were at the state fair. You know how big it gets—it's packed. I was thirteen, and I went into the food barn to get some fish sticks."

"The food barn. A crazy maze of pizza rolls, walleye on a stick, chocolate-covered bacon, and cheese curds."

"Yep. Our family went every year. My dad would give each of us kids a twenty-dollar bill and tell us to get anything we wanted.

I went into the packed food barn and suddenly, there was Hannah. She'd run in after me. Except, she didn't want fish sticks—I didn't know what she wanted. I just knew that I didn't want her tagging after me, so . . . I yelled at her and told her to go back to our parents, who were waiting outside. I wasn't angry, but I don't know . . . I was thirteen. Who knows what I said? I just have this memory of her running away from me."

Aria hadn't moved her hand, and somehow the darkness made it all easier. Outside the rain had subsided, a quiet descending throughout the hospital. He lowered his voice. "That was the last time anyone saw her."

Silence. Just Aria's breath, in and out, a swallow. "Wait . . . *ever?*"

"Mmmhmm. We think someone snagged her. Maybe offered to buy her food, I don't know, but when I came back without her, we started to look for her. Then we called the police and they searched the fair, but there were over a hundred thousand people there that day and . . ."

"Oh, Jake."

"They didn't blame me. They should have, but my parents remember her saying she was going with me, and there was so much chaos, when they looked around she was gone."

Aria had lifted her head sometime during the telling, and now settled it again against his shoulder. "I'm so sorry."

He leaned his head back, closing his eyes. "Our family just . . . we just didn't talk about it. My mom was wrecked . . . I could hear her at night weeping—it came right through the walls of my room. I know she was trying to hide it, but it . . . I don't know, it was haunting. And the worst part is that I couldn't cry. I don't know why—maybe I thought if I did, it would mean I'd accepted it, that she was truly lost."

And wow, that was a little too close to the truth, so, "It was strange, though, too, because in the daytime, we simply kept living as if Hannah was at school, or a neighbor's house. I think my parents wanted us to have a normal life, but we stopped talking about her and it made it easier, I guess, not to cry. In fact . . ." He blew out a breath, the horror of it shredding his voice low. "I've never cried."

"You've *never* cried?"

"We never had a funeral, so . . ." He opened his eyes and glanced at her. "I just feared going down, into all that pain. I thought if I did, I might never resurface."

"We all deal with grief different ways."

"Yeah. The worst part is not knowing. Really, we're pretty sure that she was kidnapped, maybe murdered."

"That's horrible."

"I don't know how my parents even looked at me after that. But my dad, he just, well, he pressed into his work. A few years later, they had another child—my sister Ellie. She calls herself the replacement."

Aria made a noise. And he remembered her words, earlier. *"I can't help but feel I'm a poor substitute for her."*

"She's not. Ellie is beautiful and smart and amazing, and a spitfire and bold and . . . well, nothing like Hannah. In a way, Ellie saved us."

"If you didn't cry, how did you deal with it?" Aria raised her head again.

He lifted a shoulder. "I don't know. I was sad."

"You blamed yourself."

"Who else was I supposed to blame?"

"How about the person who kidnapped her?"

He hadn't really thought about that before.

"You're suddenly starting to make sense to me, Jake."

"How's that?"

"Just . . . it's hard to go through life feeling like a murderer."

Her words were soft, but he winced. "My family was so impressed when I joined the SEALs. I think I wanted to prove I could . . . be a hero, maybe, instead of the guy who . . . well, scared his sister away. And being a SEAL was the hardest thing I could think to do. Ever."

"You inflicted your own punishment on yourself."

He frowned. But yeah, he supposed BUD/S could be called punishment. "Maybe. But it also gave me purpose. And brotherhood. And it made me feel like maybe I could make up for what I did."

His eyes closed. "As if that was even possible."

"You need to forgive yourself. You were a kid."

"I was thirteen. Old enough to know better."

She set her chin on his shoulder. "And young enough to be forgiven."

He said nothing. Finally, "One night, about a month after she'd gone missing, I went into her room. It was right next door to mine, and nothing had been touched. I took this little rabbit she had on her bed and I got on my knees and I prayed. And I asked God to find her. And if he had to, to take me instead."

Now his eyes burned, and probably he should just stop talking, but he couldn't seem to stop. "But he didn't, and believe me, I tried, for a long time, to make that exchange for him."

Her hand touched his face. "Jake. You're not a replacement for your sister."

He made a noise of disagreement. "I started to realize that the best I can do is just keep trying to be, I don't know, the guy who doesn't make people run away."

She touched his jaw and turned his face to hers. "I'm sorry I ran away," she said softly.

Her breath was against his lips, so close he could smell her, nearly taste her. "It was probably a good thing you ran away," he whispered.

His heart hammered, and he was suddenly very, very aware of the feel of her hand on his face, the fact that she moved it behind his neck.

Then she pulled his face down to hers and kissed him.

Her mouth was soft on his, as if comforting. Or maybe just reaching out in this darkness to connect, hold on.

Probably a catharsis for all this unwrapping of his soul, but he leaned in, her touch igniting something inside him he couldn't douse, and suddenly he had cupped his hand around her neck and pulled her to himself.

He didn't think about it at all, the rush from gentle to hungry, but all of it—the race to find her, the storm around them, the darkness, the shedding of his soul—conspired to unspool into his kiss, turn it to urgency, hunger.

Need.

Yes, that was the problem. He *needed* her. She calmed the personal hurricane always swirling inside and made him see parts of himself he didn't want to look at and somehow made it okay.

In fact, he was well on his way to loving her.

So he deepened his touch, even as the storm rose around them, the rain returning in a wild gust that roared down the hall.

She pressed her hand against his chest, moved away, her breath fast. "Jake—"

"The storm's back," he said. "We must have been in the eye."

"No, I mean, yeah, but . . . um . . . I didn't, I mean . . . I shouldn't have—"

The wind shrieked, and the entire building shuddered. Her hand turned to a fist in his shirt even as he pulled her to himself. "It's okay. We're going to be okay."

But the building continued to shake. "Something's not right. It feels like the entire building is coming down—"

Like her words might be prophecy, a terrible rending of steel and cement tore through the corridor and mixed with the hair-raising wail of gale-force winds.

The door slammed open, water slinging into the room.

Yola screamed, and next to him, Angel sat up.

Jake turned on his phone light, and the swath scraped over the gnarled arms of a tree.

Jake climbed to his feet, grabbing for the dislodged mattress when the world exploded around them.

Water, plaster, and wood barreled in from the hallway and into the room.

Angel screamed, the puppy barked. Aria launched herself over Mimi, protecting her. Yola curled next to them, hands over her head.

Jake picked up a mattress and flung it over all of them, huddling with them under the debris as the hurricane tore their hiding place asunder.

■ ■ ■

If she knew what was good for her, Aria should probably untangle herself from Jake's arms.

Again.

But he had such warm arms, and she could finally hear the tharumph of her own heartbeat. A steady beat, in her ears, reminding her that she'd survived.

They'd survived.

She, and Jake, and Yola, and Angel and, *Thank you, Jesus*, Mimi, still wheezing on her ventilator, the generators for the building still kicking, despite the wind that seemed to have gutted the second floor.

Outside, the rain had slowed, drips from the destruction of the third floor slapping against the debris. A slight wind still worried through the building, but sunlight poked between the clutter.

She could probably attribute the pounding of her heart to the fact that Jake cocooned her in his embrace, his chest to her back, his legs entangled with hers—and everyone else's. Because she cuddled up with Angel, who held her stomach, and next to her, protecting Angel on the other side, was Yola. Toby the puppy cuddled between them. Mimi lay close enough for Aria to check her breathing.

Over the top of them, Jake had built a small alcove of mattresses, a nest braced by timbers that had fallen into the chapel. By some angelic act of the heavens they hadn't been crushed in the mini cyclone that tore through the building, but rather, the timbers had piled up against the altar, under which they huddled like sacrifices.

Alive.

The air smelled of brine from the sea, but heat began to settle into the morning, a musty odor rising.

Not Jake. He smelled of the storm—rainwater, a little sweat, and puppy breath, having rescued the fella twice from running out into the torrent. The little guy had turned on Jake and slathered him with kisses.

Yeah, well, she couldn't blame him—she'd done the same thing.

Apparently, that was her MO. Get into trouble and turn to Jake. Let him rescue her.

Kiss him like she'd lost her mind.

Oh brother.

But maybe she'd wanted to rescue him a little too. *"I started to realize that the best I can do is just keep trying to be . . . the guy who doesn't make people run away."*

She couldn't help but kiss him after a statement like that. No wonder he called her Hot Lips. Something about Jake Silver simply made her turn off her brain and leap into his arms.

But this had to stop. This was a one-time, safe-port-in-the-stormy-night moment.

Okay, two-time. But now, it was time to untangle herself.

She drew in a breath, aware of his arms around her, the sinewy muscles in his forearms with blond hair that glistened in the morning sun.

He had beautiful arms.

Oh! Stop! She came to Florida to *forget* Jake Silver. To get him out of her system. To find her balance again.

His breath warmed the back of her neck.

So what if he'd shown up. In the middle of the storm. Brought her necklace.

Rescued a puppy.

And understood more than she wanted to admit how it felt to lose a sister and feel like it was your fault.

He was still a whirlwind, the kind of guy a girl met on vacation . . . and left there.

Besides, she wasn't falling for him. Not really.

He was just . . . well, someone to hold on to in the storm.

"You awake?" Jake said, his voice low and in her ear, sending a warm trickle of danger through her.

And then some. "Mmmhmm."

"You injured anywhere?"

Just her common sense, thanks. "I'm okay."

He held her a moment longer, then eased back, his hand on the mattress. "I'm going to get us out of here." He gripped the mattress above her and started to move it out of place.

A board shifted and tumbled away.

Yola sat up. "There's a wall here that looks like it could come down. It's only being braced by the timbers above us."

In the sunlight, she made out wooden joists that fell at an angle from the floor above. "We could get crushed if that comes down."

"I'm going to see if I can get out," Jake said. He climbed to his knees and moved the mattress. Another board fell.

"It's going to come down, Jake!" Yola pressed her hands against the mattress.

"Okay, I see it. There's a big piece of wood balanced on the edge and every time I move the mattress it wants to push it over." He ducked back down. "And if it goes down, it brings down a good chunk of plaster. I need to get out and move it."

What, like Hercules? Or Samson? But Aria said nothing as Jake reached up and grabbed a beam above him, tested it, then pulled himself out of the enclave like a world-class gymnast.

She rolled over and checked on Mimi. "You doing okay?"

"Oh, honey, if I had a man like that show up to rescue me, I'd be more than okay." She moved her oxygen mask to the side. "I heard you two talking last night. That man has a thing for you."

Aria shook her head. "We had a . . . a fling, sorta, in Alaska. It's over."

"It's not over," Yola said. Toby poked up his head and slathered her on the chin. "Poor man, losing his sister like that."

She looked at Yola. "How much did you hear?"

Outside their enclave, grunts accompanied the sound of debris moving.

"All of it," Angel said, grinning.

Perfect.

"I would have kissed him too," Mimi said and winked. She replaced her oxygen mask.

"He was a SEAL?" Yola said, wiping her face, then cradling Toby to herself.

"He's on a global rescue team now," Aria said.

"He rescued me," Angel said.

And me, Aria wanted to say, but . . .

Well, that was it, wasn't it? Somehow, around Jake, she became a clingy girl who had to be rescued. The old, weak Aria stuck in a bed, or, more recently, in a tent, or a pile of debris.

Frankly, it scared her how easily she relied on Jake.

The mattress lifted away, and wouldn't you know it, there Jake stood, the sun streaming down over him. His short blond hair glistened in the dawn, gold-and-red highlights lifted like he might be Thor, the god of thunder. A swatch of whiskers skimmed his chin, and his shirt stuck to every inch of his body. Standing there, grinning down at them, he appeared every inch the rescuer she knew him to be.

Her heart gave a hard, decisive, betraying thump. Proving that yes, she was very, very much alive.

"We need to find a place to shelter while we wait for help," Jake said. He reached for Angel, who practically leaped into his arms and let him lift her out of the debris.

Aria didn't need help, thank you very much. She climbed to her feet while Jake finagled his way through the debris in the room, looking for a safe place to put Angel down. He set her on a gurney in the hallway that had somehow stayed upright.

Once Aria got a good look at the destruction, how they'd survived without being crushed seemed a miracle. Broken glass, plaster, wood, and dirt littered the hallway. Above her, the ceiling rained down at an angle from torn wooden planks, a tree poking branches through the joists and plaster. It might have come through a window and crashed into the inner wall.

"That could fall any minute," Jake said as he helped Yola out of the rubble. He put her on his back and piggybacked her out of the room. "I'll be back for you and Mimi."

He disappeared then, with Yola, out into the hallway.

"He's going to be back for you," Mimi said.

Aria looked down at her. Mimi winked.

"Really? We're in the middle of chaos, stranded here, and you're . . . winking? What do you think is going to happen here? A walk on a sandy beach? A candlelit dinner? Soft music?"

"I could hum. Yola has a nice voice."

"We need to get you out of here, Mimi. I don't know how long that generator has power, and you need oxygen."

"How long do you think the gennie will last?" Jake asked.

Oh. Jake had returned, minus Yola, and Aria's face warmed, hoping he hadn't heard Mimi. "A few hours, maybe? A day?"

He nodded, the look behind his eyes far away, as if he might be formulating a plan. He turned and hunched over.

"What are you doing?"

"Getting you out of there. C'mon—climb on my back."

"No, I'm just fine."

He straightened and turned around. "Aria. Two weeks ago you seriously sprained your ankle. Don't tell me it doesn't hurt."

Her mouth tightened. But yeah, all the running yesterday had stressed it, and it had swollen in the night, sending an ache into her bones.

"Listen, Houlihan, I'm here to lift heavy things. You're the finesse. You get hurt and we're all in trouble. So, let me help you, okay?"

Aria gave Mimi a look, then turned back to Jake. "Mimi goes first." She knelt by Mimi and tightened down the oxygen mask. Met her blue eyes with something of a warning.

Mimi winked again.

Oh brother. She propped Mimi up, and Jake leaned over the mess, running his arm under her shoulders.

Then, as if he might be lifting a child, he swung the woman up into his embrace. "Stay put," he said to Aria. "The floor is thick with glass and nails."

Oh, for . . .

Aria felt like a fool as she stood there in the nest of clutter, like some kind of invalid.

She lifted her leg over the debris, setting it on the other side. Her ankle burned, but surely it would hold her. Still, heat gathered in the ankle as she eased her weight onto it.

She just had to move quickly—

Her ankle buckled, and she bit back a scream as she started to collapse.

"Oh, for crying out loud—"

Jake's arms came around her, pulling her up. "I told you to wait."

"You're not the boss of me—"

"Oh goody. Here we go again. What happened to the woman I woke up with? The nice one?"

"Ha. Listen, Thor. I don't need you to show up and rescue me all the time."

"Apparently, you do." He righted her, then turned. "What did you call me?"

"Nothing. What are you doing?"

"Climb on my back."

She stared at that wide, muscular back. And the way he glanced at her, over his shoulder, almost a little angry.

"It doesn't hurt you to admit you need help, you know."

Her lips tightened. "Fine." Aria leaned over and wrapped her arms around his neck. Oh, see, this was *not* the way to keep her heart from trouble. Jake had a wide, sturdy back, and his hands grabbed her knees and held her steady as he carted her from the room.

He brought her to the staff lounge, still intact despite the windows that had blown in. Outside, blue skies arched over a frothy shoreline, a still-churning sea. Seagulls called, soaring on the currents above.

He set her on a table. Then he stepped back, turned around, and grinned at her. "Thor, huh? I admit, I like it better than Hawkeye."

And behind her, lying on a gurney that the superhero must have found, Mimi started to hum.

■ ■ ■

Ah, Jake recognized this Aria.

The Aria *after* the storm.

The Aria who didn't want to admit that she'd needed him. That she'd clung to him when the world was crashing in. The one who, like a wet cat, turned on him when the sun rose.

He sorta liked cats. They were like sisters—independent, smart, savvy, and capable.

But he'd heard Aria's words as he'd been dismantling their enclave. *"We had a . . . a fling, sorta, in Alaska. It's over."*

No, no, it wasn't over. Not when she'd ended up in his arms again.

Not when he knew, in the deepest wail of the storm, that he'd found a measure of peace.

She was good for him.

He just had to prove to her that he was good for her too. Even in the light of day.

"I'm going to find us some fresh water and grub," Jake said as he set down a mattress he'd retrieved from one of the patient rooms. He'd wrapped Aria's ankle, despite her protests, but her limping had eased. Made him less desperate to simply carry her everywhere.

A little less desperate.

She had pushed aside tables in the staff lounge to make room, and now she eased Angel onto one of the mattresses. Angel winced, her hand on her belly.

"Are you having contractions?" Aria asked.

"I don't think so," Angel said but lay back, her jaw tight. Tough girl. Reminded him of his sisters—blonde hair, blue eyes. Quiet, thoughtful.

Against the other wall, on a gurney, Mimi lay with her eyes closed. Feisty, but rail thin in her illness, she held the oxygen mask over her mouth, as if trying to eke more air from it.

"Mimi, you okay?" he asked, the gesture stirring his concern. He walked over to her to check the ventilator. It wasn't pumping. No wonder she was fighting for breaths. "I think the generators have gone out," Jake said to Aria.

Aria came over to Mimi to confirm, then nodded. "But they should be working. Most hospitals' generators last for at least twenty-four hours."

Jake walked toward the window. Jagged glass edged the sides and shards littered the room, although he'd done his best to sweep it up. Outside, the skies had turned an eerie yet beautiful magenta, the clouds a deep purple, slashes of light yellow where the sun bled through.

Below, the storm surge had flooded the parking lot, the water over the top of most of the remaining cars. Palm trees stuck up like broken toothpicks, their fronds stripped from their trunks and floating in the water. Black shingles from roofs of nearby houses glistened in the rising sunlight, undulating in the waves.

Down the shoreline a house sagged off its foundation, the roof smashed, the waves foaming around it. The house next to it had lost its roof, leaving only the skeletal remains of the rafters.

A massive sailboat lay like a broken albatross in the middle of a nearby beach, propped up next to an SUV with a dented roof that was trapped in a pile of debris.

Aria had come to stand beside him. "Wow."

"I know. So much destruction."

"But look at that sunrise. I read somewhere once that the normal rhythm of wavelengths is disrupted after a hurricane, and the residual moisture in the air scatters them and brings into focus the colors we don't normally see."

"So, the storm lets us see something that is usually hidden?" He looked at her.

She met his eyes, then looked away. "Or it's just a rare phenomenon, never to be repeated."

"Until the next storm."

"Hopefully there won't be another storm. How are we going to get on the roof?"

Okay, so they wouldn't talk about the kiss, or the fact that he'd woken up with her in his arms. "My guess is there is an access on the third level," he said. "I'll see what I can find."

"I'm coming with you."

Of course she was.

"But first, I need to find an ambu bag."

"I think I saw one in the room I stole the gurney from." He headed out the door.

The southwest wing of the hospital had suffered the least destruction. Broken windows, but none of the ceiling had come down, the walls were still intact, and aside from the debris and the grime of the storm, the structure seemed sound. He found the room—just down the hall from the staff room—and retrieved the bag.

The other side of the unit—the northeast corner where he'd oh-so-wisely decided to take cover—had been shredded. Sheetrock hung from the ceiling, a few joists dragged on the floor, and the skinned and broken trunk of a palm tree poked like a finger into the middle of the chaos. Probably the one that landed in their door moments before the ceiling came down. The storm had shoved the tree farther down the hall, but just seeing the wicked power of the aftermath sent a fist into his gut.

God clearly had Jake's back because his instincts had nearly gotten them killed.

Jake handed the ambu bag to Aria, his hands shaking a little. Probably he just needed some coffee, something to eat. He hadn't eaten a meal since yesterday—a hamburger as he'd left Miami.

The storm had pushed the fridge from the wall, unplugged it, and when he opened it, the smell of rotting food turned his gut. And without electricity, no water emerged from the faucet.

"We need fresh water too," Aria said, as if reading his mind. She had hooked up the ambu bag to the oxygen mask and was teaching Yola how to bag her grandmother. Slow, even movements.

Yola's jaw set tight as she took Aria's place.

"Let's go," Aria said, and he followed her out the door to the stairwell.

She held the door for him, then took the stairs up to the third floor. At the top, a hinged pull-down ladder was affixed to the wall, and he easily reached it and gave it a tug.

It came down, and she reached for it.

"Let me go first. Just in case the roof has caved in."

"Which means I get to save you?" She stepped back. "Have at it, cowboy."

He still liked Thor better.

Debris blocked the rooftop hatch, but he set his shoulder against it and it finally budged.

Sunlight poured down over him as he climbed out, testing the rafters. Aria poked her head out of the hatch. "So?"

"It seems intact. And aside from a few gnarled pipes, it seems undamaged." He held out his hand to help her, but she was already out. She stood beside him, taking in the view.

And oh, the view.

"Oh my," Aria said and slipped her hand into his.

He tightened his around hers.

From this vantage point he could see the whole island, starting with the destroyed bridge out of town, swept away by the sea, waves crashing over the broken edges of pavement.

So, they were trapped. And on an island that looked as if it had been swept by the hand of God.

On every side, water had rushed over the land, the surge easily over twenty feet, swamping houses, businesses, and streets with seawater, still swirling and undulating in the aftermath of the fury. The boats in the nearby harbor, once moored in tidy stables, now piled together in stacks—skiff, sailboat, and fishing boat alike—tangled, their hulls broken, some breached and belly-up.

Farther up the island, more boats lay in curious places—one in a pool, another through a shed, another in the median of the highway. And everywhere twisted metal from the roofs of mobile homes and other houses floated like ribbons, shiny in the sunlight.

Wood, garbage, palm trees, furniture, water toys all collected in debris piles where the wind took them. Houses lay in sticks, some homes simply a smear of rubble on the land.

Other homes had been cleared completely off their foundations, the belongings tossed to the storm.

An odor rose from the debris—rot, mold, dead fish, even gasoline, and despite the salty air, the humidity stewed it together into a rancid cesspool.

Aria pressed her hand to her mouth. "I hope Drey hurries up."

Jake looked at her. "Who?"

"Drey. He was one of the doctors from the conference. He took the last chopper out but said he'd send one back for me."

"So, there might be help on the way?"

"I hope so."

Him too. "Gennies are over there." He pointed to two giant gray metal boxes side by side. "Watch where you put your feet."

"Sort of like climbing down a glacier." She followed him across the roof.

"Yeah, sort of." He glanced at her. "I thought we weren't talking about that."

"If we limited our conversation to only the things that happen when we're trying not to die, we're going to run out of things to say."

Oh, he'd probably never run out of things to say with her. Because it seemed the moment he started spending time with her, he unbuttoned his soul and said all sorts of crazy things.

But she had a point. "Maybe we should try it." He reached the gennie and put his hand on the metal structure. It hummed. "It seems to be working."

"Try what?" she said, crouching in front of the door. She unlatched it.

Inside, the motor was humming, the fuel at half-tank.

"Spending time together when we're not in trouble. The gennie looks like it's running. It's just that the switch that routes the power from the generators to the electrical system has sprung back to the neutral position. Maybe there's a blown transformer somewhere that's causing a ground-short in the system."

"A what?"

"It's a short that keeps turning off the electricity to the rest of the building. We need to force the switch into place." He reached for his belt.

"What are you doing?"

He swung the belt out of the loops and wrapped the end around the switch handle. "Now to tack it into place."

"Hook it onto this bar." She was pointing to a long bar that protected the power unit on the bottom.

He looped the belt through it and pulled the switch over, hitching the belt tight. "This should keep the ventilator and other essentials running. Probably not the lights, though. The emergency generators are usually only set up to run medical equipment."

"You're a genius," she said, and the compliment made him look at her. "A hero, even in the daylight."

"Enough to be seen in daylight with you?"

She smiled. "What does that look like—us together when we're not dodging a blizzard, or a hurricane?"

He edged back to the door. "Dinner out? Maybe I take you sailing?"

"On your cat?"

He nodded, held the door open for her.

"The one that capsized?"

Oh, she heard about that, huh? "So maybe not the cat, then. We could, I don't know, go for a drive?"

"On your motorcycle?" She descended the stairs.

Right.

"Okay, so we eat dinner at home, in front of the television, or go to a movie, or—I don't know, Aria. Not everything I do is dangerous."

She had reached the bottom of the ladder. "Really? Because

it feels like it. I mean, you're in the rescue business, Jake. Which means you run *toward* trouble."

He followed her down the stairwell. "Listen, I met you while you were climbing a mountain, for Pete's sake. Don't tell me you don't like adventure."

"I wasn't doing that for me—"

"Not true."

She stopped on the landing and turned, frowning.

He met her there, unfazed by the darkness in her eyes.

"Are you calling me a liar?"

And although he heard sirens, he couldn't stop himself. "Yeah. Because if you were honest with yourself, Aria, you know you have a choice. You like the adrenaline rush of doing something scary. Going beyond yourself—"

"What? No, I—"

"Fact is, Doc, I get you, better than you think I do. You spent the first sixteen years of your life watching your sister do and be all the things you wanted to be. Then you got her heart. And you suddenly got to live that life. But you felt guilty—of course you did. And maybe a little scared. So you said—hey, I'll go do all those things because of Kia. Because she wanted to. But that's not true, is it?"

Her eyes widened.

"It's because *you* wanted—still want—to prove to yourself that you're strong. That you're brave. That you are every inch of the daring, amazing person you always wanted to be."

Her mouth closed.

"You're testing *your* heart, Aria. Not Kia's."

Her hand went to her necklace and she shook her head. "No, I'm . . . I'm . . ."

"Not brave?"

She swallowed.

"Not adventurous?"

She bit her lip.

"Not—"

"Not Kia."

He frowned. "I know you're not Kia."

Her eyes filled. "But see, Kia was supposed to live this life, and—"

"Kia wanted you to live your life, Aria!"

She turned away.

"Sheesh. You need to forgive yourself just as much as I do." He ran his hand over her shoulders, pressed his forehead to the back of her head. "Doc, I know why you only let yourself collapse when there's a storm. Because if you were to need anyone in the light of day, under the blue skies, then you'd be weak little Aria with the broken heart again, wouldn't you? And that's why you kissed me and ran—because it wasn't Kia who kissed me, but *you*. And you couldn't live with the fact that you, Aria, get to live. To love. To feel. To be happy."

Her body trembled and his voice softened. "You get to be happy, Houlihan."

She pressed her hand to her mouth and turned. "No, Jake. I . . ." She looked at him. "I was perfectly happy before you . . . before you . . ."

"Rescued you?" His mouth quirked.

She nodded, but her eyes had filled. "And that's why it won't work, Jake. Because around you, I . . . I turn into a woman I don't want to be. Weak and needy. I don't want to be that woman. I can't go back to her."

"Aria, you're not weak—"

But she'd slipped away from him.

"Aria—"

The door closed behind her, on the second level. Jake wanted to slam his fist into the wall.

Instead, he listened to the pounding of his heart.

And the pounding in his head.

He could use some coffee. And probably fresh water and maybe some food. Which maybe he could find in the cafeteria.

Then maybe he could figure this thing out between them. Help her see how brave she was. Not needy, but capable and amazing.

The water from the first floor reached his thighs, cold and dark as he descended to the main level. Debris had propped open the door and he squeezed his way through and into the lobby. Following a sign, he headed toward the coffee shop.

The area was dark, the tables floating, the water just below the counter level. Stuffed animals floated by, soggy and grimy. The menu board boasted a fresh Caesar wrap he might have paid a thousand bucks for. Even more for a can of Spam. Funny how some things were damaged in the storm, others survived intact—like the display of wrapped cookies, neatly sitting on the counter. The paper bags of coffee, however, lay soggy and broken.

He nabbed a cookie, then went around to the back and found the refrigerators, silent. He was right—the generators only supplied power to the essential medical machines.

Still, maybe he could find something to eat.

Opening an upper door, he spotted the goodies for the next day's sale—a tray of bran muffins, some banana bread, a few warm yogurts. On the bottom rack, a supply of bottled waters. He grabbed a couple bottles and stuck them into the pockets of his cargo shorts. Then he pulled out a tray of muffins.

What he wouldn't do for hot coffee, but the odds that the makers were working seemed slim. Still, he slogged through the water to the supply of coffee and found three commercial makers, two with pots of coffee, probably brewed yesterday.

He set the muffins on the counter.

So, maybe he didn't have to rescue her. Maybe he could simply show up with breakfast. That didn't count as a rescue, did it?

More of a fast-food delivery-service guy.

No tip required.

Standing in the water, he reached for the coffeepot. His left hand touched the metal of the machine, testing for heat, and even before it happened, he felt a quiver ripple through him, something not right.

Something dangerous and lethal—

Then the voltage hit him. Two hundred twenty volts jerked through his body, tightening his muscles, zapping his heart, and stealing his breath.

Jake dropped like a rock into the water.

CHAPTER 9

THERE SHE WENT, BEING A JERK AGAIN.

The door to the hallway closed behind her to Jake's voice. "Aria—"

She didn't look back. Couldn't.

Because of course, the man had seen inside her soul. Again. *"Because if you were to need anyone . . . then you'd be weak little Aria with the broken heart again . . ."*

She stopped and braced her hand on the wall, waiting to hear Jake enter behind her.

No footsteps.

He hadn't followed her.

Which was probably for the best because . . . well, he was right about the kiss too. It was Aria who kissed him, both times. Aria who wanted to be in Jake's arms.

Aria who was falling for dangerous Jake Silver who rode a motorcycle and sailed on the wings of a cat and climbed mountains and probably skydived and did everything that both stole her breath and hummed in her heart.

He scared her. Lured her.

She looked over. He still hadn't followed her.

Huh. She stood up. Walked to the doorway.

The stairwell was empty. And then she remembered their conversation before they fixed the gennie, as he called it. Fresh water. And grub.

She debated a moment, then headed down the stairs, not sure why, but aching at the words between them.

At the fact that she'd run away from him, again.

The lobby was dark, the water nearly to her waist as she waded through it. "Jake?"

She was standing near the information desk when she heard it. A shout, quick and sharp, muffled by the water and the walls, but loud enough that it jerked her around.

The coffee shop. Of course.

She pressed through the water. The door had been shoved open, the water holding it back, and now she stared into the darkened space. "Jake?"

No one.

But she did notice a tray of muffins on the counter. And a handful of bottled waters in the display case. She pushed through the water and headed toward the case. The front had been broken, jagged glass rendering the sliding door useless, so she worked her way around the counter to the back.

She nearly tripped on something solid, and put her hand out—

Touched a body.

She recoiled. Screamed, hard and fast.

Then a cold horror swept through her as she recognized, in the dim light, Jake. His black T-shirt, his cargo shorts—

"Jake!" What—? She hauled him up by the shoulders and pulled his face out of the water.

His eyes were closed, he wasn't breathing.

"Help!" She dragged his body, with the help of the water, around the counter toward a solid wooden table in the center of the room, climbed up, and pulled him onto it.

"Help! Someone!"

But really, who else was there?

Kneeling on the bench beside him, she tilted his head back and swept his mouth. Clear.

She started compressions.

"C'mon, Jake! Don't you dare die on me!"

Ten, eleven, twelve, thirteen—

"Listen, Jake. You were right, okay? I did kiss you because I wanted to. I really wanted to." Twenty-seven, twenty-eight, twenty-nine. "Please, Jake—"

She gave him two strong breaths.

She checked his carotid artery. It seemed something might be pumping, but he lay lifeless.

More compressions.

"Jake, please. I'm so sorry. I know I can be difficult. I can be a real jerk too. But I need you, ten, eleven, twelve—"

A gasp.

"That's right, come back." She kept pumping.

He drew in another breath, this one deeper.

She checked his pulse again. Stronger.

Another breath and she stopped compressions. Leaned over him, rubbing her knuckles on his sternum. "Wake up, Jake—"

His eyes opened and he startled, drawing in another long breath.

She put her hand on his chest, feeling his heart beat, his breath rising and falling, and wanted to weep.

He lay there a long, quiet moment, just breathing, as if trying to get a grip on what had happened.

Quietly, he moved his hand to cover hers.

She hid her face under her other hand, not wanting to give herself away. But her shoulders shook, her breath hiccupping.

"Aria," he whispered, "I think that counts."

Swallowing, she wiped her face and looked at him. He was staring at her.

"What counts?"

"You rescued me. So, we're even."

"Hardly. And shut up. I never want to do that again." She turned away from him then, her hands again covering her face.

Really, she just wanted to shatter.

"Aw, Aria." He moved his arm around her and pulled her down against his soggy body. "Shh."

"I can't do this. I can't keep you and everybody else alive."

His arms encircled her. "I'll be okay—"

"You nearly died, Jake." She leaned up, her eyes hard in his. "You can't do that to me, *ever*."

His mouth tweaked on the edges. "Because you need me?"

She frowned.

"I could hear you. Somehow, even as I was climbing back through all the darkness, I could hear you. You need me. You're a jerk. And you kissed me because you wanted to . . ."

She made to get up but he caught her arm.

"Stop running from me, Aria."

She froze. Turned to him. He eased himself up from the table, to a sitting position. "Because I'm not sure I'm in any condition to run after you."

Then he cupped his hand on her face, drew it to his, and kissed her. Softly, a sweetness in it that she recognized.

Because that was the Jake she knew. Gentle. Sweet. Yes, he might have danger stamped on his forehead, but under his charming, dangerous exterior lived a man who would die for his teammates, follow his friends up a mountain, and weather a storm with a woman who professed to be angry with him.

She closed her eyes and let him kiss her. Let herself feel his gentle strength, the way his body trembled, probably the aftereffects of—

"Wait," she said as she pushed away. "What happened?"

His gaze was roaming her face, as if hungry, stopping at her lips. "Bad coffee. Got a real bite to it."

Then he kissed her again, something sweet and perfect.

Oh, Jake. She let him linger, take his time, let herself sink into the taste of him, the sense that right here, right now, they were both alive.

Whether they deserved to be or not.

And maybe, well, that was the point. Jake kept showing up in her life despite her efforts to push him away.

So maybe she'd stop pushing him away. Maybe it was time to . . . well, what he'd said—be happy.

How many second chances was she going to get? She let him deepen the kiss, kissing him back. Because she wanted to.

He finally let her go, his body still trembling.

"Jake, are you still having trouble breathing?"

"With you around—"

"Stop." She took his pulse at his neck again. His heart seemed to be pumping, but with a strange quiver at the end. "Take a deep breath for me."

He drew in, but coughed, bending over.

And that's when she saw his hand. "Jake!" She lifted his wrist, looking at the horribly burned flesh on his fingertips, blistered, already peeling back. "Can you feel that?"

He stared at his fingers, the torn skin. "I . . . yes . . ."

"Probably the water kept it from burning worse. What did you touch?"

"The coffeepot, like I said."

"The coffee . . . but . . . wait, were you electrocuted?"

He considered her words. "I think so."

"Let's get us out of this water."

"It's not the water. It's probably the fact that the electricity is still hot through the lines even though the lights are blown. I was wrong about the power only going to the essential machines. Apparently, it powers the entire building."

"So anything we touch could electrocute us?"

"Only if we are standing in water. I touched something that was hot and I was grounded by the water, and the electricity flowed through me. The water isn't electrified. But if I touch something that is, then I act as a conductor and get zapped."

"So, don't touch anything."

"Now you tell me."

"I need some light to examine this wound. And we should get you upstairs. I wish I could run an EKG, but at least I want you where I can monitor you."

"I like the sound of that."

She rolled her eyes. But she reached for him, pulling him to his feet, her arms around his waist.

"You're pretty good at this trauma doc thing."

Huh. She was, really. "My ER rotation was one of my favorites." They waded through the water, toward the stairs. "In ER, you simply stabilize and move them on to better help. But I liked knowing I saved a life."

She propped open the door and helped him through it. He'd gone quiet.

"I heard about the baby."

She drew in his words, let them settle on her. "Yeah. I was tired, and I'd stayed up all night, and . . . I don't know. I just . . . wasn't enough."

He stopped her then, one foot on the steps. "Aria, you are so enough. So, enough."

But even as he said it, his eyes rolled back, his body started to shake.

She caught him even as his knees buckled and he pitched into the water.

■ ■ ■

Fire coursed through Jake.

The kind of hot that saturated his pores and drenched him with sweat. It dripped into his eyes and blurred the sight of his MK11 scope. Worse, Afghani soil embedded his ears, his mouth, itched every inch of his body as he lay under his ghillie suit.

He was Bigfoot. He even smelled like an animal, his odor enough to turn his gut.

But two days hiding in the grime had paid off.

"HVT en route," said Danny, aka Charlie One, in his ear.

"I got him," whispered Bjorn, Charlie Three. He hunkered down in an enclave of sunburned rocks maybe a hundred yards outside the village, point sniper for this particular op, his job to take out the HVT. "Two klicks out."

Jake's job was to watch the village while the rest of the team set up a shot to take down Hamid Moussad, a ranking Taliban leader.

Just watch the village.

Nothing more.

Even as Jake settled into the nightmare, he heard a voice in the back of his head.

Wake up.

He ignored it, as if determined to watch it play out.

Again.

"Charlie Three, I have two young men headed out of the village, toward your position," Jake said.

"Copy that."

Two boys, one of them holding a kite. Jake zeroed in on them.

They couldn't be more than fourteen.

A glint of something bulky under the kameez of one of the youths had him centered on it, looking for another glimpse.

"Be advised, I think one of them might be wired," Jake said.

Next to him, his spotter, petty officer Jennings, confirmed. "And I think he might be holding a detonator."

A suicide bomber?

"We're compromised," Bjorn said. "What do you want us to do?"

No, please, they were too young to be jihadists.

Wake up!

"Sit tight," Danny said. "Let's see what they do."

"HVT has arrived," Danny said. "Charlie Three?"

"Almost," Bjorn whispered. Beside him, his spotter was whispering adjustments, his voice hissing through their mics.

Jake's chest tightened as they unfurled their kite, letting it spin in the air. Then, they bolted right toward Bjorn's position. One was reaching inside his kameez.

Shoot! "Boss!" Jake said. "They're making a move."

"Your call, Jake."

"Taking the shot," Bjorn said.

The one with the vest fell to his knees, as if in prayer. Pulled out an object.

Prioritize. Execute.

Jake squeezed off a shot.

The kid dropped, blood puddling in the sand.

"Confirmed," Bjorn said, about his HVT.

"Exfil," Danny said, and Jake would have started moving if it hadn't been for the scream emanating from the village.

A woman, middle-aged, her arms waving, ran toward the downed boy, who was now being dragged through the dirt by his panicked companion.

"Silver, move it," said Jennings, packing up.

But Jake couldn't even breathe as he watched her fall to her knees. Cover the kid's body, screaming.

"Jake, move it!"

Wailing, her body undulating in pain as the boy lay, dead.

"Jake!"

The scream tangled his brains, paralyzed him, separated him from his thoughts, his actions.

"Jake!"

The voice dragged him forward, harsh, strident, a hand on his arm. Jake burst to the surface, light peeling back the dream. And opened his eyes.

Not in Afghanistan.

And not in Walter Reed, although the smells knocked him sideways for a moment—cotton, antiseptic.

He wasn't even at the base in Norfolk, tangled in his sheets.

"Are you okay?"

His breaths tumbled over each other as he searched for the voice.

Mimi. The old woman on the ventilator, although now she'd pulled her bed close to his, had rolled over and grabbed his arm.

Probably to pull him out of the dream.

Darkness swathed the room, a stillness that, despite the hiss of the ventilators, evidenced the lack of electronics. No buzzing lights, no television, no elevator or air-conditioning hum.

Silence. Air. Heartbeat.

Breathing.

Jake swam through his memories and found nothing he could latch on to. His last clear memory was kissing Aria in the dark kitchen—no, not a kitchen. But somewhere like it.

He'd like to return there, to that dream.

That sweet dream where she let go of all her fears and became the woman who trusted him.

Called him her hero.

He winced. Because he was anything but a hero.

"You were thrashing pretty good there, kiddo," Mimi said, her voice a whisper. "I thought you were going to fall right outta bed."

Brisk, cool air filled his nose and his mouth from a mask strapped to his face. Still, sweat drenched his body, and his covers fell to his waist. The smell was back and Jake's entire body was a knot of hurt.

"War dream?"

He made out Mimi on the other bed. From the looks of it, they were in a patient room. Mimi lay on her side, a pillow between her knees, watching him.

Had she just called him kiddo?

"Van, Rollo's brother, had them after he came home. Would get up and prowl the house at night. Took to drinking to keep the nightmares at bay." She patted his arm. "You got some demon chasing you, don't you?"

He moved the mask to the side. "Just something that happened . . ." His voice sounded like he'd gargled half the ocean. Felt like it too, his throat rough. An anvil lay on his chest, and pain bloomed out from it, right in the center of his sternum. "Why am I in bed?"

"You gave us a scare." She reached out and patted his arm. "But you've been breathing for six whole hours without a hiccup, so that's a good sign."

Six hours? "What are you talking about?" He made to sit up, but flame burned through his chest and he lay back, still groaning.

"Don't get excited now. You need to lay there and let your body recover from all those seizures."

He knew he wore a sort of horror in his expression.

"You crashed on the stairway. Yola had to help the doc get you up the stairs and she gave you CPR. That ticker of yours tried to give out twice. Once in the stairwell, and once after she got you in a bed."

No wonder his chest hurt.

He didn't remember any of it.

"You had a seizure—actually, two of them—and you stopped breathing both times, so she put a tube down your throat, just to make sure you didn't die."

He touched his throat, swallowed. "What time is it?"

"Oh, it's about four in the morning, I suppose." She looked past him toward the window and he followed her gaze. The periwinkle of early morning had just begun to bleed into the vault of night.

His gaze landed on Aria, sleeping in a reclining chair next to his bed. She wore her hair down, a stethoscope around her neck, her hands folded under her cheek, her knees drawn up, and he just wanted to reach out and pull her into his embrace.

Apparently she'd saved his life over and over again for the past eighteen hours.

"She said it was a result of your near electrocution."

Electrocution. The coffee machine.

Only then did he notice his hand, bandaged. At least it was his left hand, not his shooting hand.

And weird that thought should come to him. He wasn't in the navy anymore.

He wasn't anything anymore.

Jake lay back and closed his eyes.

Mimi touched his arm. But when she said nothing, he looked over at her. She had her eyes closed, her lips moving.

"What are you doing?"

She opened one eye. "Shh. I'm praying for you." She closed her eye again.

He didn't know why her words tightened the fingers around his chest. Or why he said, "It won't work."

She opened her eyes. "What do you mean?"

"I've tried to pray it away. It doesn't work."

"Then you haven't tried hard enough."

He sighed. "I've tried, believe me." And not just prayer. He stared at the ceiling. "Maybe there's just some nightmares you don't get to wake up from."

"Lies from the devil. God wants you to live in peace. With a free mind."

His mouth tightened.

"What is so terrible, Jake, that you don't think God will forgive you?"

He blew out a breath. Looked at Aria. But she already knew the story.

He rolled over, looked at Mimi. Lowered his voice. "Fine. I shot a kid."

Mimi said nothing. Didn't even blink.

"Did you hear me?"

"I'm not deaf."

His mouth tightened. "He was thirteen."

She nodded. "I'm sure you had good reason."

"Is there ever a good reason to shoot a kid?"

She lifted a shoulder. "War. It doesn't play favorites."

He rolled back. "That's not how the press saw it. I'm not sure how, but they got ahold of the incident, and although they couldn't name the shooter they called me all sorts of terrible things."

"And you believed them."

He lifted a shoulder. "I can't get the wail of his mother's scream out of my head. It's . . . I don't know. Maybe the press was right . . . I'm a murderer." The devil.

"Jake." She tightened her hold on his arm. "That's not true."

"It is. I'm impulsive. I . . . I think I panicked. I saw this kid with a grenade and thought he was going to kill one of my teammates. So I shot him. Just as simple as that. But see, SEALs don't do things blindly. We look at all the angles. Come up with a strategy. Run scenarios. Train. We don't just . . . well, we don't just hop on a plane and . . ."

"Rescue a pregnant girl from danger? Help an old woman keep breathing?"

He rubbed his chest.

"You know what a hero is? It's someone who does the hard thing despite the cost."

"A hero doesn't kill kids."

She drew in a breath. "A kid stops being a kid when they decide to take a life."

"He made a mistake."

"God can forgive even this, Jake."

He must really have gotten the stuffing knocked out of him, because his eyes watered.

She rolled back, holding her mask. "I am willing."

"What?"

"It's one of my favorite lines from the Bible. Jesus says it to this poor man who has leprosy. It was such a terrible disease—everyone who had it was required to yell 'unclean, unclean' whenever they came into town or were around people. Can you imagine? Having to shout out this terrible condemnation of yourself?"

Jake said nothing. But yeah. He'd been shouting condemnations of himself for a while now. Say, twenty years.

"So, here is this diseased, unclean man, and he sees Jesus. He's clearly overwhelmed, and he's heard of him, probably thinks of him as a prophet, but whatever the case, he bows before him, desperate, and says, 'Lord, if you're willing, you can heal me and make me clean.'"

She drew in a long breath, her voice changed, thick with emotion. "And Jesus says, 'I am willing. Be healed.' And instantly, the man is healed, just like that. Clean."

Clean.

"I am willing. That is the posture of God, Jake. That is the posture of love. If you're looking for a hero, you don't have to look any further than Jesus. The one who, for the joy—for *love*—gave everything, including his life, to rescue us from death, even though we didn't deserve it. Or, frankly, even want it."

On the other side of him, Aria began to stir.

"Do you want it, Jake?"

"Want what?"

"To be rescued. Forgiven. Clean."

He had nothing. "I've been a Christian all my life."

"Yes, but are you clean? Because it seems to me you see yourself as dirty. A leper. Unforgiven."

"Maybe I don't deserve to be forgiven."

"None of us do, kiddo. But, he is willing."

His eyes heated. "I spent some time on my knees begging for forgiveness. I still feel like . . . well, like it's not enough."

"Then maybe you need to ask God to help you to forgive yourself. To stop punishing yourself. Because if Jesus can forgive you, if he paid the price for those sins, what right do you have *not* to forgive yourself?"

He clenched his jaw, his voice small. "I don't even know what that looks like, Mimi."

"You start by receiving forgiveness. Then, by letting Jesus rescue you every day. We think of forgiveness as a one-time deal, but really, it's a moving target. Every time the wicked one calls you names and wants to take you captive with guilt and shame, you break free by proclaiming the truth of Christ's forgiveness. Daily, hourly, if you need to. And you start blessing yourself instead of cursing yourself. You tell yourself the truth. I am forgiven. I am clean. I am loved. Say it, Jake."

I am forgiven.

"Jake?"

"I'm trying."

"Forgiven. Clean."

He stared at the light spreading through the room, the fingers of dawn.

"I know Jesus is in you, Jake. There's just too much hero in you not to see it. Now, it's time for you to open your eyes and see it too."

I am forgiven. I am clean.

Aria stirred again, drew in a long breath, opened her eyes.

And then she smiled at him, something easy, something warm.

Heat filled his entire body, sweeping with it the aches, the scratching in his throat, the fire in his chest.

Loved?

She got up, walked over to him. Picked up his wrist to take his pulse. The dawn shone behind her, turning her hair to a rich, layered brown, her eyes soft in his.

She was made for this—saving lives.

Oh wow, he saw it now.

He didn't belong in her world.

I am clean. I am forgiven.

How he wished it could be true.

He put his hand over Aria's. "Thank you."

"Now, we're even." She bent down and kissed his cheek.

Not even close. But he squeezed her hand and let it go.

Because if he loved her, he should probably listen to her.

Get her home safely.

Then let her go.

■ ■ ■

It was an old dream, really, the kind he'd tried to extinguish for years—and had successfully, most of the time.

More of a memory, really, and just as tangible, just as real as the first time it had happened.

Ham could hear her laughter lifting even before he saw her. He knew it was crazy—just showing up like this, at her cute little off-campus bungalow on the edge of Berkeley campus. In his dress whites, no less. But he missed her.

Ached for her.

And he'd just done the hardest thing in his entire life and he needed . . . well, he needed someone to care.

So he sat on the front steps next to a ceramic pot filled with lavender, listening to the wind knock leaves from the trees, and prayed she hadn't forgotten him.

It had been a long two years since the day he'd promised them a happy ending.

And then there she was, walking into view, under the dappled shadows of a towering elm. She wore a pair of linen pants, a cropped T-shirt, her blonde hair down, long and golden in the late-afternoon sun.

She spotted him, and any fear she'd forgotten him vanished in the widening of her eyes, the way she stopped.

Her book bag fell to the ground and she sprinted across the lawn and leaped into his arms.

He caught her as her legs went around his waist, her arms clutching his shoulders. "Hamburglar!"

She smelled like sunshine and home, and when she kissed him, the past two years of training dropped away, the fatigue, the fear of drowning, the taste of sand in his mouth, ever-present yelling in his ear.

He was home.

Signe bracketed his face with her hands, leaning away from him, her green eyes bright in his. "What are you doing here?"

"I got my trident. I'm officially a SEAL," he said, putting her down. "And . . . I had to tell you."

"Oh." She stepped back from him, offered a shaky smile. A woman walked up to her, held out her book bag.

"You dropped this," she said, looking up at Ham.

"Thanks." Signe nodded to Ham. "This is the guy I was telling you about. Hamilton Jones. Ham, this is my roommate, Tara."

"And you're the boy from back home," Tara said. Pretty, short blonde hair. She looked at Signe. "I'm going to the library." Then she winked.

Ham stilled.

Signe took his hand. "How long do you have?"

"A 96-er. Four days."

She opened the door to the house. A Craftsman feel on the inside, with hardwood floors, floor-to-ceiling bookshelves that flanked a tiled fireplace, overstuffed furniture covered in throws. Plants in pots lined the window alcove, textbooks were stacked on a chipped wooden coffee table.

He put his backpack down in the entryway.

The place felt exactly like Signe. Comfortable.

She took his hand, brought him into the family room. "Do you want something to eat?"

He shook his head.

She took a breath. "So, was it terrible?"

He nodded.

"Were you hurt?"

"A lot. But it was okay. I knew it was for a good reason."

She nodded, but she wore an enigmatic expression, her face a little twisted. Then she touched his uniform, first one hand, then the next. "You did it." She had smoothed her hands over his chest. "You really did it. You're a SEAL."

"Yeah. I'm just waiting for my team assignment. And then, deployment. But I'll be back, as soon as I can, I promise."

She covered her mouth with her hand, then turned away.

"Signe?"

"I just . . . I'm afraid."

He took her face, turned it back to his. "I told you, I have a plan, and it's all going to work out."

She kissed him then, and even in his dream, he could taste the urgency, the fear, the desperation in her kiss.

She was still his girl, and that truth washed over him. He deepened his kiss, and somehow, too fast, too easily he found himself stretched out beside her on the sofa, breathing hard, fighting not to trace his hands down her body. He pressed his forehead to hers. "Sig . . ."

"It's okay." She met his eyes, her face flushed, her breathing tight. "It's okay, Ham. I love you and—"

"No. It's not okay." He pushed himself off her, all the way off the sofa and walked away, to the window. Looked out it. "I made myself—us—promises."

"But we're not . . . we're not kids anymore."

He looked at her. "No, we're not. Let's get married."

The question just spilled from him, a feeling more than a decision, but once it was out, he couldn't exactly take it back. And despite the quick rush of her breath, he didn't want to. He turned to her. "Marry me. Today. This weekend. We'll go to Vegas and—"

"Yes." She found her feet. Came over to him, nodding. "Yes, Ham."

"Yes, Ham. I will marry you."

His hand moved to his chest, even in slumber, feeling the knot tighten, a sense of doom that clenched his heart, moved through his body, filled his lungs.

He opened his eyes with a quick and sharp breath, a gasp, and stared at the ceiling, trying to place it.

The early morning sunlight filtered through the linen curtains at the windows, and a slight wind lifted the heat from his body.

Ham sat up, still feeling Signe in his arms, tasting her, smelling her fragrance on his skin.

As if she'd been in the room with him.

Haunting him.

He got up, went to the bathroom, and washed his face. Brushed his teeth. He'd spent the past day looking into the yachting accident, talking to the Italian coast guard and discovering that indeed, two men had washed ashore, one matching the description of Pavel Tsarnaev. The other, his brother, Ammon. They'd owned an eighty-meter yacht named the *Romea* that could sleep twelve. Five decks, with a media room and onboard pool, and room for a crew of twenty. According to the local police investigation, the crew was all ashore for the night, just the family on board.

None of whom had surfaced.

"Are you sure the wreckage was from the *Romea*?" he'd asked the local police chief, a man in his late sixties who'd detailed him on the accident remains.

"The *Romea* was built in a German shipyard in 2015. Steel hull, aluminum superstructure, and it was designed by Bernard Tisdale."

Ham hadn't a clue who that might be, but apparently Tisdale left his trademark embedded in the designs of the yacht.

"The wreckage we recovered was a Tisdale yacht."

Ham had tried calling Jake again last night, standing on his balcony looking at the basilicas of the nearby churches and, in the distance, the expansive blue of the Mediterranean Sea. Overhead the sky arched in magnificent brilliance. Ham hung up when the call went to voice mail—no good trying to leave another message.

But as he'd stood there after his no-go call, listening to music drift up from the street four stories below, the smells of gardenias and roses twining up into the night from the trellises, the what-could-have-beens hit deep and hard.

He crumpled onto a chair, his head in his hands. Closed his eyes.

This wasn't the plan.

Lord, this wasn't the plan!

He didn't know how he ended up with his face turned to heaven, wettened, his throat raw, but he couldn't stop himself. *God, I know I've made mistakes—lots of them. But I need . . . I need answers. And help. If Aggie is my daughter, help me to be the father I should be to her. Help me to be the man Signe needed. Help me . . . help me to . . .* Let her go.

To live with a plan he didn't want.

He'd scrubbed his face, then gone to bed.

And dreamed of the moment when everything started to derail.

Now he dressed and, his stomach writhing, went outside to find a cafe.

The sun bled rose-gold fingers into the square and he headed back to Caffe Opera, bought a croissant and cheese, a cup of cappuccino, and sat at one of the umbrella tables.

In the square, vendors were setting up shops. Artists selling watercolors, oils, and pencil drawings, florists, wood-carvers selling Pinocchios and other puppets, tourist junk—including the turtle he'd purchased, T-shirts, and beach hats.

He sipped his coffee and considered his next move.

Like, home. Although, he didn't know why the idea of going home put a fist in his gut.

A little girl ran across the square, her mother quick-walking after her, the pair clearly on the way to school or daycare. She called out to her, and the little girl turned, laughing.

The pain in his gut tightened.

Aggie.

He couldn't face her.

She was afraid of him—he'd figured out that much. And wasn't that fun? His daughter preferred his teammate over him.

The one time she'd actually turned to him was when she'd nearly drowned.

But what scared him more was that he didn't have any feelings for her, either. She was a stranger.

An anomaly.

A kink in his plans.

And he hated himself for even thinking that.

The little girl had run back, grabbed her mother's hand. He watched her pull her mom through the now-busy square.

His gaze fell on a woman, also watching them from across the piazza. She stood under the shadow of a stall, wearing a light blue headscarf, a pair of long linen pants, and a blue sleeveless button-down. The wind lifted her scarf and betrayed golden blonde hair, tied back. And although he couldn't make her out clearly in the shadow and distance—

"Signe!"

He was on his feet and sprinting across the square before he had a clear thought. The place had crowded with the morning traffic, scooters and bicyclists crisscrossing to side streets. A bus had pulled up and passengers disembarked.

He kept his gaze on the kiosk, dodging pedestrians, finally cutting through into the open.

She was gone.

His heart slammed against his ribs, cutting out his breath. He sprinted up to the vendor at the stall. "Where did she go?"

The young man frowned at him, shook his head.

Ham turned, searching the crowd. So many people, faces and none of them familiar.

"Signe!"

A few people turned, but no one stopped.

He stood there. *Please, God—*

His cell phone vibrated in his pocket and he dug it out.

"Hello."

"Hamilton Jones, this is Dr. Salvatore D'amico." The coroner.

Ham stepped out into the sunshine, walking toward the giant elephant statue in the center of the square, still searching for Signe.

No one in a blue headscarf.

No one with her glorious long blonde hair.

No one with Signe's ability to breathe life back into him, make him believe that he hadn't screwed up his entire life.

"I have . . . news. The coast guard found a body last night, on shore."

Ham stopped looking. "What?"

"It's a female. She's fairly well decayed, but she matches your overall description—blonde, midthirties. I'm wondering if you have a DNA sample we might use to identify her."

Ham let out a shuddering breath. "I . . . I don't."

"I see. Well, if you want to come by and examine the remains, I will allow it."

"Thank you, Doc. I'll think about it."

He hung up and sank down onto the edge of the fountain. A little boy came up and tossed a coin into the moat around the fountain.

Ham stared at the coins inside. *"Lucky dog. He picked the right girl to follow home from school."*

Then he put his hand over his eyes and wept.

CHAPTER 10

JAKE WAS A BEAUTIFUL MAN when he was sleeping. There was a heart-aching peacefulness on his countenance Aria rarely saw in his expression. Dark lashes whispered across his cheeks and his blonde whiskers were raked by the morning sun, lifting the copper and gold from his beard. High cheekbones, a scar deep in the well of his cheek, another along his jaw, and best of all, the sweet, simple rhythm of his chest, rising and falling beneath the thin sheet over his body.

Across from them, Mimi also slept. Yola had spent the night curled up beside her on the bed, Angel in the recliner they'd found and wheeled into the patient room.

He'd scared her. Right down to her marrow. This strong man, felled by the shock to his body that seared his hand and set his heart quivering, unsure if it wanted to resume function.

Please, God, keep him alive.

Aria had slid right into praying as she and Yola got him up into the hallway, as she pumped his chest, restarting his heart for the second time, as she breathed for him, praying it was enough. He'd come back to her.

Then died again, twenty minutes later. This time, tears raked down her cheeks, and she'd begged God audibly.

He'd rebounded more quickly. And since then, kept breathing, albeit reluctantly.

She'd watched him for hours, even after she took the tube out, a dread in her gut.

She couldn't lose him. The sense of it burrowed deep, took root.

She couldn't lose him, because despite herself, she could love this man. Let him inside her heart to find a home.

Because Jake had the ability to look past all her walls and see the truth.

Speak it.

She felt most alive when she was saving lives. When she faced trauma, disaster, and the impossible head-on and fought to survive.

Maybe it wasn't Kia's heart beating inside her that pushed her to this life, but something inside her soul.

Kia's heart just made it possible to live the way she was born to.

"You're pretty good at this trauma doc thing."

His words, but with them a memory walked in, took root.

Ten-year-old Kia on her bike—the one with the fat wheels—racing down the driveway into the street. Aria, of course, sat on the steps of their home, watching, reading a book. Anne with an E.

"Are you okay, Houlihan?"

She looked over, and Jake's eyes had opened, searching her face. Clearly, this man could read her mind.

Lifting a shoulder, she gave him a wry smile. "I was thinking about my sister, and the day, well, that I decided to become a doctor."

"Yeah?" he said and rolled over, curling his injured hand to his chest. He was a big man—he took up almost all of the bed, but somehow still looked so painfully vulnerable.

Thank you, God, that she hadn't lost him.

"Yeah. It was a Saturday. I was reading, of course, and Kia took off on her bike. It was just a normal day, and I just kept reading.

Then I heard tires squealing, a scream, and suddenly, I saw Kia flip over the front of a station wagon. Scared the life out of me."

"I'll bet."

"I ran down to her, and she was crumpled on the other side of the street, screaming. The car's driver had stopped, but I got there first." She made a face. "Kia's forearm hung at this brutal angle, both her radius and ulna broken midway between her wrist and elbow. And while she was screaming, I was mesmerized."

She expected disgust in his expression. Instead, he wore a smile, nodding. "Of course you were."

See? "I grabbed her arm, right behind the break, to stabilize it. And I said, 'It's going to be okay,' although I had no idea what I was saying. I remember a neighbor showing up, shouting that she'd called 911. Kia had scraped her jaw, and her helmet bore a black scrub from where she hit it against the curb."

"Yay for helmets," Jake said.

"Always. Kia just kept saying, 'It's broken. It's broken,' as if she couldn't believe it. And I said, stupidly, 'Well, of course it is.' I mean, it was so obvious. I had no idea that she was going into shock. I think I even told her it was really gross."

She laughed, seeing Kia's dirty face, her tears, the way she looked at her, almost a spark of anger in her eyes.

"She was really freaked out that they might have to give her a shot. I told her it was like a bee sting, and then all the pain would go away."

"So, you lied."

"Yes. Although I'd had so many needles by then, I was pretty used to it. But Kia was absolutely traumatized by needles, so . . . yeah, I lied. But she was always so brave, and she was being this pansy."

Jake said nothing, an unnamed emotion in his blue eyes. She was caught in them for a moment.

"I remember the driver yelling at Kia, telling her she should have watched where she was going. She was clearly unravelling, but I think I must have gotten up to protect her, because all I remember is my dad showing up. He had come from the house, wearing his scrubs on his way to work. He worked the night shift, trauma nurse. I remember him turning to the woman and saying that blaming didn't help. But . . . then he looked at Kia and said that it was going to be just fine. That she was in good hands."

Jake made a noise, something of agreement.

"I don't know what it was about that, but I'd spent my whole life wishing . . . well, that I could be like Kia. She never needed me. And suddenly, she did. And I liked being needed."

"We all like being needed, Aria," he said quietly.

A heartbeat. A truth. She smiled, meeting his eyes. *I need you, Jake.*

He was reaching out for her hand when he stilled. "Do you hear that?"

"What?"

He held up his hand and she went silent.

A low humming rattle, in the distance, growing louder with each second.

"That's a chopper." Jake pushed himself up. "It's headed for the hospital."

"It's the rescue chopper!" Aria landed on her feet and raced to the window. "I don't see it."

"It could be on the other side of the building." Jake was getting up.

"Stay there." She put her hand out to stop him as she headed out of the room.

Yola lifted her head. "What's happening?"

Aria didn't stop to answer. She raced down the hallway and hit the stairwell door, running up to the third floor, then up the roof access ladder.

The latch on the access door wouldn't move. She banged on it and pain spiked up her hand. Banged again, not caring. The sound deepened, turned bright and coarse, roaring overhead.

She pushed the door, but it fought back.

Please!

Footsteps behind her—she looked down to see Jake working his way up the stairs.

"What are you doing?"

"Get the door open!"

She turned back, listening to the sound fade, took a step up and set her shoulder against it.

The door moved off its enclosure and broke free. She wedged it up and ran out onto the roof.

Indeed, a chopper, flying north, past them, as if it had already swept the island and was heading home.

She bounced on the roof, waving her arms. "We are here! Help!"

"That's a coast guard chopper—a Jayhawk. Probably looking for survivors." Jake had poked his head out of the hatch.

"I don't care if it's a spaceship from Mars. We need rescue!" She ran out to the edge of the roof. "Come back!"

Below, the ocean had settled, the waves an eerie green, maybe from the plankton stirred up in the storm.

"Aria." Jake's voice was soft, solid in the rattle of her frustration, which was sudden and swift and shaking through her as the orange-and-white chopper vanished. "Aria, it'll be okay."

She rounded on him then, unable to stop the rush of emotion from cresting into her voice. "No, it won't, Jake! We're stranded here, and look around us! There's no water, there's no electricity, the fuel for the generator is going out, and you nearly died. *Died.* Three times—"

"Shh." He'd walked out onto the roof now, his arms out. "Shh. But I didn't. Because of you. I'm going to be fine, and we're going to get out of here, I promise."

She stared at him, his words like hands, reaching in to grip her. Hold her.

And then he did. He stepped right up to her and wrapped his arms around her, pulling her to his chest. She rested her head against his breast, listened to his still-beating heart, and let herself breathe.

"I know you're freaking out. And that you have too much on your plate, and that you feel responsible for all these people, but I promise you're not in this alone. I'm going to get us out of here. And get you home safely."

Us home safely. But maybe he meant that.

"You should be in bed." She stepped away from him.

"I'm tired of being in bed."

She glanced at his bandaged hand.

"Oh, this?" He raised his hand. "Nothin'."

Always the tough guy. She rolled her eyes.

He climbed down the ladder after her and closed the vent, not tightly. He seemed to be walking okay, his breathing sound, but she'd like to check his lungs, listen to his heart—

"Do you hear that?"

They stood in the stairwell, the chill from the water rising to turn her skin to gooseflesh. He stilled, listening.

"What—"

Then she heard it too—the sound of a motor, a low humming, echoing up toward them.

"The chopper?"

"Sounds like a boat. It's got a high-pitched hum."

He started to descend.

She wanted to grab the back of his shirt, hold him back, but this was what Jake did. Besides, maybe it was the coast guard, on a search mission.

The sound of the motor deepened, revved.

"Jake—"

Glass shattered, a terrific cacophony that shook the entire building. It burst through the hum, a tearing of metal and steel and suddenly the motor roared through the building.

Jake reached the door. "It's a boat! It broke through the glass windows! And there's a man in it—"

Then, like the hero he was, he vanished into the disaster.

"Jake!" She followed him down into the water. Bracing and probably riddled with gasoline and other debris, it was black and murky and up past her waist.

The boat had lodged itself against the information booth, the motor still running. Jake reached it, climbed over the edge, and shut it off. A man sat in the bottom, holding his arm, groaning.

"Are you okay?" Jake climbed up onto the information desk and reached for the man. Midthirties, short, cropped hair, with a paunch around the middle and a three-day beard growth. He held his arm to himself, already wrapped in a sling.

"Is this the hospital?"

Aria sloshed up to them. "Yeah. What's going on?" Close up, he looked like he'd done battle with a wall, or a set of stairs, a survivor of the storm, with bruises on his face, a cut over his eye. "What happened to you?"

"What do you think?" he said, then winced. "Sorry. I need drugs."

"What you need is to have that arm looked at," Aria said.

"Are you a doctor?"

"Yes, she is," Jake said and reached for him. "You're in good hands."

Her throat thickened. But yeah, she was made for this. "Let's get you upstairs," she said as she helped him off the counter. "Watch out, the water is cold and dirty."

He eased into it, wincing. Up close, yeah, he'd taken a beating.

"How did you survive the storm?" She helped him toward the stairwell.

"One hour at a time," he said. "Name's Hagan."

"Well, Hagan. You've come to the right place. We'll take good care of you." They stepped into the stairwell.

"Hey!" Jake's voice stopped them. He was still standing on the information counter, the water to his ankles, illuminated in the wan light. "Can I borrow your boat?"

■ ■ ■

Jake had that knotted feeling in his gut. The one that said something wasn't right.

The man bore all the telltale marks of a beating, and Jake had seen more than a few beatings.

But what was he going to say? "Um, I don't like the look of this Hagan fella"? Because they all looked a little worn around the gills, beat up and on edge, and who was to say that Hagan hadn't found his way out of a sinking ship the way the bruises littered his face, his body.

He seemed friendly enough as he sat on the floor on one of the mattresses in the staff lounge. Aria knelt in front of him, running her fingers gently up his arm as he gritted his teeth, trying not to wince.

The arm was deeply bruised, clearly injured, swelling just above his wrist.

"I wish I could get an X-ray," Aria said. "I can't be sure. The bone doesn't feel displaced, but it could be a hairline fracture with the swelling." She got up and walked over to Jake. "I'm going to try and splint it while you're out."

Aw, shoot. Because Jake had been trying to figure out if he should take back the request to borrow the boat.

The man wore grimy black trousers, a gray T-shirt, and beneath his sleeve, a tattoo that looked like some kind of anchor symbol. Maybe he'd served in the military. He was a big man too. Over six feet tall, burled shoulders, as if he spent time outdoors or at the gym. He certainly bore a rough edge about him, something gritty about the way he glanced at Jake, as if sizing him up.

And maybe Jake might have put that aside, attributed it to some wizened sea dog who'd seen too many storms, but if he read his hands right, the guy also had a couple bruises on his knuckles as if he'd given as good as he'd taken.

Yeah, no, Jake wasn't leaving.

"We need fuel for the gennies. I can't believe they've lasted this long," Aria said. "And more water, if you can find it. We've got about six bottles from the coffee shop, and maybe twenty-four more in the supply, but who knows how long it'll be before help gets here—if they get here at all . . ."

He cupped his hand under her chin. Met her eyes. "Help will be here."

She made a face. "You don't know that."

The despair in her tone added to the roil in his gut and now he had to go. At least to find fuel.

She sighed. "Oh, what am I saying? I don't feel good about you leaving. What if you have another seizure?"

He didn't feel good about leaving either, but for an entirely different reason.

"I'll be fine. But . . ." He glanced at Hagan. "Maybe I should stay."

She followed his glance and drew a breath.

And that's when Yola came into the room, her face drawn. "Mimi's vent just died. I'm going to have to bag her again."

Right.

Aria put her hand on his chest. "Don't get killed. Please."

"I promise." He glanced again at Hagan. But the man sat with his head back against the wall, his eyes closed.

Probably Jake was simply jumpy. Overprotective. It came with the territory of being a SEAL. A big brother.

A man in love—

Nope. He could not let himself love her . . . not when he had to walk away from her at the end of this gig. So, he dropped a kiss on the top of Aria's head and nodded. "I'll be back in a jiff. I'm going to the harbor to find some fuel in one of those boats. Maybe a radio."

"Be careful." The warning came from Hagan, who opened one eye. "The prison was destroyed. There's gangs out there." He closed his eyes. "Armed."

"Lock the stairwell behind me," he said quietly to Aria.

Angel stood in the hallway. "I want to go with you." She put Toby down and the puppy scampered to Jake. He picked it up, endured a few kisses on his chin, and walked down to her.

"Angel, no. It's too dangerous. We don't know what's out there. There's debris everywhere and—"

"What if he came back for me?" Her eyes were wide. "What if Baker came back and I wasn't there and—"

He put the puppy back into her arms, then put his hands on Angel's shoulders. "How about if I swing by the youth hostel? Where is it?"

"Just a couple blocks off the harbor, near where you found me."

"I'll see if I can find it." He rubbed the pup behind its ears, and the animal leaned into his hand. "You keep this guy safe, okay?"

She nodded, her blue eyes glistening. "Thanks, Jake."

He didn't know why his throat tightened as he walked away. She just seemed so . . . lost, maybe. And oddly familiar, as if a part of him recognized her from a long-ago life.

He went down the hall to grab his backpack, wishing he had a weapon. He'd have to make do with his Leatherman. He dug it out of the pack, shoved the tool into one of his knee pockets, left the pack, and headed down the stairs into the murky waters of the first floor.

Water had continued to seep into the room, reaching his waist as he waded to the boat. A flat-bottom metal skiff, probably used to transport goods across the harbor, it slid easily back into the water. He rolled into it, then checked the motor, turned on the choke, and yanked the pull-start.

It revved on the first try. He kicked it away from the desk, sat on the bottom, and gauged the distance between the water and the top of the door.

No wonder the guy went through the glass. He'd end up with his head off his shoulders if he went through the doors. But the big paned windows still held shards of jagged glass.

Jake puttered over, then turned off the motor and eased the boat through, an eye on the guillotine above.

Outside, the water had started to recede, shiny and dark under the sun, although the parking lot still stood under four feet, he guessed. Toward the center of the island he'd probably find clear roads, but if he wanted diesel fuel, he'd need a yacht, something big.

Something that might also have a working two-way radio.

Overhead the sky had cleared, but the wind still rushed over the island, carrying a bite, something angry from miles offshore. A rank smell saturated the breeze—dead fish, decaying wood and other debris, gasoline in the water. He moved up to the seat and motored away from the building, toward the tiny harbor that edged the hospital grounds, then he turned and got a good look at the building.

A parking light had fallen into the second story and uprooted an outside transformer—and probably accounted for the terrible boom he'd heard that first night. The wind had stripped every window on the south side of the building. He motored around submerged cars and emerged at the back of the hospital. Here, the northern winds had defaced more than windows—the entire back half of the building had been sheared off, the innards open to the wind, and the lethal palm tree that had collapsed their enclave speared the end of the building.

He turned away, unable to look.

Across the harbor, the wind left pickup sticks where homes had once bordered the shoreline. Nothing but rubble—roofing tiles, wood, plaster, furniture, appliances, crushed vehicles.

He prayed there were no bodies, but he wasn't the only one who thought they could simply hunker down and ride out the storm.

Motoring out into the waterway, he headed west down the shoreline, past a school, its roof torn off, then an elementary school, the playground equipment twisted, destroyed by flying metal. A pileup of boats to his left evidenced a small harbor, but nothing except utility vessels there. He noticed an overturned speedboat with the words Key West Police on the side, and sure enough, he passed the detention center, the grounds edged by fencing and barbed wire, now a knotted tangle. The roof lay half-torn from its foundation, a wall nothing more than rubble, and the main administration building scooted off its foundation.

The prison looked abandoned.

He kept driving, his gaze skimming the shoreline, water splashing up in a fine spray. Around him, the ocean spat foam at him, driving him into shore, the sun warm on his skin.

In the distance, he spotted a seaplane. Just drifting.

The resorts had taken hits—from torn roofing to destroyed outbuildings, boats and water toys piled up on the shoreline.

No one walked the beaches, the town lethally quiet.

He spotted the Bahama Mama. The tiki roof had blown clear off and vanished, probably out to sea. And a schooner lay in the pool. A downed palm tree blocked the back entrance, right where he'd found Angel.

Seagulls screamed above him as he rounded the shoreline.

The big harbor, the one by Margaritaville, came into view. When he'd driven by, before the storm, it hosted tall-masted sailboats, massive catamarans, and three-story yachts.

Now, the watercraft were piled together like a traffic jam, bumping and hacking at each other's hulls as the waves drove them into a knot. Many of them were half submerged, others driven onto shore, across the cobblestones.

But there, down the shore, a sixty-foot yacht was moored on the beach, its beautiful blue hull embedded into the sand. He motored up to it and tied off, jumping aboard at the stern, where it sank into the water.

He went first to the captain's nest, checked on the two-way radio.

Dead.

The fuel tanks were located below the deck, but he found the latches and opened them to reveal the massive diesel holding compartments. They were intact but too big to move, so he got back into his boat, found a nearby skiff, and raided a twelve-gallon square tank off the back. Then he found a hose and siphoned off fuel into the tank.

He loaded the tank into the boat, glancing at the sun. Past noon. He should find them some food.

Nice yacht—and it had a rescue dinghy in the back, a lounge on the upper deck, complete with a stocked bar, and below deck, a fancy galley kitchen. He found the fridge empty, however.

But then . . . oh yes. Spam. He opened a cupboard and discovered three little blue tins stacked in with a can of corn, chili, and sardines.

Odd stock for blue bloods, although maybe it belonged to the staff. He went in search of a bag in the captain's roost and found another jackpot—the emergency bag.

He'd call it Christmas. Zipping open the bag, he discovered a full emergency supply kit. A dozen water pouches, a handful of protein bars, water purification tablets, flares, candles, a lighter, a whistle, and . . . thank you, Santa, a transistor radio. The batteries looked corroded, but maybe he could find more.

He packed it back up, added the canned goods, and headed back out to the skiff. The sun had dropped, hovering midpoint into the afternoon, the sky a deep, hopeful blue.

For a moment, he stood, staring out into the horizon. Blew out a breath.

So maybe he was impulsive. And made some doozy mistakes. But . . . *I am forgiven. I am clean.*

He wanted that more than he could admit.

Jake was pushing off when Angel's words skimmed through his mind. "*What if he's out there?*"

The wavering in her voice made him decide to take a look.

After double-checking his line, he got out and headed across the beachhead toward town. She'd said the hostel was near the beach where he'd found her, so maybe he'd just wander down a few streets looking for life.

Water flooded the streets, up to his knees in some parts, dry in others, as he headed out of the shopping district into the residential area. Broken tree limbs, roofing, soggy drywall, fencing, and grimy, pressed earth littered the streets. "Hello? Anyone here?"

A few seagulls cried overhead, but even the wind didn't answer. He turned down another street.

The neighborhoods in this part of town betrayed an age and character resonant of the twenties and thirties, with deep porches and fenced yards. Hurricane windows. And all abandoned. "Hello? Anyone need help?"

Oh, this was fruitless. He didn't have a clue where the hostel might be in all this mess.

And probably, Angel was better off without the jerk. Any man who took off when things got prickly . . .

No. That wasn't what he was doing with Aria. He was respecting her fears. Walking away first, before she had to run away.

He was turning when he heard it—a shout, distant but clear.

"Over here!"

Jake stopped. "Where?"

"I'm here!"

He followed the voice. "Call again!"

"On this roof! Over here!"

He jogged down the street and spotted a kid standing on the veranda of a dilapidated two-story house. Half the roof had blown off, tiles scattered on the street, and the grounds were surrounded by water, a moat around the house.

"Are you okay, kid?"

A boy with short brown hair looked down at Jake like he might be seeing a Marvel hero.

"I'm trapped. The roof collapsed and I didn't know how to get down."

"Right. Okay." Jake measured the distance—too high to jump, but maybe—"Hang tight."

He'd passed a piece of two-by-four and now ran back, pulling it up from the water. Maybe twelve feet long, it might work.

He came back and set the two-by-four against the house. "Climb down. I'll hold this and you can shimmy down."

The kid stood there, considering Jake's words.

"What's your name?"

"Bailey."

"Okay, Bailey. Just put your foot over the edge and climb down. Hang on until you reach the board. I won't let you fall."

He guessed the kid to be around age ten. At ten Jake remembered being willful, tough, and just stupid enough to put his foot over the edge and take a risk if some guy told him to.

Bailey was definitely ten. He threw his legs over the veranda wall and slid down, holding himself a long moment before he climbed onto the board. Jake braced it between his legs as he shimmied down, over the knee-high fence and onto the street.

"Nicely done," Jake said, giving the kid a quick, cursory check over. Grimy, soggy, but he seemed to be fine. "What are you doing out here?"

"I was looking for my dog. He ran away in the storm, and then it hit and I didn't know where to go, so—"

"You weathered the storm . . . here?" Jake spotted a no-trespassing sign on the fence.

"It's an abandoned house. I thought . . . it had a big claw-foot tub, so I thought maybe I'd be safe . . ." He lifted a shoulder, and that's when Jake spotted the reddened eyes, the streaks down his cheeks.

"Okay, kid. Let's bring you home. Where do you live?"

Bailey pointed deeper into the neighborhoods. "But there's nobody there. My dad works for the police department and left before the storm to evacuate people."

"He left you home alone?"

"I was at a friend's house. My mom was supposed to come and get me after her shift at the hospital, and when she didn't, I went home. But the house was empty, and my dog was gone. I thought he got out of the yard, so I went to look for him."

"They evacuated the hospital, kid. There's no one there."

From the shock on the kid's face, maybe that could have come out better. Jake blew out a breath. "Okay, let's go to your house and see if your mom is there."

Bailey nodded, a little spark in his brown eyes.

They walked down the streets, the houses turning smaller, more compact, bungalows nestled practically side by side with only fencing separating them. The storm had ravaged all the homes in some way—peeled roofing, shredded fencing, broken windows, missing front porches—and many were embedded with the litter of their neighborhood, including watercraft, motorized vehicles, and furniture.

Bailey picked up into a jog as they turned down a street littered with branches. "That one." He pointed to a small pink one-story bungalow, its picket fencing like spears littering the uprooted cobblestone driveway.

"Mom!" Bailey yelled, going through a hole in the fence and climbing onto the porch. "Mom!"

He burst into the front door.

A magnolia bush lay stripped, its petals browning in the sun. Curtains blew through a jagged front window.

Bailey's voice echoed in the house.

Jake stayed on the porch, his heart sinking.

Bailey appeared a few minutes later, head down.

"Okay, kid. Come with me. We'll figure out where your parents are."

Bailey said nothing as he followed Jake out of the yard.

"What if she came home and went out looking for me? I should have stayed home."

"Okay, listen, I get it." He resisted the urge to put his arm around the kid. But he knew what it felt like to wish you'd made a different choice. "But there's no blame here. You did what you had to in order to stay alive."

They were rounding the corner onto the main drag when shots cracked the air.

Jake froze, turned.

"Did you hear that?" Bailey said, and Jake grabbed his arm, pulling him into the shadows.

"Those are gunshots."

Bailey's eyes widened.

"Okay, let's go. Stay close to me." He started off in a jog toward the harbor. Bailey, good boy, kept up.

They somehow emerged by the Bahama Mama. More gunshots, and now Jake heard voices. "In here."

Gesturing into the destroyed lobby, he waited until Bailey was inside, then pointed to the lobby desk.

"Get down."

"What is it?"

"I don't know. Stay here."

He ran out into the parking lot and crouched behind the only car in the lot. Then, every cord in his body chilled as a cadre of men walked into view. They wore black pants, gray T-shirts. One turned.

KWDC was printed in black block letters on the back.

Key West Detention Center.

Six of them, and at least four were armed, two with Remington pump shotguns. The other two with Glocks, which they recklessly shot into the air.

Perfect, just—

Bailey was edging out of the desk area, his eyes wide.

Stupid kid! Jake waved at him to go back.

"Hey you!"

He closed his eyes.

"Hey you, kid, c'mere!"

Aw. Jake didn't want to look, but well, what was he going to do?

Bailey came out from behind the desk, his hands up, shot a glance at Jake, and started walking.

Jake didn't have a clue how this might go down, but he knew one thing.

He really, really wanted to keep that promise to Aria to stay alive.

CHAPTER 11

"YOU PICKED A FINE TIME TO LEAVE ME, LUCILLE."

Aria didn't know why the old Kenny Rogers tune kept rolling through her head, but of course, the minute Jake left, taking with him his calming, steady presence, everything fell apart.

Aria didn't like the look of Mimi's oxygen levels, and Yola looked like she might be getting hand cramps from the ambu bag. Which might not have been a problem if Angel hadn't suddenly doubled over in pain.

Please let her not be in labor.

As for Hagan, she'd searched the supply closet off the nurses' station and found a cardboard box. She doubled it over, then wrapped it to his arm and fashioned a makeshift splint.

"So, what happened to give you these bruises?" she asked after splinting his arm. A purple welt swelled his cheek, and a dark line split his lip. The ER doc in her labeled it a bar fight, but that didn't make sense.

"I was taking cover in my bathroom when the storm took out a wall. I got down but one of the joists banged me across the face." He drew his arm close. "I tried to brace it with my arm, but that wasn't the best idea." He added a grimace.

"You're lucky you weren't killed," she said, wishing she had an ice pack.

"Yeah. The tub protected me, but it was terrifying."

"You're safe now," she said. "But let's get some fluids into you." She gave him a bottle of water. "The vending machine has a few snacks left. Jake got the door open, so help yourself."

"Thank you."

Probably it was a good thing to have another man around, although Hagan didn't possess the don't-worry-I'm-here aura of Jake Silver.

Probably no one did.

In fact, Jake exuded a confidence unlike anyone she'd ever met—well, except for Kia, maybe. Kia knew how to make people laugh. Looked danger in the face. Never said "I can't."

That's what had scared Aria the most.

"I need to check on Angel," she said to Hagan. "Give me a shout if you need anything." She left him in the break room and headed down the hallway to the patient room where Angel lay on the bed Jake had inhabited, her hands over her belly, her face twisted. The puppy cuddled in her arms, whining. Aria took her pulse, then found a blood pressure cuff and scope and took her pressure.

"Are they contractions, or just one solid pain?" Aria said, feeling Angel's stomach, reaching back to her residency days in the OB department.

"They come and go," Angel said, and her breath caught, her eyes closing.

"Another one?" Aria asked.

Angel nodded. Grabbed Aria's hand.

Aria timed the contraction. Thirty seconds, then it eased.

Next to them, Yola and Mimi were watching her.

"I was in labor for two days with Yola's mama," Mimi said, her breath thin and wispy.

Aria turned to her, took her pulse. Eighty-five beats a minute—she didn't like it. And Mimi seemed pale, tired. "We should try another nebulizer treatment," she said to Yola. "I'll go back down to the pharmacy to get more."

Angel groaned again. Aria checked her watch. Four minutes. She put her hands on Angel's stomach, feeling the baby. It felt head down, ready to deliver.

"Angel, when are you due?"

"Not for . . . another month."

"Don't hold your breath. Just keep breathing, nice and easy."

"That's easy for you to say. You're not lying in a hospital bed in pain!" Angel's eyes widened at her outburst. "Sorry."

"No, I get it. And I remember very well how it felt to be helpless, in pain, and even unable to breathe." She looked at Mimi. "I was born with a congenital heart defect that kept me in bed for the better part of my first seventeen years of life."

The contraction subsided. Angel took a deep breath. "What happened?"

"I got a new heart, and it changed my life."

"Sometimes I wish I could get a new heart," Angel said.

"Oh?"

"It seems that no matter what I do, I choose the wrong men." She stared at the ceiling. "I keep thinking this is the one, and every time, I get my heart broken. And yet, I keep doing it—choosing a man who will only break my heart."

She ran her hand over her belly. "And now I really did it. But we're going to be okay. We are."

Her eyes glistened as she looked over at Aria. "It's going to be different for her. I'm going to take care of her. My mother abandoned me when I was six, and I grew up in foster homes. So I'm not sure why I think I'll be a good mother for this child, but . . . I don't know. I just can't . . . I can't give her up." She looked over at Aria. "It's the first thing I have that I know belongs to me."

She winced, holding her breath.

"Deep breaths, Angel."

Angel nodded. Breathed.

"I remember when I met Rollo," Mimi said quietly. "He was a surfer in Fort Lauderdale, and he had the most beautiful dark skin. He wore dreadlocks and looked just like Bob Marley. I fell instantly in love, and I just knew he was the one for me. And then he turned stupid."

Aria glanced at her and frowned.

"He decided to surf the maverick waves of Half Moon Bay."

"What are those?" Angel asked, her voice tight.

"They're monster waves in Northern California, just off Pillar Point Harbor," Yola said, shaking her head. "They're known for being up to sixty feet high. And they kill people."

"I was so angry with him," Mimi said, then started to cough.

"Shh. I'll tell the story," Yola said. "Rollo was determined to do it, so he piled Mimi and a couple other friends into his VW bus—"

"It had safari windows and camping gear," Mimi whispered, a sort of ethereal texture to her voice, as if she might be caught in memory.

Yola smiled. "They drove across the entire country and camped out near the beach. Rollo spent a couple weeks watching the other surfers and trying to understand how to surf the waves. See, surfing the big waves is really dangerous. If you wipe out, the breaking waves can push a surfer down for twenty, maybe even fifty feet. The wave spins them around, and they lose their sense of equilibrium, and then, when they're down there, another wave comes in to hit them. There are also currents that can slam them into rocks, or even a coral reef—it's really dangerous."

"No wonder you were angry," Angel said. She took a long breath, her contraction clearly over.

But the rhythm worried Aria. She should probably check her and see if she was dilating.

"She was furious, right, Mimi?"

Mimi nodded.

"But he was determined to do it, and so, finally one day he got a ride out past the breakers and Mimi watched from shore—"

"Worst day of my life," she whispered. "The waves were about twenty-five feet tall. It was cold, and all I could think was that he was going to drown, and I was going to watch it."

Yola wrapped her hand around Mimi's. "But he didn't drown. He caught multiple left-breaking waves and surfed them all day. People came to watch, and that night, he was a celebrity.

"When he came in, one of his buddies asked him why he did it, and he said the famous line . . ."

"Because I can," Mimi said quietly.

"Because he could," Yola said, smiling. "Mimi always said that he scared her, the way he could look at a wave and not let it chill him. He had respect for the ocean, but he knew it too. Like he was born to it."

Born to it.

Like Jake was born to rescue, to face danger, maybe.

And not just Jake. "My sister Kia was like that," Aria said, getting up to find gloves. "She wasn't afraid of anything, and it . . . it scared me. She was always living big and loud. Like her music. And her dreams—she wanted to climb mountains and skydive and . . . she wanted to taste it all. In fact, the last fight we had was about the fact that she was going to take Dad's motorcycle out without his permission."

"I love motorcycles," Angel said.

"Yeah, well, this one killed her. She was driving too fast and she skidded on a wet patch that spun her out. She hit a tree and was declared brain dead."

And that was how to quiet a room. "I'm sorry. I just . . . I understand how it feels to love someone who loves danger, Mimi."

In fact, she hadn't realized how much Jake was like Kia. Or vice versa.

Except Jake was capable. Smart. Not reckless. And he wasn't going to do something foolish and get himself killed.

"I always sort of thought that she would love me enough not to risk her life, but . . ."

"That's how you got your new heart," Mimi said softly.

Aria looked at her. Oh, her conversation with Jake in the storm. "Yeah."

"She was your twin."

"Yes. And she died. And I took her heart. And now I have a debt I'll never pay back."

Really, she should stop talking, because she wasn't sure where that came from. Maybe fatigue. Maybe the fact that Jake was out there, and she'd let him go, and if he didn't come back—

"Really, that's what you think?" Yola said. "That you owe your sister a debt because she gave you her heart?"

"No." She winced. "Okay, yes. I feel like I owe it to her to live a life that is . . ."

"Exemplary."

Aria lifted a shoulder. "At least one that is worth her giving her life." She reached for the separating curtain. "I need to see if Angel is dilating. Okay, Angel?"

The girl nodded and Aria pulled the screen.

She was at three centimeters, so not precariously past the point of no return, but, "I'm going down to the pharmacy to see if I can find some terbutaline. That should at least slow your labor until we can get help." She pulled off the gloves and tossed them in the trash.

Mimi reached out and grabbed Aria's arm as she walked past her. "If we spent our entire lives trying to pay back what we owe, we'd live in a constant state of debt. Always feeling we weren't enough, always scrambling to make ourselves better, make ourselves more." She squeezed her arm. "You are enough, Doc."

Aria stared at her a long moment before she nodded, moved away from her grasp.

The sun had cast itself past the apex of the day, long shadows reaching down the hallway as she headed toward the stairwell.

"You are enough."

She didn't know why those words slunk in under her skin, turned to an itch. But no, she wasn't enough.

How could she be?

Hagan lay on his mattress, curled into a sleeping ball as she walked by the supply room. She glanced at the dark stairwell.

She could probably use a light. And a bag. She found a pillow and pulled the case off. Now, a light.

Jake's backpack. A tiny Maglite dangled from a clip on the side. She retrieved it, spying the shoe polish canister tucked into a pocket. The one that he'd tucked her necklace in just a few weeks ago.

When he'd saved her life.

Now, we're even.

She couldn't believe she'd actually said that.

She would never be even with Jake Silver, for the way he stormed into her world, stripped away all her defenses, and made her see herself as . . .

Well, as more than she ever thought she could be.

Enough, maybe.

Entering the stairwell, she braced herself for more murky cold, the water over her waist now. It should be receding, shouldn't it?

She moved into the darkness of the lobby, half-swimming through the water as she headed toward the pharmacy. The door was still propped open, and she climbed over the chair, then over the counter to the back.

Turning on the flashlight, she skimmed it over the tall shelving, searching for the betamimetics.

Soggy boxes and packages cluttered the water, and she picked up a few, found one that contained budesonide, and tucked it into her pillowcase.

Then she flicked the light over the shelves. There, terbutaline, in bottles. She grabbed a handful and dropped them into the pillowcase.

A splash sounded behind her, and she froze, listening. Flashed her light toward the sound.

When her beam landed on a skinny, nearly skeletal man, his eyes reddened and staring at her, she let out a scream that reverberated through the building.

"Stop!" the man said, coming toward her, his hand out. "Stop screaming!"

He clamped his hands over his ears and she stepped back, slamming against one of the shelves. It wobbled. "What do you want?"

"Make it stop!" he said, his hands still over his ears. He wore a grimy black T-shirt, his hair cut short, a tattoo along the underside of his forearm.

She dug down, searching for her voice. "Make what stop?"

"All of it! All—" He lowered his hands. Stared at her, or through her.

And suddenly, she got it.

He was high. And looking for drugs. Opioids, probably. She flicked off her flashlight and felt along the shelving as she moved away from him.

"Hey! Hey. Don't . . . Where'd you go?"

She moved along the edge of the row, around the corner. Spied the door.

Made a dash for it. Except slogging through the water felt like moving through cement, her body brutally slow—

"Where you goin'?"

She'd barely reached the door when hands clamped on her shoulders, yanking her back. "No—stop!"

Her hands missed the door frame. She tripped.

Hit the water.

And just like that, she was underwater, his hands holding her down. She grabbed his arms, trying to wrench them from her shoulders.

Like claws, they dug into her neck, her collarbone. She kicked, fought, twisted, her air seeping from her.

No! Not like this!

Still the claws pressed her into the darkness, trapping her.

Her chest burned, her vision turning blotchy—

Jake!

Then, just like that, the hands released, and another hand grabbed her and yanked her up.

She hung onto the wrist of her rescuer as she cleared the water, gulping the air as it burned her lungs.

And yes, she expected to see Jake, to see the panic in his blue eyes, to even leap into his arms, and hold on with everything inside her.

Except it wasn't Jake.

Hagan had her by her upper arm, pulling her away from her attacker. He pushed her out into the open of the lobby, turned, and she could hear the smack as he delivered a punch to the young man's face.

She winced as he howled.

"The pillowcase!" she shouted, seeing a flash of it floating in the water.

Hagan fished around in the water, grabbed it, and shoved it at her. Then Hagan shut the door and shoved the chair in front of it, trapping her attacker in the darkness.

In a room full of drugs that could possibly kill him.

She stared at the dark window into the room as Hagan waded past her.

"Don't be stupid," he said to her when she didn't move.

Right.

But as she followed him upstairs, she couldn't help but glance out into the horizon, toward the setting sun.

Please, Jake, come back.

■ ■ ■

Jake could not watch another kid die.

But this could really hurt.

He drew in a breath, calculating the distance between Bailey, the prisoners, and the entrance to the resort. Bailey hadn't yet crossed the threshold—

Jake sprinted for the building. Ham was roaring in his head, telling him he was an idiot, but frankly that's how he survived. By following his impulses.

Okay, often he had to circle back around and fix whatever his impulses wrought, but right now, he had nothing else.

He launched himself at Bailey, took the kid down around the waist, rolled with him behind the door, then bounced to his feet just as a shot pinged off the door frame.

Whoever he was, Jake hoped he couldn't shoot.

He grabbed the kid up. "Run!" Pushing the kid toward the back of the building, he turned.

A man came through the door, gun first.

Jake grabbed the gun with his left hand, right by the trigger guard, and directed the gun away. With the other hand he stripped the thumb of his assailant away from the gunstock, yanking it back.

In a second he had the gun in his hand.

He turned his back to his attacker, threw out a stinging elbow, and connected with the man's nose.

The man roared.

Jake ran.

"Go, go!" he shouted to Bailey as the kid reached the end of the building. Bailey dove through the broken back entrance, over the tree, and out onto the plaza. He took off toward Margaritaville.

Jake emerged behind him, catching up fast.

Shouts, behind him.

"Faster, kid!" He caught up to Bailey and grabbed him by his jacket, pulling him along. Glanced behind him.

Five pursuers with lethal expressions, and one of them bled from his face.

"This way!"

Jake pointed across the marina, toward his little skiff, then shot out ahead of the kid. "Hurry!"

He leaped down the ramp to the dock, over the back of the beached yacht, and onto his skiff.

Turned around.

Good boy—Bailey was scrambling after him.

A shot cracked the air.

"Move it, kid!" Jake grabbed the rope, untying it from the yacht, then scrambled back to the motor and gave it a rip.

Nothing.

Please!

Another shot, and this one pinged off the water beside him.

Bailey landed in the boat.

"Push us off!"

Bailey pushed so hard he nearly unseated Jake, and he gripped the side of the boat with his left hand, pain searing through him. He'd ripped off his bandage, leaving his hand raw and freshly wounded. But he ignored it and ripped the cord again.

The motor sputtered, then caught.

He turned, grabbed Bailey's jacket by the neck, and yanked him down in a horse-collar tackle. "Stay down!"

The brute force had reached the docks, and one of them sent another shot toward the boat, this time hitting the metal skin.

Jake dropped down onto the boat's bottom and opened the throttle, turning them in the murky shallow water, praying he didn't dig the rotor into the sand.

The boat turned, nearly unseating them, and then they were shooting out over the waves, bumping hard into the surf.

More shots, and for the life of him, Jake couldn't figure out why they'd be wasting bullets.

Oh, wait. He'd bloodied one of them.

And now they were trapped on the island together.

Bailey curled on the bottom of the boat, his hands over his head.

Jake glanced behind them, saw the lot standing on the shoreline, yelling.

He turned the boat south, away from the route home.

Just because.

"You okay, kid?"

Bailey looked up at him. Sat up. Stared back along the wreckage of the island.

The sea had trapped debris and flung it back along the shoreline, everything from boats to housing wreckage to palm trees. They skimmed along the shoreline, fighting the waves, the sun casting long, dark fingers into the waves.

"Why didn't you shoot them back?"

Bailey's gaze was on the gun from the Bahama Mama, now shoved into Jake's belt.

"Why would I? I don't want to kill anyone."

Bailey looked at him. "You sound like my dad. He says he will never draw on anyone unless he intends to use his weapon. But he hopes he never has to."

"You said your dad is a cop?"

"Yeah. He works for the Key West Police."

Jake remembered the cop on the bridge, on his way into town. Hopefully Bailey's dad hadn't been caught on the bridge when the storm hit. Jake turned his face into the wind and said nothing.

"I saw you disarm him."

"You were supposed to be running."

"That was pretty cool."

Jake's mouth tightened.

"What, are you special forces or something?"

"Nope. Just a guy."

Bailey sat in silence, shivering.

Okay, fine. "I was a SEAL."

"I knew it. Have you ever shot someone?"

The kid had big, eager eyes. A sense of innocence about him that felt rare.

"Yep."

Jake angled the skiff toward the east, the bridge he'd crossed on his way to the hospital. The sea had crested it, and now just the cement edges showed. He slowed, eased them over it.

"Who was it?" Bailey asked.

"I was a sniper, so . . . more than one."

He didn't know why admitting that seemed to sear him. Like Mimi said—it was war.

"Oh," Bailey said. Then he swallowed and turned away from him.

Yeah, Jake might have had the same reaction.

He motored them past the prison, and Bailey's attention dragged past it, his head turning.

"Those men were escaped prisoners, weren't they?"

He nodded.

"Which means there are more of them. Probably roaming the whole island."

Yes. But his words sank into Jake for the first time.

More of them.

Wearing black pants and a gray shirt.

"Hang on, kid," he said and turned the throttle as high as it could go.

They practically bounced into the lot of the hospital, and he slowed just barely enough to motor into the lobby.

He leaped out of the boat and sloshed toward the stairs.

"Hey, wait for me!"

Jake hit the stairwell running. Banged out onto the second floor. "Aria!"

He stalked down the hallway, his heart in his throat. "Aria!"

The staff room was empty and the sight of that only notched up his pulse. What if Hagan had taken her captive or hurt her or—

He skidded into the patient room at the end of the hall and caught his breath. Aria stood beside Angel's bedside, administering a shot. Next to her, in the other bed, Yola held a nebulizer over Mimi's mouth and nose.

Hagan leaned against the counter, watching the proceedings like he might be supervising. Or protecting.

And Jake simply lost it. "You!" He advanced on Hagan and jerked him around, searching for the KWDC letters on the back of the shirt.

Nothing.

Because the shirt was on inside out. He yanked it up.

"Hey!" Hagan wrenched it out of his grip. "What are you doing?"

"I wanna see your shirt. Or maybe I don't have to. You're one of them, aren't you?"

Hagan stared at him, frowning, jerking back. "Get away from me."

"Show me your shirt, Hagan."

"What's with my shirt—"

"You're an escapee from the detention center down the road—"

"What?" Aria said. "Jake!"

"Stay out of this, Aria." He slid the Glock from his waist. Pressed it up into Hagan's neck.

"Jake!"

"Show. Me. Your. Shirt."

Silence, as even Mimi gasped.

"Don't, Jake," Yola said. "He saved Aria. He's a good guy."

Hagan was meeting his eyes, a darkness in them that told Jake otherwise, so he tightened his jaw, not moving.

"Fine," Hagan snapped and reached up, pulling the shirt over his head. He whipped it off, letting it dangle over his splint. "Gary's Plumbing."

Jake stared at the lettering, simple and white, on the back of the shirt. "Who is Gary?"

"My brother."

"Why is your shirt on inside out?"

"Because I was in a *hurricane*! And I had to get to cover, so I grabbed any shirt I had and put it on. Seriously?"

"Put the gun away, Jake." Aria's voice, soft beside him. She put her hand on his arm.

He stared at the weapon. Slipped it back into his belt, turned, and walked from the room, shaking.

Oh. What had he . . .

"Are you okay, mister?"

He looked over, and Bailey stood there in the middle of the hallway, soggy, wide-eyed, white-faced. Jake closed his eyes and looked away.

"Who are you?" Aria's voice. She must have followed him into the hallway.

"I'm Bailey. He . . . he rescued me."

"Are you okay, Bailey?"

He must have nodded. "But we were shot at."

Oh, great. Thanks, kid.

Aria drew in a shaky breath. "By whom?"

"Convicts," Jake snapped. "Escaped convicts from the Key West Detention Center who are armed and roaming the island."

"Bailey, go inside the room," Aria said, meeting Jake's gaze. "I need to talk to Jake."

"He's a SEAL," Bailey said. "It was really cool—he disarmed the guy with only one hand!"

"I definitely used two hands," Jake said quietly.

"Yes, Jake is cool," Aria said evenly, her gaze still not leaving Jake's. "Bailey, can you go check on my patients for me?" She looked over at him. "And then, there's some juice boxes and chips in the room. Help yourself."

"Yes, ma'am."

Jake watched him go, then turned. "What did Yola mean—he *saved* you?"

She pursed her lips, shook her head.

"Tell me."

"I went down to get medicine from the pharmacy, and there was a guy there, trying to score drugs, I think. He was high and he attacked me."

Everything stripped out of Jake. "What?"

"He didn't know what he was doing, Jake. He's sick and right now he's trapped in a room that could probably kill him if he finds the right opiates and takes them."

"Get back to the *attack* part. What did he do?"

She ran her hands over her arms. Looked away. "He tried to drown me."

The words punched him, landing in the center of his chest. "Are you . . . are you okay?"

"Mmmhmm." She turned back to face him. "But I wouldn't have been if Hagan hadn't shown up. He hit the guy and pulled me out of the water, and then locked him in the room."

"So the guy is there now?"

She nodded.

Jake ran his hand over his mouth. Turned away.

"Jake—"

"I'll get him." He turned back to her. "You. Stay here."

She gave him a look, but he responded with a little shake of his head, turned, and took off down the hallway.

Shadows engulfed the lobby as he entered, nearly swimming through the water toward the pharmacy. He should have brought his flashlight but managed to find the door and the chair with which Hagan had barred it. He moved it to the side and wrenched open the door.

"Anyone in here?"

His eyes were adjusting to the dim light, but he saw no one.

A groan lifted from somewhere in the bowels of the room, behind the shelves. He worked his way toward it. "I'm here to help. Don't freak out."

Nothing.

He rounded the last shelf and found a long countertop under a couple inches of water. A huddled figure sat on top, his knees drawn up, his head on his knees. As Jake drew closer, he saw that the man trembled. He was too draped in shadow for Jake to place his age, but he seemed to be crying.

"Dude, are you okay?"

A whimper.

"C'mon. Let's get you outta here."

He reached out to help him, but the man jerked back, lifted his head. "Don't touch me."

Jake held up his hands. "Okay. Just . . . let's go upstairs. We have a bed for you, some grub. Let us help you."

Shadows covered his face, but Jake felt the man's eyes on him, as if trying to get a fix on his words. Then, he eased out of his position and let himself slide to the floor.

Jake walked behind him as the man staggered out of the room into the dim light of the lobby.

He nearly went down, twice, and the second time, Jake grabbed his arm, pulled him back up.

The man didn't recoil but let Jake help as they walked to the stairwell.

The light on his face as they climbed up to the second floor suggested he might be in his midtwenties. He wore a scraggly growth of beard, his dark hair wet and long, tucked behind his ears, and the bones in his body suggested he hadn't eaten well for some time.

He crumpled at the top of the first landing, hanging on to the rail.

Jake reached down and scooped him up, fireman style, and carried him the rest of the way, emerging onto the second floor.

Aria was waiting by the door. Now, she leaned up off the wall. "Is he okay?"

"I don't know. Let's get him into a room."

Aria started down the hallway.

"A different room, Aria."

She looked back, nodded, and went into the room next to the end. The windows were broken and the bed was wet but unoccupied. Jake set him on the mattress. The kid flopped back, his eyes rolling up.

"He might have overdosed," she said, pressing her fingers to his carotid artery. "His heartbeat is steady, albeit fast."

"Probably just needs to sleep it off." Jake had picked up a sheet, stuck the edge into his mouth, and ripped off a long strip.

"What are you doing?"

He brought the strip to the bed, grabbed the man's wrist, and tied it to the bed rail. "What do you think?"

"Do you think that's necessary?"

He ripped another strip, then looked at her. "He attacked you."

Her mouth tightened into a thin line, but she took the proffered strip from him and tied the man's other hand. "I don't like this."

"I'm not taking any chances." He blew out a shaky breath and stared at the man, his body still trembling. A blanket lay wadded at the end of the bed and he pulled it up over the man.

The young man started to cry.

Oh, fabulous.

"You're okay," Aria said quietly. "You're safe now."

Maybe. But he had a long way to go to okay.

Jake turned and stalked down the hall.

"Jake!"

He didn't stop.

"Jake, stop. Where are you going?"

"Just leave me, Aria."

But no. Of course she was following him. He didn't slow, however, just went for the door at the end of the hallway, not sure why, but he needed air.

Fresh, free air.

He took the stairs to the third level, then climbed the ladder to the roof.

Aria said nothing, but her footsteps trailed him.

Perfect. Well, if she wanted to join him on the roof, he couldn't stop her. He pushed open the door and climbed up, letting the warm breeze sift through him, ease the thundering of his heart.

To the west, the sun was dropping into the horizon, leaving a purple smudge on the clouds, a simmering fire of orange and red. If he ignored the destruction on the island, the beauty could steal his breath.

He could believe he was in paradise.

But that was his MO, really. Ignore the destruction, keep looking ahead.

Pretend everything was okay.

When, frankly, he was as stupidly broken as the kid in the bed.

Jake leaned over and caught his knees.

"Jake, what happened back there?" Aria had climbed out onto the roof, now stood beside him.

She touched his back and he just couldn't . . . He stepped away from her.

"Okay. So—"

"You were right, Aria. I'm . . . I'm a mess."

"What?"

"And probably you're only going to end up hurt around me."

"Jake—"

"No, you don't get it. I . . . I'm that angry twentysomething guy in there. You just can't see it."

"What?"

He stood up and rounded on her. "I got in a tussle with a group of escapees, all armed, and now, they're probably headed our direction."

She frowned.

"I hurt one of them."

"Oh."

"But see, that's what I do. I act first and pick up the pieces later." He reached for the gun on his belt, drew it out, and set it on a nearby mechanical box. "Like in there. I was so sure Hagan was . . ."

He held up his hands, backed away. "See, yes, you should stay away from me. Because despite the hope that I've changed, I'm still the guy who shoots first and sorts it out later."

She frowned. "What are you talking about?"

He shook his head.

"Wait, Jake. Is this about the kid you shot in Afghanistan? The one you told me about in Alaska? He was a suicide bomber, right?"

"I thought he was wired up. And I had to choose. The kid or my team."

"You didn't have a choice."

"Didn't I? Turns out it was a cell phone. He might have been trying to take a picture."

"You didn't know that."

"Okay, maybe not at the moment, but afterward, I just keep moving it around in my head, looking at it from every angle, and . . . I can't escape the fact that maybe I should have waited."

She considered him.

"And it's always with me. All of it. My sister, and every single life I took, including the one two weeks ago, in Alaska."

"The terrorist at the hotel?"

"Yeah."

"You didn't have a choice. He was wearing a suicide vest."

"So I shot him. And yeah, I probably didn't have a choice, but it's still . . . I killed someone. And I know it's not supposed to bother me. I'm just doing my job, but . . ." He ran a hand behind his neck and turned away from her. "It sticks around, you know? When I'm sleeping, it finds me." The wailing. In his bones.

In his soul.

Overhead the seagulls cried, the waves lashed the shoreline as the sun continued to fall.

"After I shot that kid in Afghanistan, I . . . I didn't handle it well. I started drinking and fighting. I had anger with nowhere to put it. One night I got so drunk I ended up in a hospital. My team leader reported me. They shipped me home and put me in a psychiatric ward to detox. I went through treatment for six months. At the end, I was supposed to pass a psych evaluation to stay active, but I refused to take it, so they discharged me. Medical discharge. Unfit for duty."

Unfit to be a sailor. A SEAL. A hero.

"See, I was that kid, Aria." He found her eyes. "I'm still that kid, sometimes, just trying to keep it together."

"Except you mask it with all these heroics. Saving people. Jokes. Charm."

"Oh no, the charm is real." He didn't know why he said that, and winced. "See?"

"What I see is a man with a broken heart, trying to figure out how to live with it."

"Or maybe I'm just really a bad person. Maybe I'm the villain of the story, pretending to be the hero." And that felt way too real, too raw, so he turned away from her. "I shouldn't have freaked out with Hagan. But that's me . . . act first, fix later. And as much as I try and keep a lid on that, you're probably right to stay away from me, Aria. Because in the end, you could get hurt around me, no matter how much I try and protect you."

"Probably."

He turned, frowned.

She just stood there, the sun behind her, turning her brown hair to layers of amber and gold, her brown eyes holding his with so much fierceness, he couldn't look away.

"Because you're right. You *do* go looking for trouble. But not because you're a mess, like that kid down there. It's because it's in your DNA to find trouble and fix it. That makes you the good guy, not the villain. The difference between you and the kid downstairs is that you might know your weaknesses but you don't let them take over. You are dealing with them."

He stared at her, the words embedding, finding his bones. The wind teased her hair, her gaze unmoving. She had the most incredible eyes, layers of brown embedded with gold.

His voice dropped. "What I don't know how to deal with is the fact that I . . . I care about you, Aria. I came down here thinking I could convince you to give us a chance, and now I'm just freaking out that something is going to happen to you, or I'm going to do something stupid and I won't be able to fix it. And then you'll get hurt and—"

"Sheesh, Jake. Have you met me? I'm a tough girl, with a tough heart."

He drew in a breath. "Or trying to be."

Her mouth tweaked up on one side. "Yeah, that."

"I really want to kiss you right now," he said, his voice a near growl. "But I don't want to do something we're not going to continue when we get home."

"Who says we're not going to continue when we get home?" She stepped up to him, put her hand on his chest. "Wasn't that your fabulous idea—to start having conversations that don't include trauma?"

Her touch bled heat through his chest. He put his hand over hers, needing it there.

"Kiss me, Jake Silver."

Oh, Aria. He put his arm around her and pulled her to himself, searching her eyes.

Then his closed and he kissed her.

She tasted like home, sweet and familiar, a place to land, to stay.

She wrapped her hand around his neck, drawing him close, deepening her kiss, keeping it slow, sinking into him.

As if they belonged together.

Jake and Aria, kissing under the sunset, just like he'd planned.

No, hoped.

Maybe he didn't make a mess of everything. Or maybe Aria just knew how to fix it.

He just knew, as the sun set behind her, that he'd stopped trembling.

She finally moved away, her hands on his chest, smiling up at him. He drew her to himself, wrapping his arms around her, soaking in the warmth of her.

Over her shoulder, winking in the last glint of the sun, he spotted the seaplane from before, still riding the waves.

He put her away from him. "I think I know how to get us off this island."

She touched his face. "Not before I rebandage your hand, tough guy."

"Aye, aye, Doc."

He followed her back down the ladder, down the stairs, and back to the second floor.

The puppy came scrambling down the hallway, barking, high yips of excitement, clearly fully recovered. Jake caught it up and it wriggled in his arms, licking his face.

"Okay, okay, I'm glad to see you too!"

"You found him, Jake! You found him!" Bailey ran down the hall, all smiles.

"Found who?" Jake put the puppy down.

Bailey knelt on the floor, clapping his hands. "C'mere, Ringo. Here, buddy."

Aria touched his arm. "What did you say about not being a hero?" She winked at him.

Okay, maybe.

CHAPTER 12

IT FELT LIKE CHURCH CAMP. Only without the campfire.

Instead, the group huddled in the staff room around a dinner of Spam, sardines, cold corn, and a few protein bars for dessert.

Angel's contractions had stopped, and she sat in a recliner chair, her hands over her belly, rocking.

Yola was opening the packages of protein bars and cutting them into sections. Even Mimi was better and off her oxygen after her nebulizer treatment.

Hagan stood away, his gaze on Jake, but Aria had seen Jake apologize. Hagan grunted, no grace in his expression. Maybe because although Jake had tucked his weapon back into his belt when he left the rooftop, he still wore it.

It shook her, the way he transformed into spec ops right before her eyes. SEAL Jake was lethal, fierce, and willing to do whatever it took to protect her.

"Maybe I'm just really a bad person. Maybe I'm the villain of the story, pretending to be the hero."

No, he was the real deal. He now sat on the floor, leaning against the wall with his legs crossed at the ankles, and held Ringo in his strong arms, rubbing the puppy's tummy. Bailey sat beside him, glancing over at the former SEAL with what looked like hero worship.

Why not? The guy rescued puppies and children, protected the weak, and even let her inside his secrets.

And Jake Silver knew how to kiss. He tasted of adventure, but something solid and safe about him made her yearn to stay right there, in his arms.

Yes, he was very, very dangerous.

Yola passed her a slice of Spam and a protein bar. "Help yourself to sardines and corn," she said. She gave the same speech and portion to Angel, then Hagan, Mimi, and finally Jake and Bailey.

Jake handed Bailey the puppy, then got off the floor and went over to sit in the chair by the bed of the kid he'd found downstairs.

No, not a kid. A former soldier, because Jake had found a pair of dog tags around his neck that identified him as Specialist Parker, twenty-four years old.

Parker lay asleep on the bed, his trembling stopped.

"Don't you think we can untie him now?" Aria said, getting up to stand by the window. She'd made Jake wheel Parker into their common room, wanting to keep an eye on him.

"Not until he wakes up and I can see how he is."

"He's trouble is what he is," Hagan said. "Keep him tied up."

Aria looked at Hagan. He'd eaten his Spam in two bites. "He was high and didn't know what he was doing."

Hagan shook his head, looked away.

Something about him sent a chill under her skin, but what could she say? He'd saved her life.

And besides, Jake was here now.

"I think we should pray," Mimi said, and everyone looked at her. She sat in the other recliner chair, her legs crossed, the chair dwarfing her petite body. "Really. We survived a Cat 5 hurricane. And we're eating a meal to celebrate."

It did feel like a celebration of sorts. *"Who says we're not going to continue when we get home?"* She couldn't believe she said that to Jake.

Meant it.

She wanted to know Jake without the trauma, under the sunlight and blue skies.

"Okay," Jake said to Mimi's suggestion. He closed his eyes.

Yes, most definitely church camp.

"Lord, your Word says that when we pass through the waters, you will be with us. That they will not sweep over us. And it's true. You were with us in the storm. And you're with us now, on the shore, and we thank you for saving us. You are good. And you are sovereign. And we trust you. Thank you for the Spam."

"Amen," Jake said.

Good. Sovereign. The words latched on.

"Did you know Spam was served to Allied troops in World War Two?" Jake said, picking up his piece of Spam. "It's packed with protein and doesn't need refrigeration." He took a bite. "Mmm. And there is a Spam museum in Minnesota." He looked at Aria. "I'll take you there sometime."

She grinned. Yeah, he would.

"It tastes like a hot dog," Yola said.

"Oh, Yo, it's a thousand times better than a hot dog," Jake said.

Yola grinned.

Oh yes, the man had charm.

Parker stirred, groaned. Aria had started an IV drip of fluids. A sweat broke out over his forehead.

Jake stood up and came over to him. "Hey there, Specialist Parker. You're okay."

The man's eyes flickered open and his gaze darted from Jake to the others, then back to Jake. "What—" He yanked at his bonds, his expression clouding. "Let me go!"

"Shh, buddy. Take a breath there." Jake put his hand on his chest. "We don't want you to hurt yourself." He left out "or anybody else." The kid probably wouldn't remember trying to kill Aria.

"You're going to be okay. We just need you to ride this high down, all the way to the ground floor."

"He's going to be in pain if he's going into withdrawal," Angel said quietly. Aria didn't want to ask how she knew this.

"I could try and find some anti-nausea medicines," Aria said.

"You're not going back down to that pharmacy," Jake said over his shoulder. "We don't know how high the water is now."

Or, how infected with germs and the diseases of dead animals.

Jake turned back to Parker. "You'll just have to ride it out, pal. But we'll be right here with you. We're not leaving. I'm not going to lie—it's gonna be miserable. And it'll hurt. But when you're through it, you'll be able to start over. You'll be free."

Free.

For some reason, her hand went to her necklace—a reflex, maybe, of her memory of waking up after surgery, her entire body, her heart and soul in agony.

But on the pathway to freedom.

"I can't do it," Parker said. "I can't." He pulled at his bonds.

"You can, buddy. Just one breath at a time." Jake eased back. "Listen. You can do anything one breath at a time. When I was going through hell week in BUD/S, my entire body hurt. I'd had about four hours of sleep in the very distant past and I was fighting sheer exhaustion. But I was on a swim, and I knew if I gave up, I was going to die. My buddy North was with me—he was my swim buddy, and he was shouting at me to keep moving. And the only thing going through my mind was . . . this could be it. I wasn't going to quit, but I might die trying.

"And then I heard North say, 'Just one more breath. Just one more breath,' and I thought, if I could focus on that, just the next breath, maybe I could stop looking at the distance to the shore. So I did. Just one breath, a couple strokes, another breath, two more strokes, another breath. I didn't look back. I didn't look forward. I depended on North to keep me going the right direction and just kept breathing."

"And you got to shore?" Bailey asked. Aria glanced at him. Oh boy, Jake should probably start signing autographs.

"Yep." He looked at Mimi. "'When you pass through the waters, I will be with you.' That's from Isaiah 43:2. I memorized it when I left for BUD/S. I'd forgotten that. Thank you."

He turned back to Parker. "I guess what I'm saying is that you don't need to see the shore. Just take one breath at a time, and you'll get there."

One breath at a time. Like one heartbeat at a time.

Parker was whimpering.

"I'm not giving up on you, and you can't either. Set your mind to it. Do it."

Parker met his eyes. "I can."

"Atta boy, soldier."

The wind tousled the curtains around the broken window. The breeze carried the humidity of the island, even at night. Aria turned, staring into the night, the vastness of the ocean, the moon carving a finger of light across the waves, a trail to the horizon.

Yola came over to stand beside her. "You know what I love about the ocean? It's the unknown in the darkness. You know it's out there, but you can't see it. You can hear it, smell it, taste the salt in the air, feel it on your toes. Vast. Beautiful. Mysterious. But dark."

She wrapped her arms around herself, cut her voice low. "Don't tell Mimi, but I'm not going back to Queens. Even before the storm, I had decided to stay. I don't know why—just a feeling, I guess, that God has something more for me here. I sense him calling me to something big, something life changing, and I'm just supposed to stand on the shore, staring out at the sea to wait for it."

Aria stood beside her, staring out into the vastness, the stars winking down at them. She hadn't thought about just . . . well, standing on the shore, waiting. She always had to have a plan.

"I'd like to get the radio going," Jake said. "Yo, can you sit with my man here?"

Yola turned. "Aye, aye, boss."

Oh, for cryin' in the sink. Aria rolled her eyes, but really, who wasn't flirting with Jake?

Hagan, maybe. He eyed Jake as he left in search of batteries.

"Bailey, how about I make you a bed? Let's go find you a mattress." Aria headed out the door and Bailey followed her, carrying Ringo.

She knew the hallway so well, she didn't need lights to step over the debris, find her way to an empty room. Finding a mattress, she grabbed one of the blankets she'd gathered and a pillow and brought them back to the staff room.

"He's pretty cool, isn't he?" Bailey said as he followed her.

She didn't need an identifier. "Yeah, he is."

"Do you think . . . ?" Bailey held Ringo close. The animal squirmed for a moment, then settled down in his arms. "Do you think he can find my dad?" The question emerged small, almost in hesitation.

Oh. Aria didn't want to stir up a hope that might only break his heart. But, "If anyone can, it's Jake."

She entered the staff room and put his mattress down. Jake had vacated the room. Bailey sat on the bed. "Maybe tomorrow we can go looking for him," he said now, about his father.

Tomorrow she hoped to be heading home. Because Jake had outlined his plan for her after he retrieved the pack of food, as he was refueling the generators on the roof.

"I'm going to drive out to that plane and see if I can get the radio working," he'd said. "I could spend hours trying to find a yacht with a working radio, but . . . my guess is that that plane's communication system might still be intact."

He had capped off the fuel. Stood up and stared at the stars.

"I know," she said. "Reminds me of Alaska." A thousand stars arched overhead, tiny eyes watching them. She'd never felt so small. Or so aware that even so, she wasn't forgotten.

"Yeah. Same beautiful view."

She glanced at him. He was staring at her.

Oh.

But what if Mimi was right? God showed up in the storms. And saved—not from the disaster, but *through* it, even when she couldn't see the shore.

One breath. One heartbeat at a time.

So, now she tucked the blanket around Bailey. "Yes, maybe tomorrow, Jake can find your dad. Try and get some sleep. You're safe."

She found Jake at the darkened nurses' desk, the transistor humming. He held it to his ear. "Where did you find batteries?"

"I stole them from a television remote control," he said. His voice had softened. "I found a VHF maritime channel."

"Great. Uh, so . . . did you hear anything about the coast guard? Maybe a rescue mission to the Keys?"

He wore a strange expression. Drew in a breath.

"Jake, what's going on?"

"I don't think there's a rescue mission on the horizon."

She folded her arms, leaning a hip against the side of the desk. "Seriously? Why not?"

He put the transistor on the desk, turning down the volume. "On account of the tropical storm that is gathering offshore."

She stared at him. "You've got to be kidding me."

He shook his head, then reached out and held her hand.

"Oh my . . . is it headed this way?"

"It sounds like it. And from the sound of it, the coast guard doesn't think they have a window to search for survivors."

She looked around. "We can't take another hit, Jake—"

He found his feet. Pulled her against himself. "I know."

"Angel is going to go into labor, and Mimi needs more help than I can give her, and—"

"I know." He put her away from him, met her eyes. "Tomorrow, first thing, I'm going out to that seaplane. And I'm getting us off this island."

■ ■ ■

This was the last time he booked a seat in coach.

Ham checked his ticket and confirmed, yes, he was stuck in the middle of a family with two kids—the father and son on one side, the mother and a very blonde, chubby-faced little girl on the other. Both parents looked at him apologetically as the woman climbed out, grabbing up her toddler. "We need aisle seats in case we need to get out," she said. "The kids are prone to airsickness."

Ham forced a smile.

He'd been on forty-mile marches easier than this. But he stowed his carry-on and climbed into the middle, shoving his backpack into the minuscule space under the seat in front of him. His knees touched the seat in front of him, his shoulders overlapping into the side seats, and he closed his eyes, trying not to rue every second of this stupid trip.

He should have said no. Not to helping Senator White's friends, but to the impulse that told him to dig up information on Signe's death.

He'd already closed the door on losing her ten years ago. He should have simply accepted it and moved on.

Figured out a way to be a father to a daughter he didn't know.

But Ham never did well with loose ends. He didn't leave men behind, questions unanswered, and most of all, people he cared about in the lurch.

Especially if he thought they might be in trouble.

He might never get out of his head the image of the corpse of the woman he'd given his heart to—forever and only, amen—lying on a stainless-steel table in a morgue in Italy. He couldn't be entirely sure it was Signe. The remains were brutally decayed, her deformed and bloated face and what remained of her body covered in a sheet. He searched for identifying marks—she had that scar on her upper arm from when she scraped herself on a nail in their tree fort—and found what looked like a long, pale mark exactly where he remembered it. And then there was her hair, bleached nearly white, but once long and beautiful.

She was the size and weight of Signe. Had her long legs, beautiful still in his mind. And her head shape seemed the same, a heart, with a strong, stubborn jaw.

He'd walked out of the building into the sunshine, gulping air, sinking down onto the cement steps, trying to get his heart to start beating.

"That's the closest we're going to get to a positive identification," Salvatore said when he followed him out. "Do you want to sign off on it?"

He didn't, but he obliged anyway. Because he was, after all, her husband.

Then he packed his bags and headed to the nearest airport. He hopped a flight to Rome, waited eight hours on standby, and found a seat on a KLM flight to JFK.

Next to him, the little girl was kicking the seat in front of her.

"Maddy, stop." The woman wore her dishwater-blonde hair in a messy ponytail. She looked over at Ham. "I'm really sorry. We were in Italy for my brother's wedding, and it's been a long trip. She'll go to sleep after we take off."

"No problem, ma'am," he said and pulled his hat down, folding his arms across his body. It was better than a C-130, probably.

Or not, because an hour and thirty minutes into the flight, Maddy was still squirming, whining about her ears feeling yucky, and on the other side, the little boy was playing Nintendo, his tongue caught in his teeth, rambunctious as he waged some sort of war on the machine.

So much for sleep.

The service came through the cabin, and he got a Diet Coke and some peanuts, not even denting his hunger.

Maddy settled down, her mother setting her up with a movie—a Disney offering with waves and ocean, and Maddy started to sing along.

"It's *Moana*. She's a fanatic."

"I get it. I like the ocean too," Ham said.

"Nolan and I used to travel, but after the kids arrived, well . . . this is our first big trip in five years." She glanced at Maddy. "And probably our last for a while. Having kids changes everything."

He hadn't thought about that. Aggie would need someone to stay at home with her, if he needed to travel.

No, she would need her father to stay home with her.

So much for his global SAR team.

"My name is Serena. That's my husband, Nolan." She nodded toward him. Nolan was plugged into a movie, his charge now leaning against him, the Nintendo dropped into his lap, the little guy asleep.

"Looks like Dakota has had it," Serena said, laughing.

"I'm Ham," he said. "And I feel a little like Dakota, except I can never sleep on planes."

"Yeah, me either." She handed her empty glass to the flight attendant and reached for Ham's.

"I'll keep it, for the ice," he said.

She reached for Maddy's, but the little girl spotted her action and leaped for her half-finished drink.

It splashed over Serena, catching even Ham.

"Oh! Maddy!" Serena jumped back in the seat, her clothing saturated. The flight attendant handed her napkins, passed some to Ham.

Ham wiped off his arm, his pant leg, then dabbed up the moisture on Maddy's seat.

"I'm so sorry. Are you okay?"

"A little sticky, but I'll live," he said and offered a smile.

"Maddy, sit down."

The little girl had started to cry, and Serena put her arm around her. "It's okay, honey." She looked at Ham. "Do you have kids?"

He debated a moment, and then, "Yeah. A daughter. She's ten."

"Oh, I can't wait until my kids are old enough to entertain themselves."

He offered a half smile.

"Any advice?"

"Oh, uh . . . no. I'm . . . I'm not—"

And Maddy picked right then to throw up. Peanuts, soda, and

everything else she'd consumed for the past three hours simply burped out of her, onto the seat, onto the floor, and even on Ham.

"Oh—oh!" Serena unbuckled, jumping out of her seat.

Ham had grabbed the barf bag in his seat and was holding it out under Maddy's chin. "C'mon, kid, aim for the bag."

Maddy let go another round. The odor rose from the seats and Ham gritted his teeth.

"Oh, wow, I'm so sorry—"

On the other side of him, Nolan had also gotten up.

"Get some wet paper towels," Ham said to the man, who took off down the aisle, leaving a sleeping Dakota curled on the seats.

Maddy had erupted in a howl, her face and shirt plastered. The flight attendant must have seen the trouble because she arrived with a wet towel and a garbage bag.

Ham didn't move. Vomit dripped from his arm, the smell turning his gut. Serena grabbed up Maddy and carried her away down to the bathroom.

Then it was just him, and the flight attendant, and a sleeping Dakota.

Another flight attendant appeared with another wet towel, along with Nolan, who offered a handful of wet paper towels. Ham wiped his arm, threw the bag away, and eased out of the seats so the attendants could clean them up.

"Sorry, man," Nolan said.

Ham opened the overhead bin and dragged out his carry-on bag. "It's okay. These things happen."

But Nolan looked stricken as Ham headed for the bathroom.

He cleaned up, pulled off his T-shirt, washed it, then changed into a clean shirt and headed back toward his seat.

The seats had been cleaned, but the family was rearranged, with Dakota and Maddy sleeping in the center, the armrests up.

Um . . .

A flight attendant came up to him. She carried his backpack. "This way, sir. We found a place for you in first class."

Oh. Well.

He looked down at Serena. "You okay?"

She had cleaned up too, changed her shirt, but the smell still emanated from her. She made a face. "So sorry."

"It's okay."

"I guess you have a lot more practice than I do. You knew exactly what to do."

Huh.

"You do what you have to do, right?" he said. "Take care."

She nodded, but his words lingered.

It didn't really matter if Aggie was his or not.

Signe had given her over to him, into his care.

I'm sorry I couldn't find you. But I got her, Sig. I have our daughter. She's safe.

He settled into first class next to a woman who wore an eye mask, earphones, and a blanket.

He pushed his seat back and somehow fell into a deep, dreamless slumber.

The flight attendant had to wake him to land, and he was still groggy as he disembarked and stood in the passport control line.

His phone began to light up, vibrating as texts and voice mails rolled in.

He handed his passport to the agent and sneaked a look at his texting app.

A dozen or so texts from Orion, another handful from North.

Nothing from Jake, and that had Ham worried. He cleared passport control, then customs, and walked out into the terminal.

Dialed North.

"Have you heard from him?" North's voice, groggy—it was nearing midnight.

"Who?"

"Jake, man. Didn't you hear about the hurricane?"

Ham walked into a gate area and glanced at a nearby television. CNN. It showed pictures of a destroyed beach, and he wandered over.

"What hurricane?"

"Hurricane Lucy. It went through the Keys."

And no, he wasn't making the connection. "So?"

"Jake was in the Keys. With Aria."

Ham simply stood there, trying to figure out his words. "I don't . . . What do you mean? Jake's in Minneapolis taking care of Aggie—"

"No. Aggie is with the Silvers. Jake is in Florida. And we haven't been able to get ahold of him for three days."

"Jake was in a *hurricane*?"

"Yeah. Didn't you get any of my texts?"

Ham curled his hand around his neck. "And Aggie isn't with him?"

"No—she's with Ellie, she's fine, man. But Jake is missing. Along with Aria."

And the picture on the television panned over a recap of a Cat 5 storm that had washed over the island. A drone showed brutal damage, houses flattened or swept off their foundation, dead animals, debris littering the desolated island.

"Where are you?"

"Where do you think? Orion and I are in Miami. We're trying to charter a boat, but they're hard to come by. Read your texts."

"I just got off a plane. Let me make some calls. I'm on my way."

He hung up. Stared at the flight board.

At least this, he knew how to do.

Hang in there, Jake. We'll find you.

■ ■ ■

Blue skies overhead, with the slightest tufting of dark clouds on the eastern horizon. A breeze lifted mist into the air as Jake's boat skimmed through the waves. The sun burned his neck as he drove into the fingers of sunlight.

Today they would go home.

Jake had awoken at first light. If he could call what he'd done sleeping. Mostly, he'd kept one eye on Hagan, who had snored his way through the night.

He'd also risen numerous times to check on Parker. And Aria, who spent the night in the recliner by Parker's bed.

"I'm a tough girl, with a tough heart."

Yes, she was. Still, it left a pit in Jake's gut to leave Hagan behind. He didn't trust the guy, but maybe Jake was simply raw, tired, and edgy.

Especially with the weather report of another storm on the horizon. He'd heard of storms running the same route twice, but Aria was right.

They needed to get out of town before it hit.

Which meant his one focus was getting help, then getting back to the hospital.

Jake motored along the shore, his gaze on the plane. It seemed caught on something, maybe a coral reef, or a rocky shoreline, past a grouping of buildings.

As he drew closer, he spotted a three-story white building with what looked like the outline of a diver painted on the outside. About a foot of water surrounded the buildings.

Right. He'd forgotten that the Army Special Forces Underwater

Operations School was located in Key West. The place looked abandoned, from the housing to the pool area. A metal strip had been torn from the roof of the fifty-foot free-ascent tower, used for simulating ascents out of submarines or dives down to sub level. Boats and scooters lay scattered like toys on the grounds.

As he motored closer, he saw that the float plane—a white, red-striped Piper Super Cub—had gotten hung up on a jutting of the rocky shoreline of the key. The wings had been damaged with gaping tears in the fabric, along with the floats, one of them wedged onto a rock. It would sink if it got out to sea.

Jake tied his skiff to the plane and climbed out onto one of the floats. He worked his way to the door.

Inside, however, the cockpit looked intact, despite one broken window.

He opened the door and leaned into the cockpit. A black Garmin SL30 Nav/Comm transceiver was mounted on one of the overhead cross braces.

And—jackpot—it was powered by a 35-watt DC battery.

Which, once he switched it on, worked.

He toggled the intercom. "Mayday, mayday, mayday, this is . . ." He didn't know how to label himself, so, "Chief Petty Officer Jake Silver, requesting assistance at the Key West hospital."

He listened, and when he heard nothing, he changed frequencies and tried again.

And again.

On the eighth try, he got a response. The voice cut in and out but he made out a sketchy, "Received . . . nature of your emergency . . ."

He was watching the horizon, the boil of clouds eating away at the blue sky. The ocean had started to chop. "We have eight souls trapped at the Key West medical center. We need transportation immediately."

Static.

"Come in, base."

He thought he heard a voice, a snatch of sound, but couldn't get them back.

The plane began to rock in the waves.

He climbed into the cockpit, repeating his mayday through the channels. Seven hundred and sixty channels. He picked up chatter on a half dozen, giving his location and nature of emergency.

The waves jolted the plane, rocking it from its position.

"Mayday, mayday, mayday," he called again, his gaze still on the oncoming storm. The deep panes of blue evidenced rain sheeting across the horizon. "This is Chief Petty Officer Silver—"

"—Officer—"

He stilled, listening. Nothing.

"We are trapped at the medical center in Key West." He pressed the intercom to his forehead. "Please, come get us."

Static.

Then, miraculously, "Chief Silver, this is NMA. I hear your distress call. What is your situation?"

A wave slammed into the plane, and Jake braced his hand against the console. The aircraft shuddered, then broke away from shore.

And just like that, the waves took him out to sea.

"We have eight souls stranded at the Key West medical center who need immediate assistance. Please send air evacuation."

He felt the aircraft tilting, the water filling up in the floats.

"Request confirmed—"

The static resumed and Jake gave them another minute to come back.

Then he hung up the radio and opened the door.

Request confirmed.

He stared at the sky and the roil of clouds. Hopefully soon.

The water crested over the opposite float, driving the near one up, and he stepped out on it, his weight evening the plane out.

His boat had stayed on shore, his knot tethering it to the plane clearly insufficient.

The waves took him farther out. Oh joy, now he got wet—

Shots barked in the air and he stilled.

They came from the west, and he ducked down, searching under the nose of the plane for the source.

A yacht—it looked like the blue one that had been beached in the harbor—floated in the channel between the key and a shallow reef.

Aboard it, Jake made out the gray shirts of his favorite escapees.

Nice. A party boat.

As he watched, however, he spotted one of the men pointing his shotgun at a man seated on one of the couches at the stern of the boat.

He wore a ripped blue uniform and sat as if tied up.

Jake's gut clenched. The men had found themselves a hostage, and by Jake's best guess, it was a cop.

He shot a look at his boat, still moored on shore, caught on the rocks, but moving uneasily in the waves. Dive now, and he might catch it before it drifted away.

Or . . .

Another shot cracked the air. Laughter, loud and boisterous.

One of them sat on the bow, drinking out of a bottle, his feet dangling over the front.

Ah, they'd found the liquor supply.

Idiots.

Dangerous, drunk idiots.

And Jake just couldn't live with himself if he let them kill a cop.

They were too far offshore, however, to make the crossing completely under water. And they'd spot him in a second, one glance at the sea.

Unless.

He dove into the channel and swam hard for his boat, his lungs nearly on fire as he surfaced on the back side of it. He crept along the shoreline, staying low, and emerged behind the cover of seagrass and shrubbery.

Then he hoofed it toward the tower of the dive school.

He just needed a tank, a rebreather, a mask, and fins.

And maybe, if someone had stayed on base, a little assistance.

He found the doors to the tower locked, but he still had his pick set in his pocket.

Inside, the room smelled of seawater, the dank, musty odor of cement, and trapped water.

He found the supply room, with the drying fins, masks and BCDs equipped with rebreathers, and oxygen tanks. Pulling down a tank, he checked the pressure and found it full, 3000 psi. Like Boy Scouts, always prepared.

He tested the tank, confirmed air, then hooked up the rebreather lines and attached the BCD. Then, he carried the entire unit, along with the fins and mask, out to the shoreline. Toed off his shoes and threw them in a nearby boat.

The yacht bobbed in the waves, maybe five hundred yards offshore to the east.

The plane sat half-submerged in the water.

He inflated the BCD, let it carry the tank weight for him, and waded out into the water. Putting on his mask, he then slipped into the vest, adjusted the fit, tested the rig. Air, sweet and cool.

He added his fins and slipped under the water.

The world turned silent as he kicked away from shore, diving down to slide along the bottom.

So he hadn't entirely thought this through, but if he could get onto the boat, he could disarm one, or more, then use their panic to relieve them of their hostage.

An escape vessel might be helpful, however.

If Ham or North were here, one of them could act as a distraction, bring the boat alongside, posing as rescuers, while the others boarded the vessel.

Aria would kill him if this went south.

The water still hadn't cleared from the storm, but he'd pulled up the compass on his dive watch, had set a heading before getting into the water and now followed it.

He came up under the boat, twenty feet down, and sat there, thinking.

If this was the same crew as before, there'd be six. Six armed, angry, possibly drunk men.

The props of the massive engine were damaged—the boat wasn't going anywhere but where the waves blew it. Which made these chumps even more stupid. However, it did host an inflatable rescue dinghy, if Jake remembered correctly.

He could pull a dinghy from under the water, if he got the cop off the boat.

But first, he needed a distraction.

Or better yet . . .

He could sink the yacht.

Yes, this could work. He slid his fins off and attached them to his BCD by the straps. Then he unclipped his BCD. It would float in the water until he needed it again.

The Glock was still lodged in his belt. And he'd found a dive knife in one of the BCD pockets.

He hovered just below the boat, visualizing his attack.

Then, as he watched, feet appeared on the dive platform at the stern of the yacht.

He didn't have to wonder what a drunk guy might be doing off the back of a boat.

But, one target down. He kicked to the surface, held on to the ledge, and grabbed the man's leg.

Yanked.

His target fell into the water and Jake pushed him away from the boat. He didn't need him dead, and drunk was disabled.

Jake swung himself up and aboard before the man could surface and alert his buddies.

On his way up, however, he released the life raft, letting it explode out of its case on the back into the water, inflating as it went.

It made a racket, but Jake was already on board.

"Hey!"

He really needed two hands, and his bandage was soggy anyway, so he switched his knife into his left hand, palmed the Glock from his belt with the other, and squeezed off a shot toward the man emerging from the captain's desk. Purposely didn't hit him, but it shaved off decking and sent the man scrambling.

He'd reached the cop. "Gimme your hands."

They were duct-taped, and Jake slid his blade through them, barely looking at the man or the mess of his face.

Instead he sheathed the knife, grabbed him by the arm, and threw him off the back of the boat. "Swim for your life!"

He didn't look to see where the man landed.

A shot pinged the boat right next to his leg and it shook him.

Thank you, God, that they were drunk.

He turned then and fired a shot into the deck of the ship, right into the fuel tank.

Another shot from behind him, and this time it shattered the light at the back of the boat.

He looked up and spotted a man with a darkly bruised face.

Oh, hi.

The man swore and raised his shotgun.

Jake had the sense he wasn't going to miss.

Well, okay then. He raced for the back of the boat and leaped off, turning in the air. He caught his inflated BCD, barely submerged, came up fast.

A bullet skipped off the water beside him.

Please, let this work.

He aimed for the back fuel tank, the one that he'd shot through the deck and let seep long enough for fumes to gather.

Kicking hard away from the boat, he pulled the trigger.

The boat exploded. A mushroom cloud of fuel and flame and destruction.

He clipped on the BCD and dove, letting out his air. At the bottom, he slipped on his fins and searched for a swimmer.

He spied the cop struggling, twenty feet from the boat, swimming hard for the dinghy.

Good man.

Jake kicked hard, caught up, and grabbed the lead line of the dinghy. Then he emerged and grabbed the cop, towing him toward the raft.

He practically pushed the man into the boat, dove again, and like a dolphin, towed him into shore.

The flames from the yacht lit up the water.

And that's how it was done.

Hooyah.

He surfaced as he came closer to the beach, spitting out his regulator and propping himself on the edge of the raft.

"You okay?" he asked.

The man looked familiar. Short dark hair, a scattering of dark whiskers across his square jawline. The build of a linebacker.

The cop who'd let him onto the island.

"Yeah," the cop said. Except he didn't look okay. He'd been worked over, his eye swollen, a welt on his jaw, and he held his side from where a wound bled into the standing water of the raft.

He'd been stabbed.

Jake took off his fins, threw them into the raft, and towed it to shore, wishing he'd grabbed booties in his haste to get in the water. But he slipped his feet into his shoes, then reached for the man.

"What's your name?"

"Wade. Wade Donovan. With the Key West Police."

Jake saw the confirmation printed on his shirt. He helped Wade out of the raft, then shucked off the equipment and left it in the raft, keeping the dive knife. "Let's get you some medical attention."

Wade had crumpled onto shore, his face twisted. "I should have been paying attention, but they got the jump on me."

"It happens. Let's go." Jake grabbed him by the waist and helped him up. He spotted a jet ski amid the scattered boats, grabbed the dive knife from the vest, and headed for it.

"What are you—"

"Scoring us a ride." Jake grabbed the two wires protruding from the handlebar attached to the ignition box, cut them with his knife, then peeled away the rubber insulation, exposing the wires.

He tied them together. Then he climbed on and pressed the ignition button.

And voilà, God was suddenly on his side because the machine turned over.

Hooyah.

He revved it and it hummed to life.

"Get on," he said to Wade, who was leaning over, clutching his knees. He hobbled over to Jake and eased his leg over the back, groaning. "Who are you? Some kind of criminal?"

And right then, Jake heard Aria's voice, bright and solid in his head. *"It's in your DNA to find trouble and fix it. That makes you the good guy, not a villain."*

Jake pulled out, toward the inlet leading to the hospital. "Just a guy trying to help. Hold on, because my guess is that there's more than just those guys on this island. And if I don't get back, the woman I love is going to kill me."

CHAPTER 13

ARIA JUST KNEW THAT JAKE had something to do with that ball of flame on the horizon, the cloud of black smoke, the thunderous explosion that reverberated through the blue sky.

Aria stood at the window in the hallway, watching as the smoke rose in a fat column toward the heavens, her arms wrapped around her waist.

"Hope your boy wasn't on that boat," said Hagan from behind her. He'd risen early and she'd found the remainder of the protein bar wrappers next to his mattress along with three juices.

Which left two for the rest of them, along with another can of Spam.

She didn't say anything. Frankly, despite her words of defense about Hagan, he lifted the tiny hairs along her neck with the way he looked at her.

The way he looked at Yola.

Even his gaze on Angel.

She was probably just edgy and tired, having sat up much of the night with Parker. He'd fallen into a deep, much-needed sleep shortly before Jake left for the plane.

She'd wanted to sleep too, but she couldn't get her mind off

Jake and the group of angry escapees he'd described meeting earlier.

Please, God, protect him.

She didn't know why, but talking to God seemed to get easier with every plea, starting with the moment Jake nearly died under her hands.

And then there was Mimi and her simple, easy conversation about God and his love, his protection. "*When you pass through the waters, I will be with you.*"

"Oh my, is that a fire?"

Aria turned to find Mimi walking out of the staff room, Yola by her side. "Good heavens, what happened?"

"Jake blew a boat up," Hagan said.

"You don't know that," Aria said. She turned to Mimi. "You should be in bed."

"I can't sit in bed one more minute. Not when the sun is finally shining."

Aria didn't mention the new storm gathering behind them, on the eastern horizon. And it was probably good for Mimi to walk around. She looped her arm through Mimi's, Yola on the other side.

"Look at that view," Mimi said. "We came down here for the first time in '68, and Rollo took one look at that view and said he'd found home. He died free diving when he was fifty-seven, twenty long years ago. Loved what he did so much, it killed him."

Aria looked at her, searching for the bitterness in her voice, finding none.

Mimi must have sensed it. "Oh, I was angry at him, that's for sure. I couldn't believe he left me. And for a long time, I let that anger protect me. It kept me from having to feel the real grief of his loss. See, I let my heart turn to stone and thought that was the best thing for it." She patted Yola's hand.

"I locked the grief inside, scared to feel the pain. But in doing so, I didn't allow myself to live, either. I was a hard, angry woman."

She looked at Yola. "Thankfully, God says he can remove our hearts of stone and turn them to flesh. That he'll give us a new spirit. Replant what was once desolate and give us fruit. Blessings." She kissed Yola's cheek.

"I realized that I didn't want my old, broken heart, but the heart that Jesus wanted to give me. So . . . I let him give me a heart transplant." She looked at Aria and winked. "I let myself feel the pain of Rollo's loss, and in it, I remembered the great love we had. See, our pain is the residue of love. And that's when I realized God could take the hard memories and diminish them, replace them with good. In his hands, my heart is safe. He protects it. Heals it. I can trust him, because even when life hurts, he is good. And he is sovereign."

"Is he though?" Aria let her words drift into the morning. "I mean, from my point of view, it doesn't make sense."

"What doesn't?"

"All of it. But, mostly—"

"Why someone you loved had to die for you to live?"

Yeah, that.

"That's a hard conundrum. How can God be good *and* sovereign when something terrible happens? Either he's good—and has no control. Or he's sovereign and causes bad to happen, right? Panic comes when we stop believing that God is good. Or, that God is sovereign. But he is both, and that is the key to peace, even in the midst of the grief, or fear. Whatever storm life brings."

"I'd really love to believe that," she said softly.

Mimi made a humming sound. "Of course, that would mean that you aren't responsible for the fact that your sister died, and you lived. You might even stop believing that God took the wrong twin."

Aria stilled at the words.

Mimi looked at her. "I have old ears, but they still work."

Aria stared out into the horizon. "I *was* the one born with the bad heart. I was the one who was supposed to die."

"So, God made a mistake? And of course it's your job to fix it."

She didn't want to nod, but . . .

Yes.

The smoke was dissipating, turning a pewter gray, as if the fire might be dying.

"Stop fighting the new heart God gave you and embrace it, Doc," Mimi said. "You don't have to be afraid when your heart is in his hands."

Behind her, Ringo started to bark, high yips that made them turn. Bailey had been wrestling with the pup and now let it go, and Ringo disappeared out the door.

Angel appeared in the doorway. "Jake's back. I saw him pull up on a jet ski. He's got someone with him."

Aria arrived in the doorway just as Jake was struggling up the stairway with a man in tow, his arm over his shoulder.

Beaten and bloody, his shirt saturated and shiny, he appeared pale and dire. Dark hair, a thick shadow of whiskers, and he wore the blue shirt of the local police force. "What happened?"

"I found him being held captive by a bunch of convicts," Jake said.

Aria came up on the other side of the man, helping him down the hallway toward another patient room.

"You have anything to do with that explosion out there?" she asked as they reached the room.

"Dad?"

She glanced down the hall. Bailey took off at a run. "Dad!"

The man drew in a long breath, winced. "Bailey! What are you doing here?"

"Whoa, there, kid," Jake said, catching Bailey. "Wait until we get him into a bed."

They brought the man into the room and eased him onto a bed. "Yola, I need my blood pressure cuff and a scope." Aria turned to the man. "What's your name, sir?"

"His name's Wade," Jake said and stepped back.

"Dad!" Bailey pushed past Jake. "Where have you been?"

Wade was groaning, but he reached out for Bailey and pulled him to himself, crying out. "Bailey! I thought your mother took you to Miami with her!" He put him away from him, tears cutting down his face. "What happened? Why aren't you with her?"

Bailey's face paled. "I was looking for Ringo—"

"I need some room here," Aria said, and Jake put his hands on Bailey, easing him away. Jake glanced at her, frowned, but she didn't have time for family reunions.

The man was shivering, his respirations rapid, and by the sweat covering his body, she suspected that whatever had caused his injuries had led to an infection.

Even septic shock.

She opened his shirt.

"I don't understand. She must have thought you were with me," Wade said, mostly to himself, because his eyes closed. He groaned.

Jake turned the kid away from the table.

Angel came into the room and put her arm around Bailey. "Let the doc take care of him." She pulled him into the hall.

The man had an infraumbilical penetration stab wound in his lower abdomen. It seeped blood, was reddened and inflamed. The wound tracked anteriorly, but Aria couldn't pinpoint the end tract.

"I need an ultrasound machine."

Yola had returned with the blood pressure cuff and the stethoscope.

"Thanks. Can you find me a thermometer?" She took his blood pressure, found it low. Then she listened for blood in his gut.

She found gloves and snapped them on. "This is going to hurt, but I need to take a look."

Wade moaned as she put her hands on him, probing the wound. "What were you stabbed with?"

"A screwdriver."

She looked at him, then Jake. Made a face. "What kind? Do you remember how long it was?"

"I don't know—it was dark, but I remember, there were building supplies—my neighbor, fixing up his house. I saw an intruder—oh—"

"Sorry." The wound had underlying tissue showing, indicating an upward thrust. And if the weapon was long—eight inches or more—it could have found its way into the diaphragm and bisected his intestines.

She gestured to Jake, and he followed her to the window. Outside, the clouds had piled along the horizon, dark and hazy. She pulled off her gloves. "He needs surgery, a diagnostic peritoneal lavage so we can see where he's bleeding. And I'm worried he's going into septic shock."

"I got ahold of help, but I don't know from where."

She nodded. "I hope it comes soon. By the darkening of the edges of the wound, he's had it for a while—maybe even a couple days. And the fact he's still bleeding has me worried."

"So he was stabbed before he got on that boat."

"My guess, yes." Something, maybe, had changed about Jake. He seemed sturdier, more confident.

"So that was you, blowing up that boat."

Jake nodded. "The group I saw before stole a boat, which, I guess we're all doing, but I spotted them tuning up Wade here, and I just couldn't—"

She held up her hand. "I get it. It's in your DNA." She sighed though and pressed her hand to his face. "But I'm glad you're back. In one piece."

He smiled at her, his eyes warm, and right then, her heart unlatched and Mimi's words rounded back to her. *"I was so scared to feel that pain. But in doing so, I didn't allow myself to live, either."*

Oh, she loved this man. And it could really hurt. But maybe it was worth every single crazy, dangerous moment of it.

Yola returned with a thermometer in a sheath, and Aria took Wade's temperature. It was elevated to 101. "Yola, see if you can find any acetaminophen at the nurses' station."

Aria could try antibiotics until help arrived, but if sepsis was setting in, they were running out of time. "How did this happen, Wade?"

Wade groaned, his voice weak. "I was supposed to leave with Bailey, but they called me down to the station to help with evacuations. I sent him to a friend's house and I called my wife to tell her, to see if she could pick him up, if I didn't get back in time. I left a message, but . . . when I got home to get Bailey, he was gone. I thought he'd gone with my wife, but when I called her cell, I couldn't get through. I was headed to the hospital when the storm hit. I barely made it home. After it died, I went out again. I saw movement in my neighbor's garage." He opened his eyes. "I thought he might be home, and might have seen my wife pick up Bailey, so I went over. But it wasn't Gary. It was this big guy. He was wearing a Key West Detention shirt. Right then, I figured out that the detention center had been hit and he was an escapee. I wasn't sure what to do when he spotted me. We tussled and—"

"I stabbed him."

She looked up and her blood chilled.

Hagan held Bailey to himself, a scalpel to his throat.

"Hagan—" Jake started.

"You. On your knees, your face to the ground, hands behind your back."

Jake's mouth tightened into a thin line.

"Now, or this kid bleeds."

"I knew it," Jake growled, something lethal in his tone.

"You're a real whiz. Forehead on the ground, hands behind you." Hagan tossed what looked like Parker's bedsheet handcuffs at Aria. "Tie him up. Make it nice and pretty, Doc."

Jake's hands came around behind him, his wrists side by side, and she laced them tight. "Sorry."

"It's going to be okay," he said quietly.

Hagan walked into the room, still holding Bailey.

Then, he kicked Jake. Right in the face, a blow that jerked Jake back.

Aria screamed.

Hagan advanced on Jake and sent another kick into his gut. Jake grunted but curled into himself, bringing his knees up. He bled from the welt on his face.

"Bailey here tells me you're a SEAL. I've never killed a SEAL before."

No, no, this couldn't be happening. "Stop—Hagan, please—stop!"

"Sorry, honey," Hagan said as Wade tried to raise himself off his bed. "This was all going to work out perfectly, if it weren't for your hero here. He just had to rescue this nosy cop."

He kicked out at Jake again.

Jake turned, deflecting it. He grunted though, the blow landing in his ribs.

"Please stop—" Aria said, her voice breaking. "You don't have to do this. You can still get on the chopper, you can still get away—"

"You really think your boyfriend here will let that happen?"

She looked at Jake, who met Hagan's face with such a calm, dark look it shook her to the bones.

Never.

And that, really, was the truth of it.

Jake wasn't going to change. He'd always be the guy who did what was right. What was good.

He'd always be the guy who ran toward trouble, not away from it.

And that turned her entire body cold.

Especially when Hagan pushed Bailey aside and advanced on Jake.

■ ■ ■

He should have listened to his instincts.

Jake's body burned, but nowhere more than in his brain where his suspicions had simmered away for two days.

He'd left Aria alone with this man.

Aria, and Angel and Yola and Mimi and even Bailey and Ringo, alone with a murderer.

Jake stared up at Hagan as he quietly worked his hands out of the bonds, unfeeling of the blow to his face, his ribs, his shoulder.

Just feeling, really, his hands on Hagan, wringing him out.

"Please." Aria's pleading made him want to wince. *Don't beg, Houlihan.*

Because he had this. One more step closer, please . . .

Hagan smiled down at him, the scalpel in his hand. “Such a tough guy. A *navy SEAL.*”

“Not anymore. They kicked me out.” Jake cocked his head. “Said I was too much trouble. Actually . . .”

Hagan took another step. There we go, tough guy—

“They said I was *crazy*.” Jake smiled.

“No!”

Even Jake froze at the voice coming from behind Hagan. His attention jerked away from Hagan just as Yola launched herself at the big man.

Yola!

But, *hooyah*—just the distraction he needed.

Jake exploded. He kicked Hagan in the knee, twisting it, and with Yola’s weight, Hagan went down.

Jake bounced to his feet, his hands already free, and reached for Yola, who was punching Hagan’s head.

He pulled her away, handing her off to Aria, then threw his own punch into Hagan’s jaw.

His fist bloomed in pain, and he knew better, but he just needed that.

Hagan rebounded, swinging wildly at Jake, but he slapped the punch away, then grabbed his hand and twisted.

Hagan roared and rolled over, subdued by the force.

Jake threw his knee into his spine and bent Hagan’s hand back in a submission hold. Leaned down. “But it doesn’t mean I don’t remember a few things.”

Yola had bounced out of Aria’s arms as if ready to fight.

“I got him, Yo,” Jake said, barely looking at her. “But good job.”

“Cool,” Bailey said.

“Untie those wraps, Aria.” She picked up the sheets she’d used to tie him. Her hands shook. Unknotting them, she stepped over Jake as he put an elbow into Hagan's neck.

"Please move. Because I'd like nothing more than to toss you out of this window."

Hagan swore.

Jake looked at Aria. "Now, this time when you tie him up, make sure his wrists are flat against each other, not side by side." He winked. "Another trick I learned in the navy."

"He might have a broken arm, Jake," Aria said, kneeling beside them.

"Are you sure about that? Enough to risk him—"

"No." She grabbed Hagan's other arm. Hagan let out a curse, something nasty, and it took everything Jake had not to cuff him.

She tied the knots tight, then Jake got up and checked them, tightened them more.

Hagan spat at him.

Jake pulled him up to a sitting position. "I'd really like to kick you in the teeth right now."

"Jake!" Aria said.

He glanced at her, his mouth tight. "I'm not going to. Unless—" He looked again at Hagan. "Just give me a reason." Then he turned and strode over to Bailey. Knelt in front of him. "You okay, kid?"

"That was cool."

Maybe it was. He couldn't help but smile. He tousled Bailey's hair.

Aria turned to Wade, who'd sunk back down onto the bed. "I'm going to get you some penicillin and see if we can hold off this infection."

He reached out for Bailey, who took his hand.

"Hey!" Angel said as she came into the room. "Parker's missing."

"He must have left when Hagan untied him," Jake said.

Aria started out the door, but Jake grabbed her arm.

"Let him go."

"What—no, he's suffering."

"He's made his choice, Ari. You need to let him make it."

She frowned, swallowed.

"You can't fix everything."

"Says the man who collects strays."

"Oh," Yola said then, and Jake looked at her as she slumped against the wall.

Everything inside him froze. "Yola?"

She had her hand pressed to her body, blood seeping between her fingers. "I didn't realize . . . I mean . . . I think . . ." She looked down just as she fell to the ground.

Aria barely caught her. "Yola!"

"I just felt it. Maybe the adrenaline . . ." Yola's eyes widened. "This is starting to hurt . . ."

Jake rounded the bed and scooped her up. Put her on the second bed in the room.

Yola was moaning, a deep haunting of pain that sliced into his soul. He stepped back from the bed, just staring as blood began to pool out of her, saturating her shirt.

"Jake! Get me some gauze pads, or something to stop the bleeding."

Aria's voice was a slap that moved him into action. Just keep moving—he searched the drawers of the cabinets next to the bed and found a giant bed pad. He handed it to Aria, who pressed it onto the wound.

"Gloves," Angel said, but Aria just waved her away, leaning over Yola. "Just breathe, Yola. You're in good hands—I'm not going to let anything happen to you."

Yola nodded, her breath wheezing in and out.

Blood edged the corners of her mouth. No, no—

Aria looked up at him. "I need to get in there and stop the bleeding. He might have nicked her suprarenal aorta."

Jake knew enough medicine to recognize the main blood vessel to the heart. And the way the pad filled with blood . . .

Aria's jaw tightened, her voice small. "I need an operating room." Her eyes filled and she blinked hard, looked at Yola.

"It's okay," Yola said quietly and put her hand on Aria's, holding her wound. "I told you. God has something big for me. He told me to wait for it—and he was right."

Jake pressed his hands to his head, his breaths coming too fast. No—no—

"I just didn't realize it was going to be this big." A tear tracked down Yola's face.

"Jake. I need to open her up, stop the bleeding . . ." Aria said. But the way her face paled, her stricken expression . . .

They were out of resources.

"I have Mimi." Angel's voice, from behind him, and Jake turned, spotted Mimi, whose attention fell on Yola.

He stepped away, as Mimi came up to them. Angel held her hand.

"Oh, my precious Yoyo." Mimi's voice shook. She pressed her hand to Yola's cheek. "How is it that . . . that you get to see the Savior before your Mimi?" Her breath caught, even as she forced a smile. "I'm so proud of you."

Aria looked away, her face wrecked, her eyes closed.

Jake walked over to Hagan and ripped him off the floor. Stared at him as Hagan looked away, out the window.

Don't.

The voice was a thump inside him, a hard knocking against his impulses, his urges.

Don't.

Jake let out a shuddered breath and dragged the man out of the room.

Yola deserved not to die with her killer in the room.

"It was an accident!" Hagan shouted. "She jumped me."

"Shut up, before you have an accident."

He reached the supply closet and threw Hagan in, slamming the door.

Every cell in his body shook.

He turned and sent his fist into the supply room door.

Jumped back, wanting to open it.

Wanting—

Wanting to *kill* Hagan.

The thought backed Jake up, into the wall.

Jake closed his eyes. And see, he already knew the truth.

He was the villain. No different from a guy like Hagan.

Justified, maybe.

But still, a murderer in his heart.

I am forgiven. I am clean. I am loved.

Not a chance.

He blew out a breath and walked back to the room.

Silence. Mimi wept, a keening that emanated from deep inside her body. Angel held her, weeping also.

Aria had stepped away, her hands bloody, just staring at Yola.

Wade held Bailey in an embrace.

"She's gone," Jake said. "So fast?"

Aria met his gaze, nodded.

Oh, Yo. She lay there, her eyes closed, and frankly, he'd seen plenty of dead men—and women—but something about Yola looked different.

Felt different.

"That's what a hero looks like," Jake said.

"No, Jake. That's what love looks like." Mimi turned to him, drew him to herself.

He couldn't . . . didn't . . . he had no ability to reach out to her.

And for the life of him, he didn't know why his throat filled, burning with the terrible, bone-shattering urge to weep.

Instead, he pushed away from her and stalked out of the room, down the hall, all the way to the end.

He stood in the open window.

And then, with everything inside him, he yelled. A reverberation that tore out of him, ripping through sinew and bone, exploding cell and breath.

A shout that shook the air, then dissipated into the darkening swell of the horizon.

And then he slid to the floor, his head in his folded arms, letting the brisk tongue of the wind lash him, bracing himself for the next storm.

CHAPTER 14

ARIA COULDN'T MOVE, hearing Jake's agony, the evidence that finally, the man she thought was indestructible had unraveled.

Yola lay still on the bed.

"That's what love looks like." Mimi's words crashed through her, and Aria couldn't stay here. She pushed out of the room, hearing her name called—maybe by Angel, although she wasn't sure—and headed down the hallway. Blood still saturated her hands—she saw that in the print she left on the door as she exited into the stairwell, then on the railing as she took the stairs to the upper floor, and finally climbed the ladder to the roof.

With a shout, she pushed open the hatch and climbed out, her body sucking air, trying to get a grip on her emotions.

But they were spiraling out, in great heavy gasps, and as she stepped out onto the roof, she fell, her hands on the asphalt, and let herself sob.

For Yola.

For the injustice of it.

For the impulsive acts that took people's lives.

For the fact that she couldn't stop any of it.

Aria wrapped her hands around her waist, and with everything inside her, she too screamed. The sound scattered birds roosting nearby, rent the air, and hung on until she had no more breath.

Then she listened to it die in the mottled sky.

It wasn't supposed to be this way.

She did things right. She planned. She obeyed. She worked, she . . .

She fixed God's mistake.

He is good. And he is sovereign.

Mimi's words. Spoken to her in the staff room.

Spoken as Yola's spirit left her body.

Grief and joy, entwined.

Good and sovereign.

"Panic comes when we stop believing that God is good. Or, that God is sovereign."

She closed her eyes, and for a moment, Kia stepped in.

Oh, she'd missed her voice.

"Sis, I know it's not fair. And I hate that. It kills me to see you in that bed. So, I'm going to do the very best to live for you."

No, Kia. You lived for you.

The thought brought her up. Stung.

She'd wanted to assign only altruistic motives to Kia. But what if Aria had nothing to do with Kia's behavior?

What if Kia was just . . . Kia.

And Aria couldn't stop her from destroying her life any more than she could stop Yola from dying.

She wasn't to blame for Kia's death.

And she certainly didn't owe her life to her now. She could be grateful, yes, but . . .

"Stop fighting the new heart God gave you and embrace it, Doc."

Good. Sovereign. Even in the middle of death.

A distant hum lifted her head and she searched the horizon. Spotted a two-rotor Chinook chopper thundering toward them in the distance.

She climbed to her feet, waving her arms. "Here! We're here!"

It came closer, hovering over her, the giant props hammering the wind. She crouched and watched as a man hooked to a line was lowered down.

By the time he hit the roof, Jake had joined her. "It looks like they're from the Army National Guard!"

The man ran up to them. He wore a helmet, a gray-camo uniform, and yes, his patch identified him as ANG.

"We're looking for Chief Silver?"

"That's me," Jake said.

"Staff Sergeant Hines. You have eight for transport?"

Yes, still eight.

It should have been nine.

"We're on a tight leash here. The weather is coming in."

"We'll bring them up." Jake glanced at Aria, and she nodded.

"We'll send down a basket," Hines said.

Jake climbed down the ladder and Aria followed him, aware of her bloody hands.

She landed on their floor and headed to the staff room, washing with a discarded towel.

Ringo danced around her feet, barking.

"That's right, buddy, we're going home."

She found Angel with Jake.

"I'll get her up the ladder," Jake said. "You prep Mimi, okay? Get her an ambu bag, in case she needs help."

She nodded. Jake had turned military on her and she recognized the man from the day the storm hit.

The man she'd met on the mountain, trying to keep her alive.

The man she loved.

She didn't care what it cost her.

She found Mimi in the patient room, standing beside Yola. Someone had covered her body in a sheet. "Mimi, we need to go."

"Just one more minute."

Okay. Aria went to the next room, picked up her ambu bag, the quick memory of Yola's hands steady on the balloon punching through her.

"Even before the storm, I had decided to stay. I don't know why—just a feeling, I guess, that God has something more for me here. I sense him calling me to something big, something life-changing, and I'm just supposed to stand on the shore, staring out at the sea to wait for it."

She swallowed the memory away and returned. Jake was back downstairs, talking with Bailey. "Don't worry, we'll find the dog. You gotta go." He looked over at Aria. "I gotta get Wade."

"He's not ambulatory. He'll never make it up that ladder."

"They can't land in the parking lot." Jake headed toward the room. "Don't worry, I got him."

Bailey was running down the hall. "Ringo! Where are you?"

"I think he's in the staff lounge," she said and followed Jake into the room.

Jake had grabbed a sheet and was fashioning a giant sling. He pulled Wade up to a sitting position. Wade groaned, barely able to sit up.

"Jake, this won't—"

"Just help me. Put his arms over my shoulders, and the sheet under his legs. I'll tie the sheet around my chest and carry him on my back."

Yes, that might work.

She grabbed the sheet and eased it under Wade, then pressed

his arms around Jake. Jake grabbed his legs, pulling them around him.

"Now tie that sheet tight in front of me."

She obeyed, and it brought Wade up against Jake's back.

"Get the door to the stairwell." Jake took a breath and stood up. Found his balance.

"We had to do this in training," he said. "I carried North."

She raised an eyebrow.

He smiled, something brutal and sad in his eyes, and it did something to her insides.

He was such a hero. Trained for this.

God had indeed sent him here. Because he was good. And sovereign.

They were going to get out of here. Not without grief, but onto shore all the same.

He lumbered down the hall with Wade, Aria behind him. Bailey ran out of the staff lounge. "I can't find Ringo!"

"Come with me, Bailey. I'll find Ringo." Aria took his hand and they followed Jake and Wade up the stairs.

Jake took a breath, then climbed the ladder, the staff sergeant waiting at the top to retrieve Wade from his back.

"You're next, kiddo," Aria said to Bailey. She met his eyes. "Go with your dad. I'll get Ringo. I promise."

Bailey's eyes filled, but he nodded and climbed the ladder.

She didn't wait for Jake but ran down the stairs.

Mimi was next, but Jake would get her. "Ringo!" She ran down the hall.

Stopped by the supply closet.

Hagan.

She didn't know why she hadn't thought of him. Except maybe Jake planned on bringing him out last.

Or, not at all.

Okay, Jake wouldn't do that, but it occurred to her that in all the ruckus, maybe Hagan would be forgotten.

Just like Parker.

She couldn't save Parker. But Hagan should be brought to justice—real justice, not punishment by tropical storm. She opened the door.

Hagan stood in the doorway, his hands unbound. So much for his so-called broken arm. "Think you were leaving without me?"

He advanced on her, grabbed her around the throat, and pushed her into the hallway. Put his face next to hers. "Sweetheart, this dance isn't over."

Jake!

But he hadn't come down from the roof yet. Hagan grabbed her arm and twisted it around, behind her, and she let out a cry. He doubled her over and pushed her down the hallway.

"Hagan—stop!"

Please, Jake, show up.

But he wasn't in the stairwell when they entered.

And Hagan wasn't going up, but down.

He pushed her into the water on the first floor, dunked her hard, held her, then dragged her up. She coughed, sputtered, and grabbed his arm as he dragged her across the lobby. "You don't have to do this—"

"If I'm trapped here, so are you. And he'll just have to choose you or the storm."

What—? Oh, this was about *Jake.*

Hagan dunked her again, holding her down as he waded toward the pharmacy. When he let her surface, her lungs burned, and she gulped in the rank air, unable to speak.

Hagan pulled her into the pharmacy and pushed her up on a counter. "Now, don't you go anywhere."

The water lapped up to her waist. She sat frozen, coughing, gulping air as he backed away from her. "Hagan, please—"

"Doc."

"I helped you!"

"You're in the way. Sorry, but I'm getting off this island. And I can't have anybody following me."

Then he pulled down one of the shelves.

It crashed over her, into the wall, not crushing her, but pinning her to the counter. A blinding pain sliced up her leg, her damaged ankle reinjuring, maybe, and she couldn't move, the weight of the shelf pressing on her chest.

"Hagan!" Her voice emerged raspy and weak, mostly from shock.

He pulled down the next shelf. It crashed onto the first, wedging her down farther. It nearly cut off her breath.

"Please—"

He gave the third shelf a shove and it fell against the other two. She couldn't move, the weight of the three braced against the wall, pinning her.

If they all fell, it would crush her.

"Don't worry. The storm surge will be here soon."

Then he closed the door and left her in darkness.

■ ■ ■

"Okay, Mimi, just get into the basket and they'll lift you up." Jake had walked the woman up the stairs after easing her away from Yola's body. Above him, the Chinook was fighting for control in the wind as it chopped up the sea.

"We need to go soon!" Sergeant Hines shouted as he strapped Mimi into the litter. "The storm has been upgraded to a Cat 2 hurricane, and it's headed this way."

Jake held the swaying basket as Hines clipped himself to the litter and gave the signal. "I have to find Aria, and then we'll be ready."

"Five minutes, and we need to go!"

Jake gave him a thumbs-up and climbed back down the ladder. *C'mon, Aria, leave the dumb dog.*

Although he'd owned a few dogs in his life, knew that they became family.

"Aria!" He hit the second floor and found it empty.

Except for—shoot, Hagan. He went to the supply closet and opened the door.

Empty.

He stared at it a moment, just long enough to hear the grunt behind him.

Hagan swung a two-by-four right at his head.

Jake ducked and dove for the man, driving him back against the wall.

Hagan slammed his fist into his ribs, but Jake trapped his arm, blocked the punch. Delivered one of his own into Hagan's soft middle section.

Hagan whoofed and pushed off from the wall. He had a good thirty pounds on Jake, and that mattered.

But Jake had training.

Jake ducked under his arm, got him in a chest-to-back hold, his arm around his neck. "Where is she, man?" Jake didn't know why, but he just *knew* Hagan had done something to Aria.

Hagan tried to headbutt him. Jake dodged it but took a hit on his chin. He tightened his arm, curling it into a sleeper hold.

Hagan leaned up, using his height to drag Jake off his feet.

Jake held on, wrapping his legs around Hagan's body.

Hagan stumbled back, slamming him into the wall. Jake took the shock, gritted his teeth.

The big man was tiring.

"It's too late. She's trapped, and so are you." Hagan tried to headbutt him again.

Jake dodged.

Then, "Hey! What's going on!"

Jake spotted Hines, standing in the hallway.

"He's an escaped convict! And he's already killed one person—"

Hines drew his weapon. "On your knees, buddy."

Hagan dug his fingers into Jake's arm, turned, and stumbled down the hall, picking up speed.

Heading for the broken picture window.

Jake saw it happening and realized Hagan had a hold on him.

Shoot, he either went over with him, or—

He unlatched himself from Hagan, kneed him in the back, and the big man broke away.

Hagan skidded to a stop, right before the window. Turned.

Laughed. Raised the Glock, the one he'd pulled out of Jake's belt.

Jake was breathing hard, but he raised his hands. "Just tell me where she is—"

Two shots, center mass, and Hagan stumbled back, eyes widening.

Then he fell, arms windmilling out of the window.

Jake turned.

Hines lowered his gun. "I'm a cop in my day job."

Jake just bent over, grabbing his knees, not sure what to say. Except, "Thanks."

"We gotta go."

Jake looked up at him. "My girl is missing. I can't leave without her."

"There's a storm coming, and we're not going to get back here—"

Jake stood up. "This isn't our first storm. And it won't be our last."

Hines nodded but pulled a two-way radio out of his jacket. "For after the storm. We'll be back as soon as we can get in."

Jake took it. "Can I get your Maglite too?"

Hines handed over the light, then ran down the hall.

Jake listened to his footsteps echo up the stairwell.

"Aria!" Jake started in the patient rooms, searching each one, his stomach in a knot, bracing himself to find her bloodied body.

Nothing. *Where are you?*

How had Hagan disposed of her so quickly? Jake had been hung up getting Wade off his back and onto the litter, but . . .

"Aria!"

He wanted to check the third floor, but no one had even been up there, the door blocked by the tree.

Which meant—

He raced down the stairwell even as he heard the chopper thrumming away in the distance. "Aria!"

The lobby was quiet as he shined his beam over the gray water. He'd driven the jet ski into the parking lot, the water receding somewhat outside, but inside, it was deeper, and for some reason still rising. Probably the water drains in town were overflowing to the lower levels of the island.

"Aria, are you here?"

Outside, it had started to rain, light showers, the wind banging against the remains of the door.

He waded through to the coffee shop. "Aria!" He searched behind the counter, kept his hands to himself, then went into the storage area.

"Aria!"

Outside, the wind began to howl, the outer rain bands washing across the island. He didn't want to ponder what crazy luck he possessed to be trapped on an island twice during a hurricane.

She had to be here.

He was wading out into the lobby area again when he heard it, the muffled syllable of his name, maybe.

"Aria!"

He listened, and the sound came from down the hallway toward—oh, of course—the *pharmacy*.

Where she'd nearly drowned before. Hagan had a warped sense of humor. Or perhaps it was simply evil.

The door was barred with the chair, but Jake threw it away and entered the room, his light shining into the destruction.

No. Hagan had brought down the shelving in the room, all three tall metal shelves leaning against the far wall, one on top of each other.

As he scanned the light across the darkness of the rising waters, he spotted Aria, wedged back into the corner.

Oh no.

"Aria, I'm coming, honey." He worked into the room, trying to right the first shelf, but it wouldn't move—wedged into the wall with its weight and the press of the water. He gave up and moved to the end of the counter. He could barely make her out under the clutter of the metal. "Are you hurt?"

"A little. My ankle is wedged and it's hard to breathe."

He spotted the water, now up to her chest.

"It's going to be okay. I just have to figure out how to move these."

"Be careful. If you dislodge them, they'll come down on top of me."

She didn't have to say more, because the combined weight would crush her.

He got up onto the counter, his feet barely fitting on the thin lip, and put his body behind the first shelf. About eight feet wide and ten feet tall, the shelf probably weighed over three hundred pounds. He could lift it on one side, but he didn't have the leverage to work both sides.

And then the far end slipped, sliding down on the other shelves.

"Stop!" The movement pinned Aria's body deeper into the water, now up to her chin. "It's going to land on me!"

Jake's breaths raked in and out as he shone the light near her, enough to see her face. "They're too heavy. I need a two-by-four, maybe, but even then—I need help. Leverage."

"You need to get out of here before the storm comes."

He just stared at her. "What? Aria, I sent the chopper away. I'm staying."

"Oh, Jake." She closed her eyes. Sighed.

"Did you really think I'd *leave* you?"

She shook her head, looked away. "I guess not."

"We're in this together, Houlihan."

She pursed her lips and he could tell she was trying not to cry.

But he wanted to.

He climbed in between one of the shelves, working his foot through to find the counter. "I'll try and get to the center for better leverage."

But he couldn't turn around, and in a second fell hard into the water. He came up fast, turning. "Aria? Are you okay?"

"It slid. But yeah."

He found his flashlight and shined it on her. She'd lifted her chin, the water below her ears.

And it hit him that he could wait until the room filled with water, leverage the buoyancy of the wood on the shelves to help him move them.

But she'd be long underwater before then.

This was a terrible idea. But he had nothing else.

He needed time. A way for her to breathe while he figured this out.

They were in a pharmacy. He shined the light off her and around the room, searching the floating packages for tubing. Certainly—

He found rubber gloves, dressing packages, medicines, bottles, needles, and—

His hand closed on a coil of CPAP tubing. He opened it and swam over to her, as close as he could get. "Put this in your mouth. You can breathe through it. I'll attach it high so the water won't reach it."

"Jake, this isn't going to work."

"Try!"

She was crying now. "Jake, I'm sorry I ran away from you. I'm sorry you had to follow me to Key West. I'm sorry you sat through a hurricane and got electrocuted and nearly killed by Hagan, and who knows who else. I'm sorry that I didn't see how amazing you are, and that I didn't tell you earlier that . . . you scare me, Jake, but I still want to be with you—"

"Then you will, if you just stop talking and put this in your mouth!"

"I don't know why God gave me a new heart, but I'm tired of denying that it's mine. It is mine, and I do get to be happy, and . . . I want to be happy with you."

His stomach clenched, and he was going to cry too—

"Just shut up and put this in your mouth," he snapped.

She shook her head and he wanted to throttle her.

"No, you'll get stuck here too and I . . . I can't have you die for me, Jake—"

"It's not your choice!"

She winced, then coughed as water got into her mouth.

He lowered his voice, tried to find something calm. "It's my choice, Hot Lips. I'm staying with you and we are getting out of here, I promise. I'm taking you home and we're going to go freakin' dancing, and you're not going to die, because . . ."

And shoot, he didn't know why the words balled in his chest like a fist, suddenly, but he forced them out— "Because I love you. Okay? I've loved you since I met you in Alaska. I love you because you're brave and sweet and a little crazy and if you don't put this tube in your mouth and breathe and stay alive then I will . . . I will find a way to keep following you, and drive you completely crazy—"

"Fine!" She reached out her hand. "Why are you doing this?"

"Because I can't watch you die." He slapped the tube into her hand and she put it in her mouth.

She closed her eyes, her lips clamped around the tube, and he unwound it, took the rubber band on the package, wrapped it around the end, and hung it from the edge of the high cupboard above her head.

Then he grabbed her hand and squeezed. His heart stopped a moment when it took her a second to squeeze back, but she did.

Outside, rain lashed the window, and he climbed back onto the counter and set his shoulder against the shelf.

It moved, just barely, but fell back. He set his forehead against it, breathing hard. *God, right now I need a hero bigger than me. Please help me figure this out.*

He repositioned himself and tried again, ending in a shout as the shelf rocked, then again fell.

He could be crushing her, for all he knew.

Please!

"Hey—what are you doing?"

He knew that voice, and now swung his light toward it.

Parker stood in the doorway, looking gaunt but awake and sober.

"Specialist! Where'd you come from?"

"I was in the cafeteria. I found some sandwiches. They were all in little tiny bags—"

"Get in here." He jumped down from the counter. The water had reached his chest.

Parker was taller, skinnier than he was, but seemed sturdy enough. Jake grabbed his shirt. "I need your help. Can you fit into there?" He pointed to the gap between the shelves.

"I don't know, man. That looks a little precarious. Those shelves could fall and trap me."

"I know—Aria is under there."

Parker peered into the darkness and Jake shot his light toward her.

She lay like a mermaid, her hair around her, her eyes closed, and it sent a cold shard of terror through him.

"Is she dead?"

"She's going to be if you don't help me. C'mon."

Parker looked at him, frowned, something cresting over his face. "I—"

"I need you, man. Please."

Parker nodded. He climbed up onto the counter and worked himself in between the gap.

"You'll have to watch your head—the top of the shelf could hit you coming up." Jake pushed himself onto the ledge.

"Got it, boss."

"On the count of three."

Parker put his skinny arms on the upper shelf.

Please let this work.

"Three!" Jake pushed, and beside him, Parker grunted.

The shelf moved.

"Keep going!"

The leverage moved the shelf over and it rocked, then fell the opposite direction.

"Hang on, honey! C'mon, Parker. Next shelf!"

Parker nodded, galvanized, and leaned down, getting his hands on the lower shelf.

"On three—one, two—"

"Three!" Parker said and heaved.

Jake too. The shelf had farther to go, and Jake let out a groan as the weight settled through him.

"C'mon, Parker—"

Parker too was groaning, but the shelf started to move. "We got it!"

It started to topple on its own weight, and Jake felt it let go just as Parker stood up.

The shelf clipped him on the back of the head and he flew off the ledge and crashed into the water.

"Parker?" Jake shined the light on the water.

Parker lay facedown, a gash in the back of his head bleeding out.

Aw—

Jake dove in and grabbed him up, treading water to keep his head up.

"Parker, buddy, wake up."

Parker was out. Jake swam out with him into the lobby, into the stairwell, and pulled him up to the landing. Parker flopped like a fish, his head bleeding onto the cement.

Shoot. Well, the kid probably wouldn't die. He slapped his face. "Parker, buddy—"

He moaned.

That was enough. Jake took off for the lobby.

Outside, the rain sheeted down, and now Jake was swimming, stroking hard for the pharmacy.

He shined his light on the rubber tube as he came in and found it still affixed to the cupboard. He reached in through the slat and found Aria's hand.

She squeezed back. *Thank you, Lord.*

He climbed up in the middle of the counter where Parker had been standing, took a breath, and reached down to grab the shelf.

He put everything into the lift, straining, holding his breath. Felt the shelf move. But it settled back in a moment and he had to pop up for air.

The water was nearly over his head, even on the counter.

He had maybe two feet left of clearance. Which meant that . . . well, even if the room filled with water, it might not be enough to lift it.

He would not leave her.

God, please!

"I thought you said you weren't giving up on me!"

Parker.

He'd come back and Jake had no words. The kid swam right over to him and landed on the counter beside him. "On three?"

Jake took a whopper of a breath and ducked under the water.

Parker strained beside him, lifting, the weight fighting them.

Parker surfaced, gulping.

No. Jake kept holding on, fearing the weight falling on her. But his lungs gave out and he surfaced too, gasping.

The water was nearly to the top of the room.

"I have an idea," Parker said. "Let's lift it, then you pull her out. I'll hold it."

"Can you hold your breath that long?" Jake asked.

Parker met his eyes. "I'll hold it until you get her out."

Jake just knew the kid had hero in him. He took a few breaths, then, "Ready?"

Parker nodded, took a breath, and ducked.

Jake went with him, and together they pulled up the shelf, just a few inches, but it seemed enough. He turned and grabbed Aria, pulling her free, through the slats of the shelf. Her ankle caught on the edge, so he dove, working around Parker's body to free her. Then he pushed her to the surface.

Except, there was no surface, and he fought against the urge to gulp for air. Instead, he grabbed Aria and kicked hard toward the door, hoping Parker was behind him.

His vision started to darken, his body aching for air, but he forced himself not to gasp.

He found air in the lobby, with its higher ceiling. He gulped hard as Aria coughed beside him.

Alive. And breathing. She clung to him, her arms around his shoulders, her legs around his waist, and he parked them on the information desk.

Alive. Thank you, God.

Except.

"Where's Parker?" he said, searching the water for the kid.

"Parker's here?"

"He helped me." He let her go, turning to go back when suddenly Parker surfaced. He coughed out water, and Jake grabbed his shirt, holding him up.

"You okay, kid?"

Parker nodded.

"Maybe you should reenlist, join special forces."

Parker just stared at him, then a slow smile broke out on his face. "Maybe."

Jake turned back around, looking for Aria.

Found her staring at him.

"Are you okay?"

She nodded, something haunted on her face. Then, she covered her face with her hands and started to weep.

He reached for her, but she pushed him away. "Don't touch me!"

He stared at her as she turned and started swimming for the stairwell.

"Why is she mad?" Parker asked.

Oh, Hot Lips. "She'll be okay. It's just that she really wants to kiss me."

"Huh?"

"Long story, kid. I don't blame you if you can't keep up."

CHAPTER 15

ARIA WAS ACTING IRRATIONAL AND SHE KNEW IT. Jake had saved her life.

Again.

But this time . . . *this* time, watching his panic, seeing him nearly run out of air, nearly drown because he didn't know how to quit—

It turned her bones weak, stopped her heart, and frankly, she didn't know how to feel.

So angry—no, *furious*—seemed the only emotion she could get her hands around. Fury, so she didn't have to think about the other choices.

Grief.

Life without Jake.

Fear.

Life with Jake.

The fact that, no matter what she thought, she hadn't a hope of a happy ending when every time he answered a call, he might not walk back in the door.

She hit the stairwell, pulled herself up, and nearly cried out as she put weight on her stupid ankle. It slowed her down, but not enough to stop her, and she limped up the stairs and down to the staff room, not sure, really, where she was going.

She leaned against an upright chair, breathing hard.

She had to get away from him, because every cell in her body pulsed with the terrible urge to throw herself into his arms. Here she was, right back in Alaska, losing her common sense.

"Calm down, Aria."

Kia, in her head. Smiling. Swinging Dad's Harley key around her finger. *"I know what I'm doing."*

No—you don't!

"Aria, what's going on?"

Jake, behind her, still breathing hard after rescuing her and running up the stairs after her, and the poor man probably thought she was losing her mind.

Maybe.

At the very least, she was the most ungrateful—

"I know you're freaking out—"

"Thank you, Jake." She didn't look at him, just stared out the open window at the rain sheeting down, into the room, the wind lashing the palm trees. Oh goody, they'd circled back around to more drama.

Or maybe, with Jake, she'd never leave it.

"I know you saved me, again, and . . . well, I don't know what to say."

She glanced over her shoulder and the man stood there, soaking wet, his clothing plastered to him, shivering slightly, staring at her with so much worry in his eyes it could unravel her.

Don't. Don't end up in his arms.

"What's going on, Hot Lips?"

She wanted to smile at his nickname. Wow, she loved him, the way he found humor in the darkest places. But he deserved an explanation.

A real one.

"I'm scared, Jake."

"Of the storm? Aw, that's nothin', babe." He took a step toward her.

She held up her hand. "No, not of the storm. Of . . . of this." She gestured between them. "I know what I said back there—and I meant it. And then you . . . you . . . you would have died trying to free me."

He said nothing, his shoulders rising and falling.

And the fact he didn't deny it only settled the truth in her bones. "I think I told myself that you were different than Kia. That yes, you put yourself in perilous places, but you weren't reckless with your life."

"I'm not reckless with my life, Aria. I know exactly what I'm doing." He took another step toward her, but this time she didn't stop him. "I would have died trying to save you, and counted it worth it."

Her breath trembled, and her eyes filled.

"Because that's what love does. It doesn't stop to consider the cost. It just . . . acts. Puts itself out there."

She let her breath leak out. "I so want to make you promise me that you'll never do anything like that again, but . . . you can't make me that promise, can you?"

His mouth tightened into a grim line. He shook his head.

"And I know that. I thought maybe I could handle that, that I could even, I don't know, control you. But . . . I can't. And that . . . that's what scares me." She wanted to step away from him, but her ankle kept her planted. "Being out of control. Knowing that storms just show up, randomly, and even though I do everything I can to prepare for them—even stop them—I still end up—"

"Caught in the middle. Having to make choices that hurt people."

He swallowed and looked past her. "You're doing things you never thought you'd do, because you have to, and then looking in the mirror and not recognizing yourself."

She wanted to touch him, then, to soothe the words that felt ripped from the secret places inside him.

"So, what do you do, Aria? Because there will always be storms. I suppose you can weather them with me or without me." He took a final step toward her, so close he could bend down to kiss her.

The wind howled behind her, casting into the room.

"I guess I hold on," she said and reached for him.

He reached for her and pulled her to himself, off her hurt leg, and her arms slid up behind his neck, over his shoulders.

And then, she was kissing him. Because she had no other choice. Because he was here, right now, and she could.

And because God was good. And sovereign, and like Mimi said, she didn't have to be afraid when her heart was in his hands.

Jake's whiskers roughened her skin, his arms hard as they pulled her tight. It wasn't a gentle kiss, but one of resolution, of power . . .

Of the impulsive, all-out love that embodied Jake Silver.

"Whoa—and here we thought you guys were in trouble!"

At the voice, Jake broke away from her, his eyes wide, and put her down, still holding on to her.

"Am I interrupting? I could come back at another time . . ."

Aria looked past Jake as he turned.

Ham?

The big man stood in the doorway of the hospital, soaking wet, wearing a rain slicker, holding a flashlight and a two-way. Now, he toggled the radio. "I found him, guys."

He walked into the room.

Jake glanced at her, but she'd balanced herself on the chair, so

Jake walked over to him, bypassed Ham's hand, and wrapped him in a hug. "Dude! What are you doing here?"

Ham gave him a quick one-armed wrap, then looked at Aria. "You okay?"

She didn't even know where to begin, her words stripped from her.

"She has a bum ankle," Jake said.

Well, that was an oversimplification, but yes.

"How'd you find us?" she asked.

"Orion was worried about you when Lucy hit, and when he didn't hear from either of you, he called me. We met in Miami and were trying to locate you."

"You and Orion?" Jake asked.

"And me." North walked into the room, his pant legs wet. "What, you think you get all the fun?" He grinned at Jake, and Aria could see why he was his swim partner. They had the same weird sense of humor. He grabbed Jake in a hug. "Orion's down with the Zodiac, in the lobby. He's with someone else—a skinny guy—"

"Parker," Aria said.

"You took a Zodiac from Miami?" Jake asked.

"Of course not. We called in a favor from one of Isaac White's supporters, a guy from Texas named Dex. He nabbed us a yacht from one of his friends in Miami. We were already on our way down when the coast guard relayed your call. We were going to turn around, but when the chopper said you were left behind, we fired up the Zodiac. But we gotta get moving. That storm is starting to rock and roll."

Aria just stared at them. "You came all the way down here for Jake?"

"Hey, not just Jake. You too," Ham said. "One of those employee perks, Ari. Think about it."

"He's always recruiting," Jake said, shaking his head.

"Anything to keep you from reactivating," Ham said. "I can't lose you to the teams, Silver."

Outside, lightning flashed, and behind it, the low roll of thunder.

What? Jake was *reactivating*? The words blew her over, swept out any response.

Ham glanced past her, out the window. "Sounds more like a tropical storm than a hurricane, but let's get going before we're all stranded."

At the tail end of his words, however, a dog howled, maybe out of fear, but something sharp and high, and Jake looked at Aria. "Ringo."

"I got him," North said, disappearing down the hall. He returned a moment later with the wet puppy. "He's cute." Ringo was slathering his face. "He was in the supply closet, behind the mop bucket. Looked like he was scared and got himself wedged in."

Yeah, she knew what that felt like.

But not anymore. No more trying to justify her life. Time to live in freedom.

"Let's go," Jake said. And then, because he was Jake, he simply walked over, bent down, and picked her up, holding her in his arms. She curled hers around his neck.

"Back to that again, huh?" Ham said, glancing over his shoulder as he led them down the hallway.

Yes, it seemed she always ended up in his arms. Right where she belonged.

"Take me home, Hawkeye."

"Aye, aye, Hot Lips."

■ ■ ■

Apparently, Jake couldn't escape hospitals.

He stood at the window of Mimi's room, looking over the deep, calming blue of Biscayne Bay in Miami. Massive cruise ships sat at dock, tethered front to back, and just down the shoreline, sailboats, yachts, and whalers listed in the harbor of a local hotel, sun gleaming off their white hulls.

A glorious day.

Not a hint of trouble in the sky.

But that's how it was when storms hit—one moment, blue skies, the next, he was running for cover.

Picking up the pieces.

Figuring out how to survive in the sunshine.

Behind him, Angel sat in the recliner, her feet up. Aria stood at Mimi's bedside, having recapped her symptoms to the pulmonologist at Mount Sinai. "I'm just a phone call away," Aria said, her hand in Mimi's. "Once I get a phone." She gave a small, feeble laugh.

Jake turned, leaned on the window frame. Aria had been acting strange since they left Key West, first on the Zodiac, then on the fancy yacht Ham had scrounged up. She'd sat in the bow, staring into the wind, something stoic on her face he couldn't read.

He'd gotten the lowdown on Ham's trip to Italy, a short but tight-lipped recap of his mission as well as his luck finding Royal—no joy there.

Then Ham had just about broken Jake's heart when he'd stared out the window and said, quietly, "The Italian coast guard found Signe's body."

Only then had Jake realized how much Ham had been hoping that somehow, someway, Signe might still be alive.

Then again, it wasn't exactly a far-fetched hope, what with her turning up, alive, after ten years.

Jake had been there, had seen the explosion of the bunker. Had seen Ham unravel.

And the look on his face now reminded Jake too closely of his own breakdown at the hospital.

Completely losing himself, like some kind of pansy.

The memory made him want to stalk out of the room, even as Mimi looked over at him and reached out her hand. "C'mere, Jake."

And what was he going to do? So he took her hand, his fingers coarse and roughened against her fragile softness. She tugged him over.

The bed nearly swallowed her, and frankly, it seemed she'd aged a decade in the few hours since Yola's death. But her eyes glowed as she patted Jake's hand. "Thank you, kiddo."

He swallowed, his throat thick. Shook his head. "I should have—"

"No, now you listen to me. You did everything right. Yola had her own mind. And her own heart. And she followed both of them." Her eyes glistened, a tear forming in the corner. "She was always so much like her grandfather. Impulsive, yes, but so brave. She knew exactly what she was doing when she saved your life."

Jake looked away.

"Except, you think it was a reckless, impulsive, meaningless act."

He looked at her, stricken. But, yes.

And Mimi could very possibly read his mind because she met his eyes, boring in. "And what about Jesus? Was he reckless when he gave his life for us?"

"Of course not. It's just . . . No one should give their life for me."

"Says the man who is so willing to give his for others."

He lifted a shoulder.

"Because if you do, then you deserve grace, right? Deserve forgiveness for losing your sister and every other terrible thing you've done."

He looked at her. Swallowed. Angel looked up at him, as if needing his answer.

"I am forgiven. I am clean. I am loved. Say it with me, Jake."

He closed his eyes.

"I know grace is difficult to accept, Jake. It's in our nature to want to bargain for our redemption, as if we have a stake in it. But it's an all-or-nothing proposal. You can do nothing but receive it. All or nothing. I am forgiven. I am clean. I am loved."

"I don't deserve grace."

"Of course you don't. That's the point of grace. So stop acting like it's a negotiation." Her hand tightened in his. "Receive the gift, or don't. That's all that's required to be set free, Jake. To live in peace."

He nodded, aware of eyes on him. "Take care of yourself, Mimi." He leaned down and kissed her forehead.

She pressed her hand to his whiskered face and smiled at him.

He walked around to Angel and knelt before her. "You okay?"

"I'm going to help Mimi rebuild the Bahama Mama." She ran her hands over her belly. "Me and Hannah here."

He looked at her, frowned. "What did you say?"

Angel looked at him. "I'm having a girl—didn't I tell you? And I'm naming her Hannah."

He swallowed. "Really? Why Hannah?" Maybe she'd overheard him talking to Aria . . .

"I've always loved that name." She smiled. "I had a friend growing up who was named Hannah, and, I don't know . . . I just like the name."

Jake looked at her belly. "May I?"

She nodded and took his hand, pressed it on the baby. It moved beneath his hand, tiny limbs, a tiny body. Alive. "Thank you, Jake," she whispered. "Thank you for saving us."

He drew in a breath, his throat tight again, and nodded.

"I'm going to check on Wade," Aria said and Jake got up.

"If you ever need anything—ever—you call me," he said to Angel, then Mimi.

"C'mon, superhero," Aria said and tugged on his arm.

But when he turned to take her hand, she walked away, down the hallway.

In doctor mode, clearly.

Wade was sleeping, but Bailey slid off his mother's lap as Jake and Aria came in. "Jake!" He threw his arms around Jake's waist.

The woman by Wade's bedside—a pretty woman with short, dark hair—got up and walked over to Jake. She'd clearly been crying, her voice torn when it emerged. "Thank you. I can't believe that Bailey weathered that storm alone—I thought he was evacuating with Wade. I even went home to see if he was gone. That's probably how Ringo got in the car. I didn't see him and thought . . ." Her hand went to her mouth, trembling. "I don't know why I didn't get his voice mail, but by the time I got Wade's message, I was in Miami."

"He made it," Jake said. "That's what matters."

Then, for some reason, he reached out to the woman and drew her into a hug. Clearly all this emotion was infecting him. But she gave him a hard hug, and he drew Bailey in before she let go.

"Hey, where's Ringo?"

"They set up a kennel at the hospital for evacuated pets," Bailey's mom said.

"Give the little guy a rub for me, okay, champ?" He knocked fists with Bailey.

Aria was out in the hallway, chatting with a doctor as he came out of the room. Good looking, redheaded, short and lean, he wore a pressed oxford shirt and a pair of clean chinos, his arms crossed over his chest, his brow furrowed. Jake caught a "And you were stranded there for three days? Aria, I'm so sorry—I told the chopper to go back for you—"

"You're Drey?" Jake said, walking up to the man. "Let's talk about that chopper—"

"Jake."

Aria's voice stopped him from the rest. Although the rest might have included Jake pushing the guy against the wall, getting into his face about broken promises.

He drew in a breath and heard his own voice, to Bailey's mother. *"He made it. That's what matters."*

Right. They'd made it through the storm.

He tightened his jaw and turned away, spotted Ham leaning against the far wall, along with Orion and North. Ham was on his phone.

"Are you sure you want to go to Texas Children's?" Drey asked Aria. "Cincinnati is one of the top hospitals in the country for pediatrics. You could teach, run your own department . . ."

Aria laughed, but Jake's heart had turned into a hard ball in the middle of his chest.

What?

"Thanks, but I've already written my acceptance letter, so . . ." She laughed.

And he couldn't breathe.

"Hey, Jake, our Uber is here. We gotta fly." Ham cut into their conversation.

Aria was hugging Drey.

As if she hadn't just . . . wow, his chest actually hurt, right in the center.

"I can't wait to get home and get a shower," Aria said, looking at him with a smile.

But it didn't quite reach her eyes.

And frankly, he probably gave her the same half smile back.

Texas?

He followed her down the hallway, behind the rest of the crew, desperately wanting to grab her arm, pull her back, and—well, *what*?

Pull out his heart for her to finish the job?

He knew that Aria wasn't herself under stress. She did and said impulsive things she didn't mean under sunny skies.

They both did.

Like hand over their hearts.

Wow, he was a fool.

He climbed into the Uber van and sat with his hands tucked between his knees all the way to the airport.

Aria's rebooked ticket landed her in first class. He ended up in coach, squished into a middle seat between Ham and Orion.

North got an aisle seat.

"You okay?" Ham asked as they buckled in. He glanced at a kid seated across the aisle and made a face.

Jake folded his arms, leaned his head back, and closed his eyes. "Never better."

But he had the very distinct feeling that Aria was on the run.

Again.

■ ■ ■

The pit in Ham's gut had grown into a ball of fire since the plane had landed in Minneapolis. He wanted to blame it on Jake, and the fact that his number one man seemed even more despondent than when he'd left him a week ago.

What if Jake really was thinking of reactivating? Ham had meant it as a joke when he said it in Key West, but . . .

Please. Jake had just been through a hurricane and its aftermath. He needed a shower, a nap, and his feet on dry, stable land.

They both did. Because as Ham emerged out into the concourse, his backpack over one shoulder, then led the way out to the parking ramp where his jeep sat in long-term parking, he just wanted to get home, climb into bed, and wake up to a new day.

A new reality, maybe. One where the ache of missing Signe didn't feel like a fresh wound, infected and raw in his chest.

Which, frankly, was the source of the burn inside.

How was he supposed to help his daughter adjust to a life without her mother when even he couldn't bear it?

"Jenny is picking me up," said Aria as they reached baggage claim and passenger pickup. She turned to North and Ham, then glanced at Jake. "Thank you again for all you did."

"Aria, I—"

"I'll call you, Jake," she said, wearing an enigmatic expression, and that shut Jake down like a hand in the face.

He nodded, his mouth tight.

Then, to confuse the poor man completely—because even Ham was stymied—she came up and kissed Jake on the cheek.

Then practically ran for the sliding doors.

Jake sighed. "She's at it again."

"What?" Ham said, but Jake just shook his head.

"Let's go."

They dumped their bags into the back of the jeep and climbed in, the night thick and muggy around them as Ham pulled out of the ramp. Overhead the sky spilled watchlights, the moon partial and dove gray as Ham headed toward North's apartment on the west side of the city.

"See you at the birthday party tomorrow?" North said to Jake as he got out.

"What party?"

"Dinah's twins. At the Mall of America. Selah invited me—I hope that's okay."

"Right. See you tomorrow."

North shut the door and Ham noticed how Jake's gaze followed him into his building.

"So North and Selah are a thing now?" Ham said.

"News to me," Jake said. He'd slept most of the way home on the plane, and his voice betrayed it, a little sleep worn. He tapped his fingers on his pant leg, as if agitated.

"Jake, I gotta know—are you reactivating?"

Jake looked at him. Frowned. "No. I mean . . . I don't . . ." He lifted a shoulder. "I guess it's an option, but . . ."

"What's going on?"

They turned off Hwy 7 and wove through the side roads of Greenwood, towering oaks and elms scattering the starlight.

"Aria is taking a job in Texas."

Ham glanced at him. "Really?"

"Yeah. But of course, she didn't tell me—I had to overhear her talking to another doctor at the hospital in Miami."

"When is she leaving?"

"I don't know. But . . . shoot." He ran a hand around the back of his neck. "I really thought that . . . yeah, well, I guess I shouldn't be surprised. It's not like my life is trauma free. She has enough stress with her patients. I don't need to add to it."

"From what I saw, Aria isn't afraid of a little trauma."

"I think what she's been through counts as *a lot* of trauma."

Ham let his mouth curve up. "Yeah. But that's hardly on you."

"No, but she's right—I'm impulsive, and I run into danger. And it scares her."

"You are impulsive, Silver. But that's how God made you. Some would call it reacting quickly."

Jake's mouth gave a quick, wry tug.

"And running into danger is what you were trained to do. Regardless of what circumstances you find yourself in, whether you stay with Jones, Inc. Or reactivate. You see danger, you react."

Jake nodded. "Someone has to, right?"

"Do they? Because to a lot of people, the answer would be no. But that's the difference, Jake. You say yes. But do you do it because you have to—or because you can?"

Jake stared at him, as if nonplussed by the question. Then, "Is there a difference?"

"*Have to* means that if you don't, you've let someone down, probably yourself, maybe your team. *Can* means you are being the man God designed you to be, for his purposes."

"Either way, Aria gets hurt." Jake looked away again, into the darkness. "Probably, I should just call this thing quits."

"So, you two did have a thing."

Jake made a face. "I'm in love with her."

"Well, that's easy, then. You run after the woman."

"Even if she's running away?"

Ham turned into Jake's driveway. A motion light turned on, illuminating the cobblestone drive of the beautiful old house. "You really think she's running away? Maybe . . ." He swallowed, his words crawling out of his heart. "Maybe she just desperately needs to know that you'll run after her. That you won't give up on her. That you'll keep your promises."

Jake turned quiet as Ham pulled up to his door. "And what promises are we talking about, Boss?"

Ham put the car in park. Sighed. "The ones that said you'll keep her safe. Give her the happy ending she always wanted."

And for a moment he was back there, standing in her grandfather's barn, his arms around Signe as she wept, her back to him, her hands over her face. *"Shh, Signe. It'll be okay."*

Except, he hadn't a clue how to fix this, the death of her grandfather. The sense that her entire world had collapsed. So he'd opened his mouth and made promises he couldn't keep. The ones that included that he would always show up for her. Always love her. And that she'd never have to be afraid, because he would keep her safe.

She'd turned in his arms and looked at him with so much belief, it latched right into his bones.

And then he'd gone and joined the navy and shattered her heart.

Silence fell between them. Finally, Jake said softly, "Yeah, those promises."

The house was quiet as they entered, but a light shone in the back of the house. Ham followed Jake into the kitchen and found Ellie, Jake's mother, Georgia, and his father sitting at the center island.

"Hey, you two," Chuck said. "We were just watching the tropical storm hit Miami."

Ham glanced over and spotted the Weather Channel playing.

"High fun," Ellie said and walked over to Jake, putting her arms around his neck. "I was worried, bro."

Jake hugged her, then his mother. "I'm starved, what do you have in the fridge?"

"Some leftover meat loaf." Georgia let Jake go and turned to the fridge.

"Thank you for watching Aggie," Ham said.

"She's a doll," Georgia said, pulling out a glass container. "She's sleeping upstairs in Dinah's room." She set the container on the counter. "Would you like some meat loaf?"

Ham shook his head. "Thanks, but I'll just go get her."

"She can stay," Georgia said. "She's going with Dinah's girls to the birthday party tomorrow at the Mall of America. Darcy and Lola are here too."

Oh. Well. And maybe that wasn't a terrible idea. Probably she didn't love sleeping in his storage room, like she might be baggage.

Yeah, he could do better. Much better.

In fact, "Can I tag along tomorrow? I could use some help fixing up a little girl's room." He glanced at Ellie.

"I'm your girl," Ellie said, winking.

"I'm just going to go up and check on her, then I'll see you at the Mall tomorrow."

"Ten o'clock, at the amusement park. I think Dinah has reserved space near the pineapple bounce house."

Ham clamped Jake on the shoulder. "Get some rest."

Then he headed upstairs.

Aggie was asleep in a tiny ball in the bedroom at the end of the hall. He eased the door open, and the hall light fell across her face.

Such a cute face, pixie nose, her blonde hair in a tangle on her pillow. He knelt beside her bed, aware suddenly of her small hands, the way they gripped that grimy, ragged unicorn, holding it to herself.

He had the terrible urge to ease her grip open, to weave his own hand into it.

His throat burned, and he closed his eyes. *Lord, I'm in over my head here, but I want to do right by her, and by Signe. I should have been a husband—a real husband. But help me be a good father to Aggie.*

She stirred, and he opened his eyes. A smile tugged at her mouth, in her sleep, and he leaned up and whispered a kiss on her forehead. "Daddy loves you, Aggie."

Signe, I'm going to keep those promises. I will keep her safe, no matter what.

Then he got up, turned off the light, and headed downstairs—back to his darkened home.

CHAPTER 16

IF JAKE WAS REACTIVATING, Aria would have to learn how to live with impulsive. Live with danger. Live with the unknown.

Aria stood at the kitchen sink, staring out the window of her apartment at the sun lighting the skyline of Minneapolis aglow, and listening to her coffee brew. She'd said nothing—*nothing*—to Jake last night at the airport about their future, and her regret had forced her out of bed.

In fact, she'd said almost nothing since Ham's words in Key West. "*Anything to keep you from reactivating. I can't lose you to the teams, Silver.*"

The comment swept out her breath and hung around inside her heart the entire deafening ride to the boat in the flimsy inflatable raft. Then, Jake had spent the rest of the trip, at least until they got onto the plane, regaling his buddies with his three days of super-heroic-ness.

She hadn't wanted to douse his triumph with her hurt.

Jake. Reactivating.

Becoming a SEAL again.

He might have mentioned that tidbit to her when she was handing over her heart, declaring that she wanted to be with him . . .

He probably expected her to follow him to . . . where? San Diego? Norfolk? Hawaii?

The coffee stopped dripping, gurgled, and she poured herself a cup. Remembered Jake's whining about needing coffee, right before he, um, *died*.

She pressed her hand to her chest.

Maybe she would like Hawaii. And San Diego's Rady Children's Hospital was ranked twenty-fifth in the country for their pediatric cardiology and pulmonary surgery.

She could maybe help with that.

Really, Jake?

Aria had even tracked down Ham in the waiting room of the Miami hospital. "Is Jake rejoining the SEALs?" She'd kept her voice low, aware that it could carry into the ER bay where Jake's hand was being examined and redressed. She'd like him to have an EKG too, but he seemed to be just fine, the way he'd picked her up, carrying her to the chopper.

For her part, they'd put a walking splint on her ankle, but it had stopped aching.

Or possibly, it just paled in comparison to the ache in her heart at Ham's words. He'd looked at her, grinned, and said, flippantly, "After this week, I think reactivating would be a vacation."

She'd stilled.

And then Ham had lifted a shoulder, turning serious. "Not if I can help it."

But Aria knew Jake. When he made up his mind about something . . .

Maybe that's what he meant by being caught in the middle. Having to make choices that hurt people. She'd thought he meant Afghanistan, but maybe it meant her. Not wanting to hurt her when he left.

"You're up."

She turned and Jenny came out of the bedroom. She wore a pair of joggers and a T-shirt and held a shoulder bag, her blonde hair back in a braid. She looked tan and completely recovered from their adventure in Alaska.

"I probably need to check in at the hospital."

"Or, you could join me and Orion at the Mall of America today," Jenny said. "He overheard Dinah tell Jake that she was having her twins' birthday party there, and he decided he wanted to check out the amusement park."

"Seriously?"

Jenny grinned. "Sure. Why not? Pick up some cheese curds?"

And for some reason, Jake and his Spam were back in her head.

"I don't know . . . I—"

"Have had enough fun for one week?" Jenny winked as she walked over to the coffeepot. She poured a cup and leaned her hip against the counter. Blew on the coffee. "Face it, Ari. You need another vacation from your vacation."

Aria laughed. "Please. I'm not leaving the state ever again. I'm tired of storms and blizzards and *drama*."

Jenny looked at her. "Are you, though? Because according to Orion, who heard it from Jake, you were sort of a superstar in Florida. Jake said you saved his life." Jenny raised an eyebrow, as if waiting for confirmation.

"He was electrocuted. I had to restart his heart." She left out how many times.

"Wow." Jenny put down her coffee. "You two really know how to take it to the next level."

Aria felt her face heating.

"Oh . . . wow, I didn't mean—did something happen between you two?"

Aria finished her coffee. Put her mug down. "I don't know . . ."

Silence, and finally Jenny, the psychologist, rescued her. "You're in love with Jake Silver."

Aria drew in a breath. And then, because it was Jenny, "Oh, Jen, he's just . . ."

Jenny's face tightened. "What did he do?"

Oh, wait, no— "Nothing."

"Jake can be charming. And sort of pushy. And impulsive—"

"And brave and amazing and kind and—Jenny, he's not to blame for what happened in Alaska."

Jenny's mouth tightened.

"Really. I was the one who invited him to our room. I was the one who . . . well, who invited him to stay for a shower."

Jenny raised an eyebrow.

"And yes, I'm grateful you walked in, because I wasn't myself, but, well, maybe that's the thing. I was myself—at least, I was following my heart, not Kia's, and yes, I was following it way too far, but for the first time in my life, I realized something."

Jenny had walked over to the counter, put her cup on it. Met her eyes, still unsmiling.

"My heart belongs to me, not Kia."

One side of Jenny's mouth lifted up.

"And I get to be happy. And to live. And it doesn't have to be on Kia's terms, but mine. I don't owe her my life just because I had the fortune to get her heart. God arranged that. And he's good. And sovereign and I don't have to justify that gift. Kia lived her life the way she wanted to. And I get to do the same."

"And that means—"

"That I love Jake Silver."

There, she said it.

And the words sank like a balm into her soul.

She *loved* Jake Silver. Brave, impulsive, charming Jake Silver.

And she wasn't letting him go.

Jenny blinked. "Wow. Really?"

"Really." She blew out a breath. "Even if he's going to be a SEAL again."

"What?"

"Yeah. Apparently, Ham is trying to talk him out of it but I know Jake. He's stubborn—"

"And charming and sweet and—"

"Impulsive and dangerous—"

"And hot." Jenny grinned.

"And hot," Aria said. "Painfully hot, and not just because of his smile. But because he's all the way good, right down to his core. The kind of guy who doesn't think before he saves a life. And I love him for that too."

"Really?"

"I am tired of standing on the sidelines or doing the safe thing with my life."

"We did climb Denali."

"I meant emotionally, Jenny."

Jenny grinned. "Then come to the Mall of America with us."

"Why?"

"Because Jake will be there."

Jake will be there.

He'd chased her to Florida. It seemed the least she could do was to chase him across the city. And wherever his—their—adventures took them.

"Let me get dressed and make a phone call," she said.

Jenny reached for the bran cereal. "Who are you calling?"

Aria headed for her bedroom. "Texas."

■ ■ ■

Jake should have been able to sleep until the end of time the way he'd fallen, hard, into bed, his muscles asleep before he hit the pillow.

But things weren't right.

Not with Aria.

And then there was Ham's question, rolling around in his head. *"But do you do it because you have to—or because you can?"*

Not that the answer mattered, but it would have been easier to shrug away if he didn't hear his own voice echo the answer back . . .

"You're doing things you never thought you'd do, because you have to, and then looking in the mirror and not recognizing yourself."

Jake had spent his life following the have-tos, maybe.

Something he stared at the ceiling thinking about way too long.

Of course, the dream had woken him up first. A new one, but enough for him to feel it tremor over him.

He finally got up, pulled on his jeans and a T-shirt, and stopped in the bathroom for a quick brush, getting a look at himself in the mirror. He hadn't shaved when he'd showered last night, his hair askew. But at least he was clean.

And not in a hospital.

Jake headed downstairs, following the aroma of fresh coffee, and found a pot brewed in the big kitchen. Pouring himself a cup, he brought it out to the sunroom.

His father sat in his recliner, his Bible open on one arm, his eyes closed, rocking.

Oh.

Jake made to turn around—

"I can hear you breathing, so don't even try to escape." His father opened his eyes. "For a SEAL you sure are loud."

"I wasn't trying to sneak up on you." But Jake grinned. "Sorry to interrupt your praying." He'd forgotten his father got up early to pray—had ever since Jake had been a child.

"I'm done. For now." He closed his Bible, his tattered prayer list stuck inside.

Jake came over to the windows and stared at the lake. It was a deep indigo, and the sun was just gilding the waves, turning the tips to platinum. The scent of fresh-cut grass seasoned the air, the sprinklers hissing as they watered the lawn.

"Couldn't sleep, huh?"

"I slept." Jake sipped his coffee.

"You were talking in your sleep again. Same dream?"

He looked at his father. He wore an old Moody Bible Institute sweatshirt, his readers down on his nose. Now, he took them off and gave Jake a smile. "You can talk about it. Nobody's judging you."

Jake shook his head. "Different dream. This time I was swimming. I was in the ocean, and North and Ham were with me. But Aria was there too, and they were in a Zodiac just a few feet away, but I couldn't seem to catch up. And the harder I swam . . . anyway, it's just a stupid dream. I've seen enough ocean for a while."

"You used to have one about running—"

"Yeah. Back when I ran track. Apparently I like to exercise in my sleep."

His father took a sip of his coffee. "Any more . . . memories?"

Jake shook his head. But stared into his coffee. "Give it time."

"Or maybe you've let it go."

Jake gave a laugh. Only it didn't sound like a laugh.

"I've been praying for you for a while, that you'd be freed from your, um—"

"Nightmare? Thanks, Dad, but I'm not fourteen. You don't need to pray away my night terrors."

"I'll never stop praying for you, son."

He didn't know why those words burned his throat.

"I pray for all my children. Even Hannah."

Jake looked away, blinking. "Why? She's gone, Dad."

"Because I believe in hope. And miracles."

"I gave up on hope a long time ago."

"You gave up on a lot of things a long time ago. Including your belief that you deserve to be happy."

Jake looked at him, frowning. "I'm happy."

"You *act* happy. But you aren't happy, son. You mask all your pain with charm and jokes. And then you fill up all your emptiness with trouble and danger and call yourself healed. But you're not. You're angry and broken and driven by the voices that tell you that you're trouble."

"Wow, I'm glad I got up. How many cups of coffee have you had?"

"Just the three, but you know I'm right." His dad raised an eyebrow.

Jake looked at his father.

"You've lived your entire life telling yourself that you are a villain. And villains don't get a happy ending, do they?"

Jake drew in a breath. Fine. "It's hard to be happy when you know you've wrecked the lives of the people you love." He didn't know why he said that, and frankly, it was the first time, really, that he'd spoken the truth, but maybe it was time. "It's my fault Hannah went missing."

"You're the only one who believes that, Jake."

Jake's mouth tightened. "It's true."

"Then the only one who hasn't forgiven you is . . . you."

Jake closed his eyes. "I've tried. And sometimes I think I have. And then it comes right back and . . . something reminds me of . . . well, reminds me."

"That's the devil's games, Jake. He'll do anything to make you feel ashamed. Or guilty. Anything to try and tell you that you are unloved. Memories. What-ifs. Even the unkind words of others. They poke at you, unsettle you. Your relationship with God is the devil's primary target, and if he can get you to believe that you have to earn God's love, or that you are unredeemable—get you to turn away from grace—then he can block out God's voice in your life. And suddenly, your life *is* empty."

His father got up. "Forgiveness is a moving target. You have to find it and tell yourself the truth every day, as declared in God's Word. You are forgiven. Nothing can separate you from God's love."

He walked over to Jake. "Jake, look at me."

Jake felt like he might be thirteen years old again, unable to resist his father's command, as he met his father's eyes.

"You've listened to everybody else's voices. Your guilt, your shame, even other people's accusations." His father put his hands on his shoulders. "Now listen to your father's voice. I *forgive* you. I *love* you. You are my son, and I would choose none other."

"Even if that son is impulsive and runs into trouble?"

His father gave his shoulders a shake. "*Especially* because that son is quick on his feet and isn't afraid of danger. I count on him being exactly the man God made him to be."

He paused, just holding Jake, his big hands warm on Jake's body, his blue eyes in Jake's.

"You are forgiven. You are clean. You are loved."

Yes.

He breathed it in, the sunrise warm on his skin.

Finally, "Are we done here?"

Jake nodded.

"Good. Because I'm making waffles. My grandchildren will be up soon and we have a party to get to."

He let Jake go and headed into the kitchen.

No, he didn't deserve his father's forgiveness at all.

But apparently, that's how grace worked.

It *wasn't* a bargain. So maybe he should stop trying so hard to earn something he already had.

I am forgiven. I am clean.

"Hey, Unca Jake!" The voice called out his name and he spotted six-year-old Darcy bouncing down the hallway, wearing a black tutu and a red Mickey Mouse T-shirt.

He put his coffee down just in time to scoop her up as she flew into his arms. She smelled of cotton sheets and bubble gum toothpaste. Grabbing his cheeks, she kissed his nose and grinned at him. "Are you going to my birthday party?"

"I wouldn't miss it for the world, kiddo."

Three hours later, however, Jake was rethinking his answer as he stood in line for Blue's Skidoo—one of the flying rides. He held Lola's and Darcy's hands, both of them wrenching his arms as they bounced in line, their excitement sloughing off them.

At a picnic table nearby, Dinah and her husband were finishing off waffle fries, while Ellie and Chloe got pedicures with their mom at a nearby salon. They'd roped Aggie in on the fun, something Ham seemed on the fence about.

"She's ten."

"Ten-year-olds have toenails, Ham," Ellie had said, taking Aggie's hand.

Scout and Bear had taken off with their grandfather for the Avatar Airbender ride.

North and Selah had vanished too, mentioning something about a roller coaster.

Jake had always liked the Mall of America, but he remembered the Camp Snoopy days with the giant blow-up of Snoopy standing guard at the entrance of the theme park. Now, a giant Spongebob Squarepants stood in Snoopy's place, his legs the opening to a bounce house and ball pit for youngsters. Jake had stood at the netted wall watching Lola for nearly a half hour.

"What is this thing?" Ham had asked, watching Aggie jump.

"It's a giant, um, sponge?" Jake said. "Shaped like a kitchen sponge. And he lives in the ocean, in a town called Bikini Bottom, and works as a fry cook—"

Ham held up his hand. "That is way too much information."

"You'll need to brush up on your Barbie and My Little Pony chops there, Chief."

"I was thinking of taking her rock climbing."

Jake laughed. "Right."

"When Signe was a kid, she used to take in stray dogs. Maybe Aggie would like a dog?"

"Maybe you should just figure out how to take care of a ten-year-old before you start adding pets to the mix."

Ham made a face.

"Listen, you'll be fine. I'm not a parent, but there's an instinct to it. You're not her friend, you're her father. Which means you have to be the bad guy sometimes. But the rest of the time, you just tell her that she's loved. That she's important to you. That she's safe. And that you'll never leave her."

Weird to be giving advice to Ham, but he seemed to be listening, nodding. "I just . . . I haven't quite figured out what this looks like."

Now he stood in line with Jake, as if not sure what to do with himself. Poor guy, he radiated a weird tension, something so un-Ham-like it had Jake worried for him.

Still trying to figure out how to ace the dad thing, clearly.

At the picnic table, Phoebe had arrived. She carried a couple shopping bags and now sat on the bench, her hand perched on her belly.

"I missed so much," Ham said, out of the blue. Or maybe it was simply a continuation of the conversation he was having in his head.

Whatever. Jake had his back. "You're not going to miss any more."

Ham shoved his hands into his pockets.

As Jake watched, his mother, Ellie, and Chloe returned. From a distance, he could see them show off their toes to Dinah and Phoebe.

"Where's Aggie?" Ham asked.

From the body language of the ladies, his mother's sudden frown, Chloe's turning, and finally Ellie's stricken look as she met eyes with Jake, they were asking the same question.

He felt a punch, right into the center of his gut.

"Where is Aggie?" Ham said and started out back through the line.

"C'mon, girls, we have to go," Jake said, pulling them out.

"Unca Jake! No—" Lola started, but he gave her a look.

Her eyes widened, but she stopped whining.

He pulled them along, not quite running, and finally reached down and picked them both up, carrying them on his hips as he ran over to the bench.

Ham was already there, already getting a chaotic explanation.

"She was right ahead of us. *Right* ahead of us!" his mother was saying.

She met Jake's gaze.

And inside, he heard screaming.

"We'll find her, Mom," he said and practically shoved Lola and Darcy at their mother.

"We'll retrace our route," Ellie said. Ham took off after her.

Jake took a breath. "I'm going upstairs. Maybe she's in the park. I can get a better view from there."

He looked at Lola and Darcy and couldn't help a "Stay put."

Dinah had their hands in a steel grip.

Then he took off for the escalator.

Oh, how he hated the Mall of America. Or any mall, in any city.

Any crowd, really.

Please, God, don't let this happen again.

Jake took the escalator two steps at a time, pushing past a couple angry mothers, and ran out to the deck that overlooked the park.

She was wearing a pink shirt and a pair of jeans, her blonde hair in braids. He remembered Ellie braiding Aggie's hair in the kitchen this morning. Remembered her changing her shirt after she spilled syrup on it.

"Aggie!" He didn't care if he attracted attention, but it didn't matter anyway, the roller coasters and screams of riders swallowed it up. The park was a mass of colors, moving machinery, balloons, and people, too many of them children. He scanned the park, his gaze falling on a little girl—too young. Another with blonde braids—but a green shirt.

He spotted North. He was standing on the picnic table, waving his arms at Jake.

"What?"

North was pointing toward the west entrance, to the third level.

There. Right by the I Love Minnesota store, he spotted Aggie. She was holding on to the railing, staring out at the amusement park.

His breath leaked out—

Wait.

Behind her stood a man, his hand on her neck, as if he was trying to pull her free from the railing.

"Hey!" Jake shouted, but it was useless. North had already sprinted for the entrance.

Jake took off, not sure who'd get there first, but racing toward the west entrance along the second floor.

Oh, how he wished he had a weapon.

He flew up the stairs at the west entrance. "Make a hole!" And landed at the top.

Clearly, the man was trying not to make a scene, the way he had Aggie by the arm, trying to pull her away from the railing.

She was fiercely holding on but not making a sound.

So, Jake did. "Let her go!"

What felt like a thousand heads turned.

But not the assailant. White, midthirties, with a backpack.

And behind his shirt—Jake lunged for the weapon.

Too late. The man turned and pulled it out, grabbing Aggie around the throat.

"Back. Off."

Jake put up his hands.

The man seemed sober, and he bore an accent, something eastern European. Dark hair, a tattoo on his neck that snaked out of the collar of his shirt. He pulled Aggie back, away from the railing.

"Listen, dude, I don't know what you want, but let the girl go, and we can talk."

Behind him, Jake heard a voice—low, sober. "Aggie, don't be scared."

Ham.

The man looked from Jake, to Ham, then to the exit. Jake spotted a mall cop by a rack of Minnesota Vikings sweatshirts. Jake shook his head but the cop, maybe midtwenties, seemed intent on taking down the assailant.

"Listen, no one needs to get hurt here," Jake started.

But Mall Cop clearly wasn't listening because with a shout, he rushed Aggie's assailant.

"No!" Ham's voice but Jake's thought as he dove at Aggie.

The assailant turned, fired off a shot at Mall Cop. Shoved Aggie toward the railing.

Then he turned his gun on Aggie.

And then, following his instincts—or maybe just a wild impulse—Jake grabbed her and dove over the edge, just as a gunshot bit the air.

CHAPTER 17

SURPRISE! Except the joke was on Aria, because the first thing she saw as she followed Orion into the massive amusement park under the dome of the center of the Mall of America was the man she loved—yes, *loved*, and she planned on telling him that—hanging over the edge of the second-story balcony.

Hanging, one hand on a lower girder, his other hand gripping a hysterical little girl.

Aggie Jones, Ham's daughter.

And to her eye, it looked like Jake was—yes—*bleeding*.

His hand, in fact, was slipping, from the looks of it.

They were going to fall.

People were screaming.

She felt like screaming.

On a level above them, North had ahold of a man, wrestling him to the deck.

A crowd had gathered right below the balcony, around the big yellow blowup sponge. A stupid place to stand—and she had a mind to tell everyone to move.

But, exactly the right place to jump, if someone had a mind

to do that. They could, with the right angle, land on the massive bounce-house-slash-pillow.

"What's he doing?" Jenny said. She'd slipped her hand into Aria's as they made their way over to the horrible spectacle.

Yes, Jake was most assuredly slipping. She saw him adjust his grip, and then, as she watched, he pulled the little girl up to his waist and clamped his legs around her. He let her go and grabbed on to the girder with his other hand.

His *injured* hand.

"They're going to fall," said Jenny.

Aria looked at her. "This is Jake. Trust me—he's got everything under control."

Jenny gave her a look. "He's dangling from a second-story girder!"

"And he knows what he's doing!"

Okay, she might sound a little panicked, but—

But she knew it in her gut. Jake knew what he was doing. Even impulsive, even out of his element, even with his crazy schemes, Jake . . . well, Jake might follow his gut, but she'd gladly put her life into Jake's impulsive hands.

He was talking to Aggie, who put her arms around his body.

Then, he leaned down and spoke to her. Aria could imagine what he might be saying . . .

Hold on.

I'll keep you safe.

I promise.

And if anyone kept his promises, it was Jake Silver.

Jake wrapped his arm around the girl, pulled her to himself. She locked her arms around his neck. Then, as if he might be an acrobat, Jake used his legs to spring them out into the open air of the mall.

Flying, it seemed.

Voices screamed, and Jenny gasped.

Aria held her breath.

Jake landed on the giant blow-up sponge at the entrance. He cradled Aggie in his arms, falling into the sponge, then back, into the ball pit.

"That jerk," Orion said and took off, moving as quickly as he could on his crutch.

The man was brilliant. Aria hobbled after him.

By the time they reached Jake, he was rolling out of the pit, Aggie still clinging to him. Orion helped them out and then took Aggie.

"You okay, kid?"

She looked at Orion, then Jenny, and Aria—who really wanted to give her a good twice-over—and then her gaze settled on Ham, who was running across the entrance.

She burst into tears. "Daddy!"

Ham's expression broke as he scooped her up, pulling her hard to himself.

Jake sat on the edge of the ball pit, his hand clamped to his bleeding arm, watching.

But Aria was watching Jake. The look on his face, the way his jaw tightened, the way his breathing caught.

The way his eyes teared up.

"Jake?"

He looked at her, his eyes widening. Then he closed them, his head bowing.

She walked up to him, put her arms around him, and pulled him to herself as he quietly, appropriately, fell apart.

"Jake?" Orion started, but Aria looked over at him.

"I got this," she said.

Orion raised an eyebrow but nodded.

"I could use a first aid kit," she said.

"I'm on it," Jenny said.

A crowd had gathered, some of them clapping, but she ignored them as Jake's shoulders shook.

"You're going to be okay, tough guy," she said quietly. She kissed the top of his head.

A breath rattled out of him, and he pressed his hand to his face. Looked up at her. She ran her thumbs down his cheeks, catching the moisture there. "It's okay. Trauma makes people do strange things. Feel all sorts of unexpected emotions. You're going to live. Trust me. I'm a doctor."

He looked at her, smiled. "A hot doctor."

Aaaand he was back.

"What are you doing here, anyway?"

"Really? That's how you're going to greet me after I chase you . . . all the way across . . . town?"

He waggled his eyebrows. "You're chasing me now?"

She nodded, her smile falling. "I love you, Jake. No matter what you do. I love you for who you are, for the tough guy, the joker, even the guy who scares me to death. And I'll love you even if you decide to reactivate."

He stared at her. "Oh, uh . . . I'm not reactivating, Aria. That was . . . I don't know, an impulse. I guess I just wanted to do something more with my life."

"More than rescuing little girls and hot doctors?"

"No, that's enough." He reached up to touch her face but drew back at the blood. "Sorry. I got a little nick when I went over."

"My guess is that I'm going to have to get used to this."

Jenny had returned and handed her the first aid kit. Aria walked Jake over to a bench. She sat beside him, examining the wound.

"It's a pretty deep graze. You might need a couple stitches." She pulled out a gauze pad.

"Good thing I know a good trauma doc."

She pressed the gauze to his arm. "About that . . ."

"I know about Texas, Houlihan. And I'm in."

"What?"

"I overheard that doc from Cincinnati. Something about you transferring to Texas?"

"Yeah, well—"

"I'm in. If you want to go to Texas, I'll learn to herd cattle or something—"

"I'm not going to Texas, Jake."

He stared at her.

"I like my job here. I like my life. And Ham did mention he needed a trauma doc on his SAR team, right?"

"Right," Ham said. He was carrying Aggie, who held him in a death grip. For his part, he didn't seem to be letting her go.

"Who was that guy, Ham?" Jake asked.

"I don't know. But he was swearing in Russian when North took him down, so . . ." Ham looked at Aggie. Clearly, he didn't want to have this conversation in front of her.

"Let's get both of you to a hospital, make sure you're okay," Aria said.

"But what about the birthday cake?"

Everyone stared at Aggie and her question. Hadn't Jake said that Aggie refused to talk?

But then again, that's what happened when a girl stepped into Jake's world—he showed her who she could be.

Helped her become it.

Because that's what heroes did.

"C'mon, Hawkeye. Let's go. Because Aggie's right. We need to get back for cake."

▪ ▪ ▪

Jake didn't know why he was getting all emotional. It wasn't like today was any different than every other. His family, hanging out, laughing at his stupid jokes, the boys playing Monopoly with their grandpa, Phoebe and Selah sitting at the kitchen island, shopping for baby clothes online. North had left the room to take a call. Ham was at the table with Aggie and the twins, coloring a picture of Dora the Explorer, attacking it with the zeal of once-a-SEAL-always-a-SEAL. Chloe was taking shots of the birthday cake as Dinah lit it, his mother armed with a cake knife, ready to serve it up.

Except, this might be better because Aria stood in front of him, leaning against his chest, her hands running down his forearms, contented, it seemed, to stay right here.

No more running.

And he was turning into an embarrassing sap because he couldn't stop the sense of wanting to tear up, his throat still thick from his crazy stunt at the mall.

What had he been thinking?

Maybe he hadn't. He'd just—well, reacted. But not before he'd leaned down and told Aggie to trust him.

But even before *that*, he'd realized that he was going to fall. And if God didn't catch them both, they were goners.

So he'd done the only thing he could. *God, please save us both. Not because I'm a hero, but because you are.*

And then he'd grabbed Aggie and let go.

But the fact that they'd lived, that Aggie hadn't been hurt, that he hadn't broken both their necks—it all rushed out of him in an embarrassing deluge of emotion.

Tears, for cryin' out loud.

But, for the first time in longer than he could remember, he could breathe.

No, he felt washed. Baptized.

Clean.

Dinah finished lighting the candles. "C'mere, girls." She pulled up a couple benches, and Lola and Darcy dropped their crayons and climbed up to hover above the cake.

"Everybody sing—" Dinah started them off.

Even Ham joined in, his hands on Aggie's shoulders.

They were going to make it. Something had unlocked inside Aggie, and she spent the entire visit to the hospital talking about her week with the Silvers. Apparently, Ellie had taken good care of her.

Of course.

The twins blew out the candles, and his mother dug into the cake—pink, with a red crab in the center.

"I love cake," Aria said, taking her piece.

He took a plate also and headed over to the sunroom. "You're really not moving?" They hadn't exactly talked about Aria's declaration during his visit to the hospital—six unnecessary stitches in his opinion—and he wasn't sure her words hadn't been panic induced.

Aria tended to step outside her body and make all sorts of crazy statements when the storms hit.

"It's a great opportunity," he said, sitting down in one of the wicker chairs. "The next big thing in your career, right?"

She sat opposite him, her plate on her lap, her fork poised over her cake. She looked up at him, grinning. "You're my next big thing, Jake."

Oh.

"Any more adventures, I'm having with you."

"Really."

"Mmmhmm." She took a bite of cake.

And his heart just might explode.

"Buckle up, sweetheart."

She swallowed, took a sip of her soda. "I'm wearing a three-point harness."

He laughed and her eyes twinkled.

The doorbell rang and Ellie slid off her stool at the island to get it. Maybe it was Stephan—his absence at the family shindig irked him. But Phoebe seemed unruffled, so maybe he shouldn't worry.

In fact, maybe all his sisters were grown up, and not needing their big brother to hover anymore.

Or to hover less, perhaps.

Ellie came back into the room holding the hand of a tall, handsome young man with the look of an athlete. Jake gave him a hard look.

"Everyone, this is Landry. Landry, this is everyone."

He offered a grin, and even shook Chuck's hand.

Jake glanced at Aria, who was watching him. "Down, tiger," she said.

Oh. He had put down his drink, looked like he might pounce.

North had walked into the room, and Jake saw him gesture to Ham on his way to the sunroom.

"What?" Jake said, wiping his mouth.

North pocketed his phone. "That was a buddy of mine, Will Masterson, who works for Homeland. He was just confirming a hunch Ham had—that the guy who attacked Aggie was Bratva."

Jake looked at Ham. "The Russian mafia? What?"

"I saw his tattoo right before North took him down. A star, on his neck."

"Why would the Bratva be after Aggie?"

"I don't know, but I think it has something to do with Signe, and her death," Ham said. "When I was in Europe trying to track down Royal, I met with a contact who told me about a rumor that the Bratva is searching for something called the NOC list."

"That's real?" Aria said. "I thought that was something from a Tom Cruise movie. A list of undercover agents around the world? That's spy-movie stuff."

"It's real. And according to Chet, it's being auctioned on the black market." Ham looked at North and Jake. "Clearly, it's bothering me that Signe didn't contact me for over a decade, but what if . . . well, she said something to me that made me think maybe she was working undercover."

"You think Signe was CIA?"

"I don't know. And I don't know why she kept Aggie a secret from me. Maybe she didn't have a choice. Or was coerced to stay. But if she was, and she had somehow earned the trust of the man who kidnapped her—Pavel Tsarnaev—then I could see her playing a long game."

"Pavel Tsarnaev?" Jake glanced at Landry, who was accepting a piece of cake from his mother. He was laughing, his hand on Ellie's back.

"Russian-Chechen terrorist with ties to the Bratva," Ham said.

"The guy who attacked the refugee hospital?" Jake said, turning back to Ham. "He took Signe."

"Yeah. Or . . . what if she went with him?" Ham took a breath. "We did recover her coworker, Zara, easily enough."

"Do you think Tsarnaev had the NOC list?" North asked.

"How would he have gotten it?" Aria asked.

"I don't know. But maybe Signe's cover was blown, and he killed her."

And that shut down the room.

"What if Signe had the list?" North said.

"That makes sense. Because why would the Bratva come after Aggie," Jake said quietly, "unless they think she has it?"

"Maybe they think Signe is still alive, and they could use her daughter for leverage," North said, adding even more doom.

Ham leaned forward, his hands clasped. "All I know is that my daughter is in danger, and I don't know how to stop it."

"What about Royal? Didn't you have a lead on him?" Jake asked.

Ham nodded. "I missed the meet with him, but Chet gave me a number. So far no answer to my voice mail."

"Find Royal, and you might find answers," North said.

"Maybe. He might even be on the list," Ham said, leaning back. "But for now, I need to stay close to Aggie."

As if she'd heard her name, Aggie came into the room. She looked at Jake, smiling. "Can I have another ride on your sailboat?"

Jake would do anything for that smile. "Yes."

"But maybe tomorrow," Ham said. "I think we need to get home. I have a surprise for you."

She fairly beamed as Ham got up and took her hand.

North followed him out.

Aria leaned forward. "How about me, Hawkeye? Do I get a ride on your sailboat?"

"You want one?"

She nodded.

Only then did he notice a second necklace hanging around her neck. He reached out, touched the charm, a half-heart to match the one he'd returned to her in Florida. "What's this?"

"Oh." She grabbed the charms, held them together. "It's Kia's half. I thought . . . well, since I have our heart, I should wear it."

Our heart. He smiled at her. And then— "I'll meet you outside, by the cat."

He set his plate in the sink, then headed upstairs and found the shoe polish tin, still tucked in his backpack. Opening the tin, he took out his identification tags, wrapped in black silencers.

He let them dangle in the late-afternoon light, reading the designation.

Name, Silver, Jake C.

His department of defense number. Member of the US Navy.

Blood type, O Neg.

Religion, Christian.

He shoved the tags into the pocket of his cargo shorts, then headed downstairs.

The sky was a beautiful turquoise, a slight scattering of wispy clouds, the sun burning the edges with its fall toward the horizon. It would be a beautiful sunset.

Aria was barefoot, her hair down and blowing in the wind. "Will I get wet?"

"Maybe," he said. "But it'll be worth it." He stood on shore. "I gotta do something first."

He walked out to the end of the dock and pulled out the tags.

"You don't have to wear your dog tags to be a SEAL."

He hurled the tags high into the air, watching them catch the sun until they dropped into the water.

Vanished.

Nope. He didn't.

"That's in here . . ."

He walked back to Aria. "Ready to fly?"

"I'm ready, Superman." Her eyes shone.

Ho, baby, this would be fun.

She made to help him push the cat into the water.

"Whoa—I got this. You stay on shore. I'll carry you."

He half expected an argument, but she just perched herself on the dock as he unwound the mainsail, the jib, laid out the lines. The wind wanted to grab the cat, but he reined it in and brought the cat next to the dock. Then he hoisted himself aboard and reached for Aria.

She braced her hands on his shoulders and let him lift her onto the trampoline. He handed her a life jacket and hooked her into the trapeze. "You think you can hang ten with that ankle?"

"Try and stop me."

He laughed. "I know better than that."

Then he pushed them off and pointed the cat toward the glorious golden sunset.

Put his face to the wind.

And spoke the truth.

I am forgiven. I am clean.

I am loved.

■ ■ ■

When Ham had purchased the 1970s home, he hadn't envisioned a family living here.

Although deep inside, maybe his heart had beat to a different hope, because he'd purchased a *three*-bedroom home.

He'd done most of the renovations himself, vaulting the ceiling in the great room, connecting the inside to the breathtaking private view of the lake with massive sliding doors that opened to an expansive deck. Dark walnut cabinetry, hardwood floors, minimalist furniture, and sleek industrial post-and-beam construction with massive windows, including a skylight, seemed exactly the right adornment, for a man.

But not for a little girl.

Which was why he'd armed Selah and Ellie with a secret mission.

"I love it!"

The mere fact that Aggie was talking to him put a fist in the center of his chest, but her words, the delight in her voice as he opened the door to her bedroom . . .

He couldn't breathe.

Thank you, ladies.

Selah and Ellie had taken his request to decorate Aggie's room to heart. He hadn't really paid attention to the purchases today at the mall—just showed up with his credit card. But they'd gone to town on the room he'd used formerly for the storage of his scuba and climbing gear and transformed it.

Butterflies fluttered in 3-D over the double bed fluffed with fuzzy purple pillows. Over the top of the arched headboard they'd stenciled the word *Dream*. A stuffed rabbit sat between the pillows.

A disco-ball light fixture hung from the middle of the room, and a white wicker egg chair hung in the corner. Purple curtains framed the window and a fluffy pink pouf sat at the foot of the bed.

A few books were tucked in a basket next to his discarded black dresser, now covered in shiny heart decals, and a flower-shaped carpet added softness to the hardwood floor.

They'd even purchased a few items of clothing to add to what Georgia Silver had given her. A frilly nightgown, leggings, a couple of sparkly shirts.

Aggie danced into the room, tossing her worn unicorn on the bed and scooping up the stuffed rabbit. She turned to Ham. "Thank you."

He nodded, unable to speak. Finally, "Why don't you get ready for bed, and I'll come back and read you a book."

She beamed at him, nodding.

He closed the door and walked out into the hallway. It overlooked his great room, and outside twilight had begun to settle, painting the sky a deep magenta, lavender, gold.

He might have painted a different ending, but maybe this was all a guy like him, with the choices he'd made, could hope for.

"I love it."

It seemed like enough. Really.

"Shh, Signe. It'll be okay."

Yes, it would.

He walked downstairs and opened the fridge. Grabbed a container of milk and poured some into a glass. Kids drank milk, right?

"This one!"

He looked up and Aggie was wearing her nightgown, holding up a book. *The Lion, the Witch and the Wardrobe.* "You got it, kiddo."

He tucked her into her bed, sat beside her. "I love this story. Your mom did too. We used to pretend we were in Narnia. She was always Queen Susan, and I was King Peter."

Aggie was so small, tucked next to him, with her golden hair down, and in his heart stirred a memory.

Signe, at this age, sitting next to him as they lay on a blanket in his yard, watching the stars drop from the sky.

Even then, he was in love with her. Probably had been his entire life.

"Wish, Ham! Wish on a star." She pointed to one, but he didn't catch it.

"I wish for this." He nearly took her hand, but that was scary and she'd probably hit him.

But yes, he wished for her, beside him. Forever.

"Who is Susan?" Aggie asked now.

"Just the bravest of all the queens. A warrior. Like your mom was."

Aggie had tucked her grimy unicorn next to her along with the rabbit, on her lap.

"Hey, maybe I should wash this one, huh?" He reached out for the unicorn.

"No!" She yanked it away. "Mama said to never let it go."

"Nothing will happen to it, honey. I'm just going to wash—"

"No!"

He held up his hand. "Okay. Sure. No problem."

She looked up at him, her eyes filling, her mouth a tight bud. "Mama told me not to tell you."

He stilled. "Tell me . . . what?"

She clutched the unicorn to herself. Considered him. "Tell you about the phone."

The phone? "Aggie, what are you talking about?" Ham said quietly.

Slowly, she turned over the unicorn. The bottom was secured with Velcro, and she opened it.

A burner phone lay tucked in the innards, encased in a plastic baggie.

He stared at it. "What is this?"

She pulled it out and handed it to him. Met his eyes, hers wide, searching his.

"You can trust me, honey."

She swallowed. "It's so I can talk to Mama."

So she could . . . *talk* . . . to her mother?

"What?"

"Except, it doesn't work anymore."

He unzipped the bag and opened the phone. No juice.

"Aggie, when was the last time you talked to Mama?"

Aggie shrugged. "I don't remember." Her eyes filled.

Aw. He put his arm around her. "When did she give this to you?"

"On the boat. Before . . ." She drew in a breath. "She said to only call her if I was scared. And to not tell anyone I had the phone."

"Even me?"

Aggie nodded. "Especially you."

Especially him?

Signe, what are you up to?

But no wonder Aggie hadn't spoken, taking her mother's words to heart. Ham kissed her on the top of her head. "How about if I charge this?"

She nodded and picked up the book. Started to read.

"Aggie, can you read English?"

She looked at him. "Of course. And French, German, and Russian."

Oh, she was *so* Signe's daughter.

And *his* amazing daughter. "I'll be right back."

He found a cord in his junk drawer and plugged in the phone. It came to life.

And he couldn't help it. He opened it and scrolled to recent calls.

His heart nearly stopped.

A *week* ago.

After he'd brought Aggie to America, while he was in Europe.

Only one number was listed, and he pushed it.

His heartbeat hammered in his ear as the number connected.

Rang.

Someone picked up.

"Aggie?"

He braced his hand on the counter. Closed his eyes.

He could practically see her, her presence, like an electric shock through him, tremoring his entire body. Nearly feel her breath through the line.

Somehow, he choked out, "No. It's Ham." Silence and— "Sig, don't hang up!"

More silence.

"She's safe. I got her."

A quick, indrawn breath. "She's okay?"

"Yes."

"Thank God. Please keep her that way, Hamburglar. But . . . don't try to find me."

"Sig—"

She hung up.

He clenched the phone in his hand, closed his eyes.

"You'll never lose me, Hamburglar. No matter where I am."

That's right, he wouldn't.

He was bringing his wife home.

Susan May Warren is the *USA Today* bestselling author of over seventy-five novels with more than 1.5 million books sold, including the Montana Rescue series. Winner of a RITA Award and multiple Christy and Carol Awards, as well as the HOLT Medallion and numerous Readers' Choice Awards, Susan has written contemporary and historical romances, romantic suspense, thrillers, romantic comedy, and novellas. She makes her home in Minnesota. Find her online at www.susanmaywarren.com, on Facebook at Susan May Warren Fiction, and on Twitter @susanmaywarren.

"Warren's stalwart characters and engaging story lines make her **Montana Rescue series** a must-read."
—*Booklist*

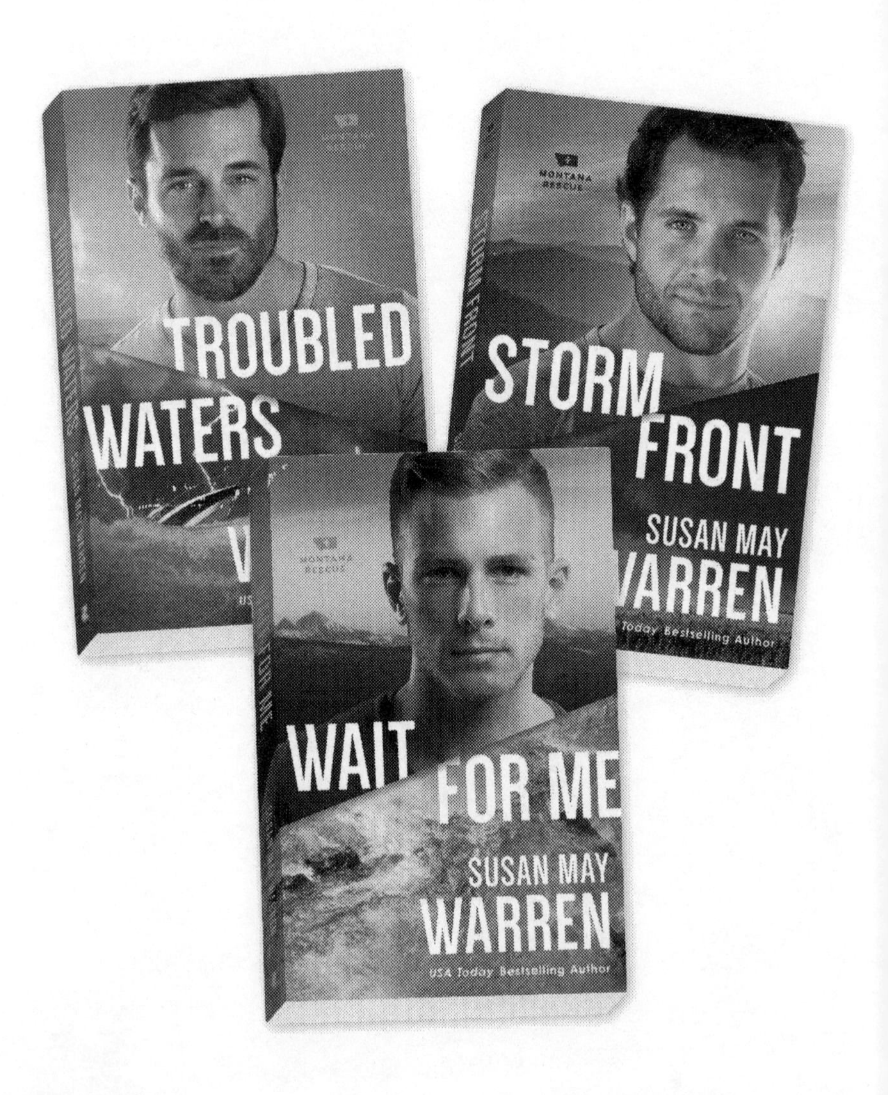

Printed in the United States
By Bookmasters